The Inscrutable Life of Frannie Phillips

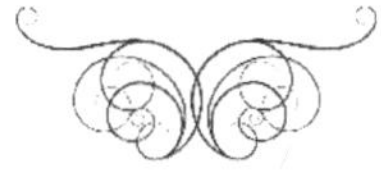

Patricia J. Parsons

MOONLIGHT PRESS | TORONTO

Cover image credit:

Illustration 111500987/Beautiful Woman © Svetlana Zdanchuk | Dreamstime.com

For information or permissions:

Visit www.moonlightpresstoronto.com

Or email moonlightpressinfo@gmail.com

Author's Note

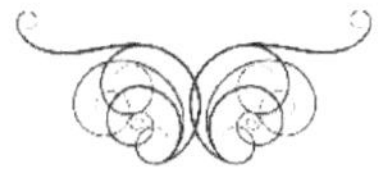

This book is number three in what is currently a three-part series that begins with Charlie's story in *The Year I Made 12 Dresses*. The story then moves backward through *Kat's Kosmic Blues*, Charlie's mother's story. Finally, the story moves even deeper into history with this one, *The Inscrutable Life of Frannie Phillips*—Charlie's great-grandmother's story.

Each one of the books is a story unto itself, but if you love complete stories and haven't yet met Charlie and her mother, Kat, you might wish to read those first. The truth is, though, Frannie's story stands quite well on its own. Enjoy!

~ PJP

Some other books by Patricia J. Parsons

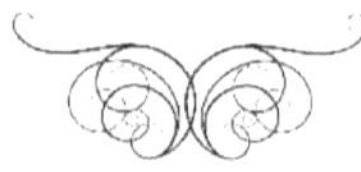

Kat's Kosmic Blues (women's fiction; *prequel to The Year I Made 12 Dresses)*

The Year I Made Twelve Dresses (women's fiction)

Plan B (lit-for-intelligent-chicks)

Confessions of a Failed Yuppie (lit-for-intelligent-chicks)

Something More Than Love (historical fiction)

Grace Note: In Hildegard's Shadow (historical fiction)

Another 'Pointe' of View: The Life & Times of a Ballet Mom (memoir)

For Art & Ian

"I am too intelligent, too demanding, and too resourceful for anyone to be able to take charge of me entirely. No one knows me or loves me completely. I have only myself"

— Simone de Beauvoir

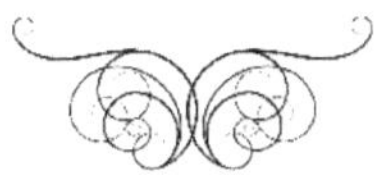

"Men should think twice before making widowhood women's only path to power."

— Gloria Steinem

Frannie

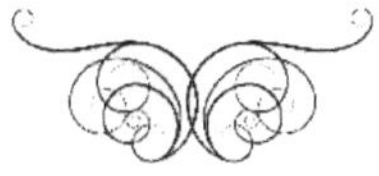

1912

FOR YEARS AFTER WHAT CAME TO BE KNOWN in our family as "the incident," my parents chose to believe that it had scarred me for life. It was convenient for them in the years that followed. It is how they explained my subsequent behaviour to friends and family, believing deeply in the necessity to maintain their good reputation. But it was not the horror of "the incident" that affected me. It was that Duff-Gordon woman. I remember every detail.

The evening before "the incident," I was dining with my parents in the first-class dining room. We had sailed out of Southampton to great fanfare one day earlier on what was proclaimed to be the world's first unsinkable ship. The RMS Titanic was a sight to behold, and the dining room was appointed in a manner that its passengers had come to expect, or perhaps to be more precise, to demand. Our dinner companions were Lady Lucile Duff-Gordon and her husband, Sir Cosmo Duff-Gordon. As my parents and I approached the table that evening, the Duff-Gordons had already been seated and were well into their first martinis. I felt Lady Duff-Gordon's eyes running up and down me as we neared the table. She had done the same thing on the two previous occasions when I had been in her company. I had accompanied my mother to Lady Duff-Gordon's salon in London. Just as before, she made a face as if she found me deficient in some way. Her sour reaction was likely because I was twelve years old, and no doubt she considered me an unsuitable dining companion. I would just have to prove her wrong.

I was secretly delighted to be sitting with the famous Lucile, as Lady Duff-Gordon was known by her public. Although my mother, ever the snob, had been less enthusiastic when she was told of our table assignment, referring to Lucile as being merely "in a trade." She objected to dining with one of her dressmakers, although I thought of Lucile as a *couturier*. I loved the sound of the French word, despite my mother telling me that it was nothing more than a fancy word for a dressmaker. In any case, despite my mother's rather harsh opinion, I was thrilled since I, too, wanted to design and sew dresses, a vocation of which my parents seriously disapproved. However, I was determined, and even at the tender age of twelve, I knew that it would be important to meet the right people.

Twenty-four hours later, I wished I had not wasted my time.

Charlie

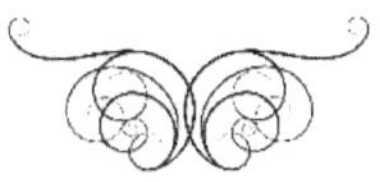

ONE

"Every new beginning comes from some other beginning's end."
~ Seneca the Younger

"WHAT DO YOU MEAN YOU'RE GOING TO MAKE your wedding dress? It's the twenty-first century, Charlie. No one sews their own wedding dress. It's absolutely archaic."

I sat at my desk gazing out into the school's quadrangle as I held my phone slightly away from my ear to avoid a ruptured eardrum. Evelyn's voice was loud at the best of times. However, whenever she took on her overbearing older sister role (which happened frequently), it had the added quality of shrillness—never a welcome addition to the dramas.

I should have known I'd get that kind of reaction from her, and I was prepared to cut her a bit of slack given her current condition. After years of proclaiming her dislike for children, my big sister was now very pregnant, and it appeared that she was ecstatic about it. In fact, both she and her obsessive husband Michael seemed to have had something of a "come-to-Jesus" moment after a turbulent year of temporary separations and crying jags—at least on her part. I can't be sure about him. The prospect of parenthood seemed to have brought both of them to their senses. And now this.

"Charlie? Are you listening to me?"

"Um-hm," I said absently as I watched a gaggle of students sitting together at a picnic table under a tree, together yet each completely separate, heads down gazing into their little screens. I had never thought of myself as old, but I felt ancient when I watched the teenagers who populated my classes.

"Charlotte Hudson! Listen to me! You're only getting married once, or at least that's the plan, so don't fuck it up."

"How's the leg swelling, Evelyn?"

"Don't change the subject. We're talking about your wedding dress, and there isn't much time."

I wasn't sure what she meant since it was now June, and I wasn't getting married until New Year's Eve. As far as I was concerned, there was lots of time—not to mention that I would be off for the summer in three days, ten hours and—I looked down at my watch—fifteen, no fourteen minutes. There was plenty of time to make my wedding dress.

"Charlie," she continued, calmer now, "I realize that this sewing thing has been consuming you since Mom died, but this is your wedding gown we're talking about. I could still fly out to help you find a dress. It might take them a couple of months to get it in stock. I'd be prepared to put a short hold on the two cases I have to finish before I go on maternity leave. I have an assistant, you know."

Evelyn was a litigator—an attorney who argued cases before a judge and jury—and a successful one, so she knew more than a thing or two about negotiation and persuasion. I, however, would not be swayed on this point. She could come at me with all guns blazing, and I still would not be moved to change my mind. This was about the third time Evelyn and I had had this discussion in the three weeks since Tom had asked me to marry him. It was her contention that the reason I wanted to take this extraordinary action (at least in her mind) of making my own wedding gown was that I wanted to make up for the fact that I'd only learned about Mom's love of sewing and design after she'd died a year and a half ago. The truth was that neither Evelyn nor I had known anything about it until I'd cleared out Mom's house and office—all of which took me just over a year. Still, I knew she might have a point.

I did have a lot to make up for, but it was so much more than that. I wanted to honour Mom in some way, and this was the best way I knew. The truth was that I also loved the idea of creating my own dress. I had found that I loved sewing. It was my Zen-like place I could retreat to whenever things got crazy, and I could sense that they were about to get crazier. I didn't know the half of it.

I looked down at the two-carat diamond solitaire sparkling on my left hand. "Evelyn, you're too pregnant to fly anywhere right now," I said. "Don't worry about it. You can come after the baby is born, and we can make the rest of the wedding plans together." I knew that, above all else, she wanted to help her sister with her wedding. Although it was entirely out of character, Evelyn had taken on a kind of maternal role since we'd learned the truth about Mom's life. Maybe she was practicing. After all, her baby was due in two months.

"This conversation isn't over, Charlie," she said. "But I have to go. I have a client meeting. Give Tom my love, and I'll call you on the weekend."

I clicked the phone off and put it down on my desk beside an open file folder holding a fat stack of pages. Even in this digital world, I always printed out major projects for a final read-through. This pile of three hundred-plus pages was the proudest accomplishment of my thirty-three (almost thirty-four years).

Kat's Kosmic Blues. A novel by C.K. Hudson. That's what the cover page of the pile of papers said. But, in truth, it said so much more. It said that, after a decade of playing around at writing a novel, I'd finally finished one. It said that I hadn't known my mother at all. It said that I'd finally found a way to honour my mother's memory. And after one more edit, it would be ready to send to my publisher, who had bought it after reading the first three chapters.

My mother had left me her diary, but she had been dead more than a year before I'd found it. It was as if she were right there next to me, whispering in my ear. *Finish it*, the little voice always said. Now I had. I had finished her story. Okay, I'll admit that it was fictionalized—big time. But it was Katherine ("Kat") Hudson's story. And now it was going to be my first novel.

I was about to close the folder when I heard a light knock at my office door. As much as I loved my students, it was late, I had a dinner engagement, and I didn't want to get into a harangue about grades. It was probably Madison, an overachieving fifteen-year-old who argued with me for every single mark. To be fair, though, I had met her parents. She came by it honestly, as the saying goes. They were both so intense that I always felt as if I needed a break halfway through any parent-teacher meeting for a drink. I opened the door with great trepidation. It wasn't Madison—it was my boss, Devin Connors, the headmaster.

"Charlotte," he began (he never did get the hang of calling me Charlie). "Charlotte, I'm so glad I caught you. I've just heard the good news." We were still standing at the door. "May I come in?"

"Oh," I said, "of course." I had hoped whatever he wanted to discuss could be done in thirty seconds while standing in the door.

"Charlotte, first, I want to tell you how happy I am that you finally took us up on our offer. We are so delighted with your work this past semester."

Did I sense a "but" coming?

He continued. "And I just heard that you and Tom are getting married. That's wonderful news as long as it doesn't mean we're going to lose you after all the time it took me to get you to come to Princess Margaret to teach." He pursed his lips and tipped his head forward to look at me over the top of his reading glasses in that fatherly way he had.

I still loved the sound of his Northern England accent. It was almost Scottish, but not quite.

Anyway, he was right. It had taken me a long time to decide to abandon a life as a full-time writer—or, to be honest, a part-time writer with a library assistant side hustle to pay the rent. Oh, and let's not omit the fact that my late mother had subsidized that indulgent lifestyle. But when I finally did make the decision to teach creative writing to private high school kids and be the writer-in-residence, I found that I was good at it. What's more, I discovered that I liked the structure it gave to my life—not to mention the regular paycheque!

Anyway, I found his concern about my pending nuptials having an impact on my role at Princess Margaret College to be charming. I suppose other young women might have found it somehow offensive or even misogynistic that an older man would still think getting married might cause a woman to rethink her commitment to her career. Call me crazy, but I didn't. Devin was a gentleman whose respect for his female colleagues was evident in every decision made at the school.

I told him I was absolutely sure that marriage would not change my commitment to my teaching, and he needn't worry. He nodded and smiled as he gazed over my shoulder (we were still standing in the doorway) toward my desk.

"Charlotte, is that a finished manuscript I see sitting on your desk?"

Devin knew that I had already sold it to an editor but didn't know it was now finished. I turned and moved back from the door just long enough for him to slide his way inside and over toward my desk. I had no choice but to follow him.

He stood over the manuscript and read the title page. "*Kat's Kosmic Blues* by C.K. Hudson." He whistled softly. "It's finished?" He looked up at me.

I nodded. "Signed, sealed and soon to be delivered."

"More good news! You must be so proud, Charlotte. I know I'm tickled that our writer-in-residence is writing! You have no idea how often people in your position fail to produce anything. This looks marvellous." He tapped the title page. "Your students will be so inspired!" He saw my backpack on my desk. "Well, I'll be going. Just wanted to give you my best wishes. I'll be off now."

I was delighted that he was so happy about me finishing my novel, but I was running late, so I was grateful that he was departing.

As he reached the doorway, he turned, his hand on the doorknob, his eyes twinkling. "You know what T.S. Elliott said about endings?" I did not know. He continued. "*What we call the beginning is often the end. And to make an end is to make a beginning. The end is where we start from.* Looking forward to reading this book, Charlotte, and the next one." He grinned and turned into the corridor.

Geesh, I thought. *The next one already.*

TWO

"One who asks a question is a fool for five minutes;
one who does not ask a question remains a fool forever."
~ Chinese proverb

AT FIFTEEN MINUTES BEFORE MIDNIGHT, Tom and I arrived home from the business dinner we had to attend that evening.

"Want a nightcap, Charlie?" he said, heading toward the liquor cabinet in the living room. One of those extravagant Art Deco cabinets with rich burl wood doors opened to reveal the most marvellous surprise within. Lined with mirrors, it housed myriad hand-blown, hand-cut crystal cocktail glasses and an array of liquor bottles that would be the envy of even the most accomplished bartender.

I'd already consumed several glasses of wine through predinner drinks and then dinner and knew I probably shouldn't have another, but it wasn't a school night, after all. "Sure," I said. "Could you pour me a tiny drop of cognac?"

"Your wish is my command," he said, reaching for two crystal brandy snifters.

I sank into the down-filled cushions of the incredibly comfortable sofa and kicked off my high heels. I wasn't really a high-heel kind of girl—that was my sister Evelyn's territory—and always opted for no higher than two-and-a-half inches. But this evening, I had made the mistake of wearing a pair of killer red heels with my ivory silk dress. The only good news about that was the fact that we'd been sitting most of the evening. Nevertheless, it felt good to wiggle my toes into the softness of the sofa as I drew them up underneath me.

"What's this?" I said, noticing a note on the coffee table. I leaned over and picked it up.

"Oh, yes, I forgot about that," Tom said as he handed me a glass, loosened his tie and sank down beside me. "Lucinda left it for you."

Lucinda was Tom's niece, late of the real estate staging business. Tom had brought her in to stage my mother's house when we were ready to sell it after she died. Lucinda was a whirlwind, and it seemed that house staging had gotten old very quickly for her. She was now on to interior renovation design. Being around Lucinda was like being inside a vortex as she swirled around from one thing to another. It made me tired just being around her, but there was no denying that she had a great eye for design. Tom had decided that his gift to me for finishing my book would be a redesign of one of the guest rooms (did I mention that this house I was now sharing with the love of my life was huge?) into an actual writing den with built-in bookshelves, a custom desk, and enough storage to hold everything a writer could possibly need—from paperclips to journals, to printer paper. It would be all mine, and he had hired Lucinda to design it.

I opened it and found a hand-written note—written by someone who so clearly didn't write often. I could hardly figure out what it said. To tell you the truth, I was surprised she hadn't texted me. Anyway, as far as I could tell, it said the following:

Getting ready for the storage stage. Need the closet cleared. I opened the boxes. Lots of dresses. What to do with dresses and other stuff?

Dresses? Other stuff? I was having trouble figuring out what she was talking about. The room had a nice-sized walk-in closet that I knew she planned to use as walk-in storage. I was excited with the possibility of having so much space to hide away my research materials and the slews of journals I kept with all manner of ideas. But I had no idea what she'd found in the closet. No one had used the room since I'd moved in just before Christmas last year, and I couldn't remember what I'd stashed in there.

"What's it all about?" Tom said.

"I guess she needs me to go through some stuff in the closet in my new office. I have no idea what it is." I yawned. "Well, it's too late to think about it now. Tomorrow is Saturday. I'll have a look tomorrow afternoon." I drained my glass.

~

By three o'clock the next afternoon, I knew I shouldn't put it off any longer. Just the thought of cardboard boxes (I presumed they were cardboard boxes), though, made me shiver. I'd spent so much of the previous year going through box after cardboard box retrieved from Mom's basement and attic that I wasn't sure I could handle any more. I thought I'd recovered, but I seemed to be wrong.

I grabbed a green garbage bag from the pantry on my way up the back staircase. I loved these old Victorians that had backstairs for the hired help.

The room that Tom was renovating for me to become my new writing den was at the back of the house overlooking the garden. The cherry trees near the house dripped with blush pink blossoms and wafted a wonderful aroma in the spring. I had experienced this for the first time this year. Once the cherry blossoms faded and the leaves of the trees filled out the space, the green blended with the swath of lawn that reached back to a gazebo at the far end of the yard. And on each side of the back garden, a long, undulating perennial border was just beginning to bloom in stages. I could hardly wait for the height of summer to experience it. By then, my new office would be complete, and my desk would be set up so that I could take in the tranquil ambience as I contemplated my next novel.

Hmm, I thought as I reached the top of the stairs, *will there be a next novel? If there is, I have no earthly idea what it will be about.* Ideas hadn't been springing up as readily as I had hoped they might.

Tom and Lucinda had consulted with me before demolition began so they could include the elements I dreamed about having in my writing den. But after that, they had bid me stay out of the whole process so that they could see me revel in the eventual "reveal" like on those television renovation shows. I was game. I knew, however, that demolition was the only thing that had happened to date, so by entering the room at this stage, there would be no spoiling the surprise.

I turned the doorknob and opened the door. Just as I had expected, the room was bare—and I mean bare. The wainscoting and baseboards were gone, and someone had gone crazy with that stuff you use to fill in cracks in plaster—the walls were so spotty they looked as if they had measles. There was no window trim anymore, and the closet doors had been removed, revealing the interior of the walk-in closet that had presumably been a nursery in the original house design.

I walked into the room and took a minute to gaze out the window, dreaming about what it would be like to sit here at my writing desk and contemplate a new story (whatever that turned out to be). Then I turned toward the closet. It was dark inside, so I looked for the light switch. When I clicked the button, the little room filled with light from a single lightbulb hanging from the ceiling. I was sure Lucinda had some fantastic lighting scheme planned to light the shelves I figured she had planned to install. Anyway, I wasn't here to contemplate the design. I was here to remove whatever it was she had found tucked away in the closet. *So*, I thought, *what dresses have you found, Lucinda?*

I immediately discovered the boxes she had mentioned in her cryptic note. There were three small cardboard boxes (dear god, more cardboard boxes) and a cardboard wardrobe—the kind movers use to hang your clothes in when you're moving. And now that I saw them, I remembered how they had gotten here.

In January, I'd had another surprise about my late mother. Just when I thought I'd finished discovering every box containing every secret my mother had, I'd uncovered another whole part of her life. There had been so much to unpack (literally and figuratively) that I'd found myself too exhausted to scrutinize yet another layer. These boxes were the unexamined layer I'd chosen to ignore at the time since they weren't directly related to my mother. What I mean is the stuff in these boxes, as I now recalled, had belonged not to my mother but her grandmother—my great-grandmother. Since my great-grandmother had died the year I was born, she had never been a part of my life, thus didn't really mean much to me. I remembered finding them in January. They had puzzled me, but I had so much to do that I then packed them away for another day. I guess that day had now arrived.

I pulled them out one by one into the middle of the floor in the empty room. I had a bit of trouble with the wardrobe—it was awkward—but I finally managed to get the boxes where I could take a closer look and decide what to do with them. I thought I'd start with the wardrobe.

I remembered that there had been a locked closet among Mom's office things, and in it had been some vintage dresses and things like hats and gloves. I then remembered being perplexed by the label on one of the dresses. As it all came back to me, I wondered why I'd forgotten about it since it had seemed so interesting at the time. I guess there had been so much else to do, particularly after reading my mother's diary. A tsunami of ideas had rolled over me as a result, compelling me forward in writing the book. Well, that was now finished, and as Devin had reminded me, the ending of one thing is the beginning of another. So, to begin.

I pulled back the cardboard top, and there they were—a rail of colourful dresses in silks and satins. I remembered the one that had struck me. It was green and gold silk, and I remembered being stunned by the label. I ran my hand over the hangers one at a time until I found it. I pulled it out from between a purple silk gown and a black jersey dress. As I pulled it toward me, I tried not to let it brush the floor, which might still have some construction dust on it. I felt a sudden instinctive protectiveness for the dress—for all of them.

As I cradled it on my arm, I looked again at the label.

PAUL POIRET À PARIS
77436 ATELIER, Mme Françoise Phillips

It appeared to be a genuine vintage Paul Poiret from sometime in the early twentieth century. I didn't know a lot about French couturiers from that time period, but I did know that he'd been one of the most famous. But what seemed even more startling than my great-grandmother owning an original Paul Poiret was the fact that this one seemed to have been created specifically for her. Mme Françoise Phillips was, I knew, my great-grandmother, but I also knew that everyone had called her Fran.

I carried the dress gently down the hall and into the bedroom, where I had my own walk-in closet. Since I wasn't a rabid fashionista, the closet wasn't full, and I had some space to spare. I hung the dress on the rail and went to retrieve more dresses. When I had removed all of them from the wardrobe box, I brought the remaining three cardboard boxes into the bedroom and put them on the floor beside the bed.

I opened the first box and saw it contained books and photograph albums. I picked up the first album. I ran my hand over the smooth burgundy leather cover, marvelling at how it still seemed so supple after all these years. The album contained those black, construction-paper-like pages held together by a shiny black cord. As I opened the cover, I saw that the photos were affixed to the pages by tiny black triangles. I peered closely at the single photograph on the first page. Yellowed by the passing of time, the black and white picture looked as if it had been a studio photograph, a formal portrait. The young woman with hair swept up into a chignon of some sort was leaning with her elbow on a high table, her chin resting on her hand, an open book on the table in front of her. Her eyes pierced through anyone who dared to look. She looked as if she might have been fourteen or fifteen years old.

As I looked more carefully at the photograph, I felt a sense of familiarity. You know that feeling when you see something that you know you've never seen before, and yet it seems so familiar to you. It's almost a feeling of understanding or closeness—almost an intimacy. Yet I knew I'd never seen this picture before. I felt like the eyes were beckoning me, and I realized why this young woman looked familiar. She looked like my mother. But this photo was clearly taken in the early twentieth century judging from the high-necked dress with the large cameo affixed to the stand collar with the frill. It had to be Fran. I was looking into the face of my teenaged great-grandmother. I began to flip through the pages.

There were dozens of photographs of this young woman—many of her alone and many of her with other people I didn't recognize. I felt as if I'd like to take some time to go through it, but there were still many more things in the boxes. There were several more photo albums, some of which didn't seem quite as old as the others judging from the fashions and one that seemed that it might be older. As I looked at the pictures of a little girl, I wondered if they were all of Fran. Just as I was about to close the album that seemed to be the oldest, I stopped at the last photo in the album.

The photograph showed a family group of what appeared to be a mother, father and young girl. They were strolling along the deck of a ship past lifeboats—I counted four of them. The picture was grainy, but I could see the ocean beyond, indicating they must have been at sea. As I peered closely, I was suddenly startled. "It can't be," I said out loud to no one since I was alone sitting on the floor of the bedroom I shared with Tom. "It's not possible." But why wasn't it possible?

"Charlie!"

I could hear Tom calling me from downstairs. I quickly checked my watch. "Damn it," I said. It was getting late, and Tom and I were hosting a couple of friends for a small dinner party. There was cooking to be done. This would have to wait.

"Coming!" I called as I shoved the albums back in the box and stacked the boxes up beside the bed.

~

Jason and Amy Kirkpatrick were becoming fast friends. Three months earlier, we had started trading off dinners with them. One Saturday evening, they would host, then about three weeks later, it would be our turn. All four of us were currently sucked into watching Chef Thomas Keller's French cuisine course on *Masterclass.* With Chef Keller in mind, Tom and I were making his chicken paillard tonight, accompanied by an arugula salad dressed with pickled red onions and Marcona almonds in a balsamic vinaigrette. Regardless of the menu on any given evening, we all seemed to enjoy ourselves.

Jason and Tom had been friends since high school and had reconnected after graduating from different universities, both of them with computer degrees. The two of them had developed their remarkably successful computer technology business together, which they had subsequently sold for what appeared to be a significant sum (maybe Tom would spill the beans on details after we were married). Tom was now a realtor, a job he adored, and Jason was in the gestational stages of a new technology business, the details for which were a bit fuzzy to me. His wife, Amy, was a very pregnant family physician whose mother owned the city's most successful women's wear shop. I knew that Amy had worked there for years when she was younger, and I also knew that she still possessed a lot of interest in (and knowledge about) current and vintage fashion. After we had finished the chicken, followed by a dessert of profiteroles from the local French patisserie and decaf coffee, we were relaxing in the living room, sipping glasses of port (Amy was sipping club soda).

"Amy," I said, "do you know much about early French fashion designers?"

"I'm no expert, "she said, "but I've certainly read a lot about them, and my mother is always on the lookout for vintage finds to add to her personal collection. I sometimes help her with the research. Why?"

I told her about my great-grandmother's dresses.

"Well, gentlemen," Amy said, carefully lifting herself from the depths of our big comfy couch, "You are on your own for a while. The ladies have more important things to do. Onward, Charlie. Let's see those dresses!"

"This could be quite a find," Amy said as we reached the top of the stairs, where she stopped a moment to catch her breath. Her due date was fast approaching, and she looked to me as if she might give birth any moment.

I settled her into the only chair in the bedroom and proceeded to bring the dresses out one by one. I started with the Poiret.

The moment I held it up in front of me for her to see, she gasped. "Bring it closer," she said, reaching out to touch the silk.

I watched Amy as she examined the dress. She started by turning it inside out and running her fingers over the seams. Then she turned it right-side out and did the same thing. Then she examined the hem. Finally, she scrutinized the label, running her hand over what had appeared to me to be hand-stitching, affixing the label to the neckline.

"Any idea who Françoise Phillips was?" she said finally.

"She was my great-grandmother."

"Wow, Charlie. Françoise must have been someone back in the day to have a dress made especially for her by a famous French couturier. What do you know about her?"

"To tell you the truth, Amy," I said, sitting down on the side of the bed, "I know almost nothing about her. She died the year I was born. I remember Mom quoting her to Evelyn and me from time to time. I remember her telling us that Fran used to say, 'If you want to make god laugh, tell her your plans,' but that's about as much as I know."

Amy laughed. "I'll have to remember that one." She patted the pocket of her jeans. "Damn, I must have left my phone downstairs. Do you have yours?"

I waved it at her. "Sure. What do you need?"

"I can't remember details about Paul Poiret. Maybe if we look him up, we can figure out where your great-grandmother might have encountered his design house. Was she French?"

"Uh-uh," I said as I plugged Paul Poiret's name into the search engine. "As far as I know, she was born in England but lived most of her life in Canada."

"Well, she could have had this dress made for her even if she lived in England, but it would have cost a lot of money."

I was scrolling through the search results. "It says here that in the 1910s, Poiret was referred to as the 'King of Fashion' in America and 'La Magnifique' in Paris." I looked at the dress in Amy's lap. "So, it must date from around that time."

"I don't think so," she said, holding it up. "It looks more like a dress from the 1920s. Doesn't it look to you like something a flapper might have worn?"

I had to admit it did. "Well, it says here Poiret closed his fashion house in 1929—something about not being able to reconcile his artistic vision with the signs of the times. Anyway, that means it definitely dates from the 1920s." My mind started racing, trying to figure out my great-grandmother's—Fran's—life. I could almost feel a story brewing in the back of my head as if cogs had sluggishly begun turning.

Amy handed the dress back to me. "You said there were others?" I nodded. "Can we take a look? If they're anywhere as fascinating as this one…"

I pulled out seven more dresses. With our heads together, Amy and I examined each one. By the time we'd scrutinized the style, fabric, and quality, we turned to the labels. There was one in flowing script that said "Lucile, 23 Hanover Square, London." There was a Jean Patou, a Madeleine Vionnet, a Schiaparelli, a Jean Muir, and an Yves St. Laurent. I lifted the last one and gasped at the label on the black silk dress with the white silk collar and cuffs. It was a Chanel, a designer I had longed to be able to wear, my lack of fashionista status notwithstanding.

"All I can say, Charlie, is that your great-grandmother was someone." She got herself up from the chair with some difficulty, and we stood side-by-side gazing at the dresses arrayed on the bed. "What're you going to do with them now?" Amy patted her very pregnant belly. "My mother would give her firstborn grandchild to own these, so promise me you won't tell her about them!" We both laughed. She looked at her watch. "I didn't realize it was so late. I guess we better get going."

Tom and I saw Jason and Amy out then sat down in the living room. I sipped on the rest of my port that I'd abandoned when Amy and I departed to look at the dresses. I told Tom about what we'd found.

"Sounds like something a great-granddaughter might like to follow-up on." He yawned. "I'm beat. You ready to go up?"

I drained my crystal glass and placed it gently on the coffee table. "You know, if you don't mind, I think I'll bring two of those boxes downstairs and have a bit of a look through them before I go to bed. My mind is racing too much to sleep."

"Of course, I don't mind," he said. "I'll help you." He smiled conspiratorially at me. "You know what happened when you found your mother's things. Maybe there's even a book here."

~

Half an hour later, I was sitting back in the living room with a cup of peppermint tea and a pile of photo albums from the first box on the couch beside me. I picked up the leather-bound one I'd last looked at and went immediately to the last page. There was that photograph of the family strolling on the ship's deck. I picked up my phone and switched on its magnifying feature. I trained it first on the face of the young girl with what appeared to be her parents. It was the same young woman as in the rest of the photographs—there was no doubt about it. It was Fran. Then I turned my attention to the grainy lettering on the side of one of the lifeboats and stared. I swallowed hard. It was just as I'd thought. TITANIC.

I closed the album and sat back. My great-grandmother had survived the sinking of the Titanic. Why had I not known this before? This seemed to me to be a spectacular piece of family history. If she had kept this a secret, what other mysteries did she take to her grave? Then, it struck me. Perhaps my mother hadn't known. After all, my sister and I hadn't known nearly as much as we thought we knew about our mother until it was too late to talk to her about it. Maybe Fran had kept her own secrets. Then I remembered the books I'd noticed when I'd packed these ones up back in January. I remembered that one seemed to have been a diary.

I got down on the floor and started rifling through the second box. I pulled out a series of hardcover books. I had spent several years stacking books in the university library to make extra money to fund my writing life before I'd taken on the teaching job. I knew antique books when I saw them. Knowing that they were so old made me especially mindful that I needed to treat them with respect and gentleness. I pulled out the first one.

It was called *The Case of Jennie Brice*. The author was someone called Mary Roberts Rinehart, and the book was published in 1913. I gently leafed through it. It seemed to be a mystery book which made me wonder if it might not have been a forerunner to the Nancy Drew books I loved as a child. I put it aside and lifted out the next one.

This one was called *The Amazing Adventures of Letitia Carberry* by the same author. I placed it on top of the first one. The next one made me gasp. It was a first edition of *Little Women* by Louise May Alcott, published in two volumes in 1868 and 1869. For the briefest of seconds, I wondered how much this one might be worth. I immediately pushed that out of my mind as I opened the first volume's cover and saw the inscription. "To Frannie with all my love, Ollie." I shivered. So, she was called Frannie back in the day, as they say. *I wonder who Ollie was*, I thought.

The next book was called *The Dressmaker: A Complete Book on All Matters Connected with Sewing and Dressmaking*. The copyright page told me it had been published in 1911. My great-grandmother was a dressmaker? That would explain her interest in all those dresses, but it would not, under any circumstance, explain how she could afford all those dresses.

There were four more books in the box. The first two were original editions of Simone De Beauvoir's feminist manifesto *The Second Sex* or, in this case, *Le deuxième sexe* since it was in the original French with a note in what appeared to me might actually be the author's handwriting—"*Pour ma chère amie Françoise. Toujours ensemble.*" "For my dear friend Francoise. Always together. Simone." My great-grandmother knew Simone De Beauvoir? How was it possible that I had not known this? The third book was called *The Memoirs of Dolly Morton*, 1899. This title rang a bell somewhere in the back of my mind. I had a hazy memory of sitting in the back of a large classroom when I was taking a women's study course in grad school. This one was mentioned in the section on women's erotica in history, as I recalled. Dear god!

And, there was another. In that same course, I seemed to remember several French authors of women's erotica from the early twentieth century. I thought I had might have read one of them, but it was hard to remember—we had been assigned so many—and since they were in French, they were more difficult to remember.

Then there were several books whose authors I didn't recognize. Two of them were in French and the third in English. The title seemed to ring a bell, although I thought I remembered it as an old movie by that name—*Life of Desire*—by an author I didn't recognize. Sounded a bit racy to me.

This was getting curiouser and curiouser, as Alice in Wonderland would have said. I was feeling a bit like old Alice at this moment. I felt like I had fallen down some kind of a rabbit hole. I just didn't know how deep it would go. The next hardcover book was hand-written. It was a diary.

I got myself up off the floor, settled myself back into the cushions of the couch and pulled a throw over me, despite the balmy June night. I took a deep breath, yawned (it was getting late, but this couldn't wait) and opened the leather-bound diary. A folded sheet of cream-coloured linen-finished notepaper fell out of the back of the book. I picked it up and unfolded it as I put the diary down beside me. I was momentarily stumped, trying to figure out what I was looking at.

It was written in the same beautiful handwriting that I'd seen on the first pages of the diary. It must have been Frannie's. But the date on the note—it was 1989. What? It was dated on my birthday—my actual birth day, the day I was born.

Dear Charlie, it began. I felt a shiver run up my spine and lodge in the prickles at the back of my neck. Despite the warm evening, I suddenly felt chilled as if a ghost had entered the room, or perhaps me. My eyelids were heavy, but I needed to know Frannie's story. *Dear Charlie…*

When I arose this morning, it was like any other day. The sun was shining, and, despite my advancing age, I felt as I have always felt throughout my life—anxious to live. But today has turned out like no other. Today I met you. I have just returned home from the hospital where I visited with my cherished granddaughter, Katherine, Kat, your beautiful mother. I had the privilege of holding you in my arms and looking into your eyes. Your eyes locked onto mine in that first instant, and I knew that you were the one. I love your older sister, Evelyn, dearly, but you are the one. You have the eyes. You have the soul—I feel it. You will be the artist of your mother's soul and of mine. I will ask your mother to keep this note for you to open on your thirty-fifth birthday. By then, you will know why.

I hope by then you know what a remarkable woman you are destined to be. How do I know this? I have just looked into the eyes of the future—your future. Oscar Wilde once said: "To live is the rarest thing in the world. Most people just exist." Existence is not enough. If you do not know that already, you soon will. I wish for you to do as I have done—live every day as if it is your last.

The Lucile

Rebel

THREE

"It is impossible, in our condition of Society, not to be sometimes a Snob."
~ William Makepeace Thackeray

IF MOTHER HAD ANY INKLING OF WHAT WOULD COME over me that day, I am confident that she would never have taken me with her. Nora, my governess, however, had a family emergency and wouldn't be able to meet me as she usually did when school let out. What was Mother to do? She had no choice but to direct our chauffeur to stop at the front gates of Notting Hill and Ealing High School and await the disgorgement of the usual gaggle of boisterous girls. She would be forced to take her often unruly twelve-year-old daughter (I know I am this and more—Mother has told me often enough) with her to her final dress fitting. However, if truth be told, there were six new gowns and three new walking suits, all of which she would require for our upcoming voyage. And it was there, in that lounge, watching the great Lucile and her assistant fuss over Mother's gowns and that I discovered the wellspring of my future. But it would take some time to get there—my future, that is!

"Get in quickly, Frances," Mother said as she held the door open for me.

I did as I was bid.

Mother peered past me at the mob as she directed me to close the door quickly. "I hope that was not that Howard girl I saw you walking with. I have told you time and again about the dangers of consorting with children from that kind of family."

I rolled my eyes, as I so often found myself doing these days whenever Mother got on one of her tirades about who was proper and who wasn't. I happened to like Abigail Howard, and yes, it was Abigail I was chatting up as we made our way to the gate. Abigail was, after all, my best friend, although I didn't tell Mother this. I considered whether I should take Mother on at this juncture or leave it. After all, we were meant to be having a mother-daughter afternoon, weren't we? We were going to spend a few hours in a fashion salon, and I didn't want to spoil it at the outset. I had also already learned that it was better to pick my battles when it came to Mother's particular inclinations.

"We need to consider very carefully where you will spend your final school years, Frances. We need to choose carefully. Your father and I have just learned of a new finishing school in Switzerland, a place I'm sure the esteemed Mr. Howard would not deign to send his daughter."

Was that a snort I heard emanate from my mother? Again, I decided not to be provoked. Mother was fond of threatening me with "finishing school," whatever that was supposed to be. And she was also fond of looking down her nose at Abigail's father, Devin Howard, because Mother thought that anyone who made his living writing novels (and novels of questionable morality, in her view, I might add) wasn't in the same category at all as she considered her family to inhabit. As for me, I thought Abigail's father was wonderful. The few times I'd met him, I'd found him to be eloquent, clever and tolerant, something that one could never say about my mother. My father? I wasn't so sure he was as supportive of Mother's oddities as he appeared to be. He had winked at me too many times for me to believe he took her views.

In any case, I was happy to be accompanying Mother to her fitting and planned to mind my manners so that this might become a habit.

When we arrived at Lucile's salon, Mother was greeted as if she might have been a long-lost friend.

"How wonderful to see you today, Mrs. Phillips," the assistant said, as if Mother's arrival might have been some kind of wonderful surprise and that Mother hadn't had an appointment. "You are looking marvellous, Mrs. Phillips. Please do come in, Mrs. Phillips."

I thought she might bow down and kiss Mother's feet any minute. It was all I could do to suppress the giggle that I could feel beginning to gurgle up. If Abigail had been here, I would never have been able to suppress it. I couldn't wait to tell her about this.

On the other hand, the woman at the door looked dubiously in my direction as Mother explained that she had no choice but to bring me. I looked up at her through my long, dark eyelashes and smiled—the picture of a proper English lady in the making. Then I looked down and stuck my tongue out at her when she wasn't watching.

The woman showed us into the salon and took our coats. Then she led us to a high-backed sofa and bid us sit down while she fetched tea and informed the great Lucile that we had arrived. The sofa was extraordinarily uncomfortable, and I was forced to sit up straight. Perhaps they were made this way so that people like my mother would not have to continually scold their daughters about slouching, a position I preferred.

Once tea had appeared, the models began to file into the room one at a time. The great Lucile—known in her other life as Lady Duff-Gordon—had yet to appear. No problem, though. I was fascinated by the whole procedure and especially by the gowns.

The dresses were ones that Mother was to examine and select as the basis for a few more dresses. Then, Lucile would arrive and begin to fit Mother into the dresses she had already chosen and that were now almost finished. All of this was in preparation for an April transatlantic trip that we would be making to accompany Father to New York. Father was a banker. To be more specific, he owned a bank in London and was working on opening one in America. I wasn't too young to recognize that the reason my mother, not being of the aristocracy, was still welcomed with open arms in places such as this was because my father made a great deal of money. Father himself had often said that money opens doors. And so, it did. I had begun to wonder if it also closed some.

I was excited at the prospect of a trip on an ocean liner, although, to be truthful, I was a bit nervous. I wasn't a fan of large bodies of water (I still could not swim), and I also felt that I didn't have the proper clothing. Mother had told me that, at my age, I needn't worry, but I had decided that, in no uncertain terms, I would not leave this salon today without the promise of at least one Lucile gown to take on board the Titanic on its maiden voyage.

I had just put my teacup down and was straining to work the cramp out of my neck from having sat up so straight for so long when another model walked into the salon. She was wearing the most beautiful gown I had ever seen. The bodice and upper portion of the skirt were lavender silk chiffon, and the lower part of the skirt was a dark purple hue. The wide neck was banded with royal blue that matched the silk sash encircling the waistline. I knew that this was the dress. This was the dress I had to wear when I entered the first-class dining room. I just had to figure out a way to get Mother to agree.

Finally, Lucile arrived. She was a tall, imposing woman wearing a black suit and an enormous, wide-brimmed hat. Under the suit jacket, she wore a silk blouse with a collar and a tie which was fastened with a gold broach, and she had three long strands of pearls around her neck. She walked to the table on the opposite side of the salon, took off her hat and placed it on the table. One of her assistants assisted her with removing her jacket. Only then did she look over at where Mother and I were sitting on the uncomfortable sofa.

"I do hope you haven't been waiting too long, Mrs. Phillips," she said, extending her hand to Mother as she approached us. Then she noticed me but did not acknowledge my presence.

If I was awed to be in the presence of one of London's most sought-after couturiers, Mother was not.

"Yes, we have been waiting some time, Lucile. Shall we get on with it?"

I had heard Mother refer to Lucile as her "dressmaker," an occupation Mother did not hold in high regard except for what it meant to her own wardrobe. On the other hand, I thought it was exciting to create such beautiful works of art. So, when Mother left the room to change into her first dress, I walked over to where three of the models were still standing. One of them was the model in the purple dress.

"May I touch the silk?" I said to the model.

"Go on," she said, never catching my eye.

I was startled at the sound of her Cockney accent. I guess I had expected the models to be from the same kind of background as I was. This suddenly fascinated me.

"What's your name?" I said to her as I gently pinched the silk between my thumb and forefinger.

"Dora." She still did not look at me.

"How long have you been here with Lucile?"

"Not long."

"Do you like being a mannequin?"

"Nothin' to like or dislike."

I wanted to know more, but Mother and Lucile had come back into the salon. Lucile set about pinning this piece of fabric here and another one there. She muttered about taking part of the skirt in and letting out part of the bodice. I was fascinated.

"It's lovely, Mother," I said, and I truly meant it. "I mean, the dress is beautiful, but it somehow makes you look even more beautiful." The dress just seemed to suit her—as if she were more herself when she had it on. It was an extraordinary transformation.

Lucile—Lady Duff-Gordon—looked over at me. "Of course, she does," she said. "It is because I see the woman. The dress must become a part of her and not the other way around. My dresses are personal. There is a lesson in that." And then she returned to her pinning.

Mother then left the salon to try on the next one.

"Excuse me, Lady Duff-Gordon," I began, "may I ask you about this dress?"

She turned to where I was standing beside the purple model.

"Do you feel it might become a part of me?"

She peered at me carefully, then at the dress. "I did not make this one for you, child."

"No," I said carefully, "but perhaps at my young age, being so inexperienced, a dress that is already created might become me. One does, after all, need to grow into one's style."

She almost smiled. "Are you accompanying your parents to America in April?"

I nodded.

"Well, then," she said, "we cannot have young ladies attired in clothing whose style does not represent one that they will most assuredly grow into someday, can we?" She nodded to Dora to leave the salon and followed her out. "Leave your mother to me. You shall have the dress."

~

"This is what it looks like," I said excitedly to Abigail when we finally had time to hide behind the staircase leading to the gymnasium at lunchtime the following week. From memory, I had taken the time to sketch the stunning dress that Lucile, true to her word, had talked Mother into purchasing for me. It would arrive the following week after the alterations were complete. I thrust my diary toward her with the page open to the sketch.

"Ooh, Frannie! It looks glorious!" Glorious was Abigail's word of the week. She said her father insisted she improve her vocabulary, one word at a time.

"Oh, Abigail, it is glorious. It is fashioned of the softest silk chiffon I have ever touched."

"I can see you in my mind's eye," she said—another device her father insisted she ought to develop. I suppose he hoped she might follow in his footsteps and become a famous novelist. He was the most progressive man I had ever met. "I see you entering the dining room on your father's arm, and every eye is on you." She had her eyes closed now. "I see you making your way to a table set with silver and crystal." We had discussed this possibility at length. "I see—oh, oh—I see a young man. He cannot take his eyes off you. Oh, and Frannie, he is glorious!"

I nudged her arm to see if I might not be able to wake her from her trance-like fantasy—although I do have to admit that I liked it. I liked it very much. Abigail had a vivid imagination. "Abigail, you tell the most wonderful stories. Perhaps you *will* follow in your father's footsteps and become a famous novelist someday. Then I can tell people I was best friends with a famous person!"

"I do love a fantasy," she said. "But you're the one with the writing journal. Maybe you'll be the novelist."

I made a face at her. I certainly did have aspirations, but ever since I'd been to Lucile's salon, they had begun to solidify around the notion of being a great dressmaker. I truly wanted to learn to create those beautiful gowns, not stories.

"I wager you can't wait to leave," Abigail said as she twirled a long blonde ringlet around her pointer finger as was her habit.

"Of course," I said. "But it's still months away.

"Still, it's something to look forward to, don't you think? I mean, an ocean liner! My father says the Titanic is the largest passenger ship in the world. I cannot even imagine it. You will tell me all about it, won't you?

"Abigail! Of course, I will. I plan to document every single minute of every single day right here in my diary." I patted the leather-bound cover of the new diary Father had given me for my birthday just days ago. It had become my constant companion. "It will be as if you were there with me when we can finally meet upon my return."

"Just as I said, you are the one who writes. Not me!"

~

I cannot remember when I first began to dislike going to church with Mother and Father. It hadn't always been that way. When I was a child of six or seven, I thought myself rather pious, sitting in my pew, my new hat perched daintily on my head. I rarely listened to what was being said up at the front—little girls aren't always that fond of lumbering old men in robes of questionable style with their booming voices raining down upon their ears. The notion of fire and brimstone, which I only later began to identify, was slightly frightening when it wasn't just dull. However, when I was about ten or so, I suppose, I began to loathe the very idea of sitting still for an interminable hour in church while someone intoned boring platitudes about things like sacrifice and pain and everlasting torment. It was more than a little girl ought to have to bear, in my view. I told my parents this on several occasions, but it was no use. They were going to church. My mother, in particular, seemed to relish the weekly preparation, taking great care with her dress, hat, gloves and even her hair. It was almost as if she were attending a social event. As far as I was concerned, even that aspect was not a saving feature. After sitting for an overly long period at the service on Easter Sunday, just four days before we were scheduled to set sail, I had had enough.

The priest had droned on interminably about doubt—how we all have it, what we can do about it, how we will overcome it. I was actually listening that day, and I realized, as only twelve-year-old girls can, that he had finally said something that made sense. Doubt. That was exactly what I felt. So, I waited until we had all sat down to Easter dinner with my aunt and uncle, my grandmother and our neighbours Sir Roger and Lady Alma Lowther-Russell and their son, Oliver, who was two years my senior. Oliver was home from boarding school, Charterhouse, which was somewhere in the wilds of Surrey as far as I could tell, for the Easter week holiday. I had known Oliver since we were five or six years old, and he was the closest thing I had to a brother. I knew he would be the one ally I could count on when I broached the subject of doubt as a dinner table conversation subject. Dinner was the best time to do it, in my view.

Father had carved the mustard-glazed ham that our housekeeper, Mrs. Groundwood, had prepared, and we were all passing around bowls of mashed potatoes, roasted squash and creamed spinach. I took only a spoonful of the vile spinach and moved right along to the dinner rolls that Oliver was now holding out in front of me. Then, of course, it was time for grace, which Ollie's father, Sir Roger, had been pressed into leading. "Amen" seemed the perfect segue—to me, at least.

"Father," I began as I smoothed out the snowy white linen napkin covering my lap. "Father, I was listening to the priest at church this morning."

My mother nearly dropped the forkful of mashed potatoes she had halfway to her mouth.

"Well, my dear daughter," Father said, reaching for his wine glass, "this is great news and something worth drinking to. Thank you for sharing it with us on this cheerful Easter Sunday."

I rolled my eyes. "I wasn't finished, Father."

He put his glass back down on the table. "Then, by all means, darling, carry on."

Ollie was snickering behind his napkin. I'd deal with him later, but now I had the floor. "Generally," I said, trying on the most grown-up demeanour I could muster, "I find the sermons tedious." I had worked at coming up with that word as I prepared myself for dinner. I looked over at my mother, who was patting her lips daintily with her napkin. "But this morning, I was taken by the notion of doubt."

"No doubt, you were," Ollie said, now in full-blown hilarity mode.

I stared at him in that way I had always been able to make other children shut up. It usually worked—even on him. At least he didn't say anything else.

"Yes," I said, nodding at Ollie then at Father. "The priest talked of doubt. He said that we all experience doubt. He said that we need faith to overcome doubt."

"What are you getting at, Frances?" Mother said. I could sense the impatience in her voice. Mother always counted on her dinner tables being calm and peaceful, accompanied only by polite conversation that I was starting to find increasingly wearisome.

"What I'm getting at is that I don't have that faith to overcome my doubt, so I believe I should not have to attend church any longer."

I heard a gasp from mother and perhaps even one from Lady Alma. Sir Roger smiled and quickly put his napkin to his lips to hide it, very likely from my mother.

My father took another sip of wine then sat back in his chair, eyeing me carefully as he often did. "Tell me, Frances, is this the only matter about which you have doubt, or are there others?"

"Others?" I said, not comprehending where he might be going with this.

"Yes, darling, others. Do you have doubts about your family? Your home? The ability of a brand-new ship to get us safely to America?"

"No, Father. I don't have doubts about those things." He was trying to best me in this conversation, and I could not let that happen—especially in front of Ollie. And where was my ally, anyway?

"So, you do have faith in some things, but you have chosen not to have faith in one thing."

"I don't see it as a choice, Father. I didn't choose not to have faith in the church. It chose me." I was rather pleased with myself at that last remark while at the same time trying to appear sad about this.

"Oh no, my dear," Father continued. "Lack of faith—with the subsequent doubt—is a choice. Everything in life is a choice. It is only a question of making a different choice."

"*'If you would be a real seeker after truth, it is necessary that at least once in your life you doubt, as far as possible, all things.*'"

Everyone at the table turned toward Ollie. He was absently lifting a fork of spinach toward his mouth, quietly ignoring the stares.

"What was that, Ollie?" I said finally.

He repeated what he had said. "It's not original," he said. "It's René Descartes."

I didn't know who René Descartes was, and I was not particularly eager to show my ignorance, but it did seem to me Ollie might be supporting my view.

"Ah, yes, Descartes," my father said. "The great philosopher. Skepticism was his weapon, was it not, Oliver? I assume you've been studying him in school this term."

"I have, sir," Ollie said. "And I think he has a point that Frannie, Frances, is demonstrating."

At fourteen, Ollie was already a great debater. He would surely become a more extraordinary barrister than his father ever would be. At least that's what he had been telling me for the past few years. It had meant little to me as a younger child, but I was now beginning to see Ollie differently, more grown-up, perhaps.

"I believe it's important to test our assumptions, sir."

"Indeed, Oliver, indeed. But if we view everything through a veil of skepticism, what is left for us to trust in?"

My mother had tired of such heady matters and moved the conversation forward by changing the subject to our upcoming trip to America. And I was left with a lot of doubt about a lot of things.

FOUR

"What the caterpillar calls the end, the rest of the world calls a butterfly."
~ Lao Tzu

We took the boat train from Waterloo Station, reaching the Southampton Terminus railway station just over an hour before the ship's scheduled departure. The station was directly on the quay where we were met by porters who whisked away our piles of luggage—enough for a month away. I scrambled down from the train's first-class carriage and took up the rear behind Mother and Father, who marched along as if they owned the place. For all I knew, perhaps they did. I stayed as close to Nora as I could as we made our way along the pier, then I looked up—way, way up.

In every life, there is a watershed moment. I suspect most people would believe that it is impossible to have one when you are only twelve years old—in those moments, you can't be aware that your future holds much more of life. But at that moment in time, I felt as if my life were about to change. It was Wednesday, the tenth of April, and I was standing on the pier gazing up at the four massive stacks on this magnificent ship. "Glorious!" I whispered so no one could hear, and I wished that Abigail were here to share this moment with me. At least I had Nora.

Mother had decided that Nora would be the best person to take along since she had been my governess since I was a baby. Moreover, she was still young enough to have the energy required to provide service on a transatlantic ocean voyage to a foreign country, and Mother liked her. Nora was also the only one of our several regular house servants who indicated that she never got seasick. And she knew of what she spoke since she had come to England from Ireland across the Irish Sea in a hurricane when she was eighteen—or so she said. I had always liked Nora and was glad of her company. She was now thirty years old and well on her way to spinsterhood, according to Mother.

Now the four of us stood there on the quay as seagulls swooped and cawed, as they do. I could smell the ocean and the tar of the docks. And the people! There were so many people!

"Look, Father!" I said, pointing excitedly at the people already lining the deck onboard the ship. They were all waving madly to everyone and no one. "There are so many people on board the ship already!"

"Those would be the passengers in second and third class. They board prior to first-class." He bent down and picked up the small valise that he had not sent along with the porter. "Come along now, ladies," he said. "We don't want to miss the boat, do we?"

The breeze had freshened, and I had to put my hand on my hat as we made our way up the gangway. Nora clutched my other hand, and I didn't mind. I suspected, though, judging by her grim expression, that holding my hand was as much for her benefit as mine. Despite her protestations that she did not get seasick and loved the idea of an ocean voyage, I suspected that she wasn't as brave as she had let on. On the other hand, I ought to have been terrified because of my horror of large bodies of water, but I was not. I was too excited—and besides, we had not left the jetty yet! I tried hard to memorize every sight, sound, and smell to imprint them on my memory so that I could write them down in my diary later. I glanced down at my carpet bag where my little diary was hidden. I would not let it leave my side.

As we stepped off the gangway and across the threshold onto this magnificent ship, Captain Smith was there to greet each first-class passenger. He seemed to know my father for some reason. After he shook my father's hand and Father introduced him to my mother, he looked down at me. "And you are?"

"Miss Frances Elizabeth Phillips, sir," I said. I think I almost curtsied. I was so taken with the elegance of the atrium and the smartness of the uniformed officers who stood behind the captain.

"Welcome aboard, Miss Phillips. I shall look forward to hearing your appraisal of this fine ship and our voyage in due course."

I smiled prettily at him. I hoped he didn't consider me dim-witted because I did, in fact, plan to provide a complete evaluation of the trip in due course.

Captain Smith nodded to a porter who immediately came forward to invite us in and lead us to our suite. As we followed him along the plushly-carpeted corridor, the porter explained that our suite was located on the B Deck—the Bridge Deck.

"You'll also find the *À La Carte* Restaurant and the *Café Parisien* on your deck," he said, his Irish brogue so obvious, I nudged Nora, who reddened immediately. He was quite a fine-looking man with his red hair and beard and dancing hazel eyes.

"And where is the dining room located, young man?" Mother said.

"Your main dining room would be on deck D, Ma'am, what we call the Saloon Deck."

I thought I heard mother sniff. Perhaps she thought it an interminable distance. I thought it exciting that we would be roaming all over this wonderful space.

We finally arrived at our suite. Our home in Belgravia was a lovely, well-appointed house, but this suite—it was something else altogether. I believe my jaw dropped just a bit as we entered the lavishly decorated space. It was so unexpected. In my young mind's eye, I had expected something far more modest, not a floating palace!

"Welcome to the B-58, the Parlour Suite, Mr. and Mrs. Phillips," the porter said.

The ornately decorated walls were covered in burgundy silk damask, and the ceilings were adorned with filigree mouldings. They reminded me of Italian Renaissance décor I'd seen in a schoolbook only last term. It had two bedrooms as well as a small room for Nora, a wardrobe room (Mother was delighted—despite her reserved response, I could tell that she was bursting!), two ensuite bathrooms with tubs and, most exciting of all, a private promenade. It occurred to me that Father must be an important person, indeed.

We had little time to spare if we wanted to be on deck for the departure. Mother instructed Nora to begin the unpacking, which disappointed me greatly. I had hoped that Nora could join us on deck. She said she'd be fine and that she would pop out onto the private promenade in due course.

We joined the rest of the first-class passengers on the promenade deck reserved exclusively for this group and took up a place at the rail where we could gaze down at the noisy crowd waving madly to see us off. At precisely noon, accompanied by two long blasts of the ship's klaxon, the Titanic began to move away from her berth. I looked down from where I was standing at the teak railing and watched as the distance between the ship and the berth began to widen slowly. That's when the first wave of anxiety began to wash over me. I did mention that I was afraid of large expanses of water, did I not? Perhaps deathly afraid might be more precise. I tried to concentrate on my excitement and my new dress that I would save for the first night after leaving our final port in Ireland. I tried to slow my breathing as the gap grew wider.

As the ship started to move, we began to pass by two large ocean liners moored just offshore. I squinted to see that one was the SS City of New York and the other called the Oceanic. It seemed that we had displaced a miniature tsunami. My hand flew to my mouth as the City of New York broke free of its mooring cables and began to swing around as if to crash into us. I watched as a tiny tugboat was able to assist in preventing sure disaster. I heard later that we had avoided a collision by a mere four feet between the two massive ships. I heard my father mutter, "Begin as you intend to continue. I sincerely hope not."

As a result of this mayhem, our departure was delayed by close to an hour. Since the wind was becoming noticeably cooler and my mother did not wish to spend the entire time on the deck, we returned to our suite to prepare for dinner. By the time we emerged at half-six, we had arrived in Cherbourg in France, where small tender vessels had begun to ferry more passengers to the ship. I begged Father to let me slip out onto the promenade deck to see the spectacle. I looked over toward Cherbourg and thought, *I am in France! It may be the first time, but it will not be the last*. That was my solemn promise to myself. I looked directly down toward the water and felt as if I might be gaining my sea legs just a bit.

~

We stayed at anchor for only one and a half hours then, as we made our way to the dining room that first evening, I could feel that we were, once again, on our way. As we entered the dining room, I found myself, as before, astounded by the grandeur. It looked like a magnificent two-story ballroom that filled the entire width of the ship. The central chandelier twinkled, resulting in cascades of diamonds down each wall. I was trying my best to imprint this on my memory when I heard my mother mutter something to my father.

"Edward, I do hope that is not who I think it is sitting at our table."

Both Father and I looked in the direction of the table to which the *maitre d'* was now leading us.

"I don't know what you're talking about, Maude." He peered in the direction my mother was trying not to point toward. "By George, I don't know who you hope it isn't, but I see Cosmo Duff-Gordon. Haven't seen him in a dog's age." Father then headed more quickly in the direction of the table where an imposing-looking man arose to shake his hand. I looked to see the woman sitting on his left and was surprised—no, shocked, really—to see the great Lucile, Lady Duff-Gordon. I was beyond ecstatic, but I knew that this would irritate my mother. Socializing with her "dressmaker" would not be her preferred way to spend a series of evenings. *Oh, this is going to be good*, I thought.

As we approached the table, it seemed that Lady Lucile did not recognize me. I'm sure that the dress I was wearing, pink satin with a large white collar and long sleeves—chosen by my mother—would have made me look the very picture of the childish school girl. I wondered how she would feel about me when I appeared in her gown in a few days. I thought I'd just pretend we hadn't met so that it could be a great surprise for her. When we arrived, Lady Lucile and her husband, Sir Cosmo, were already deep into their predinner drinks (perhaps even more than one), and I noted her looking me up and down. It seemed as if she found me wanting in some way. I thought perhaps it was because a twelve-year-old girl (even one who looked older as I expected I did) might be considered something of a wet blanket, as they say. I would have to prove her wrong.

My mother sat stiffly through dinner as I plied Lucile with questions about dressmaking. She was not the warmest person I had ever met. However, she warmed to her subject. When I asked her about her opinion of the latest designers on the continent, my mother looked at me quizzically as if to question how her daughter might know about such things. I had not told Mother that Abigail and I spent as much time as we could manage together devouring her mother's cast-off copies of *Vogue* magazine that she had brought over from America during a recent trip abroad. In fact, we had recently spent an entire lunch hour eluding the housemistress while pouring over the most recent issue. I had even copied the cover illustration in my journal. I could still see the silhouetted couple—he, wearing top-hat and tails, and she in the latest designer creation that included masses of feathers flowing from her exquisite hat. I had read the article called "Whispers to the Girl with Nothing a Year," where they showcased fashion sewing patterns to afford everyone a designer wardrobe.

Lucile had her own opinions about the new designers. "I think that many designers of the younger school are far too inclined to turn out their models *en masse*," she said. "Indeed, they seem to have no regard for the special needs of the women who will wear them. As a consequence, their designs lack personality and interest. I, on the other hand, always see the woman, not the frock as detached from her. That is why women so love my clothes. You might remember, young lady, that women are, above all other things, individual in every thought and action."

I was impressed that Lucile thought so highly of herself because I had encountered many of Mother's friends who seemed to be only their husband's appendage. I also wanted to say bravo! I did not. I could not even imagine how Mother might have reacted to that.

Later, as I prepared for my first night sleeping on board an ocean liner, I overheard Mother and Father having a rather heated conversation. The walls here were not as solid as those in our Belgravia house.

"Edward, it is mortifying in the extreme."

"What can possibly be so mortifying that you are asking me to have our table changed?"

"That woman," Mother said. "That Duff-Gordon woman. She is 'in trade,' as you well know. She believes herself to be socially on the same level as her clients."

"Well, Maude, she is *Lady* Duff-Gordon, after all. I don't know what you're so bothered about. Cosmo is great fun, and although I do have to admit Lucile does take a rather self-important stance, on the whole, I find them amusing. And Frances did seem to be quite riveted by her."

"All the more reason for us to get Frances away from her, Edward. That Duff-Gordon woman may be a bad influence."

"For god's sake, Maude. It's only for a week. Perhaps Frances can learn something. And besides, can you imagine the tongue-wagging if we were to complain about our table mates. Some might even have the audacity to call us snobs."

Of course, I was rooting for Father in this particular argument. I had many more questions to put to the great Lucile—and she had to see me in her dress.

~

We had one more stop before we began our journey across the North Atlantic in earnest. The following day, at 11:30 a.m., we arrived in Cork Harbour on the south coast of Ireland, where, once again, tender vessels brought on a few more passengers. Nora begged Mother to let her spend a few moments on deck so that she could gaze once again at her homeland in the distance. I popped out myself and spied her on deck with that young porter who, as it turned out, was called Liam and was from a village in County Cork, not far from where Nora's family still lived. It was meant to be!

Two hours later, we weighed anchor for the last time and set sail for America. I was spending the afternoon doing some sketching and writing in my diary, after which I would ask Nora to help me get ready for dinner. Tonight would be the night. I would appear in the dining room in my Lucile original, and I would no longer be a twelve-year-old girl. I would be a young woman. Of that, I was certain.

~

"Where is it, Nora?"

"Where is what, Miss Frances?"

"My dress."

"Here they are." Nora pulled open the door of the small closet in my room. "Your dresses are all here."

"The dress. The most important dress. It is assuredly not there." I almost stamped my foot, a gesture I had left behind long ago in the depths of my childhood, or so I thought. "You know which dress it is, Nora. It is the one from Lucile's salon. The purple one." I stormed out into the drawing-room of our suite past my father, who was sitting, already attired in his evening clothes, sipping a glass of whiskey, and into my parents' bedroom. My mother sat at the dressing table affixing her diamond hair clip. I ran by her and flung open the wardrobe room doors where her clothes took up two-thirds and my father's one-third. I began rifling through her dresses.

Mother stood up and pulled her silk robe around her. "Frances, stop that this instant. What has gotten into you?"

"Where is it, Mother?"

"Where is what, Frances?" She sat down again at the dressing table and stared into the glass, brushing her eyebrows with her fingertips.

"My dress. My Lucile dress!" I turned and stared at her, fury clouding my vision—or perhaps it was tears that I could feel beginning to form. I did not want to cry. That would be so childish.

"Oh, that one," Mother said absently.

My father appeared at the door, still holding his crystal whiskey glass. "Whatever is the matter with my girls this evening?" he said. "I suppose they can hear the shouting in the hall."

Mother glared at him and pursed her lips as if she were sucking on a lemon. "There is nothing for you to bother yourself about, Edward. Frances is simply having an outburst." She looked over at me. "Nothing new there," she said directly to me in a whisper.

"It's your doing, isn't it, Mother? You never wanted me to have that dress."

"Quite so," she said. "You are far too young for a dress like that. In fact, I have no idea what came over me that day. I instructed Nora to omit it from our packing. You can wear the grey velvet this evening."

"It makes me look like a child!"

"And so you are. Still." She arose and came over to where I was standing in front of the open wardrobe room doors. "Frances, there will be much time in the future for you to wear that dress. It will be far more appropriate for you when you are sixteen."

"Sixteen! I will not wait!" I am afraid that I did stamp my foot this time—just a little.

"Well, be that as it may, the dress is not here. It is far away in your closet at home. So, you will simply have to make a different choice. I am sure Nora will assist you."

I stormed out of the room, back through the drawing-room past Father, who looked far too amused for my liking, and back into my own room.

"Nora, how could you? How could you have left that dress at home? You know how much I wanted to wear it on this voyage."

"I am so sorry, Miss Frances, but you know what your mother is like." She glanced toward the open door into the drawing-room. "I had no choice. I do like my job, you know."

I did know. I knew all of it. Mother still thought of me as a child, perhaps even as an accessory. At most, I was a chattel.

I wore the grey velvet that evening and planned to wear it every night that remained on the voyage. That way, perhaps the other first-class passengers might wonder if we could not afford for me to have more clothing. Father wouldn't care at all. In fact, he might not even notice. Mother certainly would and would not like it one bit. But I would. Let them all gossip. I couldn't have cared less at that moment.

~

From then on, I found the voyage immensely dull. I still did not like that we could see nothing but water from every window, every deck, at every glance. I still held that prickly feeling of impending doom in the back of my neck and had to remind myself to breathe whenever I was outside. By the second day out of Ireland, the breeze had begun to pick up, though, so I spent little time on the deck.

The next afternoon, Father returned from a meeting with Mr. Astor. I had noted his name and image on the front page of one of Father's newspapers only two weeks earlier and knew him to be an American of great wealth. Perhaps he and my father had been doing business. I had not realized that they knew one another. From what I had overheard in the past few days, it seemed that Father's bank was a significant investor in the White Star Line and this very ship.

"I don't think anyone will be spending much time on deck for the remainder of the voyage," he began as he removed his silk scarf. "The temperature has dropped sharply."

"Oh, has it?" Mother said, looking up from the book she was reading.

"This is, after all, the North Atlantic, I suppose," he said as he poured himself a glass of whiskey. He looked over at me, where I sat on the settee, making notes in my diary. "Frances, you should have a look outside, though. There are small pans of ice floating by. It is quite mesmerizing."

I wasn't at all sure I wanted to see pans of ice, small or otherwise.

He continued. "Where is Nora? Perhaps she could accompany you on the Promenade."

"I have given her the afternoon off," Mother said.

"She is visiting Liam," I said, almost giggling. Nora and Liam, the Irish porter, had seemed to find one another quite companionable over the past few days, so she had told me. Naturally, I was happy for her. However, I wondered from time to time if she ever found a suitable young man might she leave our employ. I didn't like that idea.

"Is she now?" Father smiled slightly. Mother glared.

Dinner that evening was exceptionally boring. Lady Lucile and Sir Cosmo had decided to dine on French cuisine in the *À la Carte* restaurant that evening rather than our main dining room. I was just as glad as I had begun to find Lady Lucile to be a bit arrogant. Just the evening before, she had told me, in no uncertain terms, that she possessed something that almost all other women lacked. It was something she called 'chic.' I had never heard of it before, but it was clear that she thought it necessary for a fashionable life.

So, I was alone at the table with Mother and Father. I had oysters to begin—a choice at which Mother frowned but said nothing. If I could not dress like an adult, perhaps at least I could eat like one. I then chose the *Sauté of Chicken Lyonnaise* accompanied by *Chateau* potatoes (whatever they might be) and creamed carrots. As I read the menu, I realized that I did not know what Waldorf pudding might be and did not want to show my ignorance, so I chose the chocolate and vanilla eclairs for dessert. It was a most delicious meal. Why, you might well ask, do I remember that dinner so vividly? Perhaps because of the events that followed.

~

I said good-night to Mother and Father at 10:30 p.m. and sat up in bed against the pile of plush pillows encased in snowy white covers, reading and making sketches in my diary for some time. I finally turned off the light and lay back, feeling the gentle rock of the ship. It was exceptionally smooth sailing that evening. I peeked out the small window and could see no moon, but an array of stars shone down on the great expanse of water. I wondered who else in the world was looking at those stars at that very moment. I could still hear murmurings of my parents, who were still in conversation over a glass of brandy, even this late.

I was just drifting off into slumber when I felt a jolt and heard a scraping noise. *Odd*, I thought. *What could a ship this far out at sea possibly bump into*? I listened some more, but the only sound I heard was the door to our suite opening. I strained my ears and caught a bit of what Father was saying. I thought he said something about just going out to have a look. I could not go back to sleep.

I finally got up, pulled on my robe and crept out into the drawing-room.

"Whatever are you doing up at this hour, Frances?" Mother said. She was just pouring herself another brandy.

Before I had a chance to answer, Father returned. My father was a generally jovial man, but his face was a mask of concern at that moment. "Get Nora up and get your warmest coats on," he said as he gathered the papers he had been carrying in his valise. "Nothing to be concerned about," he continued, "but we should go up on deck."

"Up on deck, Edward? I certainly will not go up on deck in this cold. Whatever has come over you?"

He looked up. His face was as grim as I had ever seen it. "You most certainly will go up on deck, Maude. And you, Frances and Nora will go this very minute."

My mother said nothing but moved quickly to fetch coats while I woke Nora and grabbed my diary from the bureau. If something interesting was happening, I certainly wanted to be able to make notes. We piled out into the corridor as doors of other staterooms opened, people peering out, no doubt wondering what all the fuss was about. I wondered the same thing. Just as we rounded a corner, a crew member came racing down the hall toward us. "We're going down!" he shouted. "We're going down!" As we passed the first-class lounge, I could hear the musicians playing something familiar—yet, I couldn't focus enough to determine what it was.

I felt that ever-present unease in my neck begin to form into a river of anxiety as we pressed on down the corridor and up the steps to the boat deck. I could feel a rising panic not only in myself but in Mother, who had grasped my hand and was clinging to it with a vice-like grip as we followed Father. I had no desire to let him out of my sight. Nora was behind us as we quickly moved upward.

When we emerged out onto the deck, there were already so many people there. I saw Father reach for his pocket watch.

"What time is it, Father?" I said as I looked up at the still moonless sky and shivered.

"It's 12:40, Frances," he said as he looked over to where a group of passengers was gathering around lifeboat number seven.

"Will the Titanic sink, Father?"

"It well might at this point," he said. "But we shall not."

I saw Lady Lucile and Sir Cosmo closest to the rail. Father moved in their direction and beckoned us to follow just as I began to hear crew members shouting, "Women and children first!"

As we approached the lifeboat, I could see a well-dressed man I had previously seen in the smoking room as I passed by, arguing with a crew member. I could have sworn I saw him pass money to the crew member. The next moment, the man turned to the woman standing beside him, whom I assumed was his wife, and practically pushed her into the lifeboat. Sir Cosmo thumped the man on the back, and Lady Lucile, gesturing for her maid to follow, clambered onto the boat. Sir Cosmo turned and gestured to Father, then climbed into the lifeboat after his wife.

Everything happened so fast after that. The next moment, I found myself huddled in an open boat in the freezing cold with masses of inky water filling an ever-widening space between our tiny group and the massive ship. I could see people on the deck above, but their images were getting fainter and blurrier. I realized I was crying.

When I finally caught a hold of myself, I sat up a bit straighter, patted the life vest that I had somehow donned, and looked around at the group. There had been so many people clamouring to get into this boat while crew members told everyone not to worry. They'd be back on board in an hour. I had a feeling they were wrong. Despite the great numbers still on the decks that were fading away in the night, this lifeboat seemed to be half empty. I began to count. There were only twenty-seven of us. I remembered asking Father how many people could fit into each lifeboat one day as we walked along the deck. He had told me sixty-five. Sixty-five! Why was the crew member rowing away with only twenty-seven people on board? Then I remembered what I had seen. Surely the man had not bribed the crew member? But then, how did Sir Cosmo, the other man—and my father—get aboard a lifeboat when the call was for women and children first? As young as I was, I could simply not grasp it.

I did not know how much time had passed since we had found ourselves on the cold sea in an open boat. Water had seeped into the bottom of the boat, and my feet were freezing. I wondered briefly if we might not go down. I realized that my lack of swimming skills wouldn't hamper me in the least. No one could remain alive in that water for any length of time. "Father," I said, "what time is it?" I seemed to be obsessed with the passing of time.

He had some difficulty seeing his watch, but there was just enough reflection of the ship's lights on the ocean, which was still as smooth as glass.

"I make it to be 2:18, Frances."

At that very moment, I heard a distant rumbling. I looked on with horror as all the lights aboard the Titanic vanished. All that was left were the pitiful shouts of people still on board. A tear escaped my eye and slid down my cheek. Two minutes later, there was a terrifying explosion and more sickening screaming. I could hear splashing as if passengers were falling into the freezing water. I couldn't bear it.

I peered out into the blackness and should have felt the greatest terror of my life, but I saw what looked to be people swimming. Had they somehow jumped into the frigid waters and survived?

"We must go back!" I shouted at the crewman who was rowing madly, putting more and more distance between our small boat and the Titanic, which was now a dark silhouette in the distance.

"Keep rowing," came a booming voice from the back of the lifeboat. "Row as if your life depended on it, man. We'll be swamped when she goes down, and then we'll all be dead. Row, man, row!"

Who was that? I didn't recognize the voice and could hardly believe what I was hearing. Did they have no compassion for their fellows? I drew my coat closer to me and looked over at Mother, wearing her mink coat and hat, crouched beside Lady Lucile.

Lucile, squinting through the darkness, looked at her maid and said, "Oh, Franks, there is your beautiful nightdress—ruined." Franks, her maid, just looked at her with sad eyes.

My mother nodded, and I thought, *How can you endure such triviality at a time like this?* But I did know. I wished I dared to tell Lady Lucile what I thought of her at that moment. But I needn't have worried.

The crew member assigned to our lifeboat as a fireman responded for me. "You will be able to replace your property, Madam, but we will never be able to replace the people we have just lost to the sea."

I knew it just as surely as I knew that my life would, from this day onward, be different. It was just as I knew that the sense of entitlement I had witnessed this day would never be a part of who I would become—because I was becoming someone. I just wasn't entirely sure who that was. Yet.

FIVE

THE NEXT FEW DAYS WERE A BLUR OF DISCOMFORT and misery. Most of the misery resulted from my mother's constant whining about her lost clothing, her ruined mink and our general lack of opulent accommodation. I, on the other hand, felt a strange sense of freedom. It was as if I could finally see my life for what it was: the life of a child who owed her very existence to the good graces of her parents. I would have to do something about that.

I do shudder to think what might have befallen us had the Carpathia, a Cunard liner, not have been close enough to arrive before we all perished. As it was, I knew that many had indeed succumbed that night. I felt as if my life might just be beginning the moment I was plucked from that lifeboat to safety. I was far less concerned about my lost belongings (I did have to thank Mother in the end for not bringing along that dress) than I was about Nora's wretchedness. After twenty-four hours aboard our saviour ship, it was clear to her that Liam had been one of the unlucky crew members who had gone down. I tried my best to comfort her.

My father spent the three days we were incarcerated on the Carpathia meeting with others who had survived and had some business with the White Star Line. He seemed greatly troubled by the entire situation. I wondered if it was because of money—or lost souls. I was never to know.

On the evening of April 18, three days after we had very nearly lost our lives, we sailed up the Hudson River past the Statue of Liberty and on into New York. I ought to have been more upset by the whole ordeal than I was—at least that's what Mother had said several times over the three days. Indeed, I believe she thought that I was in shock of some kind. I was not. I was excited to be finally arriving in America. It was my first trip, and I vowed that it would not be my last.

As we made our way toward a berth at Pier 54, the Carpathia's home pier, for disembarkation, the ship stopped at the White Star dock to deposit the lifeboats in which we had been rescued. As we made our way closer to where we could finally stand on solid ground once again, the ship was surrounded by hordes of tugboats from which we could hear much yelling and screaming and see lightbulbs popping.

As I looked down from the deck where we had gathered to watch our re-entry into the world—or so it seemed to me—I wondered what all the fuss was about.

"Who are those people in the little boats, Father?" I said as another round of popping lights met us.

"I believe they are journalists—reporters from newspapers. I have been told there is much confusion about what transpired out there in the North Atlantic, and I believe they are looking to the survivors to tell them their story."

"Could we, Father?" I thought that telling my story to a newspaper would be the most exciting thing that had ever happened to me in my life—barring recent events.

"We most assuredly will do no such thing!" Mother seemed taken aback by the very idea. "You will say nothing to anyone about the incident while we are in America and upon our eventual return to London." She looked sharply at me. "Is that clear, Frances?"

I shrugged. It seemed to me to be a story that ought to be told. Just then, I heard some shouting from directly beneath where we were standing. "Fifty dollars for your story!" So, the reporters were even offering to pay. I would be looking for those stories for the next few days whenever I could spy a newspaper.

After we docked, Mother was agitating to disembark immediately. Father assured her that we would be next after the Carpathia's own passengers. Mother was of the opinion that since we had been through "the incident," we ought to have priority. That, of course, fell on deaf ears. We simply waited until it was our turn.

As I set foot on dry land, I looked back at the Carpathia with its lights twinkling against the night sky. "Thank you," I whispered. Then I looked down at the ground and said out loud to no one in particular, "I am in America!"

Numerous groups were offering to take those of us plucked from the sea to various shelters. However, Father had gone to see the wireless officer the day before and had telegraphed ahead to our hotel that we would be arriving. After we had settled, Mother arranged for staff from several stores to come to our hotel so that we could choose new wardrobes. That was amusing, but I would have preferred to shop along the streets. Mother said that we were not presentable but that we would get to that eventually.

We spent two weeks in New York before we had to face the prospect of another ocean voyage. Because of his work, Father was to stay on in the city for several more weeks, but Mother and I, accompanied by Nora, would have to go home.

"Are you sure you cannot come with us?" Mother said to Father. "I cannot abide the thought of another ocean voyage. And so soon. Could we not stay here with you?"

The answer was no. We were to return home and carry on as if nothing had ever happened. I wasn't convinced that Mother could do that. In any case, we did return to England on an uneventful voyage, arriving back in Southampton, where the whole ordeal had begun. When we finally arrived back at our London home, I walked in through the front door and felt as if I were in a dream world. How could any of this be real? I had heard the screams of people dying, and now I was back in the arms of indulgence. I would have to make some changes.

First, Mother and Father were to understand that I had grown up (yes, I was still twelve years old, but not all twelve-year-olds are the same). Second, I planned to spend as much time as I chose with Abigail and whomever else I liked. Finally, and most important of all, I planned to make something of myself. I had to come up with a plan.

~

Spending more time with Abigail was the easiest part. Mother had taken to her bed the moment we returned and spent the better part of each day there wearing a silk dressing gown with a mask over her eyes. I hoped that she would return to good health before Father returned from America since I knew full well that he would not be pleased with this turn of events. He indulged her in many ways, but I had also observed that he expected her to participate in his world whenever he needed her to. I had occasionally heard her suggest that perhaps she was too tired to go to one social event or other, yet he had insisted that she would do so. In any event, Mother had little interest in how I spent my time. This was how I found myself at Abigail's home one afternoon after school, holed up in her father's library—and an impressive library it was.

Since Abigail's father was a novelist of some repute, he didn't go to an office every day as my father did. He had a large, wood-panelled office on the main floor of their home overlooking the street. He also had a library. It was situated opposite his office, also overlooking the street. According to Abigail, the rooms had, at one time, been the drawing-room and dining room of the original house. Her parents had moved those rooms to the back of the house and turned the front into a writing haven for Abigail's father.

That afternoon we were scouring the shelves for books we recognized—the more scandalous, the better. I stood on my toes to read the names of the books on the top shelf and walked past rows and rows of books. Authors' names jumped out—Joseph Conrad, Marcel Proust, James Joyce, Herman Hesse. Were there no women writers?

"Where does your father keep the books written by women?"

Abigail shrugged. "I'm not sure he has any. But I have some. Do you remember when we used to love reading Beatrix Potter books?"

"Of course, but those are children's books. Surely women can write something other than books for children?"

I ran my hand down the spines on the shelf in front of me. "Do you suppose any of these whose author's names are simply initials are women?"

"Why would they do that? Why wouldn't they use their full names?"

"Perhaps because their husbands won't let them have a job," I said, thinking about Father and then about Lady Lucile being a dressmaker. Her husband didn't appear to mind that his wife seemed to be making a great deal of money from her work.

"Well," Abigail said, pulling a volume from a shelf, "then I don't suppose I want to have a husband."

"I'm not inclined toward that life, either," I said, grabbing a book randomly from the shelf.

We both flopped down on the leather sofa, which squeaked loudly.

"What have you pulled?" Abigail said as she flipped through the volume she was holding.

I looked down at the cover then opened it to the frontispiece. "It's called *The Memoirs of Dolly Morton*," I said. "It's by someone called Jean de Villet." I turned toward Abigail. "Do you suppose that's a woman's name?"

Abigail leaned over and read the full title out loud. "*The Story of A Woman's Part in the Struggle to Free the Slaves, An Account of the Whippings, Rapes, and Violences that Preceded the Civil War in America, with Curious Anthropological Observations on the Radical Diversities in the Conformation of the Female Bottom and the Way Different Women Endure Chastisement.*" Abigail's eyes widened. "I think not, Frannie. I don't think a woman could write that."

I shrugged then looked at it carefully. "Heavens, Abigail. It sounds marvellous."

"It sounds indecent, maybe even lascivious." It was her latest new word.

"It sounds perfect. I'm taking this one. Will your father miss it?"

"Look around, Frannie. He would be unlikely to notice if we took a hundred books!"

And that was how I came to accomplish my first rebellious act: to read a shocking book—at least my mother would have been shocked!

~

I had been something of a minor celebrity for the first few weeks after I returned to school. Even girls who had previously thought me too smart or stuck-up (I knew this because you just know these things when you are twelve years old) wanted to hear the Titanic story. I happily held the spotlight for a while, then grew tired of it. Being a "survivor" was not the way I wanted to be viewed, nor was it how I wanted to live my life. And the more I thought about it, the more I realized that I did want to live—really live. I just had to find something to live for.

I first heard of Emmeline Parkhurst when I spied Father's newspaper one morning and saw that there had been an explosion of some kind in Regent Park the day before.

"What is the 'Women's Social and Political Union'?" I asked as I reached for the toast rack across the breakfast table.

My father looked up from his eggs and raised his eyebrows. I detected a small smile. "Frances, I wouldn't let your mother hear of your curiosity about Mrs. Pankhurst's group."

I was now slathering butter on a fat piece of toast that was already cold from sitting in the toast rack for too long. "I won't tell if you won't."

This made him laugh. He put his coffee cup down on the table. Since his return from New York, I noticed that he had taken to drinking coffee rather than tea with his breakfast. I would have to remember to ask him if I could try it, but I didn't want to distract him from my question right at that moment.

"Well, Frances," he said, picking up the newspaper with the story about the women's group. "It's a group of women who work to gain more rights for women."

"What kind of rights?" I really didn't know what constituted rights, but I was sure I'd be able to figure it out if Father continued to discuss this with me.

"Foremost, the right to vote," he said. "These ladies are what one calls suffragettes."

"I'm not sure I understand."

"Suffrage means to have the right to vote in elections where the people select the leaders who govern the country."

"But if they are supposed to be selected by the people, why don't women vote already? Women are people."

Father sat back in his chair. "That's where it gets tricky, my darling daughter. Women are explicitly not permitted to vote by virtue of laws that were passed in the 1830s."

"I don't understand. Men are people. Women are people. They are the same. They should be able to do the same things."

Father sighed. "Unfortunately, Frances, there are a great many things women are not permitted to do—or rather are often discouraged from doing. You will learn this as you get older."

"If I must learn such a bone-headed thing, then I do not wish to get older."

Father shrugged. "And yet you must. It is inevitable."

"Do *you* think that women should not be able to do all that men do?"

Father pulled his watch from his pocket. "Good heavens! Look at the time. I must leave, or I shall be late." He got up from the table, then turned back and picked up the newspaper, which he tucked under his arm. He kissed the top of my head as he left the breakfast room. I sat there chewing on the hard toast and thinking about what he had said. I felt that I would have to learn more about this women's suffrage thing.

~

Over the next year, I tried to follow the story of the women's movement in the newspapers whenever I could, but I found them becoming more and more dire. First, they would hold parades, after which many women would be arrested. Then, when in jail, they would go on hunger strikes. I had planned to find a way to attend a parade or two, but the opportunity never seemed to arise. However, I also recognized my love for fashion and my desire to make dresses. After seeing the grainy newspaper pictures of Mrs. Pankhurst and her army of women, it seemed that this desire for beauty and artistry in clothing might put me at odds with them. I felt that I would have to find another way to make women equal. But, first, I had to hatch a plan.

I began by gently broaching the subject of learning to sew clothing with my parents. Predictably, Mother was adamantly against such an endeavour. As she had often told us, she found women 'in trade' to be slightly *gauche,* regardless of their social status. Consequently, she had no desire for her daughter to enter their ranks. However, I wasn't to be deterred.

I had seen a beautiful, black sewing machine with a foot treadle (it did not need to be hand-cranked) in the window of a shop one day in early October. I was determined that it would be my Christmas present this year. I figured that Father could be persuaded, but Mother would be more difficult.

I began by dropping hints about a sewing machine for Christmas. Then, one evening when Mother and Father thought I was upstairs studying, I overheard a conversation.

"Edward, Frances cannot be permitted to have a sewing machine."

"What harm could there be?"

"Harm? I fear she will end up like that crass Duff-Gordon woman."

"I must admit I wasn't all that fond of Lady Lucile, but Frances isn't a bit like her. But, in any case, it might well be a good skill for her to have—as a wife and mother in the future, I mean."

"I think not. It is better for her to focus on being presented to society." Mother sounded adamant.

That was when I decided I would begin a campaign to convince Mother that I was planning to attend the women's suffrage marches regardless of her directives against such behaviour. I was relentless—although I never did have the courage to participate in a march. Finally, one day when she and I were alone in the drawing-room, I casually said, "I suppose if I learned to sew, I might not have time for those marches." Or something like that.

The sewing machine and a book called *The Dressmaker: A Complete Book of All Matters Connected to Sewing and Dressmaking* from The Butterick Publishing Company in America appeared under the tree that Christmas.

~

Over the next year, I spent every moment I could find immersed in *The Dressmaker* and trying to figure out how to construct a simple skirt. Abigail and I had also found several more shocking books among her father's stacks, and we had each devoured them in private, getting together to discuss them whenever we could. We learned so many things about life, love and especially boys. It was a bright day in the summer of 1914, the news full of whether England would go to war with Germany (something I found exceptionally dull) as I sat in our back garden reading a less lascivious book, lest Mother should catch me (she seemed to have almost recovered from "the incident") when Oliver Lowther-Russell himself materialized beside me.

"Well, Frannie Phillips, whatever are you reading?"

"Ollie!" I jumped. "You startled me. I believe it to be quite impolite to startle a young lady."

"I don't suppose I did startle a young lady," he said. "I suppose you are young but are you a lady?"

He sat down in the empty chair beside me and kicked off his shoes into the grass. He picked up one of the books I had discarded. "Well, what do we have here?"

Ollie was now sixteen years old, very tall and quite handsome with his floppy blonde hair and blue eyes. I had often wondered if he had ever been admonished to get a haircut by either his parents or his school. However, he was so charming that I supposed he could somehow get away with it.

I looked over to see what book he was holding. I could feel my cheeks begin to redden as a blush—no doubt an ugly one— rose from my neck upward. He was holding a book called *The Autobiography of a Flea*. It was one Abigail and I had found among her father's books and

I had discovered—but had not yet had a chance to tell Abigail—that it was the story of the rather shameless behaviour of a young girl named Bella as told from the perspective of a flea who observed it all. It was an old book—published in 1887. I hoped Ollie was not familiar with it. I hoped in vain.

"Have you studied this one?" He said, grinning widely. "I know I have."

"Ollie, we have been friends since we were children." I held my hand up to silence him as he began to open his mouth. "And we are no longer children. I would solemnly request that you keep your thoughts about this matter to yourself." *Well*, I thought, *that should do it.*

He began flipping through the book. "I would much prefer to hear your thoughts about this book," he said. Then, to my great mortification, he began to read a passage. *"Bella was a beauty—just fourteen—a perfect figure, and although so young, her soft bosom was already budding into those proportions which delight the other sex."*

"That will be quite enough, Ollie," I said, getting up from my chair in as dignified a manner as I could muster. I grabbed the book out of his hand, lest he find it necessary to continue to embarrass me. Then, as I stood there clutching the book to my chest, watching his surprised face looking up at me, I realized that I was acting precisely as he might have expected—like a child. I then thought about his question on the topic of whether I was a lady. I decided to take a different approach to stave off any conclusion he might draw about my childish ways.

"Well, Ollie, if you would have me question whether I am, indeed, a lady, please tell me your definition of a lady. I am sure you have one."

He sat up a bit straighter and folded his hands in his lap. "This is an interesting question, Frannie. I suppose, first and foremost, a lady is one who displays impeccable manners." He looked at me. "For the most part, you have good manners." I nodded, willing him to go on. "A lady dresses well." He looked at me and nodded. "I suppose a lady is true to her word and always does what is required of her."

"And what, precisely, is required of her?"

"To be slightly superior to men, I suppose, in some ways. Morally for certain."

"Morally? Why should a woman be expected to be morally superior to men? Which suggests that men are expected to be morally inferior to women."

"Frannie, I didn't say that a *woman* should be morally superior. I said that a *lady* should. Isn't that what we're talking about? Although, on second thought, perhaps it is the case that all women are expected to be morally superior. As for men's moral inferiority? I shall leave that up to you to observe as you mature." I rolled my eyes. He continued. "Anyway, a lady ought never to be vulgar."

I laughed then sat down in the chair again, still clutching the book, almost as if to protect myself. "Why is it that so much is expected of women—ladies—and so little of men?"

"I beg to differ. There is a great deal expected of gentlemen these days, Frannie. It's just that it is different." He twisted in his chair to face me. "For example, my family expects me to go up to Oxford and become a barrister like my father. I really have little say in the matter."

"Do you not want to go up to Oxford? I should consider it a great honour if my family expected such a thing of me." I tried not to pout.

"I don't think you understand, Frannie. Yes, I do wish to become a barrister. And I consider this to be a great benefit to me in my life—wanting what my family wants or rather expects. I have friends who don't wish to follow their family's expectations, and yet they must. In life, I believe that we all must do some things that we may not want to do."

It was at that moment that I realized how very wise my childhood friend had become.

~

In early August, mere days after Ollie and I had discussed ladies, England was at war. I had no idea what this might mean to me, my life, or anyone in my family. By the middle of September, the newspapers I saw every morning on the breakfast room table next to my father's chair were full of war updates. Every morning, I tried to get into breakfast to read the front page before he realized I was doing so and before he took the paper with him to his office. Of course, Mother would never have approved of her daughter learning the details of a war that she expected to have no impact on our lives.

We went about our business. Father went to work, I went to school, and Mother continued to visit her friends and gossip about gowns and parties. I began to wonder what war was all about until January of the following year when I read in Father's morning newspaper about something called conscription.

"Father," I began when he arrived in the breakfast room, once again complaining about the cold and drizzle outside. "What is conscription?"

He frowned at me. "What makes you ask about conscription?" Then he glanced down at the folded newspaper beside his plate and saw the headline. *Conscription to begin.* "Oh, I see. You've been reading my newspapers, have you?" He sat down and poured himself a cup of coffee. "Well, Frances, it means that young men must sign up to serve in the army and go to war." He lifted the paper and read for a moment.

"All men? You, Father?"

He laughed. "No darling daughter, not me. I fear I am too old." He pointed to the story. "It says only those between eighteen and forty at this time."

I thought for a moment. "But Ollie turns eighteen this year." I felt a shiver wend its way up my spine.

"I suppose he does," Father said. "But he goes up to Oxford this summer, so I shouldn't expect he will be called up any time soon."

"Any time soon?"

"Perhaps not any time at all, Frances. It's too early to tell. Besides, I'm sure Oliver would be only too happy to serve his country."

I wasn't as sure about that as Father was, and I certainly did not wish to see any friend of mine go to war. I was, however, grateful that I was a woman—perhaps even something of a lady. I knew how hypocritical that was, but I didn't care.

And so, the war seemed something abstract to me until the very end of May. That was the day when everything changed. That was the day when a kind of cold fear settled itself in my neck and stayed there for a very long time.

I didn't see it coming. I didn't see it land. We were shielded in our classroom, studying something that later seemed so trivial. But we heard what sounded like a faraway explosion, and out the window, we could see smoke rising in the distance. The Germans had finally made their way to London with their airship bombs—their Zeppelins—and all at once, we were afraid. The war had arrived on our very doorstep. It was no longer some abstraction of a faraway newspaper story.

We never knew when one of those cigar-shaped harbingers of terror would appear in the distant sky. We never knew where the bomb might drop. We never knew if we would live to see the end of one day and the sunrise of the next. But the worst day for me was the day in September when the biggest bomb yet fell on the financial district—while Father was at work.

I arrived home from school to find my mother in a desperate frenzy. I had rarely seen Mother so agitated in all my life. She had asked our housekeeper Mrs. Groundwood to dispatch her husband, our gardener, to find Father.

"I have no idea where your father is," she said, twisting the handkerchief she clutched in her hands. "I have no idea if he is alive or dead!"

I tried as best I could to comfort her, but she was too overcome.

It was a long afternoon and evening. Then, finally, Father appeared. Dirty, tired and bedraggled but very much alive. The bomb had hit a building at the end of the block from his bank. According to his description, only the walls remained standing. There was rubble everywhere, but everyone in his bank managed to get out unharmed. For that, he was grateful. But the experience had solidified a notion that he had mentioned once or twice before this day. He wanted Mother to take me out of the city into the countryside as far away as possible from the horrors of a German siege on London. I didn't want to go. In the end, I was given little choice.

~

Father arranged for Mother, Mrs. Groundwood, and me to take shelter from the war in Oxford with his spinster sister, my Aunt Mary. Aunt Mary had visited us on several occasions in London, but I had never been to Oxford to visit her. Mother said that it was an unsuitable place for a child. I wondered why it was suddenly suitable. Perhaps she no longer considered me to be a child.

Over the years, usually just before Aunt Mary would arrive for a visit, I had overheard Mother and Father talking about her large house and her two cats. Mary was Father's younger sister, and I had always thought of her as something of a free spirit. Her style was so vastly different from Mother's.

Mother was ladylike (there it was again), and she dressed in the finest of modern fashion. Mary was what I would call a Bohemian. She had never been married as far as I knew (thus the spinster moniker), but I had heard Mother mention men in Mary's life from time to time. It seemed that she was not often invited to visit us in London because Mother could never be sure of whether she might appear with one man or another. Mother had always taken a dim view of this. I found the prospect of getting to know my aunt better a very appealing idea, so I agreed to relocate to Oxford for the duration of the war, which I hoped would not last long. I also had a friend in Oxford, as you might recall. Ollie was at university, and I hoped to see him from time to time as a kind of connection to my London life.

I was to study at home for the interval—I was not to be enrolled in a school in Oxford. I wasn't sure how I felt about this. On the one hand, I would miss seeing the other girls. Or would I? I would only really miss Abigail if truth be told.

On the other hand, Aunt Mary was an intelligent, well-read woman of substance. When we arrived, I realized that this wouldn't be much of a hardship for me since Aunt Mary had an extensive library, almost as massive as Abigail's father's. I was missing Abigail, but I relished being in Mary's circle. I had also brought my sewing machine and piles of fabric I had convinced Father I had to have. It seemed he couldn't turn down any of my requests after I agreed to leave London without too much argument.

Marys' life in Oxford was hugely different from our life in London. Whereas she did benefit from the money Father and she had inherited from their parents (I only knew this because my mother mentioned it as we approached the house), she spent her money differently.

Once we had settled into our adjoining bedrooms upstairs in Mary's house, Mother rapped on my door and asked me to sit beside her on the bed.

"Frances, we do need to have a bit of a chat as we begin our temporary life here in Oxford with your Aunt Mary." I sat down. "Mary is—how can I put it—different. That is to say, she lives her life very differently than the life her brother, your father, lives. It is…" Mother hesitated for a moment as if trying to find the right word. "…unconventional. Perhaps even *avante-garde*. Do you understand this, Frances?"

"I suppose so, Mother. But isn't everyone different from the next one?"

"Not in the same way your aunt is. She has never married." I knew this. It didn't seem so odd to me. Mother continued. "Yet, she does have men in her life. I only hope they will not be around much while we are here. Furthermore, she is," Mother coughed slightly, "an artist of sorts."

"I don't really see the problem with either of those things, Mother."

Mother sighed heavily. "Frances, you are a young lady who should not have to be subjected to oddities of others' lives."

I thought Mother was entirely wrong. I thought it might be the very best thing that had ever happened to me. And I was planning on making the best of it.

~

"What are you doing there?" Aunt Mary rapped gently on the door frame to announce her presence and pulled her silk kimono closely around her as she approached me in the corner of my room. "May I see that?" She reached for the piece of fabric on the desk beside the sewing machine. "I had no idea you were interested in sewing. Did your father tell you that I used to sew when I was your age?"

This piece of information about my aunt came as a great surprise to me. She went on to tell me that her parents, too, had discouraged her from sewing. So, she took up painting. That pleased them more until they realized she was serious about it—that it wasn't simply something a lady might do in her spare time. She meant to follow her bliss, she said.

Aunt Mary sat down on the side of my bed. I noticed that her feet were bare—a state Mother would have found improper. I found it exciting to think about being able to do whatever one wished.

"Fran," she began. When I was younger, she had called me Frannie—never Frances as my parents did but had started calling me Fran now that I was older. I liked that. "How serious are you about this sewing?"

I turned from my sewing desk and faced her. "I believe I am very serious, Aunt Mary."

"Do your parents know?"

I laughed. "Mother thinks that it would be scandalous for me to pursue it past a hobby. Father just finds it amusing. I think he finds most of what I do amusing."

"Knowing my brother and his wife as I do, this doesn't surprise me at all. You know, Fran, I have a friend here in Oxford who is a dressmaker. Her name is Odile. Odile Fremen. She makes the most wonderful day dresses for the local elites. I'm sure you'd like her. I can arrange for you to spend some time in her workshop if that would be something you'd like to pursue while you're here."

"Do you think she would be willing to teach me some things? I have this book," I pointed to *The Dressmaker*, one of the books I had brought from London, "but I can only learn so much from drawings and words. If someone could show me…"

"Then it is settled," Aunt Mary said as she got up. "And remember what Sir Thomas Browne once said. *All wonders you seek are within yourself.*"

I took a moment to digest her words. "But what will Mother and Father say?"

"Leave them to me, my dear niece. Just leave them to me." She smiled broadly.

~

Oxford was a wonderful little place. Decidedly provincial in its ambience (at least according to Mother—I found it charming), it was a world apart from the grit, and grime and general rushing that were so much a part of London—the London I loved. Oxford had its historic buildings with their twelfth century and beyond pedigrees. So did London. Oxford had its genteel, almost relaxed character, and that is where they differed so much. And that's why I never really did feel at home away from the city. I hadn't realized how much I loved the mood of the big city, despite its grime, until I spent those next few years held captive by a war I was beginning to feel had gone on quite long enough. Having said that, I realized that I probably could never have learned the things I did if the sojourn hadn't happened. For that, perhaps I had to thank the war and the warriors who caused it.

True to her word, Aunt Mary arranged for me to meet Mme. Fremen. From the minute I met her, I loved everything about her. I even had an opportunity to try out my school French. In fact, it was one of the school subjects that I had been concentrating on since our banishment to the countryside. Even Ollie, whom I managed to see every week or so, assisted me by speaking French (or at least trying to) whenever we were together. He said it helped him as much as it helped me.

"*Mon dieu, mais tu es belle!*" was how she greeted me. "My god, but you are beautiful!"

Her compliment was something of a shock to me, the schoolgirl who had always considered herself to be smart but rather plain. Oh, yes, I did love beautiful clothes, but perhaps only to the extent that I had figured out that the best clothes could make you more beautiful.

"Je ne crois pas que je suis vraiment très belle. Mais merci, Mme. Fremen," I said in my very best French. "I don't believe I'm really very beautiful. But thank you."

She went on to tell me (and Aunt Mary) that women in England didn't really know what beautiful was. "The English do not seem to know when something is quite exquisite unless it conforms to their standards."

"A narrow one, perhaps?" Aunt Mary said.

"C'est très possible. It is very possible." Mme. Fremen's eyes glowed as Aunt Mary told her about my interest in garment construction. When Mary was finished, Mme. Fremen looked at me. "Well, mademoiselle, let us see what you have been able to teach yourself." With that, she led me to the back of her shop, where there were three sewing machines, all vacant. She told us her assistants had already left for the day.

She turned to a worktable and pulled from it several pieces of deep green fabric that looked to me as if they had already been cut from a pattern of some kind. She passed the pieces to me.

"See what you can make of these," she said.

I took them from her, running my hand over their smoothness. I then picked up a small piece and rubbed it between my fingers. There was no doubt about it: this was pure silk. I had learned the trick of feeling the slide of pure silk from a book and confirmed it with Lady Duff-Gordon. I shuddered slightly at the remembrance of the vile woman who made such beautiful dresses.

"But I don't know what it is meant to be," I said, looking at the pieces.

"That is precisely why I have asked you to see what you can make of it. That will be how I will know about your skill level."

"What if I ruin it?" I was deathly afraid of making a muddle of the pieces such that they couldn't be saved.

"You will not."

And I didn't. I figured it out—at least insofar as I made it into something that fit the pieces. It was a bolero jacket when I had finished.

Mme. Fremen, who by this time had implored me to call her Odile, was satisfied that I could be taught. She did not wax poetic about my current skill level, only that she believed she could help me develop my skills. That was good enough for me.

It was a kind of schooling wherein I felt as if I were learning a trade. I adored my work with Odile, but I also longed to return to London. Of course, as expected, Mother complained for the entire three years about what she perceived as a lack of social interaction and her own desire to return home. Finally, Father appeared in late August of 1918 with the news that he believed it might now be safe for us to return. I had left London a child and was returning a woman. I knew this after Ollie appeared at Aunt Mary's door one afternoon shortly after Father's arrival. He had heard the news that we were leaving Oxford and wished for me to spend the afternoon with him. I agreed.

After that afternoon with Ollie, I began to fully realize that I had grown up. I also realized that I had never even worn my Lucile dress—a dress selected by a child. I also knew I would never wear it.

~

Ollie had one more year left at Oxford, after which he would return to London and take up his position at his father's law firm. Since I wouldn't have many opportunities to see him over the next year, I was happy to be spending one of my last afternoons in Oxford with one of my best friends.

As we walked amiably along toward the centre of the town, Ollie began to sound like a tour guide, telling me about the university and how the city of Oxford itself as a whole was the campus since Oxford was a conglomeration of individual colleges.

"Ollie, I know all this. You and I have walked these streets so often since I've been here." He didn't seem quite himself. "Are you feeling all right?" I was genuinely concerned.

"Of course. What makes you think I'm not feeling well?"

I rolled my eyes, and at once, it occurred to me that perhaps he had been called up for military duty, although it appeared as if the war might be almost over. I was petrified.

"Let's go in," he said, gesturing toward the Randolph Hotel in the city centre. "We could have a drink."

I wasn't sure that "ladies" were welcome here, but perhaps they were more open-minded since it was a hotel. I followed him into a dark, wood-panelled space furnished with oversized, deep burgundy velvet chairs. He led me to a table in a corner next to an enormous fireplace which, thankfully given the heat of the day, wasn't lit. But I could imagine it roaring on a winter night.

Once we had sat down and he had a pint for himself and a glass of wine for me (I looked like an adult at least), he took a long gulp of his drink then looked at me, his face a mask of what looked to me to be terror.

"Frannie, I've been to see your father. He has agreed. Will you marry me?"

The Poiret

Flapper

SIX

"Care about people's approval, and you will be their prisoner.
~ Lao Tzu

I FELT MY JAW DROP AND MY EYES OPEN WIDE. I was, for one of the first times in my eighteen years on earth, speechless. Had Ollie just proposed marriage to me? His best friend? A woman who had often spoken of her opinion that marriage was a prison for women? I looked across the table at this man who, by the way, I did love—as I would love my brother—and could think of not a single thing to say in response. I certainly wasn't planning on saying yes, so I said the first thing that entered my head.

"You've spoken with father? About me?"

"Frannie, I know how traditional this sounds—"

"Traditional? It sounds downright medieval to me, Oliver Lowther-Russell. I am astounded at you." I was stalling for time. I was avoiding the question. I was falling off the edge of a cliff.

He hung his head, and I felt the stirring of a tear behind my right eye. I would have to stave it off at all costs. But I had no idea how my refusal—because refuse I must—would affect him or our friendship. There would have been a time when we could simply have laughed this off and gone on to other, lighter subjects. But I had a feeling that this was not one of those occasions. He looked as if he genuinely meant it, but I had no idea where this was coming from. And I had no idea how he would respond. This was uncharted territory for me—for both of us.

"Frannie, you know how much you mean to me, and you know how traditional your family can be. And mine, if you must know. My father would have tarred and feathered me if he ever found out I asked you to marry me without asking your father's permission."

"Permission?" I could feel my hysteria growing. "Permission for what? To take over control of one of his chattels?"

"This isn't going well, is it?" Ollie said quietly. "It's not at all how I pictured it." He hung his head further if that were possible. "I've messed it all up, haven't I?"

I had never seen my handsome, powerful, self-confident friend so miserable. My heart went out to him.

"Ollie, listen to me," I said, reaching over the table for his hands. "Please look at me. At your friend." He did. There, in his eyes, was not the teasing, mischievous childhood friend I had known and loved for so many years. He seemed to know what was coming next.

"Ollie, I love you. I have always loved you—even when you tease me mercilessly. But I have always thought of you as my best friend, as the one I could call upon if ever I needed a friend. I thought we'd be friends forever."

"And so, we can, Frannie. If we marry, we can be friends forever. What better way to start a marriage?"

"I fear you don't want the same things in life that I want."

"Surely you want a family, a home."

I took a deep breath. "That's just it, Ollie. I'm not sure I do want those things."

"Everyone needs a home, Fran."

"I suppose so, but everyone's idea of a home isn't the same as everyone else's."

"And what about children?" he said, draining his pint of beer.

"To tell you the truth, Ollie, I can't see myself as a mother at all. Every time I try to look into my future, I don't see children. I don't think I ever want children. That wouldn't be something you could live with, would it?"

He said nothing. I knew Ollie wanted to have a big house that he could fill with children. We had never discussed this specifically, but over the years, we had talked of so many things that dreams and hopes surfaced in conversation from time to time. He didn't seem to have noticed mine, however. At that moment, I realized that the sad thing for me was that I might now have to change one of my plans. It was a plan that involved Ollie.

For the past several months, whenever I wondered when we would return to London, I worked on a plot for an experience I wished to have once we got home. It wasn't something I could realistically accomplish in Oxford. I hoped that Ollie would be inclined to help me. My problem was that I no longer wanted to be a virgin, and I could think of no one I would like to help me rid myself of that particular affliction. Now, I wasn't so sure he'd be willing to help. In fact, I wondered if he might not be a bit scandalized by the idea. As much as I wanted to blurt this out, I thought it might not be the best time.

By the time we had finished our conversation, we seemed to have reached a kind of détente. I wasn't at all sure, though, that Ollie believed or accepted my view of my future. He told me that he understood, then suggested we speak again when we were in London. I just let it go.

~

And so, we returned to London. The minute we walked in, Mother instructed Mrs. Groundwood to open all the rooms. Father had stayed in the house for the duration with Nora there to assist him, and it now appeared he had used very few of them. It wasn't long before discussions of dress-fittings and parties and social obligations began. So, too, began my Mother's campaign to ensure I married. And soon.

"Frances, you are eighteen years old. In fact, you will soon be having your nineteenth birthday. The war has forced a delay in you moving into your future, but all is not lost." These were her words at dinner within the first week we were home.

Both my parents were scandalized by the fact that I had not immediately jumped at the prospect of becoming the wife of a well-placed young man with a bright future. They fully expected a wedding soon to be followed by grandchildren. My mother simply could not seem to stop talking about her friends' grandchildren. Isn't there an expression that says, *be careful what you wish for*? But I'm getting ahead of myself.

The war was officially over on the eleventh of November. The next day, I began to search in earnest for a position in a dressmaking establishment. Of course, I told my parents none of this.

It wasn't easy to find dressmakers who didn't know my mother. To tell you the truth, it wasn't easy to find dressmakers who were still doing any amount of business at this point. The war had been difficult for many of them since there had been little need for new dresses while women assisted on the home front in various non-social ways. As far as I was concerned, though, the most important characteristic for a place of work for me was that they were not acquainted with my family. I needed help here.

Abigail and I picked up our friendship just where we left off. Abigail, who had spent the balance of the war in Scotland with her father's cousins, knew of a few dressmakers. She offered to set up appointments for me with them, so, with the armistice still so new, on Tuesday, November 12, while the celebrations continued, I presented myself first at one, then the other. Each of the dressmakers occupied unprepossessing premises, which made me feel a bit unwelcome. I realized that any mention of my family would put them on their guard, wondering, and rightly so in the current situation, why someone like me was looking for a job.

After the second interview, I was stumbling along looking for something in my handbag when I bumped headlong into a threesome of soldiers who were just leaving a pub. They were in high spirits—naturally.

I looked up at them and realized that they were American soldiers. One of them kindly helped me to pick up the keys I'd dropped. As we arose, he began to apologize for their inattention. I locked eyes with him and was immediately swallowed up in their darkness. I could hardly breathe. He was the most beautiful man I had ever laid eyes on. As he took my hand to assist me to my feet, I looked up and noticed that he was well over six feet tall and possessed of a muscular build that was evident even under the U.S. army uniform. Handsome does not even come close to describing him.

The next thing I knew, the three of them were asking me to join them at the next pub they planned to visit. They had much to celebrate, they said. And besides, they felt as if it was the least they could do—that is, helping a young lady recover from a near-death experience at the hands of visiting military men. I knew I ought to say no, but I simply was unable to muster the words. And so, I accompanied them down the block and into the Cock and Bull where they bought me a drink, and we all sat at a table together. As I took my first sip, I suddenly felt as if I might have made an error in judgment. Just on a stop-over from France on their way back to America, these young men might be looking for more from the company of a young lady (woman?) than a simple drink. I began to feel that little tickle of dread. This time, though, the tickle didn't last long. It turned out that all they really did want was to have a drink with a woman and feel normal for a while. They were perfect gentlemen.

As we parted ways an hour later, Elliott, of the deep dark eyes, drew me aside.

"Fran, I'm only in town for a few days, but I'd really love to see you again before I ship out back home. You wouldn't consider having dinner with me tomorrow night, would you?"

I had to think fast. There was nothing I would rather do tomorrow evening than have dinner with Elliott, but I would have to be able to explain my absence from the family dinner table to my parents.

I told him yes. We were to meet at the Savoy at seven p.m.

I chose my clothing carefully that evening. I had only one outfit I considered suitable for dinner at the Savoy. I had made it in the spring from a sewing pattern I had copied from the *Butterick* catalogue. It had taken the catalogue months to arrive, so by the time I completed it, the weather had turned too warm to wear it. It was long-sleeved green chiffon with an overdress of green velvet. But the *pièce de resistance* was the fringe. Oh, how I loved fringe, and it was all the rage this year. It trimmed the bottom of the overskirt that stopped a few inches above the chiffon. A wide velvet belt wrapped the waist, and to finish the ensemble, I would wear a wide-brimmed hat with a matching band.

I did, however, have to ensure that no one would see me leave the house. For that, I conscripted Nora, whom I considered to be a friend (since I had not needed a governess for some years), and she was more than willing to help me when I told her about my adventure. She agreed to tell my parents that I felt unwell and wouldn't be joining them for dinner. She kept watch as I crept out of the house.

When I walked into the Savoy, I felt as if I had walked into the rest of my life. Elliott was sitting in the lounge waiting for me while a group of musicians serenaded with a violin, a cello and a piano. He greeted me with a handshake, then kissed my hand. I was somewhat taken aback. After all, he was an American. They simply didn't have any manners, or perhaps I had been mistaken all these years. I had only ever heard this from Mother.

He had ordered himself a martini, and I thought that was the most adult thing I could drink, so I asked for the same. When I lifted it to my lips for the first taste, I was greeted by a pungent smell that caused my nostrils to flare. I had to steady myself so that he didn't see how inexperienced I was. Then I sipped. I'm not sure what I expected to taste, but that wasn't it.

"Too dry?" Elliott said, preparing to ask a waiter for another.

I didn't know what "too dry" could possibly mean. It was very wet as far as I could tell.

"Sometimes they don't put enough vermouth in them," he said. I could see a small smile playing about his lips. He knew. He knew that this was my first martini.

I took another sip. This one went down much more smoothly. *I could get to like these*, I thought. I began to relax. We went from drinks to dinner and talked non-stop for two hours. Elliott was from some place in the state of New York (I had only thought of New York as the city I had visited after "the incident") called Rochester or something. It sounded suspiciously like an English town name. His father was a doctor, and his mother a housewife. He had two older brothers and a younger sister. I asked him what it was like to have siblings, so he regaled me with funny stories about Christmas mornings and Easter egg hunts.

By the time we had reached dessert, and many of our fellow diners seemed to have retired for the night, we looked at each other. I suddenly realized that I would not need to broach an awkward subject to Ollie—I would no longer require him to accomplish the goal I had set for myself before leaving Oxford. I could accomplish it tonight.

By the time I crept in through the back door and up the back staircase with Nora's help, it was almost five a.m., and I was no longer a virgin. And I had learned something unexpected about Elliott.

As he retrieved his uniform jacket from the back of the chair in the hotel room where he had placed it earlier, two photographs fluttered out and onto the floor. As I bent down to pick them up for him, I noticed that they appeared to be pictures of Elliott with his family.

"What a lovely photograph," I said, gazing at the first one. Pictured was a younger version of Elliott alongside two people I expected were his parents and an older black woman. I wondered if she might be a family servant. "And who is this?" I had said to him, pointing to the older woman.

He looked at me closely. "My grandmother," he said, watching my face.

I had been surprised but not shocked in any way. I thought it quite liberal. "Lovely," I said. As he turned to pick up his hat from the table, I slipped the photo into my handbag—a souvenir of sorts.

Elliott smiled at me and kissed me on the cheek, and I left. As I walked out through the Savoy Hotel's lobby, I smiled as I thought about my scandalous encounter. And I knew I would never see Elliott again.

~

By Christmas week, I still had not found a job working with a dressmaker. Every single one of them either had no work or seemed to be apprehensive about my background, and perhaps even a bit suspicious of my motives no matter how much I tried to reassure them that creating beautiful garments was my passion. I had told Abigail that I was becoming discouraged, so she suggested we have tea at the Savoy as a kind of pre-Christmas treat. I agreed but suggested that we go to Claridge's instead. The Savoy would always have a special place in my heart, and I did not wish to revisit it so soon.

On the twenty-third of December, as we walked arm-in-arm through Claridge's front doors heading toward the tearoom, I was suddenly overtaken by a question. "Abigail, why in the world do we have a meal between lunch and dinner? The Americans have given it up." I knew this from my hours of conversation with Elliott.

As it turned out, Abigail knew the answer. "It seems that in 1840 the Duchess of Bedford often found herself hungry at about four o'clock in the afternoon and unable to wait for late dinner at eight p.m. as was their habit then. So, afternoon tea."

"How do you know this fact, Abigail? You never cease to amaze me."

"Oh, there are things you don't know about me," she said, laughing.

I was glad of her company. The past few weeks had been difficult for me since I seemed to be having something of an existential crisis. I had been blocked from my dream of finding a job as a dressmaker and had turned down Ollie's proposal. What was I to do with my life? What would become of me?

I was prattling on to Abigail about the origin of tea only because I could feel my mounting anxiety. I hardly noticed the glittering mirrors on the walls or the chandeliers or even the fine bone china adorning the table. I heard only as if in a dream the tinkling of sterling silver spoons stirring tea in those china cups or the quiet murmurs of the other guests. I didn't taste the Irish breakfast tea I ordered or the cucumber sandwich I had bitten into and placed on my plate. I sat with my hands on my linen napkin on my lap as Abigail chattered. I hardly heard a word.

"Frannie, are you listening to me?" Then, unlike Abigail, she actually snapped her fingers in front of my face causing the woman at the next table to turn and gaze sourly in our direction. I only noticed this as I came to and apologized for my daydreaming.

"What's gotten into you, Frannie? You can't possibly be so downcast because of not getting a job. You'll find something to do eventually." I still said nothing. "What is wrong, Frannie? Tell me this minute."

"I'm pregnant," I said. The look of horror that passed across Abigail's face was more than disheartening. It was heart-breaking for me. Would I not be able to count on support from any corner of my life?

"Is Ollie the father?" Abigail's horror seemed to be mounting by the minute, no doubt because she was considering all the possible consequences for me, her friend.

"No. No, Ollie is not the father."

She seemed to let out the breath she had been holding. "Well, who is, then?"

"That's not important—"

"Not important? It most certainly is important. He will have to marry you!"

I laughed quietly, one of those hollow laughs that comes when you realize that the joke is on you. I had made my bed, so to speak, and I would now have to lie in it. I would have to face the consequences of my actions. At that moment, I realized that I had never been in this position before. I didn't like the feeling.

"Abigail, I will not be marrying anyone. I have to figure out how I'm going to handle this with my parents, and I had hoped for your support."

She leaned across the table and took my hand, which was now resting beside my plate that held my discarded sandwich. "And you shall have it. I will do whatever I can to support whatever happens. Won't you tell me who the man is?"

I shook my head. There was no point in anyone ever knowing about Elliott. I made a promise to myself at that very moment that I would never divulge this secret. But I would have to tell my parents about the impending birth of a grandchild. That would not be an easy conversation.

~

Abigail agreed to be visiting when I told my parents, but we would wait until after Christmas. I figured that Mother was far less likely to become hysterical with a "stranger" in the room in any case. I had no way of predicting Father's reaction. I expected that disappointment might be his primary response. I knew that both of them would feel somewhat ashamed that their daughter had found herself in this predicament because that's not how things were done in their social circle. I didn't feel that way, although I knew I should. It was an odd feeling. I had no idea how the next few months and years of my life would unfold, but then, does anyone ever know?

I managed to make it through Christmas with Mother, Father and Aunt Mary, who had joined us for the festivities. I had considered taking Aunt Mary into my confidence, but in the end, I felt I owed it to my parents to tell them first. By the first of January, Aunt Mary had left, and Abigail was to join us for New Year's Day lunch (Mother had finally accepted that we were friends), after which we would host a dinner party, as was my family's New Year's tradition. Ollie and his parents were to be among the guests.

After lunch, Mother, Father, Abigail and I were gathered in the drawing-room with a glass of port when I felt it was time. I looked at Abigail, who nodded to me, so I plunged in.

"Mother, Father, I have something to tell you."

Mother looked at me with what appeared to be great anticipation. I believe she thought I was about to announce a new male friend. Father simply sat back in his wingback chair by the fire and puffed on his pipe.

"I am going to have a child."

"What? Whatever do you mean?" Mother looked genuinely puzzled.

"You are to become a grandmother."

There was an uncomfortable pause in the proceedings as my parents digested this news.

"I will become no such thing. My only daughter is not married. I'll have none of it!" Mother was, as predicted, beginning to sound hysterical.

Father got up from his chair to sit beside Mother on the sofa. He put his arm around her to calm her. "Maude, let's all just take a breath, shall we? I'm sure Frances has an explanation for this."

"Explanation? What sort of explanation can there possibly be? She has finally gotten herself into a situation from which there is no escape. We will be ruined!" Mother began to sob. "I knew that she hasn't been quite right since the incident."

"We will certainly not be ruined," Father said sternly to her. Then he turned to me. "You better tell us everything, Frances."

I did, and I didn't. I told them when it had happened and how I knew it to be true. I told them I had visited a new doctor in Harley Street, and he had confirmed it. He had told me to expect the birth early in August.

"And what, precisely, do you expect us to do with this news, young lady. Although I can hardly call you a lady, can I?" Mother was now beginning to sound vindictive.

"We will work it out, Maude," Father said. "Frances, I believe that you will need to go somewhere to have this baby. I can make arrangements for you to stay in Oxford with Aunt Mary once again. I'm sure she will at least be sympathetic. Arrangements for the child can be made later. There is no need for that now." I wasn't sure what arrangements Father was talking about, although I could imagine.

"We can tell our friends that you have gone away to help your aunt," Mother said.

I was suddenly gripped by terror. "I can't go to Oxford! Ollie is still studying there."

"There is no situation in which I can imagine that the two of you would cross paths with you in that...condition," Mother said. "Ollie is a fine upstanding young man who will keep to his university activities. Of that, I have no doubt. It will be up to you to be sure you stay indoors and do not parade around the town."

So, Mother's plan was for me to spend the following months as a prisoner, as it were. If it meant that I didn't have to face Ollie, I would try my best. At least the short-term issue had been settled. Now all I had to do was make it through New Year's dinner with Ollie and his family.

~

Dinner was interminable. I sat through the first few courses pretending to enjoy the company, then slipped away after dessert to spend a few moments alone in Father's library. That's where Ollie found me.

"I know," he said as he walked over toward where I was sitting in the window seat.

I turned to look at him. "What do you know?"

"I know that you're pregnant."

"Abigail."

"Yes, Abigail let it slip. But don't blame her. I'm your friend, remember?"

I nodded.

"Frannie, marry me."

"What?" I was sure I hadn't heard him correctly.

"I don't care who you've been with. We are good together. Marry me, and this will all be settled."

The offer was a good one.

SEVEN

AT THAT MOMENT, IT WOULD HAVE BEEN SO EASY for me to accept Ollie's kind—but incredibly stupid—offer. Ollie and I were certainly friends, but we were not meant for each other, a situation I thought we had settled back in Oxford. I had always known that regardless of how difficult my path would be in the short term, I could not settle for a life that I had not chosen, and I unquestionably couldn't ask Ollie to do so, either. It was wrong. I loved him even more for offering to sacrifice his life.

"Ollie, that is wonderful of you. And I know you are serious, but I just can't," I said. "It wouldn't be right for either of us. I have always cherished our friendship, and I always will. But I cannot ask you to do this. It would be wrong for both of us, and I think you know that."

I had expected him to be a bit sad, perhaps, when I turned him down again. I had even expected an offer such as, "Let me know if I can help," or even, "I'll be there for you." But I never expected the reaction I received.

"I know nothing of the kind!" he said, his face reddening with rising anger. "I've always known that you were selfish, Frannie. I guess I just didn't know how much. I loved you anyway and thought I could overcome it over time, but I see now that I was wrong. You, Frannie, can never see what's right for anyone but yourself. If you ask me, you will always be alone. When you told me you could never see yourself as a mother, I should have listened to you, but this changes things, doesn't it? Now you have no choice."

He stormed out of Father's library, leaving me there alone to pick up the pieces of my shattered ego. I knew in my heart that he was right.

I left for Oxford the following week without mentioning to Ollie that we would be in the same town for some months. Snow fell lightly as Mother and Father packed me off on the train alone, promising to visit me in August. That was such a long time away. I suppose they figured that if they never saw my growing pregnancy, they could just pretend it had never happened. That would be extremely difficult, though, once a grandchild was right there in front of them. I wondered how they would handle this in their social circle. But it wasn't my problem.

My problem was that I was indifferent to the whole notion of having a child. I hadn't been at Aunt Mary's a week when she broached the subject.

"Is it too early to talk about the baby, Fran?"

"What do you mean?"

"Well, you do have months to term, but have you begun to consider what you will do after the child is born?"

We were sitting in her sunny breakfast room, enjoying a second cup of tea. It was cold outside, but I could still see several small birds (I had no idea what variety they were—not a topic I knew a lot about) cavorting among the bushes. I had come to respect Aunt Mary's wisdom and her way of embracing life. It occurred to me that it was so unlike my mother's way. She seemed to sense that I had been harbouring a fear in my heart—a fear about my future.

"Aunt Mary," I began, taking a deep breath, "I am not at all sure I can ever be a mother."

She took a breath and sat back. "That's not really what I asked, is it, Fran? I know this is a lot for you, but it is of your own doing, as you have told me over the past week. I have the impression that you are quite prepared to accept the consequences of your action, which is a response I respect. But have you considered what you'll do?"

"I can't be a mother, Aunt Mary," I repeated. "That is all I know about what I will or will not do after this child is born." I considered her words. "You are right. I have and will continue to face the consequences of my behaviour—which, by the way, I don't regret in the slightest. But I know I'm not cut out to be a mother. I am far too self-centred. I was told this by a close friend only two weeks ago. So, I know the idea of me being a mother to this child is ludicrous and wrong. Wrong for me, and so very wrong for this poor little child who did nothing to deserve a mother like me."

Mary nodded. "I'm not judging you, Fran. I'm only trying to determine what lies ahead—what I can help you with."

"Can you help me find a suitable home for this child? I mean, a really good home."

Aunt Mary got up from her chair and came around to where I was sitting. She leaned down and embraced me in a warm hug. "This child will be well taken care of. Mark my words."

I sighed with relief.

~

Aunt Mary and I settled into a kind of easy friendship. I knew that my parents intended for her to be my guardian, but we felt more like sisters, friends. She never tried to tell me what I ought to do or how I ought to behave. She seemed to accept me for myself. At the same time, I accepted her for the artist she was.

As the days melted into weeks and the weeks into months, I realized that I had far more in common with my aunt than my parents—especially my mother. Every week, despite my increasing awareness of my growing bulk, I attended, without fail, Aunt Mary's salons. I had heard about such things in Paris from reading Father's newspapers regularly (unbeknownst to him, I have to say). I did not, however, realize that they were something that took place in such small places as the town of Oxford in England, miles away from the metropolis of London. But they did.

Oxford was rife with intellectuals, and it seemed to me that they were more than willing to share their intellectualizing on all manner of subjects. Aunt Mary, however, tried to focus on art and literature. Each week, a parade of local intellectuals arrived—professors, writers, painters, and even a fashion designer: Odile. I sat with my flowing skirts wrapped around me as if to hide the fact that I would give birth within months, listening and making notes. Someday, I wanted to contribute to these kinds of discussions, to prove to the world that I had more to offer than simply being someone's daughter, wife or mother. After each session, I made furious notes about what was said and what was not said.

I noticed early on that there was much innuendo. There were references to sensuality in literature with nods to one another—nods I didn't understand. In any case, I wrote them all down. Perhaps they would come in handy someday, and they kept my mind off more pressing matters.

I was detached from the fact that I would give birth to an actual person. After Aunt Mary and I talked about finding adoptive parents for the baby, I decided that it would not be wise for me to become attached—for the baby's sake and mine. As a result, as I look back, I realize I might have erred on the side of too much indifference. But it would be a very long time before I could look back on this interlude in my life in any kind of rational way.

~

I spent my time in Oxford as feverishly occupied as I could manage. I returned to Odile's studio, where I honed my dressmaking and now tailoring skills. I went each day to the studio, where I helped Odile and her seamstresses on various projects. My favourite project was the design, fitting and construction of dresses for an upcoming London wedding. I loved learning to embroider, although I had to rearrange myself time after time due to the growing bump I carried around. And that's how I often thought about it.

I had learned to drape and stitch together dresses of various sorts, but Odile believed that learning to tailor a jacket would stand me in good stead.

It was complicated. I had never in my life considered what goes between a jacket's beautiful tweed exterior and that interior silk lining.

I had never wondered how those shoulders sat so perfectly on the wearer's shoulders, raised just enough to straighten that shoulder slope ever so slightly. I had never wondered why the collars stood so perfectly against the back of the neck and curved around and ended in precise lapels—or revers as Odile called them. I knew none of this, but Odile was determined I should find out. And I did. I found the process difficult, though, and wasn't sure if my hand-sewing skills would ever be as perfect as I hoped they would.

It so happened that we were expecting my parents to arrive from London the next day—I had mixed feelings about their impending visit. I was engaged in pad-stitching the undercollar of a lady's hunting jacket on a hot morning in early August. My pad-stitching skills had improved so much that Odile now left me to my own devices. The pad-stitching was designed to hold the layers of fabric in the undercollar together, giving the final product a bit of body. I was so immersed that I hardly noticed when the contractions began. I simply changed position a few times until I could no longer ignore the pain. It was time.

It was time, in the sense that labour had begun, a condition which lasted for the next thirty-six hours before I finally gave birth. The less said about the process of labour and delivery, the better, I think. Suffice it to say that it happened. The baby was a boy I was never supposed to see—it was better that way.

True to her word, Mary had worked on finding a family who wanted to adopt a baby, and she had. They were a family located in Manchester—a childless couple who had been married ten or more years. He was a GP and his wife a nurse. As far as I could figure out, they would be perfect. I was happy with this turn of events. Then Mother arrived at the hospital to visit me.

"I have just seen him, Frances. He is beautiful. All those dark curls! He's quite magnificent. I believe he looks like my father."

I didn't know how to respond to Mother's odd reaction to her grandchild— one who was about to meet his new parents in six days. I looked at her carefully and noted a look about her eyes that was unfamiliar. They were almost sparkling.

She sat down on the chair beside my hospital bed and removed her gloves. I had no idea why wearing gloves on a hot summer day was necessary even for the most fashion-conscious.

"Frances, we need to talk."

Oh no. what could she possibly be on about at a time like this? "What is it, Mother?"

"I have made a plan. First, his name will be James Wilson Phillips."

I was so baffled, I couldn't speak. *Who will be James Wilson Phillips?* I thought.

She continued. "He will grow up never knowing the truth."

"The truth, Mother? What are you talking about?"

"The baby, of course," she said. "Our baby."

"What do you mean, *our* baby? You're not making any sense."

Mother sat up straight and looked directly at me. "Frances, I believe that I'm making more sense right now than I have for many years. Must I repeat myself? The baby will never know the truth. As far as he will be concerned throughout his life, your father and I are his mother and father. And so, we shall be. You, Frances, will be his sister. And he will carry my family name as his second name."

The horror of her idea had finally caught fire in my brain. "You can't be serious, Mother. Aunt Mary and I have made well-considered arrangements. The baby has a family waiting for him." I stopped for a moment and let the idea of me acting as if I were this baby's sister sink in. I looked at the self-satisfied smile that was beginning to play upon my mother's lips. "Have you given one second of consideration to me? Of how I might feel about this?"

She stood up suddenly. "How you feel is of no importance. You gave up that consideration when you presented us with this problem. Now, there is nothing more to be said about the matter, Frances. We will be taking James home with us tomorrow. You will follow next week after you have recovered. And do something about your hair. We expect you to attend a gallery opening with us the week after next. Don't worry. I have procured several dresses from that French designer called Chanel. They are very forgiving, so you need not worry about your figure just yet."

I was appalled—perhaps even more precisely, sickened. This could not be happening. I had taken great care for this child to have a solid family to raise him, and now this! Mother must have gone mad. She had never really been herself since the incident, now eight years in the past. I was so tired, but I knew that I'd have to talk some sense into Father. This simply could not be allowed. As the mother, I believed that I must have some rights in the decision.

"Oh, by the way," she said just before opening the door to leave. "I almost forgot. Ollie is marrying that Abigail friend of yours. I suppose that will be fine. Ollie's mother has told me that a Christmas wedding is planned. In any case, we will be attending their engagement party in three weeks, and you are expected." Then she vanished.

Mother's last remark knocked all the remaining breath out of my body. I was reeling. Ollie and Abigail? It was preposterous. And why? Why not? I loved both of them and wanted both of them to be happy. Why not together? Why not, indeed.

It turned out that I did not have rights as the birth mother. Mother had somehow convinced Father to call in a favour from one of his barrister friends, and the papers had been drawn up. It seemed that Father had gone along with her in this preposterous charade, and I was being forced to become complicit. James Wilson Phillips was now my brother. My son. My brother. I thought my head would explode as I sat alone on the train on my return journey to London the following week.

Aunt Mary had done her best to help me to cope with Mother's capricious decision. She had been as taken aback by it as I had. I didn't know how I would manage the lies. So many lies.

Aunt Mary saw me off at the station. Just before I boarded, she thrust a piece of paper into my pocket. "This is from Odile," she said. "If you ever find that you can't cope, she will recommend you for a job. You may have an escape."

I took the paper and, without looking at it, stowed it in my pocket. Aunt Mary hugged me so tight I thought I might stop breathing, a situation that I considered to be almost preferable to the one I would face in London. "Aunt Mary, I don't think I can do it. I don't think I can face the rest of my life."

"Fran, darling," she whispered in my ear as she held me. "You feel life more than any young woman I have ever met. I've watched you over the past years, and I know this: You would rather live a life full of missteps than arrive at the end of your life and find that you have not lived at all. In that, we are alike."

I nodded through my sobs. Being compared to Aunt Mary wasn't the worst thing in the world.

Aunt Mary pulled away from me and held me at arm's length. "My darling niece, remember something that Irish playwright Oscar Wilde once said. *To live is the rarest thing in the world. Most people exist, that is all.* You and I, Fran, don't want to simply exist. You'll find a way. I know you will."

I could barely see Aunt Mary through the tears that threatened to overflow at any moment. I nodded my thanks and stepped up into the train.

~

I sat slumped against the window, gazing mindlessly out at the trees and houses rushing by. I wondered what it would be like to have a simple life like I imagined the inhabitants had. A home, a job, a family. No worries. No ambitions. And I realized that this was both my gift and my burden—I had ambition, something my mother found unattractive in a young woman. I knew this because she had told me so on numerous occasions over the past eight years, since the day I told her I wanted to craft beautiful clothes.

I wrapped my arms tightly around myself despite the heat and heaved a deep sigh as I burrowed deeper into myself. I hadn't noticed the young man who had slid into the seat beside me. His voice jolted me out of my daydream—or perhaps more precisely, out of my wallow in self-pity.

"Everything all right, ma'am?"

I wasn't sure which surprised me the most—the fact that he called me ma'am as if I might be some old woman or the fact that his accent was so foreign and yet familiar. Finally, I turned to look at him.

I was immediately caught by his startling dark eyes that had a kind of puppy-dog look about them as they gazed at me with apparent concern. He couldn't have been more than four or five years older than my current nineteen, and yet he seemed to have a kind of worldly aura. His golden-brown hair was parted precisely down the middle and slicked to perfection, revealing perfectly shaped ears. His beige-linen (I could discern the characteristics of linen by this time) suit was well-cut and seemed to fit his broad shoulders faultlessly. He was, in a word, dazzling.

"I am sorry if I bothered you, ma'am. I just thought…"

I sat up straighter, trying to place his accent, hoping he might say something more. "No, not at all," I said. "I was just thinking."

He smiled and looked down at the white, flat-topped straw boater hat he held in his lap. "I know all about that. I spend a lot of time in my own head, too," he said.

I finally placed the accent. It wasn't exactly the same as Elliott's, but there was no doubt that he was an American. I looked at him thoughtfully. "Where are you from?"

"Minnesota—America."

I nodded, smiling. Americans always thought we British knew everything about their states. We didn't, but I did happen to know that Minnesota was somewhere in the American Midwest. I wondered what this well-dressed young man was doing here so far from home on a train making its way from Oxford to London when it occurred to me that he was probably a student at Oxford. So, I asked him what he was studying.

He laughed. "No, I'm not a student. Anymore. I left Princeton a few years back to join the army. I never did get a chance to fight, though. I've just been visiting a friend in Oxford on my way to Paris.

How about you? What's a beautiful young woman like you doing alone in a train car watching the world slide by?"

That's exactly how I felt—as if the world were sliding right by me. *Quite a metaphor*, I thought. I laughed at his perceptiveness. "I suppose I'm just watching my world get away from me." I had no idea why I had said this to a complete stranger. But it felt right.

"Oh, now, that sounds ominous. The loneliest moment in someone's life is when they are watching their whole world fall apart, and all they can do is stare blankly."

"Who said that?"

"I did," he said, looking a bit taken aback that I should question its provenance.

"Sorry. But you've just met me—actually, we haven't formally met. Anyway, what makes you think my world is falling apart?"

"Just a hunch. But if you're watching your world get away from you—your words—it's probably because your world isn't turning out the way you had hoped."

I said nothing as his words sunk in. Perhaps my world *was* falling apart. "What is it that you do for a living?" I asked.

"I create worlds."

What? So enigmatic, I thought. Before I had a chance to delve into this mysterious pronouncement, we were interrupted by the conductor telling us that the train would pull into St. Pancras station shortly.

As I gathered my things and made my way toward the exit a few minutes later, the young man shook my hand, sliding a small calling card into it as he did. "This is me," he said, tipped his hat and turned to leave.

I looked down at the card he had placed in my hand. It said, "F. Scott Fitzgerald, Writer."

~

The minute I walked back into my parents' home, I knew that life, as I had known it here, was over. But, even more than the immediately apparent changes in how the house was run were the changes I could feel within myself. I was no longer the child or teenaged girl who ran circles around Mother's staff. I had grown up—of that, I was certain.

Several new house servants were milling around—Mrs. Groundwood had retired and in her place was a new housekeeper called Mrs. Smithson, a dour woman with a long face and a very prominent beaked nose. Nora—my Nora—had taken over duties as governess to the new baby, James. I immediately wondered what nonsense my mother had told Nora about the baby's provenance. There was also an additional staff member—a maid called Enid. I wasn't clear about her duties, although it appeared that she worked exclusively for Mother. At least there was one thing that had not changed—I was back in my old room, and everything was just as it had been.

I sat down at my desk and gazed out at the garden with my diary open in front of me. I wanted to tell my journal how I was feeling at that moment, but the words wouldn't come. My mind was muddled. That's when I first heard the crying. I could hear "James" wailing somewhere in the nursery at the back of the house. The familiar cold unease began to make its way up my neck and lodged there. I put my head in my hands and wept.

During dinner a week later, Mother began prattling on about the upcoming engagement party we were all to attend. As I had expected, Abigail's parents were not hosting the party. The hosts would be Sir Roger and Lady Alma, Ollie's parents. My mind was wandering as it had been most of the past week when Mother's voice brought me back to the present moment.

"Frances, are you even listening? Have you tried on those dresses yet? There are likely to be several eligible men at the party, and I want you to be at your very best."

Ignoring her, I said to Father, "What exactly have you told everyone about the baby?"

"Ask your mother," he said, focusing all his attention on his glass of wine.

I turned to Mother, who was smirking again. "Well, Mother? What have you told them? What lie am I to support?"

"Frances Elizabeth Phillips, I will ask you to mind your manners. There is nothing wrong with a small fabrication to smooth the edges of social refinements. This is a lesson I wish you would learn. You will need it as you move through life. We have told our friends and acquaintances that my cousin, a recent widow in Manchester, died in childbirth, and we graciously offered to take the motherless child in and adopt him as our own." Mother then picked at her salad on the Royal Doulton plate in front of her. "And mind you, Frances, you are never to talk to James of his parenthood. Never. Are we clear? He need not know we adopted him."

I was stunned. "Surely you realize that someone is bound to tell him in time? You have told this—how did you put it?—small fabrication to friends and acquaintances. No one can keep that completely to themselves."

"You clearly know little about your own social class, Frances," Mother said. "No one would ever breathe a word. It would be unbecoming in people of our calibre."

I shook my head. This was so wrong in so many ways.

"Another thing, Frances," Mother continued. "You cannot put off indefinitely meeting your new brother."

I had managed to avoid the child altogether. I simply could not bring myself to see him. I didn't want to see him. But I knew that if I were to continue living under the same roof as my own flesh and blood child, I would have to see him at some point and come to terms with the situation. I just had to figure out how to prepare myself for that.

Before I had a chance to think any more about it, I received a note from Abigail. It was so unlike her to send a note as if she were already the daughter-in-law of Sir Roger and Lady Alma. I had thought that she and I were much more alike in our disdain for conventional lives. I wondered what her father thought of the whole situation. Declan Howard, renegade writer, had never had much good to say about our country's class system. He built his novels and his reputation on the very notion of questionable upper-class morality and laughed all the way to the bank doing it. His books were must-reads and had been for two decades. Surely, he must find this situation as absurd as I did. In any case, Abigail had invited me to join her for tea. She suggested Claridges once again.

There was nothing I wanted to do less than go to tea with an old friend (who I missed despite it all) and listen to her talk about her upcoming marriage to my former best friend who had asked me to marry him—twice. I wondered if she knew that. But I had no legitimate reason to say no to her, so I ignored my dissonant feelings and agreed to see her.

Abigail looked radiant. Already seated at a table among the glittering silver and pristine china, she looked the very essence of a lady—in every sense that her soon-to-be husband and I had discussed so many years ago. I approached the table with mixed feelings.

The moment she spotted me, she stood up. She smiled, and I detected a bit of a question in her eyes. Perhaps she was more aware of things than I had thought.

"Frannie, I am so happy to see you," she said, embracing me warmly. "I...I wasn't sure you'd come."

"Why on earth wouldn't I come?" I said as I settled myself on the plushly padded chair. "I have missed my best friend." And I realized that I was sincere.

I wish I could say that we immediately fell back into our comfortable camaraderie, but that would be a lie. I did, however, feel a new sense of comfort building. Things would never be the same, but we could move on. But I knew something was bothering her. I had always been able to tell.

"Abigail, what is it? What are you not saying?"

"You know me too well, Frannie. It's just...it's none of my business..."

"You want to know about the baby. My baby."

Abigail was the only person outside my family who knew about the pregnancy.

"It's just that, well, your family has just adopted a baby."

I nodded. Despite Mother's warnings, I knew that Abigail had already figured this out and, as my friend, deserved to know the truth. "I think you've already figured it out, Abigail. And, before you ask, it was most certainly not my idea."

"Oh, Frannie, how are you coping?"

I then told Abigail about the arrangements Aunt Mary and I had made for the child and how Mother had blindsided me with her plan. When I finished, I could see a small tear escape from her eye. I was barely holding it together myself. Then I told her that I was sworn never to mention any of this to James. She nodded sadly as if understanding.

We had been talking for over an hour when I realized that we had yet to broach the subject of Abigail and Ollie. It was the elephant in the room. I decided it was time to jump in and asked her directly.

It turned out that she had been harbouring a secret crush on Ollie for years. She had met him through me and knew that we were best friends. I remembered her asking me several times if I thought he and I would ever get together as more than friends. I had repeatedly told her that we would not. (This did explain her evident horror when she had asked me if Ollie might not be the baby's father.) Thus, she felt she could pursue a relationship with Ollie when she returned from Scotland after the war. The romance had evidently been a whirlwind.

"The only problem now, though," she said, "is that every time I bring up your name, Ollie shuts me down. What happened between the two of you?"

I couldn't tell her. She seemed so happy with Ollie and oddly seemed to be looking forward to a life as the wife of a London barrister, a member of the minor aristocracy. I couldn't tell her that Ollie had told me he loved me and had wanted to marry me. I couldn't let her feel that she was second best. (Was she?) So, as unlike as it was for me being who I am, I held my tongue. She would never find out from me. But that didn't change the fact that Ollie evidently wanted nothing to do with me. I would have to find some excuse for not going to their engagement party.

I had to figure out what I was going to do with the rest of my life. I knew that Mother still expected me to marry and give her grandchildren, but that was never going to happen. I had given her a grandson and look how that worked out. No, I would have to find employment and some kind of a future for myself.

~

The day of the engagement party dawned wet and drizzly. When I awoke, I looked over at the dress my mother had insisted I would wear, where it hung on the outside of my wardrobe. There was no way on god's earth I was going to wear that dress. I got out of bed and walked over to my desk. Beside my diary were two pieces of paper. One was the calling card that the strange writer had given me on the train. The other one was the piece of paper Aunt Mary had given me as I boarded the train.

I sat down and picked up the note from Aunt Mary. I unfolded it slowly and began to read. The note was, as Aunt Mary had said, from Odile who was telling me that should I wish to pursue my dressmaking and tailoring at a couture house in Paris, she would provide me with an entrée via a friend of hers who worked as one of *"les mains,"* literally translated as "the hands," the name given to the women who worked at couture houses in Paris stitching together the designer gowns. The friend's name was Madame Lesage, and she was the head dressmaker at the House of Poiret. Before even washing my face, I sat down and began a letter to Odile, then prepared one to Madame Lesage. I would not attend the party this evening (could I feel a head cold descending upon me—I hoped it wasn't the Spanish flu, I said to Mother), but I would be going to Paris—the very moment I could organize my destiny.

EIGHT

"Victory is reserved for those who are willing to pay its price."
~ Sun Tzu

AS IT TURNED OUT, DEALING WITH MOTHER'S anger about not attending the engagement party was much more onerous than making arrangements to change my entire life. The week after the party, Mother paid me little attention, and Father was so busy at the bank, I hardly saw him. It seemed that the end of the war had resulted in something of a windfall for the financial sector, of which he was a more significant part than I had realized. In past years, I might have enlisted Nora to my cause to assist me or at least be someone I could talk to about my plans without fear that they would make their way back to Mother or Father. That time was over.

Nora was plainly mad about James, the baby. If she knew his provenance, she didn't let on. As his governess, she had specific duties, and she seemed to take them very seriously, acting on every occasion as if she might even be the mother. I suppose Mother didn't mind since, despite her intentions, she wasn't much of a mother to this little thing. So, I was able to write letters, visit the bank to arrange for foreign access to my family trust money, pack a trunk to be sent on sometime after I was settled in Paris, purchase train and boat tickets and even shop for a few new outfits. No one noticed.

I thought about simply leaving without a word or perhaps leaving a note. In the end, the adult within me prevailed. Besides, it wouldn't be long before Father got wind of the fact that I had accessed more than the usual amount of my trust fund monies. In the end, I asked our new housekeeper to arrange for me to speak with my parents on the evening before I was set to leave.

"What's this all about?" Father said as he entered the drawing-room. He went immediately to the bar to pour himself a glass of something brown—probably whiskey. He nodded as if to ask if I wanted one. I shook my head.

"We'll just wait for Mother," I said, settling myself in one of the two oversized chairs flanking the fireplace, the chair where my mother usually sat. "Why don't you sit there, Father?" I said, pointing to the sofa across from me. He looked puzzled—it was his habit to sit in the chair that matched the one I had taken over—but he did as I asked.

When Mother finally appeared in the doorway, she, too, looked puzzled when she noticed me. It was likely because I was taking up her usual place. I asked her to sit beside Father on the sofa. She did as I asked, but not before pouring herself a glass of sherry.

"Well, Frances, we are here," Mother said. "The question is, why are we here? I have a great deal to do this evening. And if you were smart, you would have much to do as well. You owe the Lowther-Russell's a major apology, and I think it would be in your best interests if you put whatever petty differences you have with Ollie out of your head. It's highly likely that he has friends—friends who will be looking for a wife—"

My father held up his hand to silence her. I was more inclined to slap her to get her to stop her infernal blathering. I sometimes wondered if I made her nervous. "Maude, please," he said. "Frances has asked to speak with us. Let's let her speak."

Mother picked up her crystal sherry glass and took a sip without saying a word.

"Frances, the floor is yours," Father said with a flourish of his hand.

I took a deep breath and plunged in. "Mother, Father, I have news."

Mother's face went ashen. I immediately suspected she feared it was the same news I'd given her nine months before James's birth. I smiled slightly at that. I couldn't help myself.

"I am moving to Paris." No point in beating around the bush, I always say.

The silence that followed my proclamation was deafening. You could have heard a pin drop in the room. Immediately, I could hear the tick-tock of the grandfather clock in the corner, a sound I hadn't noticed since I was a child. I could hear the clattering of dishes far away in the kitchen where I knew Mrs. Smithson, the housekeeper, would be overseeing the washing-up being carried out by the newest member of staff: a tiny, shy young woman Mother referred to as the parlour maid, whatever that was. (As far as I could see, she was being trained to do all manner of menial kitchen work.)

After a moment had passed and there was no response from either of them, I continued. "I have an address of a women's hostel in Paris where I will stay, and I have a job." They both looked startled. "I will be working as one of *"les mains"* in the atelier of the great Paul Poiret." I knew that Mother would know who he was.

"Is this some kind of a joke, Frances?" Father said. "It isn't really that funny, you know."

"*Les mains*?" Mother said. "You cannot be serious. That's labour. You are a lady, Frances, and no young lady who is my daughter will go off on her own and take up a job doing god knows what in some god-forsaken foreign hamlet."

I started to laugh at the absurdity of Mother considering Paris, the centre of the fashion universe, to be a god-forsaken anything. Although I did have to admit that I knew Mother had visited Paris several times while I had never set foot in the city yet.

Father drained his glass and got up to pour another one. "You're serious about this, aren't you, Frances?"

"I am, Father. And I have already made the arrangements."

His eyebrows shot up. "You have already made arrangements? What arrangements?"

So, I told him about Odile and how she had provided me with an introduction to Madame Lesage at the House of Poiret. I told them it was all settled.

"You will need money," Father said. "I can help."

Mother looked at him angrily. "You will do no such thing, Edward. You cannot mean to encourage this. It's absurd. I will not have it."

"Maude, I believe she has made up her mind." Father peered at me closely. "Frances, you have always had a kind of rebellious streak. I know that it has worried your mother, but I have always felt that you would probably be able to rein it in and use it to your advantage. I hope I'm right."

At that moment, I was more grateful to my father for his moral support, as grudging as it might be (and I suspect it was more grudging than he was letting on), than for any material support he had ever provided over the years—and that had been substantial.

"When does all this happen?" he said.

"Tomorrow." They both looked like they might faint. "I'm booked on the ten o'clock train to Dover."

My mother arose shakily, smoothed her dress and stood looking down at me. "Well then, Frances, I suppose it's goodbye. I shan't be here in the morning. I have a dress fitting."

Father got up, came over to where I was sitting, raised my hand to his lips, kissed it, and then followed Mother out.

Father was waiting for me in the foyer the next morning and accompanied me to the train station, where he saw me off after thrusting a leather pouch into my hand as I stepped up into the train. When I settled myself into my seat, I opened the pouch. It was stuffed with French francs.

~

There could never have been a single person in the history of the world who was as excited as I was as the train neared Paris, and I could just barely make out the silhouette of the Eiffel Tower. I had never felt so free in my entire life. When I finally found myself on the street in front of the Hostel St. Germain, a stone's throw from the *rue. Faubourg St. Honoré*, I began to feel slightly disoriented. I could speak passable French by this time, but the sights and sounds all around were so foreign. I liked it, but I didn't really know what to make of it—or of how I might fit in. I looked at the people passing by, and it was clear that I would be pegged as a tourist for as long as I lived here unless I did something about my wardrobe. And I hoped that would be a very long time. I had ambitions beyond sewing in someone else's atelier.

I gathered my belongings and trudged up the steps to the reception desk beyond the grand wooden doors with their brass fittings. A slightly older woman with a bright red scarf tied artfully around the neck of a striped pullover (I'd seen these in magazines but had never known anyone to wear such a daring style) sat behind the desk languorously smoking a cigarette. It looked so…sensual. In my very best French, I told her my name and that I had a reservation. She immediately responded in French that was so fast I caught only a word or two.

She looked at my face and started laughing. Then she started again, this time more slowly. I finally understood. Yes, she had my room ready. These are the breakfast rules and hours. These are the rules about cooking in the rooms. Oh, yes, and no men beyond the sitting room that happened to be in full view of the reception desk. I nodded and thanked her, then made my way up two flights of stairs, dragging and juggling my cases. There was a tiny elevator with one of those mesh doors, but it appeared to be in use as three young women crammed into it laughing and chatting in rapid-fire French. I would have to improve my French as fast as possible. I finally found room "205" after remembering that the floor numbering in French buildings was such that the first floor was never numbered. Instead, it was called the *rez-de-chaussée*, the ground floor. The second floor was the first floor and the third floor, where my room was located, was the second floor.

The room was small but well-appointed. I was used to spacious surroundings, so this would take some time for me to acclimatize. I had often thought that we had far too much space in our house in London—far more than we needed—although Mother disagreed.

The pale blue damask wall covering matched the drapes perfectly, and the brass bed was covered in white linens and a blue duvet. It looked very inviting to a travel-weary newcomer. I settled in as quickly as I could and then ventured out into the street. Cafés lined the street, each one looking more enchanting than the one before. I walked along, reading menus as I went until I found a small bistro on the corner where the rattan chairs and tables clung to the wall to let pedestrians pass by safely. It was too cold for outdoor eating as far as I was concerned, but the weather didn't seem to bother the Parisians. They sat at tables, drawing their heavy coats around them and tightening their scarves from time to time, all the while smoking odd-smelling cigarettes. The smoke wafted from every table.

I took a table outside anyway and proceeded to enjoy my first evening alone in Paris. I took the time for two glasses of very fine house wine as a kind of bolster for my courage: tomorrow, I would present myself at the grand atelier of the famous M. Paul Poiret.

~

When I wrote to Odile that I would kindly take her up on her offer to provide me with an introduction to Madame Lesage at the atelier of M. Poiret, she also provided me with much information to smooth my arrival in Paris. So, the following day, I took out her letters and found the one where she detailed the instructions about how to walk from my lodging to the atelier. I now clutched it in my hand as I made my way down the steps and out onto the street where everything was bustling on this cold morning.

I was excited. Perhaps that would be something of an understatement! I was so much more than excited. I was energized in a way that I hadn't felt in a very long time. I suppose I should have been nervous, and to be completely honest, perhaps I was, but the excitement of really being on my own and having complete control over what would happen to my life was exhilarating. I was too young then to realize that this was nothing more than an illusion. It would not take me long to learn my first lesson.

I arrived at M. Poiret's boutique and atelier on *rue St. Honoré* at precisely nine a.m. as I had been directed to do via a note from

Madame Lesage, which had been waiting for me upon my arrival at the hostel. As I entered the door, a small bell rang, and I was immediately swallowed up in a riot of *tromp l'oiel* walls suggesting that I had arrived not in a dress shop but on a tropical island. The wall coverings were a mass of what appeared to me to be waving palm branches (I had seen palm trees in several paintings so knew what they looked like), and the ceilings were so high that I thought there might, indeed, be a palm tree somewhere. There were mirrors with arched tops that reached almost as high as the ceilings. I stood there, taking it in.

A tall, thin woman wearing a white coat over her dress emerged through an arched doorway. *"Puis-je vous aider, mademoiselle?"*

Of course, she would want to know if she could help me. I thought for a moment and then told her I was looking for Madame Lesage. *"Je cherche Madame Lesage."*

She then walked over to me and lifted my hands, examining them closely. "I am Madame Lesage. And you must be Mademoiselle Phillips. I see your hands are not so well-suited to long hours of work in M. Poiret's atelier, but we shall see. In future, please use the entrance at the back. We reserve this one for our dear clients."

I nodded and followed her far into the back of the boutique until we reached the atelier, what would have been a spacious workshop with massive windows letting in natural light if it hadn't been so stuffed with bolts of fabric. There were shelves everywhere, each one more overflowing than the one before. Even the cutting tables in the centre of the room were piled high with more bolts of colourful fabric in addition to what appeared to me to be works-in-progress. I could hear hushed voices coming from the back. Madame Lesage led me deeper into the space until we found the dressmakers.

Eight seamstresses sat around an enormous table, each one poring over a garment. I watched as their fingers manipulated the needles and thread so quickly it made my head spin. And most of them were whispering to one another in conversation as they worked, often appearing to not ever look at what they were doing. For the first time since I had decided to start a new life in Paris, I wondered if I was up to the task at hand.

I had spent many long hours toiling in Odile's workshop, assisting with creating dresses for local matrons and a few Londoners, but I now stood in the atelier of a famous Parisian couturier. As my eyes moved across from one garment to the next, I realized that they were fashioned of the finest of silks and that my work would have to be outstanding for me to keep up. However, almost at once, I realized that Madame Lesage meant to start me out on less demanding pieces. She led me into an adjoining room where four younger women sat at sewing machines, their feet pumping up and down as the cotton muslin fabric under the machine needles moved along. They were creating the toiles—the test garments made from plain, cotton muslin fabric that would be further fitted to mannequins then taken apart to make the patterns from which the final fabric would be cut. I heaved a sigh of relief that I would not be starting as one of *"les mains."*

Madame Lesage assigned me to one of the young women who was charged with creating the toiles. She appeared to be not much older than I was, with a plain face and hair caught in a severe bun at the back of her head. Her name was Virginie. When Madame Lesage introduced me to her, she hardly looked at me, simply grunting and pointing to the table where I would assist her in cutting out a toile. I couldn't put my finger on it, but there seemed to be something slightly hostile in the jerk of her head and her expression as she nodded to me to follow her.

Over the next two weeks, I worked alongside Virginie, following her one-word instructions as best I could. I tried to engage her in conversation but to no avail. I wondered if she thought I couldn't speak French, but I suspected it was more because I was English. That seemed enough to engender a certain degree of coolness from many of the young French working women I met during those weeks. It seemed it was going to be harder than I thought to make friends.

After two weeks of cutting out toiles, Madame Lesage came to me and told me that I would be working on the sewing machine for the next week, sewing the toiles together while one of the girls was out sick. I had experience working with a sewing machine and wasn't worried about my skills there. So, for the next week, I took the pieces the cutters provided and sewed them together. I had not yet met the great M. Poiret. I would encounter him soon enough.

On the Monday of the following week, I was assigned to assist the mannequins in donning the toiles. As it turned out, the mannequins were not the wooden dummies I had been used to using in Odile's studio. They were real, living, breathing mannequins onto which M. Poiret had initially draped the muslins to create the designs. This was such an interesting approach to design. I was fascinated.

I finished pinning the mannequin named Clarisse (the mannequins were much friendlier than the seamstresses) then watched her as she entered the atelier's outer area where M. Poiret was due to arrive at any moment to make the final adjustments to the designs. We could then make the patterns.

I peeked through the archway and saw him enter. He was a portly man, perhaps in his forties, with a dark beard and a potbelly that protruded from under the vest beneath his suit jacket. I watched as an assistant helped him remove his jacket and don another short, white jacket which he buttoned up to protect what I expected was a bespoke shirt. He then turned toward Clarisse and two other models. The other two models were wearing almost finished dresses.

He walked around each of them, lifting a hem or a neckline to examine it more closely. Then he stood back and stared at the toile on Clarisse. He looked over at Madame Lesage, who lurked in the corner. *"Qui a fait cette toile?"*

He wanted to know who had made the toile. I hoped it was because it was especially well done. Madame Lesage pointed to me, then crooked her finger to beckon me to enter the room. I stepped through the archway.

M. Poiret took a deep breath as if holding something in, then said, *"Il est faux. Ce n'est pas ce que j'ai conçu."* It is wrong; it is not what I designed. He turned toward me and continued in French so fast it made my head spin. "I am an artist. You are a dressmaker. It is a dressmaker's job to bring the artist's vision to life. It is not the dressmaker's job to alter that vision in any way."

I could feel my face reddening from my neck through my ears, which were now burning, to the top of my head.

"She has made a mistake, M. Poiret. That is all," Madame Lesage said, eyeing me out of the corner of her eye as if to say she would deal with me later.

I could see him trying to calm his fury, and I realized that I had, indeed, altered it. The truth was that I had not made a mistake. I had thought that the way he wanted to attach the sleeves to the bodice would result in an ugly fold under the arm, so I had recut it and attached it so that it was smooth. It occurred to me that it would probably be in my best interests not to explain it to him in that way. After all, he was the artist.

Later, after the great one had left, Madame Lesage scolded me for my "mistake" and told me it should never happen again. I stood there, taking my punishments, as the rest of the staff looked on with what I could only interpret as smug satisfaction. The English girl had been reprimanded.

We were now well into the winter in Paris. I longed to see leaves on the trees and to sit outside with a *café au lait* and a croissant, but it was still too cold for me. I had yet to really meet anyone. At the end of each day, I was so tired that I could hardly even consider that I seriously lacked any social life. I had exchanged simple pleasantries with several of the girls who were also staying at the hostel in passing or at breakfast, but they, too, seemed to always be in a rush to get somewhere. I promised myself that I'd make an effort to meet some people as the spring weather arrived.

One evening as I trudged up the steps on my way back home after a long day, I almost ran headlong into one of the girls who was just leaving. I dropped my handbag, which proceeded to roll down the steps, spilling out its contents onto the sidewalk. "Oh, *mon dieu, je suis vraiment désolé*!" she said. "I am so sorry." Then she bent down and began to help me gather my belongings.

As she stood up to pass me several items that she had collected, she said suddenly, "I know you. I have seen you before."

Her French was perfect, but I thought I could detect a slight foreign accent. I looked at her to see where I might have seen her outside the hostel. Perhaps she had just seen me at breakfast.

"Yes, of course," she said. "You work at M. Poiret's atelier. I have seen you." She took my hand and pumped it up and down. "I am Kiki."

I shook her hand and introduced myself. I looked at her closely and realized that this statuesque beauty with long, straight dark hair and graceful limbs was one of the boutique's mannequins.

"I am going to meet some friends at *Le Select* for a glass of wine. Would you like to accompany me?"

I was a bit flustered, as unaccustomed as I'd become recently to social invitations. "I'd really love to, but I have to change."

"But, of course. It is but two blocks in that direction," she said, pointing. "We will be there for hours. Come when you are ready."

I told her I would, and that was the beginning of my social introduction to Paris.

NINE

"There are only two tragedies in life: one is not getting what one wants, and the other is getting it."
~ Oscar Wilde

HALF AN HOUR LATER, I WALKED DOWN THE STREET just as the March sun was setting behind the buildings. I quickly found *Le Select* in precisely the direction Kiki had pointed. As I walked, I wondered where in the world Kiki had gotten that name. Surely that had not been the name given to her by her parents? But then, what did I know of the world beyond Belgravia and Oxford? I knew very little—but I felt I was poised to find out.

There were three steps down to the entrance. Before I reached the heavy wooden door, I could already hear laughter, music and clinking glasses wafting out onto the street. Several young men and women, each more strikingly beautiful than the last, were milling about, rearranging scarves and smoking those awful-smelling Gauloises. I would have to learn to love that smell, I feared.

My heart was thumping wildly as I pulled open the door and stepped into the dark, wood-panelled space lit by a few gas lights along the sides and candles on every table. The place was crammed with wooden tables, each covered by wine and beer glasses, full, empty and everywhere in between. I scanned to see if I might pick out a familiar face. I spotted Kiki at a table with three other girls far across the room. I had to pick my way past laughing, smoking, drinking people, but I finally made it.

"You came!" Kiki said as she caught sight of me. She stood up and embraced me as I came closer, coming in for the double-kiss. Immediately, she began introducing me to her friends.

It was so noisy, and my French comprehension was still a bit slow that I had to concentrate to catch the names. They were Julie, Lucie and Rose, each just as stunningly beautiful as the one before, and each possessed of long, straight hair, beautiful long necks, and long, slender limbs. As Kiki introduced them, each one leaned over and gave me the double kiss of welcome. I had always considered myself acceptable, but I felt downright drab beside these paragons of beauty. Before I had a chance to ask them if they were all models, Kiki had left to find me a drink, and the other three began peppering me with questions about London between drags of the ever-present cigarettes.

When Kiki returned, I gratefully took a glass of wine from her and finally had a chance to ask about the four of them. Kiki, as I already knew, was a mannequin at the House of Poiret, as was Julie, although I didn't remember ever seeing her before. Rose also worked as a mannequin, but she was employed by the great designer Monsieur Jean Patou.

"I was lucky," Rose said as she told me about her work. "Monsieur Patou just reopened his salon six months ago. It had been closed during the war." She took a long drag from her cigarette. "He is designing such unusual things these days. They look like sweaters as dresses." She began to giggle.

"I am hoping to work for M. Patou," Lucie said. "I am sick to death of teaching those little girls."

"What do you teach?" I said. This sounded intriguing.

"But, of course, I teach ballet," Lucie said, looking at me as if I should have known that.

"So, you're a ballerina?" I said.

Kiki began to laugh. "Of course, you would not know, Françoise." She looked around at her friends. "We are all ballerinas."

I was so shocked I almost choked on the wine I had just sipped. However, it did explain the long limbs, the extraordinary posture and the elegant way they gestured while talking. "But then, why are you all working as mannequins?"

"Because, *chère* Françoise, the ballet in Paris is all but dead." Kiki crossed her long legs, took an elegant drag from her cigarette and continued. "We have all studied at the Paris Opéra Ballet School and hoped that the ballet company might have a life of its own. I am sad to say that most of our work is dancing in those *divertissements* that classical opera is so fond of." They all rolled their eyes.

"What's wrong with that?" I said.

"Wrong? It is so wrong," Lucie said.

Kiki leaned toward me. "Of course, you would not know. How could you know? But, have you been to the opera recently."

I thought about it for a moment. "I think it's been several years," I said. "I seem to remember attending a performance at Covent Garden with my parents some years ago."

Lucie leaned in. "Did you enjoy it?"

I wondered momentarily how I was expected to answer this question. I didn't want to insult anyone, and since I didn't know them well, I might do so regardless of what I said. I decided that honesty was the best approach. "To be truthful," I said carefully, "it didn't strike me as an experience I would care to repeat."

They all laughed. "How polite," Kiki said. "As far as I am concerned, the sopranos sound like dying cats, and they are all so smitten with themselves."

"It is beyond horrible to be one of the dancers in an opera," Rose said. "We are considered low-class supports of the grand divas." She rolled her eyes again. "I cannot tell you how many times I have wished to slap one of them."

"Well, perhaps someday we shall all find an *abonnée* as the ballet used to have. There are still many men who mill about when the company director tells us to mingle in the lobby after performances," Kiki said, laughing.

"What is an *abonnée*?" I said, puzzled by the term.

"They are men who seek to provide patronage for artists. In years past, when the ballet was strong, there were many such male supporters. I suppose we should consider ourselves flattered," Kiki said. "They are much more interested in the girls of the *corps de ballet* than they are in the fat singers!" They all laughed uproariously. "Of course, they expect much in return." She winked. And I understood.

As I lay in bed later, I stared up at the ceiling and wondered: *What will I be expected to provide in return for my dream?*

~

In the months that followed, I often wondered who had decided that I should be assigned to assist the senior dressmakers as they put together the silks and satins. I wondered if someone had known that I might be out of my depth. I wondered who had ensured that I would be assigned to help with the work on a green and gold evening dress that had to be stitched together with gold thread and heavier needles. I wondered who knew that my dexterity wasn't up to handling them, and I wondered if someone had predicted that I would prick my finger one too many times, resulting in a drop of blood falling onto the hem of a dress.

When the event happened, I didn't realize it at first. And the very worst of it was that Monsieur Poiret himself had just walked into the workroom—something he rarely did—when one of the other dressmakers let out a blood-curdling scream. I had been concentrating so intensely that I hadn't even noticed that I had gouged my finger quite deeply, and yes, it was bleeding. Most of it was bleeding onto my lap, but there was no doubt about it. A single drop of blood had lodged itself on the gold trim along the silk chiffon hem.

Madame Lesage was there in a heartbeat, dragging me away from the worktable. As the chair moved back from the table, the dress dragged along on my lap and fell to the floor. I watched as Monsieur Poiret's eyes widened in horror. Someone—I didn't notice who—picked it up and tried to smooth it out on the table. Monsieur Poiret walked over and picked it up, looking long and hard at the drop of blood that was ruining the hemline's perfection.

He crumpled the dress in his hands and threw it back on the table. "It is now hers," he said angrily, nodding toward me.

I was now standing up straight alongside the back wall beside Madame Lesage. M. Poiret came over and stood directly in front of me. I could feel his eyes travel up and down me. "*Oui*," he said. "Yes, it shall be hers." He turned back to the table and said to the girls still sitting there, "One of you, please bring me the ruined dress."

When he had it in his hands, he held it out in front of me. The tragedy of it was that the dress was almost finished. It lacked only the finishing stitching and the bespoke House of Poiret label. "What is your name?"

"Françoise Phillips, *monsieur*." I was shaking as I stood there with the hem of my white coat wrapped around my hand to staunch the bleeding.

"Well, Mademoiselle Phillips, go. Put the dress on and return. Quickly."

I took the dress and fled. I needed no encouragement to get out of there as fast as possible. The only problem was that I had to return. I did so, but now I was wearing the dress. I glimpsed my reflection in the mirror as I made my way back into the workroom. It was stunning.

When I once again stood before M. Poiret, I felt stronger. After all, it was just a dress—just a tiny imperfection. Everything has flaws, does it not? Evidently, couture dresses did not.

He looked at me then silently walked around, looking at me from every direction. "Mademoiselle Phillips, you will complete this dress by yourself, and you will prepare and affix the label. It will say, PAUL POIRET À PARIS, 77436 ATELIER, Mme Françoise Phillips. Do you understand what I am asking?"

I nodded. I thought better of telling him that I was, in fact, a mademoiselle, not a madame.

"You will then take it home and wear it to a marvellous party."

I heard a swooshing sound as everyone in the room seemed to take in a breath all at once over this astounding proclamation.

"But," he said, "you will never again stitch one of my dresses. Is that clear?"

I nodded while trying to hold back the tears that were forming. Of course, the other girls would like nothing better than to see me cry. Of that, I was certain. But he wasn't finished.

"No," he continued, "you will not sew. But you will be one of my models for the parade we will have this spring for my new collection. Is that also clear?"

It was clear. And so, my career as a dressmaker was, seemingly, over. But I had my second couture dress to add to the Lucile that hung, unworn, in my wardrobe. I vowed that I would wear this one—and soon. The opportunity presented itself sooner than I could have dreamed.

~

After meeting Kiki and the rest of the girls, my social life took a turn for the better. When they were not in rehearsals—with those hateful opera divas as they liked to remind me—or standing for fittings in a salon or parading new styles in front of customers, they loved nothing better than a good party. A weeknight glass of wine at *Le Select* was the fall-back only on the evenings when there had been no other invitation.

Lucie had been hired as a model at the House of Poiret several weeks after I had begun this new stage of my career. That meant that Kiki, Lucie and I could chat endlessly as we got ready for fittings or parades. We discussed which of the pieces we loved and which ones we thought hideous. We considered which of the customers were well-mannered and pleasant and which were disagreeable and cold. There was a surprising number of the latter.

We also came to know one another much better. Kiki, as I had suspected, was not her real name. Her real name was Elke, a name that didn't strike me as very French. It turned out that her mother was German and her father French. Kiki was born in Berlin, but her father had longed to return to France, so they moved to Nice when she was five. That explained the slight accent I had noticed when I first heard her speaking French. Her family then moved to Paris when she was ten years old. That was when she decided that a German-sounding name was not what she wanted. So, she became Kiki and entered the Paris Opéra Ballet School, where she met Lucie and Rose, both from rural areas of France. All three of them had decided that they would take as big a bite out of Paris as they could before they were too old. That explained the parties.

After the sewing disaster, I was happy to have a job, even as a mannequin. Still, I chafed every time the seamstresses, customers or even Monsieur Poiret himself spoke about us as if we were those wooden mannequins—as if we were not even there. We were not permitted to speak, and we certainly were not allowed to have opinions about anything. I still had money from Father and my trust, so I didn't have to work so much, but I felt I did. I needed to be around people in the industry. I still believed that I might have some more fulfilling role to play.

Each night when I sat alone in my bedroom at the hostel where I was still living, I wrote in my diary. I also bought myself a new journal where I began to write more detailed stories of life in Paris. It was one creative outlet that helped ease the discomfort of being thought of as a vapid dimwit, unable to hold a single thought in her pretty little head. But it wasn't the only outlet I'd created.

My sewing machine, which I'd had shipped from London, had finally arrived. Until I had it set up in my little room, I had not realized how much I'd missed it. I'd missed creating my own garments. So, I once again began to design and craft my own clothes. My sewing skills might not have been sufficient to work in a couturier's atelier, but they were nothing to sniff at. And I had ideas. Before long, the other mannequins began to notice my clothes, and they started asking me where I got them.

It didn't take long before they began asking me if I could create dresses for them, and I had something of a cottage business, as the saying goes. They all loved to party and dance and drink and needed beautiful dresses that shone and sparkled. I cut the hems short to permit movement, and the girls loved them. They had all recently bobbed their hair, except for the ballerinas, who moaned about the fact that they needed to be able to create the "ballet bun," as they called it. The day I arrived home with my own new sleek bob, Kiki began sobbing.

"Oh, how I long to be able to do as I wish." She rubbed her eyes with the back of her hand and brightened up. "On that note, we have been invited to a party this evening. All of us are invited, and you are coming, *non*? It will be very posh."

I had no intention of refusing, and I knew exactly what dress I would wear. It was time to break out the Poiret.

Later, as we approached the elegant townhouse, I could see lights glittering from the windows, but even more exciting, I could see dazzling dresses on women coming from all directions.

"Whose house is this?" I said as Kiki slid her arm through mine. I looked up at the three stories of beautiful grey brick with masses of curly ornamentation. I had never seen anything like it before.

"It belongs to Monsieur Gaston Reneau."

"How do you know him?"

"He is one of those men I told you about. He lurks in the lobby after opera performances hoping to meet pretty young ballerinas."

"Oh, he sounds revolting, Kiki. Are you sure this is a good idea?"

"Don't worry, Frannie," Kiki said. I knew I was one of them when the girls began to call me Frannie. She continued. "He is not like that. You will see. He is quite young. Well, younger than the rest anyway. And he has recently lost his wife."

"His wife died recently, and he is having a big party?"

"*Mais oui*. What better way to get over a loss than to have a party and find someone to fill the hole in one's heart?" She winked at me, and all became clear. Kiki had designs on this Gaston. It seemed to me that the French treated such loss quite differently than the British. I thought I might like their approach better.

I was thinking about the name Gaston Reneau as we reached the door. A uniformed butler greeted us with a silver tray of champagne coupes and beckoned us to take a glass and enter. Just then, a tall, handsome man, perhaps thirty-five years old, spotted Kiki and immediately came over, grabbed her hand and kissed it gently.

"*Ma chérie*," he said. "You came. I am beyond delighted." He turned toward me. "And who is this ravishing beauty accompanying you?"

I think I blushed, and I suddenly remembered where I had heard the name before. Looking at him closely, I realized that he was probably closer to forty, but he had been perhaps in his early thirties when I had last seen him. I had noticed him because he was by far the most handsome man on the Titanic, in the view of a twelve-year-old girl. Gaston Reneau was a French banker, an acquaintance my father had introduced to us in the dining room the evening before "the incident." I hadn't realized that he had been among the survivors. It was clear he didn't recognize me. I was glad of that because I had no desire to ruin the evening by having to explain "the incident" to my friends.

The party was something of a revelation to me. I had lived with wealth and consorted with wealthy people throughout my childhood, but it had always been my parents' world. I had never felt comfortable with the superficiality and forced civility of society activities. There was little doubt that Gaston's guests were wealthy (at least most of them—then there were the people like us), but the French seemed to carry their wealth differently. They seemed to be more at ease with it. As I mingled throughout the various rooms, each one more extraordinary than the one before, I realized that the glamour was real, and the attitude was one of "*Je m'en fiche*," roughly meaning "I don't give a…" And they didn't. They didn't seem to care what anyone else thought. It was thrilling to me, who had spent so many years as the very picture of a proper English lady-in-the-making, all the while boiling beneath the surface. I realized that it was no longer necessary for that to simmer. I could be whatever I wanted to be here in Paris.

As I approached a knot of particularly rowdy young people gathered around the piano, it didn't seem possible, but I thought I saw yet another familiar face. I took a cigarette from some young man who offered me one in passing then leaned in to let him light it for me. I did not smoke, but that wasn't going to stop me from looking the part. With my green and gold silk Poiret and matching green shoes, my sleekly bobbed hair caught all around with a green silk headband (I had absconded with fabric scraps from this very dress I was wearing and had turned them into a headband), I felt as if I belonged. I also knew that the large gold filigree (fake, to be sure) broach I had borrowed from Kiki to hold the headband in place and the dark eyeshadow I'd just learned to apply made me look a bit exotic.

The piano player began a rousing piece I didn't recognize, yet I could feel the beat of the Charleston. I'd seen the dance a few times since it made its way across the Atlantic from America, but I had never had the occasion to try it. Suddenly, I could feel a hand pull me toward the open space in the large room where dancers had begun gathering. Then they started—arms and legs flying, long strands of pearls coming dangerously close to walloping someone in the face, skirt fringes dancing, catching the light here and there. I was a quick study and soon had the rhythm of the moves. Then I finally looked at my partner. There was no doubt about it—it was Scott Fitzgerald. What in the world was he doing here?

TEN

"When I let go of who I am, I become what I might be."
~ Lao Tzu

"WHATEVER ARE YOU, A PROPER ENGLISH LADY, doing here in this den of iniquity?" Scott said, laughing as we breathlessly finished our dance.

"I could ask you the same question."

"I like large parties. They're so intimate. At small parties, there isn't any privacy."

I looked at him and laughed. "That's quite a line, sir. Where did you pick up that one?"

"Again?" he said, feigning a pout. "Again, you think I'm quoting someone else. If you must know, it's a line from one of the characters in my new book." He looked quite pleased with himself.

I noticed him glancing over toward a group of party-goers where a captivating young woman stared out from a pair of hawkish eyes that could bore into you. She took a long, sensual drag from the cigarette in her left hand, then sipped from the champagne coupe in her right hand. I was fascinated by her long, white cigarette holder and the fact that she could accomplish all of this while still holding her stare in our direction. I wondered who she was. Then I realized Scott had mentioned a book.

"A new book? Goodness, that's marvellous. It's published?" Other than Abigail's father, I hadn't ever known anyone else who wrote books. I was particularly impressed that someone as young as Scott Fitzgerald had written a book.

"It's just out. You should read it."

"What's it called?"

The Great Gatsby. You'll learn lots about Americans who do this kind of thing." I must have looked puzzled. "Glittering parties like this," he said.

"I certainly will read it," I said sincerely. "By the way, Scott, who is that beautiful woman who is staring daggers at you?"

He glanced over, then laughed. "That's Zelda. My wife."

I think I was probably a bit surprised to hear that he was married. However, I was even more surprised that I felt a tinge of jealousy.

"Fran, isn't it?" I nodded. "I have someone I'd like you to meet."

Scott Fitzgerald dragged me over to the group of young partiers still surrounding the piano and placed me in front of a young man wearing a beautifully cut tuxedo and holding a glass of milky, white liquor. I wondered if it might be absinthe. He was shorter than Scott but slightly taller than I was with dark, wavy hair and a small moustache. He had one hand tucked in his pants pocket.

"Fran, I'd like to introduce you to Jean-Christophe Lemieux."

"*Enchantée, mademoiselle,*" he said, bowing slightly and kissing my hand. I did so love these French manners.

Scott then explained that Jean-Christophe (who told me to call him Christophe) was a newly appointed editor at the French publishing company Scott hoped would translate his new book into French. I found this whole new world of writers and publishers fascinating.

Scott left us alone, and I began peppering Christophe with questions. He was born and bred in Paris and had studied at the Sorbonne. He aspired to write but found that he was better suited to finding writers and editing their work. I thought about my own aspiration to become a couturier and how my talent seemed to veer in a different direction from my dream. Perhaps we had something in common.

Before I knew it, the party had begun to empty. Christophe and I had been deep in conversation for two hours. I looked around and noticed that Kiki was plastered to Gaston's side, so I needn't worry that she wanted to leave soon. It was Christophe who finally looked at the ornate grandfather clock in the corner and said, "*Mon dieu*, it is getting late. I have a meeting early tomorrow morning."

"But tomorrow is Sunday," I said.

"No rest for the wicked," he said as he got up and smoothed out his clothes, then ran his fingers through his hair.

I was almost disappointed that the evening was over, but I had enjoyed it immensely.

"My dear Françoise," he said. "It has been such a pleasure meeting you this evening. I must thank Scott for introducing us. Would you do me the honour of dining with me next Friday evening?"

And so, we did.

~

That first summer I spent in Paris was hot—blisteringly so. Each morning when I awoke, I could feel the mantle of heat settling on me before I even arose. My attitude was puzzling to many Parisians whose habit was to flee the city for the summer because I loved it. For someone who had spent as many drizzly summers in London as I had, the very idea of escaping even for a month or two was beyond comprehension.

By the time August was upon us, much had changed. Kiki had, indeed, gotten her wish. She was now living with Gaston, and she had recently told me that he had hinted that a marriage proposal might not be far off. She had given up dancing to take on the hostess's role to Gaston's many parties and had become a client of the couture houses rather than an employee. Thankfully, I had not had the awkward chance yet to be a mannequin on parade when she was a customer—she had told me she would avoid Monsieur Poiret's salon for the foreseeable future. Rose and Lucie were cast as extra dancers for the *Ballets Russes* performance of *Sleeping Beauty*, and they were thrilled to be part of a real company, even if only for a short run. They both had new men in their lives.

As for me, I had found myself a beautiful flat to rent on the Left Bank, not far from the Sorbonne. That meant that many of my neighbours were students who were given to noisy street parties to while away the hot summer evenings. I had expected them to leave for the summer, but it seemed that their dedication to their studies, not to mention their drinking, knew no bounds. Despite the occasional noise, I loved my flat with its Juliette balcony from which I could see the spire of Notre Dame. I was truly in Paris.

I spent as much time as possible with Christophe and often wrote about our encounters in my journal. I loved the sound of Paris on the page. He had introduced me to classic French literature, and I had been reading the works of the great writer Honoré de Balzac. He once wrote, "*Whoever does not visit Paris regularly will never really be elegant*," and I now knew this to be true. I believed my elegant days were only just beginning.

I awoke with a start one hot Saturday morning. I had been dreaming and was drenched in perspiration. Christophe, who had spent the night, was startled by my sudden movement.

"Whatever is wrong, *chérie*?" he said, raising his head from the pillow slightly.

"It's nothing," I said. "It's early. Go back to sleep." But it wasn't nothing.

I got out of bed and walked over to the balcony. Christophe had fallen back to sleep, and I was alone with my thoughts. It was exactly one year ago that I had given birth to James, and I realized that I had not thought about him or my parents much, if at all. Instead, I had spent the past year with my nose stuck firmly in my own navel. When had I become so selfish? Perhaps Ollie had been right about me.

I looked over at the bureau where six unopened letters from Mother sat. I hadn't wanted to read them, although I knew it was unfair to her and my father. Twice I had sent word to them telling them I was fine, but I didn't want to know what was happening in London. My only fear had been that one day my father might appear. He occasionally came to Paris on banking business, but over the past year, he had not appeared. In truth, I may have been a little disappointed.

But this morning I was thinking about James. I was his mother, and yet I wasn't. I wondered how I'd feel when, inevitably, I'd have to see him again. There was no possible way that I could avoid encountering him at some point. And I realized at that moment that I didn't want to. I wanted to know how he was doing. I wanted to know that he was going to be all right.

I sat down at my desk and took out my letter opener. I opened all of Mother's letters and laid them one on top of the other according to date. I read each of them carefully. By the time I reached the end, I could feel a tear escape my eye and slide onto the last page. I took a blank page from one of my notebooks and began writing. By the time I had finished filling five pages and was now writing notes in my journal, Christophe awoke and sat up on the side of the bed.

"What are you doing?"

"Writing."

"Writing? I didn't know you liked to write. What are you writing?" He got up and came over to stand beside me to peer over my shoulder at the desk.

I slammed the journal closed and pulled the letter to Mother toward me. "A letter. To my mother."

"That sounds lovely," he said. "After what you have told me about your rift with your parents, I am glad to hear that you are mending it."

I may have told Christophe about my parents, but I had never mentioned James to a single soul in Paris—not even Kiki.

When I got up and told him I would take a bath before we went out for coffee and croissants, I had no idea my life was about to change direction.

~

We settled ourselves at a table closest to the street, where there was a slight breeze. It was our favourite café for Saturday morning coffee. We could watch the families stroll by with those giant prams the French (and English) liked so much, the older children running along beside. Today, though, they weren't so rambunctious—it was too hot. Regardless of how hot it was, though, nothing could make us miss our coffee, which the waitress had just placed in front of us when Christophe began talking.

"Now, *chérie*, please do not be angry with me. I have done something most reprehensible in some ways."

I could not imagine this kind, considerate, intelligent man doing anything the slightest bit objectionable. This was intriguing.

"When you were in the bath this morning, I noticed the leatherbound book on your desk. I confess I did not know it was your journal." He cleared his throat and sipped his coffee. "I must confess to reading some."

"What? Reading—some?"

"What I mean to say is that I began reading and was immediately enthralled—perhaps one might even say titillated."

"Christophe, those are private!" I could feel my anger rising. "You can't just—"

He held up his hand to stop me. "Please, dear Françoise, please let me finish. Then you can be as angry as you wish."

I breathed out and stopped. I would hear him out, although, at that point, I couldn't see how this could possibly be anything but a betrayal of trust.

"I have read what you wrote about your life in Paris—about our…how should I put this, encounters."

I knew I was blushing. I busied myself with pulling apart pieces of croissant and watching the flaky crumbs fall to the plate. Christophe was right. I had written about our love-making—in graphic detail. I suppose I wanted to remember it clearly, in case the day came when he was no longer a part of my life, a day I hoped was far off.

"Fine, Christophe. Now you know that I like to write smut. In my personal journals. My private journals."

"But it is not smut, Françoise. It is erotica. Do you know the difference?"

I began to think back to the times Abigail and I spent in her father's library, reading passages from erotic novels to one another. I particularly remembered a book called *The Memoirs of Dolly Morton*. Oh, how we had blushed and giggled at that one. How could he possibly be comparing what I'd written with that?

"I'm not at all sure I do, Christophe. What is the difference between smut and erotica?" *If we are going to have this conversation, I might as well be in it,* I thought. *There is no point in pretending to be a prude.*

"The difference is in nuance. In pornography, or smut as you so delicately put it, there is no idealization of the human form as there is in erotica. Erotica appeals to all our senses, not just bodily functions. It is more like a gentle sensuality. As a woman writing erotica, you reclaim your power over your body—and your life."

I shook my head. "Christophe, I have no idea where this is going. You read my personal diary, and now we're discussing the difference between erotica and smut." I angrily bit off a piece of croissant. "You know I am infuriated."

He reached across the table and took my hand. "Please don't be. The point of this discussion is that I believe you should rework your diary entries into a story and submit it to my publishing company."

"I can't do that! I'm not a writer."

"Oh, but you are. You truly are."

~

A part of me thought that Christophe was stark raving mad. Another part was intrigued by the idea. My head told me that the idea was absurd, but my heart told me that a door had opened, a door of opportunity.

As far as I was concerned, the worst part of being a mannequin was the necessity to remain silent at all times, permitting everyone around to conclude you had an empty head. However, now I realized what a gift that could be. So, I spent every session during the following two weeks considering Christophe's preposterous suggestion.

For the first few days, I spent all my time considering the absurdity of the whole thing. For the next few days, all I seemed to be able to think was, Why not? Why couldn't I do it? For the next few days, I thought about whether I *wanted* to do it. Finally, I spent the last few days putting together stories in my head. Then I was ready to discuss it further with Christophe.

Christophe's idea was simple. I would take on a *nom de plume*—I could not be Frances Elizabeth Phillips. Instead, I would be a French writer of indeterminate sex. Anyone who wished to assume I was a man was welcome to do so. I would then extract my Parisian stories replete with ghastly details—prepare the manuscripts with his help, then reap the benefits. According to Christophe, the market for such writing was voracious. He assured me I could make a decent living from it. I wasn't so sure. Oh, and I would have to write the novels in French. That's where he came in with his editorial skills.

In the end, I agreed. And so, after much deliberation, I became F.E. de Plessis. I liked the sound of that.

The Patou

Artist

ELEVEN

"Women who seek to be equal to men lack ambition."
~ Timothy Leary

F.E. DePLESSIS. YES, I WOULD HAVE A NEW IDENTITY. The very thought of it was exhilarating. I knew that the word *plessis* meant "a fence made of interwoven branches," and I liked the thought of that. I was nothing if not an interweaving of many different strands, or branches and perhaps this new venture would stand as a kind of boundary between who I was and who I might become. Well, that's what Christophe said, and he was very persuasive. The exhilaration didn't last long.

It had never occurred to me that writing a book would be so torturous. Once I warmed to the idea that my journals and the various juicy bits of my life that I wrote about (and perhaps embellished just a bit) could make interesting reading for others so inclined, I thought it would be easy. It was not easy for several reasons.

First, the parts of the story I thought would be of interest were often not the parts Christophe thought best suited to publication. The second reason was that I had no process for developing an actual story to connect the bits and pieces. I certainly wasn't going to write a memoir!

For the first few months of our collaboration, Christophe would go to his office five days a week while I wrote or worked for M. Poiret through the day. Then, each evening and on the weekends, we would meet at a pub or coffee house, or sometimes at my flat, put our heads together and try to work through my writing. Finally, one evening, after two fruitless hours and several glasses of wine, I had enough.

"Christophe! For the love of god, just let me write!"

He looked at me, startled by my outburst. "But my *chère* Frannie, this is what I am doing all these months. Are we not making progress?"

I felt a bit guilty about springing this on him like this since he had been nothing short of a miraculous partner for me as I learned to write a book. The truth was, however, that I was beginning to find his oversight suffocating. I just wanted to try my hand at writing without too much interference. I thought I would use his editorial skills later in the project. The other part of the problem was that working all day and then rushing to get together each evening and weekend was beginning to wear on each of us. We had not attended a party in some two months, and our friends were starting to wonder about what we were up to. And we couldn't tell them.

Christophe had sworn me to secrecy. He had told me that it would be difficult for him to propose this project to his employer to consider publication if they knew a woman was writing it. I bristled at that, but I had agreed. That was not easy, either.

"Yes, Christophe, we are making progress, but now that I know the direction I should take my work, I think the story would flow better if I could just write. And all this running back and forth between pubs and bistros and my flat, well, it's exhausting. I'm sure you feel the same way."

He put aside the page he had been making notes on and sat back. We were sitting on the floor of my flat with masses of pages scattered all around us. He leaned back on a cushion and sipped his wine. "Frannie, I believe you may have a point. I believe you may be ready to work more independently. And as for the running around from one place to another, we indeed have little time. And we need to see friends again. I have a proposition." Then he smiled impishly.

And that was how I came to move in with Monsieur Jean-Christophe Lemieux, rising publishing star.

~

By December 1921, I had completed a draft of the book. Christophe determined that it was ready for his publisher, and so he took it. And I waited.

I was tiring of working as a mannequin at Monsieur Poiret's salon. However, I had no other evident skills, so the best I could do was look for a change of scenery. Lucie had begun working for Jean Patou as she had intended, but I'd had little time to speak with her—or anyone else for that matter. I had heard rumours that M. Patou was in the process of ridding us of the flapper style. I wasn't at all sure how I felt about that. He seemed to have an idea that women looked better in longer dresses, but I had heard that he was working with the new sportswear that I longed to be able to try. When I told Christophe that I was thinking of going to work for M. Patou, he was less than enthusiastic.

"I do not know why you even continue with that activity," he said one morning as we had breakfast at our local bistro. Neither of us was inclined to eat our *petit dejeuner* at home even now.

"Well, *Monsieur* Lemieux," I said in my most formal French, "we do not all have the luxury of a position with an esteemed publishing house as you do."

He rolled his eyes. "Frannie, you will very soon have the money from the many books you will write, which I know will be successful from the very first."

"You know nothing of the kind," I said, slathering butter on my croissant. I pulled my scarf tighter around me to stave off the cold March wind. Like all sturdy Parisians, we were sitting outside in the elements at a sidewalk café. "In fact, your publishing house has yet to give me an answer about the first one. It's been three months, Christophe. I do need a job."

The following week, I gave my notice to Madame Lesage at the House of Poiret. I presented myself to M. Patou's salon, after which I was immediately taken on as a mannequin. It wasn't work that required any cerebral ability, but I was good at it, and it afforded me uninterrupted time to think about my writing. I found that the stories I was writing were occupying more and more of my thoughts as I went about the business of my days. I no longer minded being ignored as a person when parading for customers or standing to be fitted into a new outfit. Being ignored was perfect for contemplation.

The idea for my second book came to me as I was walking into the salon wearing a new three-piece suit-like outfit consisting of a yellow pleated skirt that ended just below my knees topped by a lighter yellow blouse with a matching jacket, all fabricated from a soft knitted silk. It felt glorious to the touch. I usually didn't even notice the faces of the customers who waited in the salon for the mannequins to approach. However, on this day, I was riveted by the astonishing beauty of the bored-looking young woman who sat at the end of one of the massive sofas fanning herself with what appeared to be a pair of leather gloves. She had glossy blonde hair that fell in undulating waves to her shoulders, bright blue eyes and a bow-shaped mouth that she had carefully lacquered with red lipstick. I immediately began imagining a story where the beautiful mistress of a count or marquise or some other member of the French aristocracy appears at a couturier's salon to select a dress for an upcoming tryst with her lover when she meets an extraordinary woman and her husband. The three of them strike up a conversation then begin a lust-filled relationship. Unbeknownst to the young mistress, the man in question is her own lover's wife's lover—the possibilities and potential misunderstandings were endless. She had inspired me.

I was busily writing down as much of the idea as I could remember later that evening when Christophe rushed through the door of the flat. He was so excited he seemed out of breath.

"You've done it, Frannie. By god, you've done it!" He was waving an envelope at me as he tried to unwind his scarf.

"What exactly is it that I've done?"

"You've sold your first book—and your second and third!"

At that moment, I began to think of myself as a writer—and that I had much work ahead of me.

~

Rather than having me attend his publishing office to sign the contract, Christophe brought them home to me. Christophe was determined to make this an event and had brought along with him a bottle of champagne. I was sure it was something extraordinary, but I was too excited to examine the label. All I wanted to do was see and sign the contract to get on with my life as a real writer. Imagine! They wanted to publish my first book and the next two I would write!

I sat patiently, tapping my toes on the rug while Christophe opened the champagne with a great flourish and a pop that I was sure the neighbours could hear. He then ceremoniously poured each of us a coupe and offered a toast.

"To F.E. de Plessis. May she write many successful books in the years ahead. Bravo to you, Frannie!"

So, we toasted and sipped, and then I insisted that we begin reading the contract.

"All right, all right!" he said, laughing. "You are very anxious about the paperwork, *non*?"

"Yes!" I scooped up the first sheaf of papers and began to read. It was practically Latin to me. The prose (if you could call it that) was so dense that I could hardly make out its meaning. Christophe explained to me that it was simply the way legal contracts were drawn. There was nothing unusual about it. He held out a pen to me as my eyes moved down the page.

"What's this?" I said, pointing to a paragraph buried in the middle of page five (or six, or seven). I read it to him. *"L'auteure s'engage à conserver son identité dans la plus stricte confidentialité."*

"Just standard," he said, appearing to ignore it completely.

"Standard or not," I said, "it seems to say that I, as the author, am required to maintain my identity in the strictest of confidence. It seems to be saying that I am not permitted to tell anyone that I am, in fact, the author of these books. Ever."

"I cannot imagine that you would want to, in any case, *chérie*."

I put the pages I was holding onto the table in front of me, sat back and crossed my arms. "So, your admonition to me to keep this confidential until you had a chance to present it to your superiors was only the first volley."

"I am sure I have no idea what you're talking about." Christophe was taking great pains to avoid looking at me.

I sat there and waited. Finally, Christophe threw up his hands as if in defeat. "I concede. It is true. My superiors are thrilled with your work and agreed immediately to offer a contract. When I mentioned to them your real name, they hesitated. They said they could not, under any circumstance, publish these books as written by a woman. It would be a scandal. This was the only way they would consider it. I am sorry. I know this would be important to you, but it may well protect you."

"Protect me? Protect me from what precisely?"

"There are those in certain social circles—"

"You know that means very little to me."

Christophe turned toward me and pried my hands out from under my arms. He held them as he spoke. "Frannie, there will come a day when this will not be a problem. I am asking you—no, begging you—to allow this for these three books. You can begin your career, and by the time you are well established, what a coup it will be to announce that you are indeed a woman."

I knew that he was making many good points. It would, indeed, be easier in many ways not to be the subject of such gossip as there would no doubt be about my personal life simply because of the nature of my stories. A woman writing erotica must undoubtedly be a harlot at best. It wasn't the worst thing in the world, but it did occur to me that it might get in the way of serious acceptance of my work. In the end, I grudgingly agreed and signed the contracts. I imagined that in due course, I would proclaim my identity to the world. In the end, I never did.

~

My book was due to be published in June of 1922. While I waited, I did not sit idle. I worked feverishly on the second book and continued to walk the fashion parade in M. Patou's salon whenever they called upon me to do so. I intended to give that up at some point but had done nothing about that as yet when Kiki walked into the salon one afternoon and perched herself on a sofa with her legs primly tucked beneath her.

She had kept her word and never appeared at M. Poiret's salon as a customer while I was there, but I had not spoken with her in some months (Christophe and I were just emerging back into our social life). On this warm afternoon in early June, as I appeared from behind the heavy velvet drapes wearing one of M. Patou's latest creations—a silk jacquard cocktail dress in black and bronze fashioned with silk chiffon flutter sleeves and a deep fringe at the bottom of the hem that brushed my calves as I walked—I spied her.

Of course, we were not permitted to make eye contact with the customers, so I did as I had been taught. I did, however, notice that the moment Kiki recognized me as a mannequin, her hand flew to her mouth, and her eyes went wide (I suppose I did make eye contact with a customer at that moment!).

There were two other customers in the salon, each on their own sofas. As I walked by them, I could hear them murmuring about the dress—how elegant, how *avant-garde*. As I walked past Kiki, she hissed, "Sorry!" Then, as I made my way out through the heavy curtain on the opposite side of the salon from where we had entered, Kiki got up and ran over to follow me.

She threw her arms around me. "Oh, Frannie, I have missed you so much. Where have you been? What have you been doing? You didn't run off with Jean-Christophe, did you? I did not know you were working here."

I was equally glad to see her, but I sincerely hoped that none of the staff witnessed this. It was certainly not permitted.

At that very moment, M. Patou himself emerged from the office at the back and stopped in his tracks when he saw us. "Madame Reneau, is there something wrong?"

I was so astonished at his reference to her as *Madame* Reneau that I forgot I wasn't supposed to be conversing with the customers. "Kiki! You and Gaston?"

She held up her left hand, and I almost had to shield my eyes from the dazzle of the diamonds and rubies she was wearing on her finger. "I tried to contact you. We were married in Biarritz last month. It was a bit impulsive. I am here for my trousseau—better late than never!"

"Mademoiselle Françoise!" Both M. Patou and Madame Vachon, his assistant in charge of the mannequins, spoke in unison.

I whispered to Kiki. "I'm not supposed to speak to customers or wear the garment for any longer than it takes for me to walk out that doorway and back in through this one."

Kiki looked at Madame Vachon and Monsieur Patou. *"S'il vous plaît, pardonnez-moi.* Please forgive me. I am so sorry to have accosted Mademoiselle Françoise, but I wanted to see the dress. I wish to purchase it." She pretended to be fascinated by the fringe. "I shall take it with me today."

"But we will need to fit it on you." Madame Vachon looked at me then at Kiki. The dress fit me like a glove, but it would most assuredly not fit Kiki the same way. We were different shapes, and she was about two inches taller than I was.

"No, no. I shall take it. Wrap it up for me, please!"

Later, I met her outside the salon. We were laughing and catching up, although I had to carefully talk around what I'd really been doing with my time. "Anyway, what will you do with the dress?" I said. "Do you have a good dressmaker to make the alterations?"

"Yes," she said. "I do know one." She looked straight at me and smiled. She was still holding the dress in its carrier bag over her arm while a young man who appeared to be her driver offered to take it from her. She shook her head at him.

"Oh, no," I said. "I would never consider reworking one of the great Monsieur Patou's designs."

"No, no! You will not have to rework it at all. It fits perfectly."

I suddenly understood. "No, Kiki. I can't take it?"

"Why not? You have been a great friend to me, and I wish to make a gift of it. Besides, there is a catch." She stopped and began to smile conspiratorially. "You must wear it to our wedding celebration. It is one month from Saturday. Since our friends were not with us in Biarritz, we are bringing Biarritz to them! I will send you a formal invitation, but I will expect you and Jean-Christophe there no later than eight o'clock. I want to catch up with you before everyone else gets there. It's a date?"

"It's a date!" I hugged her tightly then watched as she sped away in her car—with her private driver. Oh, how things had changed for all of us! I had no idea.

TWELVE

A WEEK AFTER MY REUNION WITH KIKI, I arrived home one afternoon to find Christophe already ensconced in the living room, champagne at the ready. Again. A small package was sitting on the table in front of him, wrapped in brown paper and tied with a string. I dropped my handbag on a chair and rushed toward it.

"Is it here? Is this it?" I said, grabbing the package and beginning to tear off the wrapping.

"It is, indeed, *chérie*." Christophe popped the cork and filled the coupes to the brim.

Once I had removed the brown paper, I just held it in my hand, looking at it, feeling the weight of it. The slim book with its hard cover was dark blue with gold embossing that I could see peeking out from the dust jacket. The paper dust cover was also dark blue, with gold lettering and a line drawing of the silhouette of what appeared to be a naked female body. The cover proudly proclaimed the title— *La vie secrète d'Adaline*, translation: *The Secret Life of Adaline*— a novel, F.E. de Plessis. I could feel jolts of electricity assault me. I was more excited about this than I had been about anything in my life. My book was finally here.

We celebrated alone for obvious reasons. Once I had recovered from the initial excitement, I began to bristle again at the thought that could tell no one about this singular accomplishment of my life so far. I couldn't even share it with Kiki, who I knew would be just as excited. Then I thought about Abigail. I hadn't seen or even talked to her in years. She was the friend who had been with me when I first read those forbidden books. Abigail would be so thrilled. Or perhaps she wouldn't, now that she was the wife of an important barrister. Then I wondered what my father would think of the whole situation. I didn't even have to wonder about Mother. She would probably faint away. But father—he was different. I longed to be able to tell him. I longed to be able to tell anyone. I thought I might burst! But I kept my secret because I had a contract that forced me to do so if I wanted to keep publishing. And I certainly did want to keep writing and publishing.

"Next, there will be the critics' reviews," Christophe said, pouring more champagne.

I had forgotten about that aspect of writing. There were, indeed, reviewers. I hoped they would like it, but I was more concerned with readers. Would they like it? I didn't have to wait long to find out.

The publisher had sent advance copies to the critics, so the first review appeared the following day. Christophe brought the first of the lot home, and we perused them over dinner.

"A new author, this de Plessis fellow might well have bitten off more than he can handle. After all, he describes a woman's carnal response in such a way that might be questioned by his fellows…"

"The story is a lustful frolic the like which most men would long to accomplish. I look forward to more of the same from this author who knows the mind of men so well…"

They all made me laugh. The critics, of course, thought a man had written the books. And the notion that anyone would question my female perspective? Well, that was beyond the pale. It was laughable in the extreme. Laughable, perhaps, but it didn't help me deal with the gnawing feeling I might not be able to keep this secret forever. In all honesty, though, I suppose I wanted to be able to take the credit if the critics (and readers) liked the books. Perhaps I would be less enthusiastic about doing so if they did not. In any case, whenever I mentioned this to Christophe, he went a bit pale.

"Frannie, *chérie*, please do not even contemplate such a thing. Your writing career will be over before it is even begun."

"Why is it that so many people cannot take a woman's perspective seriously?"

"Frannie, I assure you that it is taken quite seriously—by me at least. However, it is this type of writing—this topic, that others might misconstrue coming from a woman."

My head understood his perspective, but my heart (and perhaps ego?) was having difficulty coming to terms with it.

"What about this Gertrude Stein I've been hearing about around town?" I fiddled with my dinner fork. "I understand that some of her work has been quite scandalous, and yet everyone who mentions her seems to hold her in quite high esteem. I've heard that she is living here in Paris and holds literary salons regularly."

Christophe placed his wine glass down on the table and delicately wiped his mouth with his napkin. He raised his eyebrows slightly. "Have you read her work, Frannie?" I shook my head. "Do you know anything about this Madame Stein?"

"Only that she is an American writer and that she now lives here in Paris."

"Are you aware that she lives here with her…" Christophe cleared his throat "…companion?"

I scowled at him. "Of course, I am. I know her—companion— as you so delicately put it, is a woman. I also know that you would be only too happy for my next book to be about just such a thing."

Christophe shrugged. *"Eh bien, ma chère, peut-être aimeriez-vous assister à l'un de ces salons.* Perhaps you would like to attend one of these salons. Madame Stein holds them regularly."

I was delighted at the very thought. "Could you arrange such a thing?"

"I could. But you would have to promise me that you will not tell anyone that you are a writer no matter what happens. Or at least, not that you have written *The Secret Life of Adaline.*"

I agreed, and so Christophe made the arrangements. I was overjoyed.

~

Before I had the opportunity to attend one of the celebrated literary meetings, Christophe and I were expected at Kiki and Gaston's wedding celebration—an after-the-fact kind of celebration. Just two weeks earlier, I had finally given my notice to Madame Vachon. I would no longer be parading Monsieur Patou's dresses in front of customers. I had a secret hope to be one of the customers before long. According to Christophe, initial book sales suggested that this might happen sooner than later. Thanks to Kiki, I would be wearing a Jean Patou couturier creation to this party, which made it even more exciting.

As expected, the party was a glittering affair. Instead of holding it at their grand townhouse, Gaston had booked the Grand Salon Pompadour at the Hotel Le Meurice in the first *arrondissement* across from the Tuileries Garden on the *rue de Rivoli*. I had never had any reason to have been in the hotel before, and I had high expectations. The hotel and the grand salon did not disappoint.

As Kiki had directed, Christophe and I arrived at eight p.m. and met them at the bar to catch up before the onslaught of guests. They had invited some two-hundred and fifty people. Imagine knowing that many people! I couldn't. But, as you know, Gaston was a banker, and I remembered the times that Mother and Father had entertained at hotels in London. I had never attended, but now I realized that this must have been what their parties had been like. Mother had always left the house looking ravishing in a gown from one designer or another. I wondered if my Patou would be enough with its deep fringe and golden threads shot through the bronze silk. Kiki assured me that it would.

As the evening progressed, Christophe took to pointing out various luminaries of Parisian society. All of them seemed to be enjoying every minute of Gaston's generosity, the flowing champagne, the delectable food and the dancing. Yes, there was dancing.

The band was called Louis Mitchell and his Jazz Kings. I suppose I had expected something more sedate, perhaps even a classical group—at least more French. But it was an American jazz group here in Paris, playing the most extraordinary jazz that made everyone want to get up and show off their best dance steps.

I had been so focused on my new writing project for so long that I had forgotten that jazz culture was such a big part of Paris these days. And I had the perfect dress with the perfect fringe to take to the floor with Christophe. I had improved since that time when Scott Fitzgerald pulled me onto the dance floor at Gaston's party.

As Christophe and I breathlessly returned to our table after a particularly energetic round of the Fox Trot, I happened to hear snippets of conversation around us. "Christophe," I said, taking a large sip of the martini that I was enjoying, "I seem to hear a lot of American accents."

"But of course. There are many Americans in Paris. You have heard of prohibition, have you not?"

I had heard talk that the American government had outlawed liquor a couple of years earlier, but it had never occurred to me that these laws had pushed Americans out of their own country. It seemed absurd to take an ocean liner all the way across the Atlantic just to have a drink. But I really had little knowledge of Americans at that point in my life except for my brief rendezvous with Elliott and meeting Scott Fitzgerald on two occasions. I looked around, half wondering if he might have been here. I suddenly felt a camaraderie with a fellow writer despite not being able to tell anyone.

Just as I was about to ask Christophe about the identities of several of the people at the next table, people began clapping. It seemed that someone was taking over the piano and everyone—except me—knew who it was.

"How marvellous," Christophe said.

The man, resplendent in white tie and tails, sat down at the grand piano that had just been vacated by the band's pianist when they began their break. He turned to acknowledge the audience and started playing a tune I had never heard before. Judging by the reaction of the rest of those in the ballroom, I was the only one.

"Who is that?" I whispered to Christophe.

"You do not know?" He laughed. "I believe I have been keeping you far too busy with your writing. We will certainly need to get out more often. That, my darling Frannie, is American songwriter Cole Porter. Is he not marvellous?"

This Cole Porter did seem to have a way with an audience. According to Christophe, everyone expected him to have a Broadway hit in New York one of these days. In the meantime, he was living in Paris, playing host to expatriate American celebrities. I felt as if I were entering a foreign land that I fully expected to fall in love with.

"Who is that lovely woman standing by the piano?" I was looking at a tall, handsome (for that was the best word to use to describe her) woman wearing a rather demure gown with several long strands of pearls wound around her neck. Her hair was impeccable, and her dress looked like it might have been from the House of Poiret.

"Oh, that is Linda. Porter's wife." Christophe then snorted.

"That was a rude sound, Christophe. What's wrong with her?"

"Oh, nothing. Nothing at all. In fact, I haven't met her, but I have heard that she is a wonderful woman. Perhaps just not his type."

"She seems devoted. Look at how she looks at him. And I'm sure I can see that he is just as infatuated with her."

"I suppose, in their own way, they are devoted to one another. But I say again: not his type." Christophe nodded toward a young man lurking behind the piano, sipping a cocktail. He had one hand in a pocket as he lounged against the wall. "There," he said, nodding in the young man's direction. "That one. More his type."

I looked at the young man thoughtfully. He was one of those young men who could only be described as beautiful. He was wearing an impeccably cut tuxedo—white tie and tails, of course, as specified in the invitation. His languid expression was barely visible from under the fringe of wavy blonde hair that threatened to drown him.

"He is a ballet dancer, so I am told," Christophe said quietly into my ear. "There is a rumour that Porter is writing a ballet. Perhaps it will be for this one." He gestured toward the young man who was staring at Porter.

I wondered if this young man's presence at Kiki and Gaston's wedding celebration was related to her short-lived career as a ballet dancer. I found the whole thing utterly fascinating and immediately wondered how I could incorporate this into a book. I was beginning to feel like a real writer, always on the lookout for ideas. I would ask her about it at our next lunch, which we had set for two weeks hence. I would, however, have to be careful I didn't give away my real reason for asking. The lunch would be an excellent opportunity to practice this skill that would undoubtedly become essential as my career progressed.

~

True to his word, Christophe arranged for us to attend a literary gathering at the famed Gertrude Stein's home. These gatherings were referred to as salons. If three years earlier, someone had told me I'd be excited at the prospect of spending an evening with a group of literary elites in Paris, I would have said they didn't know me very well. The furthest thing from my mind at that time had been doing anything more than fabricating beautiful garments. I hadn't even been terribly concerned about designing them myself. I just wanted to sew. Now, here I was, creating stories and characters and dubious situations for the reading public's pleasure. Truth be told, it was also for my personal pleasure—I loved the process of creation. In any case, here we were. We were on our way to 27 *rue de Fleurus*. I had no idea what to expect.

As usual, I was concerned about what to wear. What kind of impression did I want to make? When I asked Christophe for his opinion on the matter, all he said was that the less of an impression I could make, the better. He suggested something dark and unobtrusive. I bristled at the thought of having to blend into the background.

"Perhaps I should find out what her wallpaper looks like," I said peevishly after discarding the third outfit from my wardrobe. "Then I could simply choose an outfit the same colour—or even the same print. Then no one would notice me for sure."

Christophe looked up from the paper he was reading and rolled his eyes. He put down his paper. "I may have forgotten to mention that her partner, Alice, often takes the wives and girlfriends of the writers attending to another room and hosts her own salon."

"Are you telling me that I am your appendage? The appendage of a great and soon-to-be-famous editor? That I, the actual writer of the books on which you will coast to stardom, must be relegated to the children's table? I'm telling you right now, Christophe, I won't have it."

Christophe sighed. "Then we shall see what we shall see, I suppose."

I settled on a simple black dress made slightly dramatic by the fact that its back dipped almost to—well, you can imagine. I pushed my hair up into a cloche hat and wound a purple velvet wrap around me, and we made our way to the apartment.

Upon our arrival, the door was opened by a large woman with a severe hairstyle tightly plastered to her head. She appeared to be a servant of sorts. She said nothing. Christophe said, "Hello. My name is Jean-Christophe Lemieux, and I was sent by Monsieur Dadot of *Editions Dadots*."

"*Entrez-vous*," she said and showed us into the salon where a lively group had already begun to gather.

"How many servants does Madame Stein have?" I whispered.

Christophe laughed. "That was not a servant, *chérie*. That was the great lady herself."

I felt my face flush. "Wait," I said. "How did you know? I thought you had never met her before."

"I have not, but Monsieur Dadot has. He told me how we would be greeted and that the introduction by someone known to her was somewhat irrelevant, but it is something of a ritual. It amuses her, I suppose. And, anyway, you are supposed to know her. She is that great."

Christophe found a seat, and I took a chair and practically hid behind him. I had no intention of leaving the men to join the ladies in another room. In any event, no one seemed to notice me. Then, the great lady came into the centre of the group, turned to look around and took up her seat at a high-backed chair, gathering her voluminous black skirt around her. She nodded that it was time. And so, the discussion began. Gathered that evening was a group consisting of several writers, two critics, and a number of painters.

"You see that painting on the wall over there?" Christophe said. I nodded. "It was painted by that man over there."

I looked at the painting then over at the man. The man was probably in his early forties, with a deeply lined face as if he had spent much time in the sun. He was bald, and I wondered if he had shaved his head or if he had lost his hair. The painting was unusual. I could see in the light and shadow, and the muted colours of grey and orange, the inklings of a building and palm trees. I looked back at the man then said to Christophe, "It seems an odd way to look at the world."

"Perhaps," he said quietly, "but finding new ways to express the world—or perhaps create a world—is the purview of great artists. He does it with oils. You will do it with words."

"What is the artist's name?"

"Pablo Picasso."

Just then, someone looked over at us, and I ducked my head, hoping I looked enough like a boy that they would ignore me. Thankfully, they did.

"Who among us has read this new author de Plessis?"

I was stunned. Members of this esteemed group were going to discuss my book—my smut book, as some might have called it.

It appeared that a smattering of those present had heard of it, but only two had read it. I held my breath.

The first gave a short summary of the book (not highlighting what I considered its finest points, I have to say) and what he deemed its "literary style." I almost giggled.

"Of course," he concluded, "it will be deemed pornography by some, but I read it only to appreciate the textual richness of the narrative."

Christophe squeezed my hand as if to ensure that I would remain silent. I certainly would. This was fascinating.

The second man who had also read it didn't share that view. "What utter nonsense," he said. "I read it for the—how can I put this delicately?"

"No need for delicacy here." Gertrude Stein herself had spoken.

"I read it for the sex."

The gathered masses laughed uproariously. Someone passed a copy of the book to Madame Stein. She opened it to a page somewhere in the middle while I held my breath. She was reading something—I had no idea what.

"Literature—creative literature—unconcerned with sex is inconceivable," she said as she looked up. "Perhaps I will read it."

Perhaps she would.

When we left the salon, Christophe was elated. "Frannie, this is wonderful. You are on your way." He took my hand as we practically skipped down the street through the twinkling Parisian nighttime. "Marry me, Frannie."

THIRTEEN

"Everything is hard before it is easy."
~ Goethe

IT TOOK AN ENTIRE SIX MONTHS to get Christophe to stop asking me. I wouldn't agree to marry him—not because I did not love him because I certainly did. It was because I never intended to marry. Never. He kept telling me I would change my mind. I knew I would not. I also knew that I risked losing him. But I knew in my heart that it was better to lose a lover than to lose myself.

I worked feverishly on my second book, and by early 1923, I had completed the draft of *Secrets of the Pas-de-Trois*. My publisher loved it and planned to ensure publication by the summer. When I had completed this second book, I took some time for myself. I told Christophe that I needed some space, so I bought a train ticket to Nice. I had decided that a few weeks in the south of France at a hotel facing the beach would be the perfect balm for my weary mind. I also hoped some time apart would make Christophe realize that he and I did not need to be married to have a full life. I also wanted to be sure that having children was not part of his plans because that was not something I ever planned to do. Again. He still did not know anything about James.

While I was in Nice, I walked miles every day. I learned every nook and cranny of *Vieux* Nice, the old quarter where the narrow streets wound from here to there in no particular way. I walked the *Promenade des Anglais*, the boardwalk along the Mediterranean that stretched from one side of the city to the other. I ate at wonderful bistros where the special of the day—the *plat du jour*—was the only

152

thing on offer. I drank wine every day and even took a dip in the Mediterranean. I spoke to no one except the servers and the hotel staff.

When I felt refreshed and ready to return to Paris, I checked out of the hotel and boarded the train. I had never been a great fan of train travel. Other people seemed to find the constant noise of the train clacking along the tracks soothing. I did not. I found it irritating, and the longer the train trip, the more irritated I could become. Thus, the overnight journey from Nice to Paris grated on every nerve fibre. By the time we pulled into the station, my mood was reflected at me in the dreary fog that had settled over the city, dulling the landscape as well as my disposition. It seemed as if all the head-clearing I'd been able to accomplish in a couple of weeks on the Mediterranean had evaporated in the plume of steam rising from the train's stack. This was my mood as I turned the key in the lock of our apartment. The moment I stepped over the threshold, I realized that giving Christophe space and time may have been a serious miscalculation

As I dropped my large case on the floor in the foyer, I could hear muffled voices coming from the drawing-room. I stopped to listen for a moment. Yes, I could hear two voices and laughter. One of the voices was certainly Christophe's. The other was an unfamiliar woman's voice.

I pulled off my cloche and placed it on the hall table. I then moved slowly toward the drawing-room where the double door was slightly ajar. Later, when I thought about that moment, I wasn't sure why I didn't call out to Christophe as would have been my habit. I wasn't sure why I stood there, hidden from sight, for a few moments before entering. I wasn't sure why I thought I ought to listen for a few moments before making my presence known. I didn't know why I did any of those things. I only know I did them.

"It would be wonderful if you could," Christophe said. Then there was a clinking sound as if two wine glasses had touched.

"*Bien sûr, je peux, ma chérie.*" Of course, I can—my darling.

I stiffened. My darling? Who was this? I didn't recognize the voice, so I considered standing there longer. Somehow, though, I realized that I'd lurked long enough. I opened the door to a lovely tableau. A young woman who looked somewhat familiar to me was sitting in the oversized wingback chair in front of the fireplace that glowed hospitably. Christophe sat on the floor at her feet, gazing up at her. She was holding a glass of wine as she gazed down at him. Her dark hair hung around her shoulders, demonstrating a complete rejection of the current bob style that I sported. She wore a dark blue dress that seemed to float around her shapely ankles crossed beneath her. In a word, she looked expensive. Neither of them had noticed me yet, so enthralled they seemed to be with one another.

I was tired and probably bedraggled from my long train trip and in no mood to entertain. "Good evening, Christophe," I said finally.

They both looked up, clearly startled by my presence.

"Françoise," Christophe managed as he placed his wine glass on the table and unwound himself from the floor. Christophe rarely called me Françoise these days. He had always said it sounded too formal. "You are home early."

"Perhaps it does seem that way," I said, sitting down on the sofa. I reached for the almost empty wine bottle and looked at the label. It was one of Christophe's special bottles for which I knew he had paid a lot of money. "None left for me?" Was I being deliberately petulant and rude? Perhaps a bit, but somewhere deep inside, I knew what was coming.

The young woman, whose identity I now realized I did know, said nothing.

"Where are my manners?" Christophe said. Where indeed? "Françoise, may I present Mademoiselle Sabine de Rochford."

I held out my hand to her. "I am delighted to meet you, mademoiselle." She took my hand but said nothing. I wondered if she recognized me because I now remembered where I'd seen her before.

It had been several years since I had last seen her, but I knew in a moment that she had been the daughter of Madame (the Countesse) de Rochford, who had frequented Monsieur Poiret's salon. On several occasions, the daughter had accompanied her mother when I had been one of the mannequins on parade. If she did recognize me, she kept it to herself.

"Sabine and I are just…" He didn't finish his sentence, so I wondered what he and Sabine were just doing.

"Well," I said, getting up, "please carry on. I'm exhausted from my train trip and will just go to bed."

Sabine put her glass down and started to get up. "I had better be going, I think," she said.

"No, no," I said. "You stay. I am the one who interrupted your evening. Until we meet again." And with that, I left. I wondered how long it would be before my leaving was permanent.

~

A month later, I moved out of Christophe's apartment into my own new space on *rue de Vaurigard* near the Luxembourg Gardens on the left bank. I had bought a flat all on my own. The gardens were across the street from my corner turret on the third floor, where I could look out and see lovers strolling arm-in-arm through the leafy pathways, in love as people are always supposed to be in Paris. I was in love with my freedom and my work. It took me only twenty minutes to walk practically anywhere I chose. I could walk to the bank of the Seine in twenty minutes or to the bookshop *Shakespeare and Company* that I loved. I was also even closer to the Sorbonne, where I frequented the libraries.

I still had to work with Christophe, who was planning to marry the young Sabine, as far as I had heard. I was happy for him since I knew he wanted a more conventional life than I had imagined for myself. I also knew he wanted children, which was a situation that could never have happened if we had stayed together. Once I had recovered from the shock of finding that he had moved on even before we had finished, I accepted the situation and realized that we would always be friends. I was happy enough with that.

Now on my own, I plunged into the life of a writer as I envisioned it. I spent my mornings writing furiously at my new desk situated in that little turret overlooking the gardens. I wandered bookstores and libraries in the afternoons, taking the time to stroll down the embankment weekly to peer over the shoulders of so many of the artists I saw. I bought oil paintings from several of those whose work I admired, wondering if they would ever be famous someday. I even managed to find a tiny Picasso. At least once a week, I attended a literary salon. I had some legitimacy now since I had started publishing small pieces (not related to my regular work) under my own name in magazines. But I didn't write all my magazine pieces under my own name.

I discovered that the weekly magazine *La Vie Parisienne* had just the mix of subjects that I loved—despite its reputation as a bit of smut reading (primarily for men). My experience of working for two of the couturiers in the city provided me with a background and some connections that made writing about fashion for their readers fun and fulfilling since I loved the idea that all the readers thought I was a man. I also loved the fact that reading my work (as F.E. de Plessis) in a magazine sent many of them off to bookshops to find my books. The money was beginning to become embarrassingly respectable.

I have to admit, though, that it was a self-absorbed part of my life. As I looked back on it years later, I realized that I had little consideration for anyone but myself at that time. It gave me pause to reflect on whether all artists must somehow be required to be selfish to pursue their work. Perhaps that was so, but I still felt different from the other artists I encountered at the weekly salons (apart from simply being a woman). When Christophe and I stopped being a couple, I thought I would have to end my attendance at the literary salons. I think the thought of losing that part of my artistic life made me sadder than losing Christophe. However, since we still worked together from time to time, and we had become good friends, he insisted that we continue attending the salons together. Thus I had ample opportunity to consider how I truly was not the same as the rest of the attendees.

Every week, as I entered the salon and took my place, I looked around at all the men (for they were almost entirely men), noting that most of them carried a kind of haunted look in their eyes. It was only when I saw them with a glass or two of whiskey in them at some café or another that they seemed to loosen up. This was one thing I did not have in common with them. I was not haunted in any way by anything, or so it seemed.

I occasionally thought about my parents and James back in London. These thoughts usually rose to the surface after a letter arrived from Mother or Father. Instead of discarding them unread, as I had done for so long, I now read them and occasionally penned a reply.

In the summer of 1925, both Mother and Father began a campaign for me to visit London, both imploring me to return. I wondered if one or the other of them might be ill. As I sat in my turret one evening, the sun setting over Notre Dame Cathedral, I looked at the two letters on my desk and wondered. *Is it time to return?* I could not yet answer that question.

~

Earlier in the year, Kiki had given birth to her first child, a daughter named Juliette. She told me it was after Shakespeare's Juliette. Kiki was a bit of an anglophile, always asking me about details of life in London, so her reference to Shakespeare's Juliette was hardly surprising. Every time I visited after Juliette's birth, I immediately saw that motherhood would suit Kiki well. She was a natural. Now, as the fall days grew shorter and the shadows in the afternoons lengthened, when I visited, I saw that as Juliette grew, so did Kiki's skills—and her contentment with her life.

I watched her as she rocked and cooed to her little girl, now almost six months old, all the while still talking with me. We kept our voices low and well-modulated, and little Juliette seemed to find the girl talk soothing. She soon fell asleep. Kiki adeptly took her baby upstairs to the nursery and told me to come along. I watched as she gently placed her little daughter into a sumptuous cradle with a large lace canopy. I was appalled at the tiny touch of jealousy I felt. I had never felt this kind of bond with James, although, under the circumstances, I felt that this was to be expected. Nevertheless, there was a bit of nostalgia for what might have been and what would definitely not happen in the future.

I followed her back down the stairs, where she poured us each a glass of wine, then she picked up the bottle, and I followed her into the library. Tucking our feet up under ourselves on the massive, deep leather sofa, we settled in to catch up.

"When will you have one of your own?" Kiki said.

"One what?" I said, oblivious to the obvious.

"Frannie! A baby!"

"First, as wonderful as you make it look, I have no intention of ever having a child. And second—" I held up my hand to silence her, "and second, there would need to be a man involved. There is no one."

"We can fix that," Kiki said, sipping her wine. "Gaston and I are planning to entertain at the beginning of the Christmas season a mere four weeks from now. You will, of course, return to the land of the living—or at least the socially living—and attend. There will be at least one eligible bachelor there." Her eyes sparkled. It seemed clear to me that she had been thinking about this bachelor and me for some time.

"Oh, Kiki, that's lovely of you, but I don't know…"

"Of course, you do. I will not argue with you against such an undertaking. You have been spending far too much time with those artists and writers since you started writing for that magazine."

"Whatever are you talking about?" I could feel mild panic begin to creep up into my neck. How could she know I was writing for magazines? I had now written dozens of pieces as F.E. de Plessis, but only two or three articles under my own name in magazines women didn't read—or so I thought.

Kiki put her glass on the table and reached under a pile of newspapers to retrieve a copy of the most recent issue of *La Vie Parisienne*. "Well, there may be more than a whiff of gossip that surfaces at our Christmas *soirée*. That juicy gossip might well make its way onto the pages of this very magazine if a certain secret writer, known to her closest friends as Frannie, would deign to write about it." She feigned a pout.

She was clearly referring to my pieces written *not* under my own name since F.E. de Plessis penned the only articles I had in that issue. I began choking. Kiki immediately began to pound on my back. I stared up at her as I reached for a napkin from the table to wipe my mouth. To say I was stunned would have been something of an understatement.

"How?"

"How do I know that my dear friend has been keeping secrets from me?" She pouted. "I have friends, you know, from back in my days at the ballet. Many of the patrons are well-placed and gossip shamelessly—and all of them read these magazines regularly. And if you must know, I do as well. There has been talk. And really, Frannie, I am not a stupid woman." She smiled demurely at me from under her eyelashes.

"What do your friends know? Tell me!"

"Only that there is a new writer—this de Plessis person—who seems to know the inner workings of the female—how shall I say it—desires. There has been speculation, and I have read those pieces. You have been absent from society for months, doing god knows what. But I believe I know. I have listened to you for long enough to discern your voice and to be certain of my conclusion."

"Does Gaston know?"

"You must be joking!" she said, laughing. "He would be mortified that such a lovely specimen of a woman could write such things."

"Are you?"

"Am I what?" she said, refilling my glass.

"Are you mortified?"

"Don't be silly. I am in awe of you, if you must know. I always knew you would do and be something special. And here it is." She put the magazine on her lap and stared at the cover for a moment.

It was the newest issue. The drawing on the cover was a clever one—if you could bring yourself to look past the nude woman with her arms held high in a great V shape. The illustrator had depicted the comely brunette, wearing only a red garter on her thigh, emerging from an inkwell. The fact that I had two pieces in the October thirty-first issue that Kiki held made the illustration all the more tantalizing to me. The naked woman, no longer merely the object of admiration for her physical form, was using the inkwell to write. The fact that no one (other than Kiki, it seemed) knew that one of the writers was a woman wasn't of great consequence to me any longer. The whole situation was working for me.

"N'est-ce pas une illustration audacieuse? Isn't this a daring illustration, Frannie?" I couldn't argue with that opinion. She then flipped through the pages. "I suppose it is not all smut," she said seriously. Then she looked up and smiled in a conspiratorial way. "However, I do love this article about what the sensual Parisienne women will be wearing this year."

I grabbed it from her. "But you are a mother now, Kiki. That's all in your past."

"Oh, my dear Frannie, you have not yet met the right man. Such things can never be in one's past." She took the magazine back. "I believe I know how the secret writer came to know of the conversations between customers at the couturier salons. Perhaps even how the writer came to know the thinking in a woman's head."

She referred to the article about women's secret thoughts as they watched the mannequins parade through the salons. It was quite good, at least in my opinion—and that of the editor (who also was unaware that the writer was a woman).

I put it down between us and sighed. "Kiki, it is very important to me that no one ever know my secret—at least until I'm ready to tell. And I have no idea when that might be."

"Your secret is most certainly safe with me, Frannie, but remember that there have been whisperings that it is a woman behind this F.E. de Plessis."

"I still don't understand how you could have figured it out."

"Simple, my dearest friend. When I read this article, I simply knew. It sounds just like you. In fact, we had a conversation about this same observation you had made. There could be no other author."

"Do you read this magazine regularly?" I had thought it was a men's magazine.

She shrugged. "Gaston almost always buys it, and he likes it when I read it. He says it keeps me more in tune with the world." She put her wine glass down on the table in front of us and picked up a book from the side table. She placed it on her lap and looked down. Then she looked up and smiled. "And I did so enjoy this one." On her lap was a copy of *The Secret Life of Adaline*.

And so, Kiki became the newest member of our little clique of people who knew the true identity of the hottest writer currently in France. I trusted that Christophe would tell no one since it was in his own best interest to keep my secret—and I had a contract. At least there was not much chance any of this would get back to England since no one there read French. At least those were my thoughts when Christophe came to me with a new proposition.

FOURTEEN

"It's a funny thing about comin' home. Looks the same, smells the same,
feels the same. You'll realize what's changed is you."
~ F. Scott Fitzgerald

CHRISTOPHE AND SABINE HAD MARRIED quietly at her parents' home in
Reims. I understood from him that they were private people, unlike
their daughter, who had left to live in Paris when she turned eighteen.
Perhaps she and I did have some things in common. They invited me
for dinner at their new apartment—Christophe had thought it better
to start his new life with a clean slate, and for that, I was grateful. I
don't know how I would have felt that evening when I walked into
their foyer if I had been walking into my former home. As it turned
out, Christophe was becoming a solid friend and editor, and Sabine, a
most genial hostess. As the evening progressed, I even thought she
and I might become friends.

As we sat in Christophe's library, each cradling a snifter of
Calvados, Sabine suddenly got up and said in English, "It has been a
most pleasant evening, Fran. I shall look forward to our next
rendezvous. We have much in common, it seems." She insisted that we
speak English all evening so that she could practice. I was impressed,
but it seemed clear to me that she was leaving us alone.

"Christophe," I said as soon as she had left, "Sabine doesn't know
about my writing, does she?"

He looked shocked. "Of course not. That would be contrary to
your contract. No one must know."

I shivered slightly, hoping that Kiki was as true to her word as I
trusted she would be. I watched Christophe as he very deliberately put

162

his glass up to his lips and took a single tiny sip. I put my glass down on the table to my right. "All right, Christophe, what's on your mind?"

"What makes you think there is something on my mind?"

I rolled my eyes. "Because I've known you too long and too well."

He rolled his glass between his palms as if to warm the fluid. "I have a proposition for you." When I didn't speak, he continued. "It is about your books." I had thought as much. "It seems that Monsieur Dadot is in conversation with another publisher."

This sounded ominous. Monsieur Dadot, as you will recall, was my publisher and Christophe's superior. If he was in talks with another publisher, I immediately wondered if they intended to shove me off to some smaller firm. But my books were selling so well that this didn't make any sense. Of course, I was getting ahead of myself—and Christophe. I allowed him to continue.

"The talks are with Monsieur George Doran." The name rang a bell in the back of my mind. "Of New York City." Christophe paused for a moment as if to let me remember what I already must have known.

Suddenly it came to me. This man was an American publisher. I felt a bit of a tingle at this possibility—a tingle of excitement tinged with terror.

"Frannie, they wish to publish English versions of your books."

I was astonished on several levels. First, the fact that one of the largest American publishers who had published so many well-known writers was interested in me was stunning. I had just finished reading Virginia Woolf's novel *Night and Day*, which they had published a few years earlier. My second concern, though, was a bit more troubling. Americans, by and large, were not known for their acceptance of the kind of erotica I wrote. I asked Christophe how that might work.

"It seems that they plan to translate the works into English," he cleared his throat, "and make some minor editorial changes for the American market."

I sat back and thought about this for a moment. I could feel anger rising within me. "And who will make these so-called minor editorial changes?"

"Oh, I believe they have an American writer with whom they will contract. He knows the market."

"*He*? *He* knows the market? A *man* will make changes in my work?" My anger was about to boil over. Then Christophe told me how much money would soon be in my bank account if I signed the contract. It was in that moment that I realized everyone has a price. Mine just happened to be expensive. Very expensive.

~

Although I still had money from my family trust, I had never before seen such a sum of money. I realized that I had choices to make. I could buy a new apartment, or perhaps even a townhouse. I could take trips. I had always wanted to experience the Orient Express. I had dreams of visiting Munich (Kiki's hometown—perhaps she would come with me), Vienna and Budapest on the way to Istanbul. Istanbul! The very thought of it conjured stories I could write about. Such a trip would be manna from heaven for a writer. I could host parties at my new townhouse and invite all the literary and political luminaries in Paris. I had heard that Scott Fitzgerald and his wife Zelda were returning to Paris. I could attend couturier salons and buy anything I chose. I could be the best-dressed Parisienne woman—all financed by money whose provenance I could never divulge. There would be rumours. Of that, I was certain. No, in the end, I realized that I could spend some but not all of this windfall. The rest I would invest. I just needed to find someone who was discreet. I couldn't ask Gaston for a recommendation, but Kiki was another matter.

As it turned out, I had already met the man Kiki eventually recommended as a financial adviser. Just as she had said, she and Gaston hosted a pre-Christmas party that year. I had made one small indulgence in preparation for the party—I had purchased my first couture dress. Yes, I had worn couture before, but I had never paid for it myself. I had heard whispers about Madame Madeleine Vionnet, who had reopened her fashion house two years earlier after a wartime closure. I had seen a wonderful fringed silk dress illustrated in a recent edition of *Vogue* magazine (I was no longer working in the industry, but I maintained my interest). I would have one of her dresses.

So, I made an appointment, dressed in my most fashionable coat with matching cloche and shoes and presented myself at her salon on Avenue Montagne. This occasion would be my first experience of being a customer rather than a mannequin. Two other customers were there that day, each on our own sofas as Madame Vionnet's staff plied us with tea and cakes. I was too excited to eat anything, so I sipped daintily on my tea, awaiting the first dress.

And then they came, each more beautiful than the one before. The day dresses (in which I had little interest) were lovely, with this exciting new bias cut making them drape beautifully from the waist, but that was not why I was here. Finally, the evening dresses began to parade.

I dismissed the first one as being a bit too old for me. This conclusion was underscored when the woman on the next sofa moaned with ecstasy when she spied it. She must have been at least fifty years old, and the lace on it seemed to appeal. Then the black one appeared.

It was flowing silk chiffon with a handkerchief cut hem—a style I had never seen before—that would sweep my calves. I could almost feel it as the mannequin walked past me. I asked her to stop.

I felt the fabric, rubbing it between my fingers as Odile had taught me to do all those years ago to determine if it was pure silk. It was. The neckline dipped down in a kind of V-shaped plunge. Dripping down in a tear-drop shape from the point of the V was a panel of embroidery in gold thread. There was a matching patch of embroidery at the dropped waistline. I had to have it, and so, I did.

When I told Madame Vionnet's assistant that I would have the dress, the woman herself happened to walk over to meet me.

"If a woman smiles, her dress must also smile," she said. "I believe that this one will smile for you."

~

I was wearing the Vionnet at Kiki's party when she introduced me to Clifford Benjamin. The moment he began to speak, I knew that he was neither French nor English. He was American. When he heard my accent, he lapsed into English.

"Delighted to meet you, Miss Phillips," he said.

"Fran, please," I said as I reached out to shake his hand. He immediately lifted it and brushed it lightly with his lips. *Well-mannered for an American*, I thought.

"Cliff," he said.

I couldn't help but stare. Well over six feet tall, he had a broad smile that seemed lit from within. He had that almost-but-not-quite brash bearing that I had so often seen in American men. He reminded me a bit of Scott Fitzgerald. He looked to me to be in his mid-thirties, but I was never very good at guessing people's ages.

Kiki introduced him as one of Gaston's colleagues in the world of finance. As we began chatting, Kiki, ever the good hostess aware of her other guests, excused herself and left us alone.

"You interested in something other than this lightweight stuff?" Cliff said, waving his half-empty coupe of *Moet et Chandon* champagne (I had seen the label). "I could use a bourbon or even a martini."

I gladly went along with him, and before I knew it, we were sitting side-by-side on a settee in Gaston's library, sipping and talking. I hadn't spent this much time with a man since Christophe. It felt good. In fact, it felt so good that we didn't leave one another's side until late the next morning. When Cliff threw his jacket over his shoulder and kissed me good-bye, we had already planned another *rendezvous* for the following Saturday. Later that day, when Kiki telephoned to ask what had happened to me (she was worried), she laughed and said that she was happy I'd already become intimately acquainted with Cliff since he was her recommended financial advisor. She immediately went ahead and made me an appointment to see him (professionally) early in the new year about my investment considerations.

~

Kiki invited me to spend Christmas day with her and her little family—not so little, though, when you counted Gaston's parents among the guests—but I demurred. I preferred to spend the day alone.

I was sitting in my living room opening presents that my parents sent from England when there was a knock on the door. I was surprised to see Cliff standing in the hallway holding bouquet of flowers and a bottle of gin.

"Merry Christmas. I hope I'm not interrupting," he said as he crossed the threshold and pressed the flowers into my hands. "I'm assuming you have vermouth, olives and a cocktail beaker?"

I did.

"I took the liberty of asking Kiki if she knew how you would be spending your Christmas," he said, stirring the martinis with my long-handled silver cocktail spoon. "I don't go home for Christmas much, either, so I thought we could commiserate." He smiled in a kind of lop-sided way as he expertly poured the cocktails into the glasses, dropped in the olives and offered me one.

We sat down near my small Christmas tree, and he began talking. On our first encounter, we hadn't spent much time talking about our backgrounds. He was from somewhere called Geneva, New York, which, according to Cliff, was famous only because it was home to the Geneva Medical College from which the first woman doctor in America had graduated. That impressed me. He was the oldest of five children, and his late father had been the town doctor himself. His mother still lived there in the big family house and wrote to him regularly, imploring him to return home. It had been several years since he'd even visited, he said. We seemed to have that in common.

I told him that I'd been subject to a similar campaign from my parents. As we talked, it struck me that it had, indeed, been a long time since I'd set foot on English soil. Chatting amiably with him in English almost made me nostalgic for home—the places, the sounds, the smells and, yes, even the people. Perhaps it finally *was* time.

~

With Cliff's help and his promise of absolute confidentiality (he knew only that I had accumulated such a sum of money from writing books, the nature of which I did not reveal, and he did not ask), I organized my money safely in what I hoped would be successful investments. He also suggested that I invest in real estate as a safer place to lodge money. I agreed, and he went ahead to make arrangements to find appropriate properties for me. I left that to him. We would discuss it in the spring after he'd had a chance to gather together a portfolio. In the meantime, I arranged to go to London for a month. My father's last letter indicated that he was overjoyed that I was returning and insisted that I stay at the house despite my plans to stay at the Savoy. I would see how that worked out. Before I left, though, Cliff said he had a surprise for me.

"I have a client I'd like you to meet," he said. "Perhaps you've heard his name. Jacques Guerlain."

Of course, I had heard of the famous perfumier, Monsieur Guerlain. I had heard much whispering about his most recent fragrance—I heard it described as sensual, voluptuous, exotic, even erotic. It almost sounded like a description of my writing! This new perfume had debuted earlier in the year at the International Exhibition of Modern Decorative and Industrial Arts, but I had yet to smell it. I told Cliff this.

"Well, then, I have a real treat for you."

He took me to Monsieur Guerlain's boutique, where he had arranged for me to meet the man himself. When I first encountered Monsieur Guerlain, I found it difficult to tell his age. Blind in one eye, he had been injured in the war but had continued his work when he returned home to Paris. He was gracious and seemed to like Cliff.

When I told him I had heard marvellous things about his new perfume, he lifted a bottle from a counter and held it lovingly toward me. "It is a beautiful bottle, *non*? It is of Baccarat crystal and inspired by eastern gardens. Exotic, *non*?" Exotic, yes.

He lifted the blue fan-shaped crystal stopper from the bottle and asked for my wrist. He placed a drop and asked me to sniff quickly, then wait until it dried to sniff again. I did. The fragrance was indefinable—and yes, erotic.

Monsieur Guerlain then reached for a wrapped package from behind the counter and handed it to Cliff, who bowed slightly and offered it to me.

"For you, *mademoiselle*." And that is how I became addicted to *Shalimar* perfume.

~

As the ferry from Cherbourg approached Dover, I stood at the rail watching the soaring white cliffs emerge from the ever-present fog. I breathed in deeply, and every memory I ever had of growing up in London flashed through my brain. That smell of English fog was both indescribable and distinctive. For a moment, I thought, "I'm home." The very next thought was, "Am I?" We would soon find out.

Father had offered to come with a car and driver to meet me at the boat, but I preferred to take the train and have him meet me at the station. I knew I'd need just a bit more time to compose myself before I returned to the bosom of my family.

Father was waiting on the platform when the train pulled in. He didn't see me at first, so I had a moment to examine him. He had aged, but not much. It had been six years since I'd seen him, so ageing was to be expected. I supposed that I had aged more than he had. When he spotted me, he began waving furiously, a wide grin breaking across his face.

As we approached one another, he stopped briefly as if to be sure it was me. Then he hugged me fiercely. I was happy to see him.

"Welcome home, Fran. Welcome home." There were tears in his eyes.

When we arrived at the house, Nora greeted us at the front door, took my valise and threw her arms around me. According to Father, Nora had been elevated to housekeeper since James was now in school and didn't need a full-time governess. I had been in the house less than an hour when I began to doubt the soundness of this decision.

Mother was sitting in the drawing-room, waiting for my arrival. As I entered the room, I could see that she had carefully arranged her skirt around her as she sat demurely on the edge of a high-back chair with her ankles carefully crossed beneath her. Her dress was black with a white collar, and she wore three strands of pearls of varying lengths around her neck.

"Finally," she said, not getting up. "You have demonstrated the good sense to return. I trust that you will be staying."

I looked at Father, puzzled by this suggestion. I had no intention of staying and thought I had made that clear when I told them I was coming home. For a visit. Just then, Nora arrived at the door of the drawing-room holding the hand of a small boy. He was wearing short pants and a navy blue sweater with a school crest on his left breast. Nora was smiling tightly—almost as tightly as she seemed to be holding the boy's hand. James. It was James.

"Who's that?" James said rudely, pointing to me.

"James," Mother said, "what have I told you about pointing?" He scowled. "James?"

"You think it's rude. Anyway, I don't care." He stamped his foot and tried to prise his hand from Nora's, who kept an iron grip as if to prevent him from hurtling forward. It appeared that this little boy certainly did still need a governess if this demonstration was characteristic of his usual behaviour.

"This is your sister, James," Mother said. I winced. "Say hello to Frances."

James looked up at me. If he hadn't seemed so ill-mannered, I might have said that he was a handsome child with dark eyes and masses of dark curls. But it is often hard to see the beauty of something that appears so insolent.

He finally broke free of Nora and stood there, arms crossed, looking up at me. "You're too old to be my sister. Anyway, I don't want a sister."

Oh, this was going to be fun.

Mother then told Nora to take James to the kitchen for dinner, which is when all hell broke loose. James began running around the room yelling, "I don't want dinner. You can't make me have dinner. I'll do what I want!" As he ran past the piano, he put his hand up and deliberately brushed the small bust of Beethoven to the floor, where it crashed into pieces. Father's face was florid, and he was clenching his fists.

"Stop that right now!" Father said as he lunged for James, catching him as he ran past toward the open door.

"Now Edward," Mother said, arising for the first time, "he's just exerting his independence."

Father glowered at her and took a snivelling James by the back of his collar out into the hallway. He returned several minutes later.

"Did he do any more damage?" I said as Father poured himself a glass of what appeared to be scotch from a crystal decanter on the far table. Father shook his head. "Pour one for me, too, Father?" He smiled slightly and nodded, bringing me the heavy glass, which I accepted gratefully. It had been a long day.

"Good heavens, Frances," Mother said. I could hear the disapproval in her voice before she said another word. "Ladies don't drink scotch."

"This one does. Or perhaps I'm not a lady anyway," I said, feeling the warmth of the liquid as it slid down the back of my throat. I had an unsettling feeling this was going to be a very long month.

~

I had been home for four days, and every day had been much the same. Father fled to his office at the bank as early as possible and returned as late as he could manage while not being late for dinner. Mother spent her days having tea with her friends in the drawing-room. At her request, I attended one such gathering but found the conversation stultifying. Nora took a sullen James to school every morning, and when he returned in the afternoon, he thrashed through the place, yelling that he could do what he wanted. I had also noticed that he didn't seem ever to make eye contact with anyone.

At first, I thought it was just that he didn't like me—or perhaps strangers in general. After four days of this, I noticed that he made eye contact with only one person—my mother. And he did that in defiance of everything she asked. Then, instead of insisting he do as she wished, Mother most often acquiesced to him, as if that might be the only way to keep the peace. It was now Saturday, and Father was at home for the day. He asked me to meet with him in his library.

"I'm not sure what to do with the child." Father was sitting behind his desk. Surrounding him was a mass of rich dark wood panelling, the kind that makes you feel as if you are in a warm cocoon. I had always loved this room. "The child is incorrigible."

"Mother doesn't seem to think so," I said as I ran my hand along the dark wood on my way to the chair facing his desk.

"Yes," he said, tapping a pen on the leather blotter in front of him n the desk. "Fran, I don't quite know what to do—how to handle this."

"Father, I never meant for—"

He held up his hand to silence me. "Fran, none of this is your fault. Yes, you did make a mistake, but you handled it. It was your mother who insisted that she had to have this child. A son."

"Perhaps to make up for having a daughter who seemed to defy her wishes."

Father shook his head. "Perhaps. But as much as I love James, he is a handful."

"More than a handful, Father." I stopped and looked at the haggard expression on his face. "Father, have you ever wondered if James is—quite right?" Father looked at me with a puzzled expression on his face. "What I mean is that his behaviour doesn't seem quite normal to me. He is never happy. He raises his voice constantly. He pays no attention to what anyone tells him. And, Father, have you not noticed that he never looks you in the eye?"

Father shrugged. "I suppose. But he may, after all, be frightened of me."

"That child is frightened by no one," I said almost to myself.

Father told me that Mother had never allowed him to discipline James, and now that he was in school, they received a summons from the school almost weekly. Father feared that James might be expelled. Only the week before, he had allegedly bitten one of his classmates.

"Perhaps he needs medical attention," I said.

"Perhaps. I don't think your mother will be pleased about that possibility, but I will talk to her about it. Just being able to discuss sit with you makes it much better." He then brightened up. "And you, my dear Fran. Are you happy?"

I told him I was, then, of course, he asked about my social life. "Your mother has been needling me to ask, although I told her that you are a grown woman and would tell us if you have someone special in your life. Do you?"

I laughed. "I'm not sure how special he is, but I am seeing someone. He amuses me."

"Ah, a French man. Your mother will be disappointed, but then, what can she expect since you live in France."

"Well," I said, "as it turns out, he's not French. He's American."

Father's eyebrows shot up. "American, you say? And what does this American do in Paris?"

"Well, Father, you'll be delighted to know that you and he have something in common. He also works in the financial world."

Again, Father's eyebrows moved heavenward. "Does this Paris-based American financier have a name?"

I hesitated for a moment. "His name is Clifford Benjamin."

Father didn't speak for a moment. "Clifford Benjamin, you say?" I nodded. He pursed his lips and put his hands together, forming a steeple with his fingers. "Has he told you much about his wife?"

My jaw dropped slightly, and my neck stiffened, caught by the bolt of electricity flowing quickly up my spine.

"I have met Clifford Benjamin," Father continued. "I'm surprised he didn't mention this to you. It does seem something of an oversight, don't you think?" I didn't know what to think. "As it turns out, I had the occasion to meet Mrs. Benjamin. We had dinner in New York a few years ago. That would have been before he decamped to Paris. Divorced, perhaps?"

I had no idea, and I would have to wait a while before I could confront him and confront him, I certainly would.

Later that afternoon, I took a walk through my old Belgravia neighbourhood. I was thinking about Cliff and considering the probability that he might still be married. Did I care? I finally concluded that I did not. I had no interest in marriage myself, so his marriage might, in fact, work in my favour. I was lost in this thought when my reverie was broken.

"Frannie? Frannie Phillips, is that you?"

I looked up to see a lovely young mother pushing the largest baby pram I think I have ever seen. The lovely young mother was Abigail.

The new baby, three months old, was Oliver Lowther-Russell II, and he was the spitting image of Ollie. Can a baby that young really resemble an adult that much? I thought so.

When Abigail approached me on the street and threw her arms around me, I felt none of the previous uneasiness I'd had about her (and Ollie) when I'd heard that they were to marry. Any animosity that I might have harboured (as unwarranted as it might have been) seemed to have evaporated. Abigail was the same, but it was clear to me that I had changed. I was genuinely happy for her and surprised myself by accepting her invitation to lunch.

The following day, I dressed carefully, wondering how it would feel to see Ollie in his new life. More to the point, however, I wondered how I would feel. I worried needlessly.

As I sat down with Ollie and Abigail in the dining room of their lovely, spacious apartment, I felt the most at home since I'd arrived back in London. After the noise and confusion running rampant in my parents' home, this was a relief. Ollie and I picked our old camaraderie right up where it ended, it seemed. Abigail smiled indulgently at the two of us as we reminisced about those carefree days before adulthood had settled in. It appeared that she approved of our friendship. When I left them that afternoon, we had mended a damaged bond. They also promised to visit me in Paris as soon as they could leave little Oliver. I looked forward to it.

On my last day in London, I happened to encounter James sitting by himself in the breakfast room, deeply engrossed in the paper on the table in front of him. I stood at the door for a moment, watching him as he scribbled furiously with a pencil. He didn't notice me as I came closer and quietly sat down across from him. This was the first time I'd seen him so quiet and still—if frantic scribbling can be called still.

Before he looked up, I was able to see what was on the page in front of him. I had expected to see scrawls the way he was going at it, but I was surprised—perhaps shocked even—to see that columns and columns of numbers covered the page along with what appeared to be sums. They were tiny and meticulous. As I edged closer, his concentration broke, and he noticed me.

"What are you looking at?" he said, his eyes narrowing with suspicion.

"I'm interested in what you're doing," I said quietly.

"No, you're not! You're just like all the rest of them!" He started to crumple the paper into a ball.

"What do you mean—like all the rest of them?"

"They all make fun of me. And Mother tells me to stop. I won't!" He threw the piece of paper across the room.

"I won't make fun of you, James. I'm interested in what you're doing. Would you show me?'

He eyed me suspiciously, and I could see he was on the verge of tears. "No!" he said, getting up from the table quickly. "I won't," he said, much more quietly. Then he left the room.

I picked up the crumpled paper then sat down at the table and spread it out. It was incredible. He had written a series of numbers that seemed to follow in some kind of sequence. I was now convinced that there was much more to this child than Mother, or even Father, had been able to figure out. I folded the page and took it up to my room, where I was packing to return to Paris. I tucked it into my handbag. A half an hour later, Father called up to me that he was ready to take me to the station. The next day, I was back in Paris.

FIFTEEN

"We must find our duties in what comes to us,
not in what we imagine might have been." ~ George Eliot

I WAS SO ABSORBED IN MEETING MY PUBLISHING DEADLINE for a new book and finishing three magazine pieces that I completely ignored Cliff's ongoing campaign to get me to spend more time at one after another of the glittering parties to which he had been invited. He was also most insistent that I attend *les Follies Bergère* with him to see a new dancing sensation from America by the name of Josephine Baker. I told him that I would, all in good time.

And what about his wife, you might reasonably ask? Did I ask him about her? Not at first. I thought I'd give myself a bit more time to get to know him and permit him the occasion to tell me. In the end, it was out of our hands entirely.

One Saturday evening, we were dining at *Les Deux Magots* when an older couple, clearly American, judging by their dress and rather loud demeanour, approached our table.

"Clifford? Clifford Benjamin?" the woman said. "It *is* you! Your mother told me you'd come to Paris, but I never in my wildest dreams ever thought we'd run into you!'

Cliff dabbed at his lips with his napkin and cleared his throat. "Mrs. Armstrong. Mr. Armstrong. How delightful to have run into you."

"How are you, son?" Mr. Armstrong pounded Cliff on the back. "Nice to see a fellow countryman in these parts. Can't even read the damn menus, but Eunice there does love the French things."

I coughed slightly and held my napkin in front of my mouth to hide the smile that was erupting. Mrs. Armstrong began to look

176

around the restaurant as if she might be searching for something. "Where is your lovely wife now? We haven't seen her in years. I'd love to see her."

Cliff looked at me, and I shrugged. "Margaret isn't in Paris, Mrs. Armstrong."

Mrs. Armstrong then turned and set her sights on me. "And you are?"

"Pardon my manners," Cliff said. "Mrs. Armstrong, may I present my friend Miss Frances Phillips." I thought I heard him cough slightly when he uttered the word "friend."

After a few more awkward moments of small talk, I gleaned that the Armstrong's were friends of Cliff's parents—friends they hadn't seen in some years. After they took their leave, I poured us both another glass of wine.

"Now, Cliff, don't you think this would be the time to tell me about Margaret?"

A great cough immediately erupted from deep within Cliff, causing a stream of deep red wine to spew forth. I suppose I could have waited until he had swallowed, but what fun would there have been in that?

A waiter immediately appeared, offering damp napkins to reduce the size of the blood-red stain oozing toward the edge of the lily-white tablecloth. Cliff was on his own to attempt to minimize the damage to his obviously expensive suit.

I casually picked up my wine glass and took a dainty sip of the exquisite wine. It was a 1921 Château Margaux, opulent and decadent, I believe was how Cliff had described it only a half-hour earlier when he ordered it, no doubt to impress the young, naïve woman with whom he was dining. I had to admit it was a lovely wine.

I placed my glass back on the table in front of me and sat back with my hands in my lap. "Well? I'm waiting."

"Frannie, darlin'," Cliff began, then he stopped as if he had nothing more to say.

I just sat there and smiled at him. "Now would be the time, Cliff. Right now."

He finished wiping up the wine. I wondered if the crazed look in his eyes resulted from my question or of having spilled this eye-wateringly expensive vintage. It had been an excellent year for wine four years ago, in 1921. Finally, he seemed to get a hold of himself. The waiter had brought him a clean glass and poured an inch of wine in it. Cliff now took a sip then stared at me.

"I am so sorry about the Armstrong's. They do get confused about things sometimes. As I said, old friends of my family."

I suppose they are confused about Margaret being your wife?"

"That. I'm sure it must have come as a shock to you, and for that, I am so sorry, Frannie."

I casually sipped my wine again as the waiter placed my escargots in front of me. When he had left, I said, "Not really. You see, Cliff, I already knew."

His eyes widened as if I had somehow managed to uncover something of a major conspiracy. "How could you possibly have known, Frannie? No one here in Paris knows."

"So, you thought, Cliff. And such a big secret, I might add. If you must know, I heard the news from my father when I was in London visiting my family."

"Your father? How could your father possibly have known about me, much less Margaret.?"

"Because my father has met you. My father is Edward Phillips."

"Edward…your father owns…"

"Yes, he does. My father is that banker from London."

It was his turn to sit back. "Well, that explains a lot."

"What exactly does that explain, Cliff?"

"Let's just say that I've never questioned the source of your investable income. The apartment, the clothes. It's been a bit of a mystery, but I suppose we're all entitled to our secrets."

I bristled at the very thought that he had concluded my father was financing my lifestyle—that I was incapable of supporting myself. I was so incensed by this that I almost blurted out my secret—my secret identity. But I didn't. As Cliff said, we're all entitled to our secrets.

Anyway, I didn't care one bit that he had a wife. I just wanted to see how he would react.

"As it turns out, Frannie, Margaret and I have an arrangement."

"And, I suppose Margaret knows this, does she?"

Cliff scowled at me. "Why would you even ask that. We've not been living as man and wife for many years."

"Husband and wife."

"What?"

"Never mind, please continue. This is fascinating."

"Frannie, I never meant to hurt you. I'm starting to fall in love with you."

That was enough for me. It was time to move on. I held up my hand to silence him. "Cliff, I don't need you to love me. I just prefer honesty." Who was I kidding?

So, it was true. I was someone's mistress. The more I thought about it, the more I liked the idea. And the minute I arrived home that night, I tore off my wrap and headed directly to my desk, pulled a sheet of paper from the stack I kept in the top drawer and rolled it into my trusty Erika typewriter I'd had shipped from Germany after the publication of my first book. I sat down and began typing. My new novel would be about a French mistress of an American in Paris—with lots of details, of course. I wondered what Christophe would think of it.

~

Cliff and I carried on with whatever it was we were doing together for the next several years. I attended glittering, jazz and gin-fuelled parties with him as my escort. I sometimes even spied Scott and Zelda, who had returned to Paris and rented an apartment a block away from me on *rue de Vaurigard.* They were developing something of a reputation, partying constantly. I had not seen Scott sober in a very long time. The other part of my life, however, was off-limits to Cliff.

I was a peripheral member of the literati set. I still wrote the odd article under my own name, which gave me a certain amount of credibility. But I watched other writers as they sat in cafés, writing, drinking and smoking day after day, and realized that wasn't who I was. I gravitated toward bookshops and libraries. This was a part of my life Cliff knew nothing about.

My favourite library was the arts and letters section at *Bibliothèque de la Sorbonne*, a short walk from my apartment. I loved the ambience of the halls of higher learning. Every time I walked in through the front doors of the magnificent edifice, I could feel the atmosphere of intellectual achievement envelop me. As a young woman who had not had the benefit of higher education, this was thrilling—a thrill I could feel riding up the back of my neck every time I entered. I would find myself an empty chair at a table among the great stacks of volumes and volumes of literature and felt as if I might be in good company. Then I would pull out a few pieces of paper and begin to write long-hand, inspired by my very surroundings. I was engaged in just such an activity when I looked up one Tuesday afternoon to see a young woman with an armload of books leaning over the table, gazing at my own stack that I had gathered in front of me.

"Excusez-moi, utilisez-vous ce livre en ce moment?" she said, pointing to the book on the top of my stack. She wanted to know if I was currently using the book. I wasn't using it at that moment, so I offered it to her.

She put the stack of dusty tomes she was carrying down on the table beside me with a thud and picked up the one she wanted from my pile. She mumbled *"merci"* and sat down at the adjoining chair, unwinding her scarf as she did so.

Through a sideways glance, I tried to take stock of this young woman interested in nineteenth-century female erotica, which was the topic of the book she was now paging through. She looked to be in her early twenties, some years younger than my current twenty-nine years. Oh, where had the years gone? A kind of classic beauty with an almost heart-shaped face and an aquiline nose, she possessed exquisite bone structure. And her skin—flawless. I couldn't see her eyes, but they were framed with heavy, dark eyebrows that were the same dark brown of her mass of hair she had held off her face by a headband of sorts.

I looked at the spines of the books she had dropped on the table. One was Virginia Woolf's *To The Lighthouse,* which I had read when she published it two years earlier. In my view, it was an odd book, written as what I could only describe as a stream of consciousness (but a well-crafted one) with an attempt at philosophical introspection. I hadn't liked it.

Another book was *Lady Chatterley's Lover* by D.H. Lawrence, which I had yet to read (banned in England but available in Paris). I had heard discussions of its eroticism and hoped to read it at some point but considered it likely to be just another of the same by yet another man writing about sex. The others were heavy-handed philosophy books, neither of which I had read, philosophy not being my interest. The fact I even recognized the title resulted from the evenings I had spent with Christophe at Gertrude Stein's literary salons. Often, one or more of the discussions ended up being a debate about different philosophies of life. One of the books I recognized was *On the Genealogy of Morals* by Friedrich Nietzsche, and the other was *On Liberty* by John Stuart Mill. They were all English versions.

I looked at this young woman again, so absorbed in the book she'd just removed from my own pile and wondered what kind of young woman did such heavy reading. Finally, she closed it and offered it back to me.

"Merci bien," she said. "I had to check something." She leaned over my paper as if to try to read what I was writing. Her eyebrows shot up, and she looked at me. Did I discern surprised respect? At least it wasn't disgust—my jottings were quite graphic.

I held my hand out to her and introduced myself.

"I am Simone," she said. "Simone de Beauvoir."

Simone and I began chatting amiably until other students nearby had shushed us one too many times, and we left together, continuing our conversation over a glass of wine at a nearby bistro. She was, indeed, studying philosophy and seemed to me to be much more intelligent than any of the men I had heard discussing these topics at the salons. She was about to graduate from the Sorbonne. I found her ideas tantalizing—her belief that women were only ever what men said they were. That was the undercurrent of her thoughts. I didn't have her level of education, but we did seem to hold similar beliefs about women in the world and had a shared experience of mothers whose wishes—perhaps even demands— of us were not what we wanted to do with our lives. I could tell from her passion and intellect that she would accomplish great things in her life.

Simone and I began meeting regularly for lunch or dinner. When she asked me what I had been writing, I was vague and always turned the conversation back to her work. I was learning so much from her. She had just met a man with whom she had begun a relationship. Whenever she talked about this Jean-Paul Sartre, it was with a reverence that I thought was reserved for much older people. When I asked her about this, I was surprised to hear that he was a mere three years older than she was. Nevertheless, she did seem quite taken with him.

I broached the subject of the four of us—Simone, Jean-Paul, Cliff and I—having dinner together. The thought of Cliff and all his financial American-ness dining with two intellectuals and me—who seemed to be the bridge—made me giddy. But it was never to happen.

~

It was October 25, 1929, and the French newspapers were full of the stories of what they were calling the worst financial disaster in history. The American stock market had crashed only the day before. Parisians seemed nonplussed by the whole thing, but I began to worry about Cliff and, oddly, my father. I had no idea whether this would affect the banks in London, but I was reasonably confident they would affect Cliff.

Cliff was too busy to see me for the next ten days, so I had to worry by myself. I kept myself occupied with my new manuscript and was thinking about meeting Simone for a glass of wine when I opened the letter from Father.

"Dear Fran,

I do hope all is well with you. I suppose you have heard about the financial difficulties across the pond, but please know that they have not affected me in any material way. However, I do fear for the workers hereabout who will most surely lose their jobs. I fear the situation will become quite dire for many here in England. But that is not why I am writing.

Your mother is ill. I am at my wit's end with her and with James, as you can appreciate. I do hate to write to you about such matters, but I would like you to consider returning to England to assist me at this time.

I have not asked a great deal of you in recent years. You have free rein to do as you see fit, but I am begging you to consider your duty. I am begging you to consider your obligations as a daughter, at least.

I shall await your response."

A daughter, at least. There was as much Father wasn't saying as what he was saying. I put the letter down on my desk and sat back, thinking. Simone was right. We had been sipping wine only last week when the topic of our fathers arose. She said, "Fathers never have exactly the daughters they want because they invent a notion of them that the daughters have to conform to."

I was certainly not exactly the daughter he wanted. The question was, would I conform at this late date?

The Vionnet

Socialite

SIXTEEN

"Selfishness is not living as one wishes to live. It is asking others to live as one wishes to live."
~ Oscar Wilde

Cliff sat on the side of my bed, watching me as I placed dresses in a wardrobe box to be shipped back to England.

"I do love that dress," he said as I placed the black silk chiffon Vionnet into the box. As he spoke, I was wondering when I would ever wear it again. "I must come to visit you."

I knew that this was simply something people said. I never expected to see Cliff again. He was the sort who could see only in front of him. If something—or someone—was no longer in his field of vision, she could expect to be forgotten. I suspected that this was how he dealt with the wife situation.

Cliff's fortunes hadn't gone as badly as he had thought they might. His American banking partners, however, hadn't been that fortunate. One of them had even stepped off the roof of his apartment building in Manhattan. It seemed that Cliff had transferred his personal resources to Switzerland, or so he said. In any case, I would miss him mainly because he represented a part of my life that was now coming to an end. I did know, however, that the ending of one part of one's life marked the beginning of a new one. Sometimes that thought gave me comfort. At other times—like now—it brought sheer terror.

I telephoned Christophe to let him know about my relocation plans. I knew that this news would not please him and was grateful that he wasn't in his office to take my call personally. I left the information about how to contact me with one of the publishing assistants and later sent him a letter so that he would know that I was not likely to be writing anything for the foreseeable future. As Christophe had proposed, we had recently signed the contract with the George H. Doran Publishing Company in New York, and they were translating four of my books into English. I expected that this would create a significant stream of income. My French books also continued to sell, and there was recent talk of Italian translations. I felt that Italians might take to them almost as well as the French had. I didn't expect them to be sold in England any time soon, which was fine with me. I needed to be someone else now—precisely who that was had yet to be determined.

I would keep my Paris apartment. For the time being, it would remain empty, perhaps awaiting my return. I knew that I could always lease it or sell it if my new situation became permanent, a state of affairs that triggered mild nausea every time I thought about it.

Cliff saw me off at the station, declaring endless love for me all the way. I was glad to be clear of him as I boarded the train en route to Cherbourg and the ferry to Dover. It would again be a long day.

~

"Are you settled in your room?" Father was already in the breakfast room, reading his newspapers and sipping coffee when I appeared the first morning. He put his paper down on the table and reached for my hand as I sat down opposite him. "Fran, I know this isn't ideal for you, but you need to understand how grateful I am for your help. I don't know much about your life in Paris, but I'm happy you were able to leave it behind."

No, he didn't know much about my life in Paris, and that situation would not change—ever. And I wasn't at all sure that I had left it behind, as he put it. Father had no idea about me or, as it turned out, Mother. Whether she was ill was unclear, but she was certainly not herself. I had seen Mother only briefly the night before, immediately after I arrived. She was propped up on a pile of pillows in her bed in the master bedroom that she had commandeered for herself. Father had been relegated to one of the rooms that had previously served as a guest room. She looked pale but didn't appear to be in any kind of discomfort, at least no physical discomfort. She (or perhaps her nurse or maid or whatever the hovering woman was) had done her hair up in a beehive, and her face was made up. I didn't quite know what to say, so I had said hello, kissed her cheek, and left her alone with her nurse.

I was too tired to ask Father many questions that first evening, so here we were having breakfast as if I had never left, yet I had so many questions—mainly about what I was doing here.

I took a piece of toast from the silver toast rack and placed it on my plate. I reached for the butter and jam. "Where is James, Father?"

"Oh, Nora has taken him to school. We'll all have dinner together this evening. You'll see him then."

"How is he?"

Father looked puzzled. "What do you mean? James is fine. It's your mother who is ill."

"About that, Father," I said as I bit a small piece from the corner of the toast triangle. "What exactly is wrong with her? She doesn't seem to be in any discomfort."

Father took a deep breath and sipped his coffee. "Yes, or no. I mean, there doesn't seem to be much that's physically wrong with her."

I rolled my eyes. "Are you telling me that whatever is wrong with her is all in her head?"

He shrugged. "The doctors can't seem to find anything else." He gazed out the window for a moment as if lost in thought. "I think that the situation simply became too much for her."

"Are you referring to the situation that she took great pains to get herself into? The situation with James?"

"The child is too much for her, Fran. I think that was obvious to you several years ago. It's only gotten worse."

"What's gotten worse? James or Mother?"

According to Father, James was difficult—something I already knew. Mother had wanted the perfect little son, possibly because she had failed in her quest for the perfect daughter. I had always thought this was an insufficient reason for adopting a child. As we sat there talking, I was trying to figure out how I felt. I didn't really feel guilty because I had dealt with my situation before James was born. I had taken responsibility and made arrangements. If we had gone through with those arrangements, he would be with a loving family in Manchester at this very moment. Instead, he was the pampered, insolent brat that Mother had somehow created. And yet, he was a brat who wasn't what she really wanted. No, I didn't feel guilty; I was angry. A child was not a chattel to be owned and manipulated. A child was a person. Alongside my anger was a serious dose of pity for the child I had brought into the world. Perhaps I did have a duty here.

~

Over the next few months, I found James to be more sullen than insolent. Yes, he was rude, and now that he was ten years old, he was also beginning to see himself as his own person. No one was in charge of him—at least from his point of view. So, we settled into a kind of cold détente.

Father relaxed visibly over the first weeks that I was home and settled back into life. He had decided that despite the country's current climate of financial uncertainty, it was not the time to give up life as he had known it. He decided that we should re-enter the social circles that had all but disappeared over the past year, and we should entertain. I became his *de facto* hostess as Mother continued to languish upstairs. She bathed and applied makeup every day, then returned to her bed in a silk dressing gown, reading magazines and eating macarons she had sent in every day from a French pastry shop she liked. She had gained a noticeable amount of weight, and I wondered when (or if) this would stop.

I had also wondered what would become of the accumulation of couture dresses that I was amassing, but I needn't have been concerned. There were many occasions to wear them. Father and I stepped out as a couple, or so it seemed, to attend the symphony and dine with his business associates. What he really wanted to do, however, was to re-establish himself as a host. So, we planned a party.

We set the date for Saturday, the fourteenth of June, to begin at eight p.m. I helped Father prepare the guest list. There were almost one-hundred-and-fifty names on the list when we had finished it, including Ollie and Abigail and Ollie's parents. The house was large, but I didn't think it could accommodate that many. Father suggested a tent in the back garden, so we sent invitations to the complete list.

I hired a trio of musicians—a flutist, a cellist and a violinist from the London Symphony Orchestra. They set up in the garden to begin playing the moment the first guests arrived and had accepted a coupe of champagne from the waiter stationed in the foyer to welcome. A jazz pianist sat at the grand piano in the drawing-room and would begin his first set as the guests filtered in.

An hour before the first guest arrived, I stood in front of my long mirror in my bedroom, holding up one and then another dress in front of me. There was no contest—it would be the Vionnet. After I dressed, I rapped on Mother's door to see how she was doing—not that she would say anything other than, "Fine, Frances, fine," as she did every evening. This evening, Mother sat up in bed and looked at me. "Is that what you're wearing, Frances?"

I was so surprised that I was momentarily speechless. First, I was surprised that she even noticed and remarked. Second, what in the world could be wrong with what I was wearing? (Her tone clearly suggested that this was what she was really saying.) Third, could she not just be gracious to me for once in her life?

"Yes, Mother," I said through gritted teeth, "this is what I'm wearing. Have a lovely evening." I fled just as her nurse appeared in the doorway with her evening sedative or whatever the doctor had prescribed this month and what looked like a glass of port.

I made my way down the stairs, my mood improving with every step. The minute I arrived in the foyer, the doorbell began ringing.

The chatter soon began as guests began to avail themselves of the overabundance of food the caterers had set out and the copious amounts of champagne and other libations at the three bars Father had commissioned—two in the house and one in the garden.

Father was once again in his glory. He had a knack for this kind of socializing. I, too, had learned to enjoy a party while in Paris, but I wasn't used to being the hostess. Abigail and Ollie arrived about nine p.m., and I was glad to see a few familiar faces. Until then, the only familiar guests were Ollie's parents, who had arrived early and were, by this time, already three or four champagne coupes into the evening.

I had made the rounds of the guests, introducing myself to the surprise of most. I guess they thought Edward Phillips's daughter was lost to Paris forever, but here I was. I approached the bar and asked for a glass of cognac. I was warming the glass between my palms as I stood on the periphery of the gaggle of guests. I was leaning into the draperies in the drawing-room, making myself invisible and staring into the sea of faces, when I felt a gentle nudge on my arm. I turned. It was Ollie.

"Frannie," he said, "you look incredible. Paris has been good to you. And that dress? What can I say? It's extraordinary."

I thanked him, and we began that kind of party chit-chat that people do when they don't know what else to say to one another when Ollie abruptly turned to me and said, "Frannie, I've missed you so much. You have no idea what my life has been like without you."

I frowned. "I'm glad you haven't forgotten me, Ollie, but I think you're being over-dramatic. You have a wonderful life with Abigail and little Oliver and the new one—what's her name?"

"Elizabeth," he said. "her name is Elizabeth. Do you want to know why we called her that?"

I couldn't think of anyone in his family named Elizabeth, so I presumed it was because they liked it, although they may have named her after one of Abigail's relations. Other than her father, I didn't know any of them. Perhaps they had even called her after little Princess Elizabeth, who was now about four years old.

"We called her Elizabeth because it's your second name."

I looked at him, perplexed. "Why would you and Abigail name your baby after me?"

"Abigail doesn't know it's your second name." He stared expectantly at me while I thought, *She should know my second name. We were best friends, after all.*

I felt uncomfortable about where I thought this was going. "Ollie, I'm very happy for you. You have a wonderful life with your family and your career. I have heard great things about your skills as a barrister. I understand you're developing something of a reputation. It's what you've always wanted."

"What have you always wanted, Frannie?"

I stared at him—through him. "Not that, Ollie, and you know it."

Ollie stood slightly away from me, sipped his drink that looked as if it might be scotch and leaned back against the draperies beside me, his free hand jammed into the pocket of his tuxedo pants, one leg crossed over the other at the ankle. "James is your son, isn't he, Frannie? The timing fits."

A cold fear began creeping up my spine. "Enough, Ollie. You're drunk."

He seemed to crumple. "Frannie, I still love you. I have always loved you. You know this. Our lives could have been so different."

I was spared from having to respond as a fracas seemed to have broken out in the foyer. We both immediately headed in the direction of the sound of raised voices.

When we rounded the corner and emerged through the archway, Father was standing at the foot of the staircase while Mother's voice boomed from where she stood halfway down the stairs. She was dressed in a bright red silk chiffon dress that resembled one she had worn on the Titanic all those years ago—one that had been lost in "the incident." Her makeup was darker than usual, with black kohl ringing her eyes, a look I'd never before seen on her. She was dripping with jewellery. It looked to me as if she had emptied one of her jewel cases onto her bed and snatched up every piece—she wore several necklaces, four bracelets that I could discern, rings on almost every finger.

"No one can host a party as I can!" Mother began slowly stepping her way down the remaining stairs. She clutched the bannister with one hand and her skirt with the other. I noticed distinct wobbling.

The look on Father's face was pure horror. "Maude, you're not well."

"I am as well as I've ever been, and I will not have that whore of a daughter of mine hosting a party that is mine to host." She had reached the bottom of the stairs and began to greet the shocked guests.

I could hear that inevitable collective intake of breath whenever someone of so-called breeding causes a scene. I was mortified. *Is that what she really thinks of me?*

Ollie, who was standing beside me witnessing the fiasco, whispered in my ear. "Don't worry, Frannie. I'll help your father with her."

He then went over to Father, who was trying to stop Mother's progress. Between the two of them and the nurse who had finally appeared, they managed to get her up the stairs and out of sight. Within minutes, guests began their good-byes, no doubt itching to get home and telephone anyone who hadn't been invited to let them know of the circus that ensued.

I gazed up the stairs and saw James, in his pyjamas, peeking around the bannister. He had witnessed the whole sordid affair. At that moment, I realized we would have to do something about Mother.

SEVENTEEN

*"England is the most class-ridden country under the sun.
It is a land of snobbery and privilege, ruled largely by the old and silly."*
~ George Orwell

IT DIDN'T TAKE LONG FOR NEWS OF MOTHER'S APPEARANCE at the party to wend its way through the social circles of the London elite. Whenever I visited a boutique in Regent Street or the dining room at the Savoy to treat myself for lunch, I could feel the eyes on me. Abigail had rung to ask me to join her for lunch on three separate occasions, and I had declined in each case. I wasn't sure how I could look her in the eye after Ollie's declaration.

Month after tedious month slipped by. We managed to get Mother to spend a month in a sanitarium where we hoped they might find out what was wrong with her, although I suspected there was nothing wrong with her except her family, and her life had not turned out as she had commanded it to do. When she returned home (still without a solid diagnosis), Mother remained in her room, and Father went to his office every day, staying away from the house for longer and longer periods of time. James was almost silent but erupted several times a week, loudly demanding that Mother return to the land of the living.

"What is wrong with her? Why are you here?" he would shout at me.

He spent a lot of time alone in his room and didn't seem to have any friends. However, I noticed a decrease in the number of calls from his school regarding his insolent behaviour. For that, I was grateful. It was only later that I realized that this was merely the calm before the storm.

~

This time it wasn't a call from the school. I had been doodling in my diary, toying with the idea of perhaps writing something again one afternoon when the bell at the front door rang. I left my papers and pens on the table in the breakfast room where I had been sitting with a cup of tea and answered the ring.

When I opened the door, standing on the steps was a large constable wearing a scowl with his hand firmly planted on the young boy's shoulder—it was, of course, James. To the constable's right was Miss Hawthorn, the headmistress of James's school.

"What's going on? What's the matter?" As I spoke these words, it became clear to me what probably happened.

"You the young man's mother?" the constable said, digging his fingers deeper into James's should so that James flinched slightly although he never moved his eyes.

"No, I'm his…sister," I said. "His mother is indisposed. What seems to be the matter?"

"What seems to be the matter, Miss Phillips," Miss Hawthorn said, "is that James has been expelled."

I looked at James, who was still staring straight ahead. "I think we should all come inside."

The constable followed me, his hand still firmly planted on James's shoulder. Miss Hawthorn brought up the rear. I led them into the drawing-room, where we all stood there looking at one another. "Perhaps you better tell me the details," I said to Miss Hawthorn. "Expulsion may be a hasty choice with serious ramifications."

"I assure you, Miss Phillips, that there is nothing hasty about this decision, and there is no choice in the matter whatsoever. James shall never again set foot in our hallowed halls of learning."

I took a deep breath. "I think that we should call my father. He should be here for this discussion."

"Am I not making myself clear?" Miss Hawthorn said. "There is no discussion. James has been expelled. That is all. I am here only to relay this information to you and to tell you to come by the school tomorrow at ten a.m. to retrieve his belongings and sign a form. The rest is the constable's domain."

That's when I started to worry. I asked them both to sit down and offered tea. They declined. James stood beside the far wall, his arms straight down by his sides, his fists clenched tightly. He continued to look straight ahead as if he were in some kind of stupor. The constable began.

James and another boy had gotten into an argument during a mathematics class. This revelation seemed like old news to me. Hardly a week went by—at least that's the way things used to be—that James did not find himself arguing with someone. If it wasn't at school, it was at home. This time, however, things escalated. According to what the other boys had told the teacher (who, by the way, had been chatting with the headmistress in the hallway when the altercation began), James began pounding the other boy's head with a textbook. The other boy fought back, and James doubled down. It had been unprovoked.

"That's not what happened! They're lying!"

"What happened, James?" I said quietly.

"It doesn't matter. No one believes me."

"There were witnesses," Miss Hawthorn said. "The entire class saw what happened."

"Well, it was just a fight. Surely these things happen from time to time." I was beginning to get the impression there was more to this than what had been said to this point.

Miss Hawthorn looked over at James, the hatred in her eyes almost palpable. "No, Miss Phillips. These things do not happen in my school. On my watch."

The constable then completed the picture. James had not only hit the other boy with a textbook, but he also had, according to witnesses, bludgeoned him to the point of unconsciousness.

"I did not! He fell! He hit his head on the desk!" Tears now rolled down James's face, and his eyes had a caged animal look about them. "No one ever believes me!"

"How did the fight start, James?" I said. I refused to believe that it was unprovoked.

"He started making fun of my numbers—my ciphers. They always make fun of me—how I look, the things I like. No one ever believes me! I want to die!"

I turned to Miss Hawthorn. "What happened to the other boy? Is he all right?"

"He awoke almost immediately," she said. "He will be fine."

"He was faking," James said, much more quietly now.

I turned to Miss Hawthorn, who ignored his comment.

"As it turns out, his parents will not be pressing charges," she said, "but the constable says they could consider them in any case. We cannot have children running around, battering one another with textbooks and getting into fights. I expected more of a Phillips child."

And there it was—that snobbery as if people of our standing couldn't have issues like everyone else. In any case, I found myself believing James. The other boy probably did fake the unconsciousness. If his parents weren't pressing charges for assault, then there had to be a reason. We would simply have to find him another school. When I explained this later to Father, he had only two words. "Boarding school."

~

It took surprisingly little effort to arrange it. Father called a friend who called a friend who was on the governing board of Tonbridge School. A month later, I found myself alone with James on the train headed south to Tonbridge Wells, taking him to his new life.

James had seemed strangely more settled since his expulsion. Whenever I thought about what he may have endured at the hands of such a pack of bullies, I began to seethe, almost as if he were my own son—which, of course, he was. Despite Mother's incapacity and inability to provide mothering to this lost child, she was apoplectic when we told her that he would be leaving for boarding school. She wailed and called him "my darling boy," as if he had been the model son.

I had always felt that James didn't like me, so I thought he would be angry that I was the one depositing him at this new school, but he didn't appear to be. He seemed almost relaxed as we sat in our compartment in the first-class car of the train as it trundled its way through the southern reaches of London and on into the countryside. I hadn't been in the country since my Oxford years, and it occurred to me that I missed it. This surprised me.

We were met at the train station by a porter and driver from the school. The driver dropped us off in front of the main school building, promising to leave the luggage in James's dormitory. We stood for a moment at the end of the long walkway, both gazing down toward the long, low building. In the modern Gothic style, the impressive building had been built in the nineteenth century, with its two long, two-story sections divided in the middle by a kind of turret rising four stories, looking for all the world like a castle. Flanking this grand walkway leading to the golden sandstone edifice was a carpet of clipped grass that looked as if it had been freshly painted. I felt James slide his hand into mine as we both took a deep breath and moved in the direction of the imposing doors.

The headmaster's secretary greeted us and led us to a waiting area outside the office. Finally, after ten minutes, she looked up from her work, glanced at the clock on the wall and said, "Mr. Sloman will see you now."

Father had told me that Mr. Sloman was a decorated war hero who had left his position as headmaster at the Sydney Grammar School to serve in the Great War where he had been wounded. As we entered, I noted that he was probably close to fifty years old, with a pleasant face. I wondered what this seeming geniality covered up. I had heard stories about the rigours of boarding school and wondered if James was up to it.

He adjusted the small, wire-rimmed glasses and asked us to take a seat. He spent a moment reading the file open on his desk. Presumably it was about James (I wondered how complete it was), then he looked up. "Phillips," he said, addressing James directly, "we have high expectations of our boys here at Tonbridge. I trust you will be up to meeting these expectations."

"Yes," James said.

"Yes, what, James?"

James looked at him directly. "Yes, sir," he said.

An hour later, I found myself walking back down that walkway alone, having just left James in the capable hands of a dormitory assistant who looked as if he could handle just about any boy who walked through the door. I felt that this school would be good for James—that it would help him grow into himself. At that moment, I considered this a good thing.

EIGHTEEN

"My mind rebels at stagnation. Give me problems, give me work!"
~ Arthur Conan Doyle

I RECEIVED A LETTER FROM CHRISTOPHE every two months like clockwork. Sometimes they contained a royalty cheque, but mostly they were letters imploring me to return to Paris or, barring that, at least to start writing again. He wanted to see a new book. He told me how much the reading public needed my work. I knew, however, that his upward climb in the publishing world depended at least in part on the cash that would flow in if I were to write a new book.

I had, in fact, already begun to make notes on a new work when the doorbell rang one day. I opened the door to find Christophe standing on the porch in the flesh, leather case in hand, his eyes begging me to let him in out of the pounding rain.

As he shook off his wet coat, I placed his dripping umbrella in the stand behind the door with the rest of our collection of umbrellas. As he fussed over arranging his tie and his jacket, I watched him and realized I had missed him. *Do I miss my life in Paris?* I thought. *Maybe I miss the carefree days that are over.* I sighed.

"Christophe, whatever are you doing here?"

"Oh, Françoise," he said, embracing me warmly, "you know perfectly well what I am doing here in this god-forsaken city. *Mon dieu,* it does rain."

Christophe had told me often enough about his loathing of London and its rainy weather. It could not have greeted him more predictably if it had tried. I smiled.

"I'm not sure I do know why you're here, Christophe, but it is good to see you, in any case. Tea?"

He nodded gratefully and followed me into the drawing-room. Nora poked her head around the door and asked if she could bring it.

"Please," I said quietly.

"This is a very pretty room," he said, looking around at the warm hues of the wallpaper that perfectly matched the fabric of the draperies hanging luxuriously from the twenty-foot ceiling to pool on the floor. He then placed his damp leather case on the floor and turned to me. "As expected, you look marvellous. But Françoise, *chérie*, I am here to beg you to return to Paris. And if I fail at that, you must at least begin writing again."

Nora brought in the tea tray and left it on the sideboard. I poured Christophe a cup of tea and dropped two sugar cubes in, just the way he liked it. I passed it to him, and we both sat down facing one another.

"How is Sabine?" I said, sipping my tea.

"Sabine? Sabine is fine," he said. "She is fine."

"No children yet?"

Christophe coughed slightly. "No children. And you?" He squinted at me. "Well, if we are to play this game, let us play it."

"No, Christophe. No children. You know me well enough to know the answer to that question. And no to the next question as well. There is no man in my life."

"I find that very difficult to believe," he said.

"Well, believe it. Now, about the writing."

He placed his cup down on the table and looked at me expectantly.

"As it turns out, I have already outlined a new book," I said.

"*Mais c'est merveilleux*! Marvellous. Monsieur Dadot will be thrilled, as am I."

I had no doubt that they would be thrilled, but then, so was I. I had missed Paris and Christophe and writing. I think I missed the writing the most. I had almost thought I'd lost the ability to think since spending so much time as a domestic of sorts. Before we could discuss the direction of the new book and the future contracts, I heard the front door close and Father's voice calling out to Nora for assistance, no doubt with his wet things. I was immediately alarmed.

"Christophe, my father's home. I hadn't been expecting him so early. You must not tell him why you're here." Christophe looked puzzled. "I will introduce you as a friend from Paris. You may tell him you are in publishing if he asks, but not a word about the writing. My writing. He cannot know." I stared at him. "Now, you must promise."

He nodded. "But of course!"

Father came into the drawing-room rubbing his hands together as if to warm them. He looked surprised to see that I wasn't alone.

"Father, I'd like you to meet my friend Jean-Christophe Lemieux. From Paris."

Christophe was his usual charming self, and Father seemed happy to meet one of my French friends. Father asked Christophe to stay for dinner, which he accepted. I had hoped he might decline and that we could meet at his hotel the next day, but I was thwarted and had to spend the evening avoiding the main reason Christophe and I knew one another.

Later that night, as I lay awake in bed, looking up at the ceiling and listening to the rain as it beat on the window, I made a decision—a decision that I did not take lightly. I wasn't sure how I would tell Father, but I could worry about that later.

Christophe and I met for lunch at his hotel the next day. The sun was now shining, and he was feeling much more tolerant of London.

"Christophe, I've made a decision," I said as we settled into our chicken confit, the only thing on the menu Christophe would consent to order since it was French.

"English cooking is an abomination," he said. "Now, this is acceptable. What decision have you made?"

"I'll need your help." He put his fork down and looked at me expectantly. "Can you get my apartment ready? I'm moving back to Paris."

I had decided that since James was safely tucked up in boarding school and Mother was at least appearing for dinner several times a week, my family no longer needed me. I could plan to visit London regularly and keep control of James's school situation.

Christophe was elated and promised to do anything I needed. I decided to complete most of the arrangements for the move before I told Father. I wanted it to be a *fait accompli* before I gave him the news. I sensed that he would not be happy, but I hoped he'd understand. I never did have to tell him.

~

The doctors concluded that it was a stroke. Mother's behaviour in the days before suggested this. In the end, it really didn't matter what caused it. It never does, does it? All we're left with is all that needs to be done when someone dies.

Despite all that she had done and said in recent years, Father was devastated by this sudden loss. I had never realized how much he truly loved her—and thus the reason he put up with her idiosyncrasies for so many years—until I watched him approach the coffin after the funeral when all the mourners (if their friends could be called that) had filed out of the church to the strains of the choir singing *Jerusalem*. I had thought it an odd choice, a hymn written in 1916 at the height of World War One, with so many references to England's pleasant pastures and things like God, King and Country. It didn't seem much like Mother to me, but it did seem like Father. And now, as I watched him place his hand gently on the coffin and gaze into the waxen face of my mother's body just before they closed it for the last time, I wept. I had never before seen such anguish in my father's eyes. I hoped never to again.

The bottom line was that I now realized I was not moving to Paris—not now, and perhaps not ever. I simply couldn't leave Father alone to deal with James and life in general. And as I anxiously read the newspaper each morning after Father left it on the breakfast table for me, I became increasingly anxious about the situation in Europe—and my friends in France.

It seemed as if war clouds were once again gathering. There had been murmurings about Germany rearming in defiance of the Treaty of Versailles that had ended the Great War, and then the news of their creation of an air force—something they were calling the Luftwaffe—emerged. Germany's chancellor, Adolf Hitler, had spent the past few years establishing something of a dictatorship, and I wondered how far he would go. Perhaps I was better off staying in England for the foreseeable future.

I wasn't sure whether Mother's death had affected him or it was the school's influence, but when James returned from school for the Christmas break in 1935, he seemed different. He was less outrightly insolent, yet he seemed much harder. There was a harshness about him that I could see in his eyes and the rigid set of his jaw. He almost seemed to me as if he were always on the verge of eruption, but that eruption never came. He was also sixteen years old now, and I was beginning to worry about what he would do when he was finished school at Tonbridge.

James was an unremarkable student, especially in language arts. He was passing, but just, and it seemed from his tutors' remarks that he was barely literate with no interest in reading or writing. I was surprised how much of a blow I felt at this. His science marks weren't much better, but his mathematics marks soared. Perhaps that was where we should steer him for his future. At least we hadn't had any calls from the headmaster regarding James's behaviour. For that, I was grateful.

These were the things on my mind when Christophe telephoned from Paris. No one ever called from France—it was far too expensive. Indeed, the only reason most people ever called from abroad was if someone had died. Even then, a telegram would work just as well. But Christophe called. And he had news.

"Fran, it is so exciting. Our partners in America, your publishers over there, are interested in speaking with you about a new venture. I do not have details, but you will need to go."

"Go? Go to New York?" I said. The thought was tantalizing.

"I have taken the liberty of booking passage for you aboard a new ship. You will leave on the Queen Mary on May 27. It is done."

NINETEEN

I HAD NO IDEA WHAT KIND OF PROPOSITION I WOULD FIND facing me when I arrived in America, but I was inspired to write as I never had before—perhaps in preparation or to prove to myself that I still could. Then, when I faced my American publisher, I could be ready for anything.

James was safely tucked up in boarding school, and Father seemed more relaxed as he went about his daily life, working and coming home at a reasonable hour to have dinner with me most evenings. As we sat at dinner one evening a few weeks before I was to leave for New York, I noticed his hand shaking slightly as he raised his wine glass to his lips.

"Fran, my dear," he said, "how are the preparations for your upcoming trip proceeding."

"They're going well, Father." I peered at him across the table as I cut a small piece of steak. "How are you, Father?"

He ignored me. "I still don't understand why you have to go. What is so appealing about New York?"

This conversation was not new, nor was it a new line of questioning. I suspected that Father thought I had a man in New York, and I was simply refusing to talk about him.

"I told you, Father. I am going to do some shopping. I'm planning a new wardrobe for the upcoming season. Surely you can understand that?"

"I could understand it if I thought you had the slightest interest in our social life. Besides, I should think you would be better off going to Paris."

"I have always adored clothes, Father. You'll remember my passion for creating them. I practiced so hard, and, in the end, I wasn't good enough. You know all this. But I've never lost my interest in fashion." Although, to tell the truth, Father had a point. As far as I could tell from my continuing interest in fashion magazines, most elite American women did their shopping in Europe. In any case, telling him the truth was out of the question.

Father shrugged. "I suppose you need a break from me." He picked up his wine glass again, but his hand was shaking so much, he immediately put it back on the table. "Unless, of course, you are planning a *rendezvous* with that American man we discussed."

"Clifford still lives in Paris, not in New York, if you must know. And, no, I am not planning a *rendezvous* with him or anyone else." I dabbed my mouth with my napkin and put it back on my lap. "Father, I've meant to ask you about that shaking in your hand."

He looked at me, lines forming between his eyebrows. "What shaking? What are you talking about?" He wouldn't make eye contact with me.

"You know what I'm talking about. You're not getting any younger, and I think you should see a doctor." I didn't know exactly how old Father was—I hadn't known Mother's age, either, until I had to arrange to have her headstone carved. Father had been forced to tell me. I suspected he was in his early sixties, a time when he ought to be slowing down and considering retirement, a subject he refused to discuss.

Father looked at his wine glass, then picked it up carefully, looking at his hand. The shaking was almost imperceptible, but it was there. "I'll see someone in Harley Street while you're in America. I'll provide you with a full report upon your return. In exchange, I want you to provide me with a full report of America when you return."

It was a deal.

~

Three days before I was scheduled to board the Queen Mary in Southampton, I arrived home in the afternoon after running errands to find Father pacing in his study.

"We have a problem, Frances," he said as he noticed me lurking in the hallway. He hadn't called me Frances in quite some time. *The situation must be serious*, I thought.

I walked into the room and noticed that his hands were shaking more than usual. He appeared agitated, not a state in which I generally found my father. "What is it, Father?"

"It's James. He's in some kind of trouble at school."

I sighed and sat down. "Am I going to need a drink for this discussion, Father?"

"Perhaps. And if you don't, I do." He went over to the drinks cabinet beside the bookcase and poured two drinks with shaking hands. He walked over to where I was sitting, handed me one and sat down. "Mr. Sloman, the headmaster called. I had been hoping James might have grown out of his temper, but it seems he has not. He instigated an altercation. I'm afraid it seems that it was quite nasty."

"What was it about?"

"I didn't quite understand what Mr. Sloman was talking about. It seems one of the other boys teased James about his curly hair, and the next thing they knew, fists were flying. According to the headmaster, James was screaming some very unfortunate epithets about black people. I have no idea what this might possibly be about. All I know is that James is suspended for a fortnight."

I breathed in and held my breath. This couldn't be happening.

Father gulped his drink. "And all of this while you're going to be in America. James will be here with me. Just me."

"And Nora," I said.

"Thank god for that." Father turned to me. "I don't suppose you could possibly put off this shopping trip?" The way he emphasized "shopping," I felt strongly that he suspected that wasn't the real reason for my journey across the pond.

I assured him that I could not, but I offered to talk to James when he arrived home the next day.

I met James at the train station the following afternoon and accompanied him home. He was silent, so I was, too. When we arrived at the house, he stomped up the stairs, with me directly behind him. When he reached the top of the stairs, he turned to me, fury patently visible on his face and said, "You don't need to baby-sit me. I know what I've done, and I don't regret it."

I was still wearing my gloves and holding my handbag as I followed him into his room. I stood at the door and watched as he flung his suitcase on his bed and tore off his school jacket and tie.

"What exactly do you want?" he said.

"What I want, James, is an explanation of your conduct. The story we heard seems to suggest repugnant behaviour on your part." I could feel the red tide of anger rising to a level where I felt I might not be able to contain it.

"I don't owe you an explanation. You're not my mother!"

"Yes, I am!" The words were out of my mouth before I had a chance to give them a single thought. My hand flew to my mouth as if I could somehow take them back. But I could not.

James stood there, his dark curls wild and his mouth in the shape of a sneer. He seemed speechless. Then he slowly looked at my face and said, "Liar."

I sat down on the side of his bed and grabbed the knob on the footboard. "Yes, James, I am. I have been since the day you were born. I have been a liar. But that doesn't change the fact that I am, in fact, your mother."

His anger burst out of him, knocking my handbag to the floor where its contents spilled out in an array between us. I carried three photographs in my handbag. One was of Mother, Father and me—a formal portrait taken when I was about five years old. There was also a photograph of Christophe and me in front of the Eiffel Tower. The third one was on top. It was the photograph I'd taken from Elliott. It was the picture of Elliott with his parents and grandmother.

"Who the bloody hell is that?" James said, looking down at the mess on the floor.

I could have said nothing. I could have lied again. I chose not to do that this time. Instead, I leaned down and picked it up, then held it out to him, pointing at Elliott. "It's your father, James. His name was Elliott. He was an American soldier."

James grabbed it from me. "Liar!" he said again.

"Not this time, James."

"And who the bloody hell is that?" he said, pointing to Elliott's grandmother. "The family maid?"

My jaw hardened. "That, James," I said slowly and deliberately, "is your paternal grandmother."

I had never before heard anything like the cry that escaped James's lips. It was like an animal caught in a trap.

"Get out!" he yelled. "Just get out!"

James refused to come out of his room for the next three days. Then, I left.

~

I decided to stay overnight at a Southampton hotel the day before I boarded the Queen Mary for her maiden voyage (was I foolish to be embarking on the maiden voyage of yet another ocean liner?). I chose a hotel that Abigail recommended. She and Ollie had stayed there before their trip to, oddly in my view, Quebec City in Canada on the Empress of Britain to celebrate an anniversary a few years earlier. I had expected them to vacation in the south of France or the Costa del Sol in Spain, but Canada? I had never known anyone to visit Canada by choice. In any case, here I was, the night before my voyage, sitting in a snug little pub on the main floor of the small hotel, contemplating the last time I left Southampton for an ocean voyage.

My recollection of the month after that fateful voyage was becoming hazier in my mind. Every year in April, on the anniversary of the Titanic's sinking, I thought about that peculiar incident. And every year, as I read others' recollections that the newspapers inevitably published, I found my own story receding further and further into the background. I had taken a ship back to England after the disaster, so this was not my first time on a ship since then. But it had been twenty-four years now since I'd turned my face toward America and considered what lay ahead.

My reverie was interrupted by an eruption of laughter coming from the far side of the fireplace. Since the room was so small, I felt almost as if I were a part of the group. I counted five men, ranging in age from early twenties in my estimation to probably fifty or so. As I began eavesdropping on their conversation, I concluded that they were American journalists who had been tasked with covering the Queen Mary's maiden voyage.

There was a half-full pitcher of beer on their table alongside two empty ones. It was clear they were making the most of this social time. As another round of laughter erupted, two of them looked over at me with that kind of apologetic look people had when in public with recalcitrant children whose behaviour they could not control. I didn't mind. It was nice to have the company, even if I wasn't a part of it.

I stayed in the bar until the barkeeper came over to tell me it was last call. I finished my second glass of wine then gathered my handbag and coat. I realized that I was reluctant to move and thus edge closer to the voyage. I didn't expect to feel this way.

The following day, Wednesday, May 27, 1936, I lingered over my full English breakfast, something I rarely, if ever, ate—sausages, two fried eggs, tomatoes, mushrooms and fried bread. I had never considered fried bread before that day. It was oddly satisfying. I realized, once again, that I was procrastinating. I would eventually have to bring my cases down from my room, find a taxi and make my way to the dock.

A few hours later, I found myself standing at the bottom of the gangway, looking up at yet another magnificent ship. As I gazed upward at her colossal dark hull, the first thing that struck me was that this ship was noticeably larger than the Titanic. There were three red smokestacks, each with a black border at the top. I seemed to remember that the Titanic had four stacks. I briefly wondered if that was a good thing or a bad thing. Perhaps it was, after all, just a thing.

I had given over my two cases to the porter and would see my bags again in my stateroom in due course. As I watched the other passengers excitedly spill out of taxis, they all seemed to have a great deal more luggage than I did. I was once again in the company of the first-class travellers, all of whom could be expected to have enough baggage to contain several changes of clothes each day. I would be somewhat more restrained. There was one thing that I did feel comfortable about, though. I was alone. I had not realized how much I needed to be alone sometimes. Now, I would be alone for several weeks—on my way to New York, at a hotel, and on my return. It seemed like bliss. For the first time since I'd arrived in Southampton, I began to relax and considered the fact that I just might enjoy the trip. After all, I was making history yet again—on a maiden voyage. I expected this one to have a somewhat different outcome.

~

I stood leaning on the gleaming railing on the deck, alone in the middle of a cheering onboard crowd as we waved at an even more excited crowd far below, bidding us farewell from the pier. An armada of boats had assembled to accompany us as we made our way out of the port and into the English Channel on our way to the open Atlantic and New York City.

"I am so sorry."

The voice was very close to my ear as I felt something hit my arm sharply. I looked up to see that I'd been hit by a camera that was dangling from the neck of a tall man standing beside me at the railing.

"Damn thing got away from me. I hope you're not hurt."

The accent sounded vaguely American, at least I thought it did, but there were so many American accents, I realized I couldn't place it. But I was able to remember where I'd seen the face before. The tall (and did I say handsome?) man standing beside me in a rumpled overcoat was one of the men I'd identified as journalists the evening before at the pub. He was the one who had looked over at me apologetically. He suddenly seemed to recognize me.

"Hey," he said, "I know you. Well, I don't mean I know you, but I know you. I mean, you were the woman in the bar last night. Sorry for my colleagues' behaviour. They can get a bit rowdy."

"No harm done—on either count," I said. I glanced widening space of water between the ship's hull and pier and shivered. When I glanced up again, the man had disappeared.

I stayed up on deck for the next half hour as we made our majestic way out of Southampton—or as majestic as a ship can be when disappearing into the fog. I drew my coat around me to fend off the dampness and watched as the crown on deck dispersed, wondering why so many people were going to New York. I suddenly had an idea for a new novel set on an ocean liner in the middle of the Atlantic Ocean. *Well,* I thought, that should keep my mind busy for the next four days. *And god knows, I need something to keep my mind off that.* I turned and looked once again at the darkening water. I took one more glance above me at the lifeboats that hung just above me on the open promenade deck (wondering if there were enough) and followed the crowd inside to dress for dinner.

~

My stateroom, as expected, was luxurious. Located on the "A" deck, it was more of a suite than a simple stateroom consisting of a bedroom, a sitting room and a private bathroom. The bathroom's tub was outfitted with a selection of water choices: hot or cold fresh water and hot or cold salt water—the four taps lined up one above the other. I wondered what a bath in warm salt water would be like. I had plenty of wardrobe space and a dressing table with a large mirror and recessed lighting, a nice touch, I thought.

The décor, while not as decadent as I remembered the Titanic being (and after all, my father had been one of the important people on board that ill-fated vessel), was luxurious just the same. Rather than heavy wallpapers, the walls were warm wood with burl wood inlays surrounding the dressing table. My sitting room had two portholes, and my bedroom had one. The carpets were warm and dark, and the whole place seemed to envelop me like a cozy sweater. The thing I liked most about this was that I was utterly alone. I was a woman travelling solo, and it felt sumptuous. It was time to dress for dinner.

The suite steward had unpacked my two cases. I suspected the reason he smiled so indulgently when he came by to ask me if I needed anything else was because it hadn't taken him much time to hang my few dresses in the wardrobe and place a few other things in the drawers. I had seen how much luggage other first-class passengers were bringing aboard.

I now stood in front of the wardrobe and contemplated the several dresses I had brought. Two of them had matching jackets that I expected to wear for meetings with my publisher in New York. I also had an appointment with a literary agent, a meeting Christophe had recommended I take. I had no idea why I needed a literary agent, but I would attend the meeting anyway. Perhaps it was an American thing. Anyway, I had suitable business wear but had brought only two cocktail-type dresses. I pulled the first out of the wardrobe, held it up against me and decided against it. The only other choice was the Vionnet. It was, in fact, one of my favourite dresses and it would have to do.

Once I was ready, I picked up my new evening bag, a small indulgence that I had custom-made based on my design. It was a small clutch fashioned of jet-black beads that shimmered whenever you turned it in the light. A magnetic clasp—one of the very newest of handbag closures—held it closed. I looked down at it in my hand against the black silk of my dress and surveyed the image in the mirror. It was missing something.

I rummaged through my drawers to see where the steward had put my long silk scarf. I knew it would be a bit retro, but I wanted to wear it wrapped around my head like I had done so often at parties in Paris. I found it and wound it around, securing it with a black onyx and diamond brooch set in platinum that I had inherited from my mother. I looked in the mirror again. Now, I was ready.

I made my forward on the Promenade Deck, where the steward had told me I would find the bar. By the time I arrived and stood in the doorway, it was already buzzing. It was a beautiful, sleek space with a curved railing that divided the upper bar area from the lower table area that looked out at the great expanse of water ahead. You could barely see the water as it was illuminated only by the lights reflecting from the ship.

The décor was strictly art deco, that new-fangled aesthetic that I so adored. I couldn't see an empty table, so I took up a seat at the bar where the smartly uniformed bartenders stood in front of a large piece of artwork that stretched from one side of the massive bar to the other. It hung just above the glass shelves that held myriad bottles of liquor that reflected in the gleaming metal wall behind them. I ordered a dry martini with olives, placed my clutch on the bar and contemplated the mural.

It depicted a group of dancers, but it seemed to be saying much more. Some of them were in evening dress, while others were in work clothing or uniforms. There appeared to be aristocrats and barmaids, soldiers and everyday people, holding hands in a grand circle, dancing as if their lives depended on it.

"It's great, isn't it?"

I was so startled by the voice at my elbow that I spilled a bit of my martini that the barman had just put in front of me and that I had begun to lift toward my lips.

"God, I'm so sorry," he said. "Let me help you with that."

I looked up from the small drop that had landed on the front of my dress to find myself staring into a pair of ice-blue eyes under a mop of red-blonde hair. It was him. It was the journalist from the deck—and the bar.

"I think that may be the third time you've apologized to me," I said, laughing, "and we haven't even been introduced."

"Sorry," he said, then caught himself and laughed. "I guess I come by it honestly. I'm Samuel McLeod. Sam." He held out his hand.

"Fran Phillips," I said as he held my hand just a millisecond longer than he needed to. "And what about coming by your apologies honestly?"

"Canadian, at your service, Fran Phillips. I think we have a problem with all that apologizing."

That did make me laugh. I hadn't ever met a Canadian before, and it seemed rather exotic. That, too, explained why Sam's American accent wasn't recognizable to me. It wasn't American at all.

Sam ordered himself a rye whiskey on the rocks and slid into the seat next to me at the bar. "Anyway, you were looking at that mural."

"Yes. I'm not sure I'd like it hanging on the wall in my drawing-room, but it's interesting. Do you know anything about it?"

"As a matter of fact, I do. We journalists got advance information about much of the ship before we boarded so that the stories we file about the new Queen Mary when we get to New York are at least accurate."

"You're a journalist?"

"For the *Toronto Star*." Sam took a sip of his whiskey. "In Toronto." He smiled while I rolled my eyes. I couldn't help it. He continued. "This mural was painted last year by someone named Alfred R. Thomson. It's called *The Royal Jubilee Week*. Ever heard of that artist?"

I thought the name rang a bell, but the bell was faint. "Not really."

Sam sipped his drink. "Evidently, he's deaf and paints lots of portraits."

That was where I'd heard of him. One of Father's friends had mentioned the name at a party sometime over the past two years. She had commissioned a portrait.

By the time we had finished our drinks, we could hear the dinner bell ringing.

~

I was assigned to a dinner table with two older couples. They were already seated when I arrived. As I neared the table, both men jumped to their feet to hold out my chair while the two wives, both of whom had accessorized their cocktail outfits with an eye-popping array of glittering gold and diamond jewellery, eyed me critically. I was having *déjà vu* from the dining room on the Titanic when Lady Lucile had disapprovingly assessed me as a twelve-year-old.

"Will your husband be joining us?" The woman to my left patted her hair slightly while gesturing toward the empty place beside my chair.

I couldn't decide how I wanted to play this. It was clear that me being the odd-woman out was going to be a bit of a problem for these two women, judging by how they were eyeing me then looking daggers at their husbands. It could be fun to play up my single status, but that could also get me into the kind of trouble I didn't wish to engage in during this trip. I was just about to respond when the chair beside me began moving out.

"Sorry I'm late, honey." Just as he had done back at the bar, Sam slid into the chair beside me and smiled. "I'm Sam," he said, reaching across the table to shake hands with the other two men who looked slightly disappointed while their wives both brightened considerably, smiling at this handsome man through batting eyelashes.

Honey? I looked at Sam and smiled tentatively. "Are you at the right table?" I whispered to him while everyone else pondered the extensive menu and ordered champagne.

"I am now," he said. "What are we eating?"

What could I do? I examined the menu, ordered the Dover sole and a glass of Sancerre, and enjoyed the little deception. As it turned out, Sam was a charming dinner guest with an ability to talk authoritatively about a vast array of subjects. As he discussed the current political situation in Europe with the two husbands, the wives gazed at him, and I wondered if he'd ever heard of the writer F.E. de Plessis. After all, he did seem to be knowledgeable about a lot of things.

Overall, dinner wasn't at all like the dinners on my last trip to New York. The group turned out to be engaging and fun. The two other couples—Americans through and through—had travelled to

London from America to take the Queen Mary's maiden voyage back to New York. They were friends who lived in Georgia, where the two men were both in the tobacco business, and the wives seemed to run everything cultural that Atlanta had to offer. At least it sounded as though their money did, and they sat on boards, giving out advice. Once they concluded that Sam and I were a married couple, they seemed to accept us. I wasn't sure why I didn't immediately correct their mistake, but Sam looked so dashing in his tuxedo after ditching the tweedy, rumpled journalist attire that I couldn't bear to give up the charade, so I played along and enjoyed myself.

Once dessert was over, the other two couples excused themselves and left for the smoking room while Sam and I stayed behind to finish a glass of champagne.

"Now, that was fun, wasn't it, Fran?"

I laughed and told him it had been, but I wasn't sure we could keep up the charade of even knowing one another, much less being a married couple.

"Of course, we can," he said. "Besides, I have a feeling that it won't always be a charade." Then he leaned in close and said, "Oh, by the way, you look fantastic in that dress."

~

The four days flew by in a whirlwind of new sights, sounds, and feelings. As one of the invited journalists aboard, Sam had access to many parts of the ship, which he gladly took me to see—the second-class amenities, the kitchen (a revelation of people, speed and tons of food), and even the engine room. We drank champagne and whiskey (he introduced me to Canadian Club Rye whiskey) and dry martinis (I introduced him to the pleasures of a martini, stirred with ice and three olives) at the bar. We danced to the orchestra in the main ballroom every evening before winding down with the pianist playing a bit of late-night jazz in one of the more intimate bars. Much of the journey was so bumpy that we often had to cling together to avoid being hit by flying barware whenever we hit a particularly nasty wave. Many of the passengers had retired to their beds for long periods to treat seasickness, but that didn't seem to afflict either of us. And we talked—about everything.

Sam was born in Toronto and had lived there most of his life, except for the two years he spent in France during the war. When he returned home with a shoulder injury that he said only bothered him in damp weather (like at sea on the Queen Mary), he attended the University of Toronto and studied English. His interest in politics and the world led him to the editorial offices of the *Toronto Star*, where, as a war veteran with an English degree and a knack for seeing things from a variety of perspectives, he was hired on sight.

"I now have my pick of assignments, so here I am." He gestured around the almost empty room where even the pianist had given up an hour ago. Aboard the Queen Mary, though, first-class passengers were never booted out of bars.

"Yes," I said, cradling my late-night cognac, "here you are. I've been wondering about something, Sam. I hope you won't take this as British upper-class snobbery, but I have to admit that I'm surprised that a newspaper has bought one of their reporters, no matter how good he is—a first-class ticket on the Queen Mary. Or was it given to the newspaper?"

"No offence taken. It does seem like a reasonable question. First, Cunard-White Star did provide tickets to news outlets—second-class tickets. Second, I'm not travelling first class." He looked at the puzzlement on my face. "You see, Miss Fran Phillips, I deduced a couple of things about you the evening I saw you in the pub in Southampton. First, you were single—alone in a bar, no ring. Second, I also deduced that you would be travelling first-class. You probably don't know it, but there's a special something about you that just screams money. I suspect you try to tone that down, but it's not really working. You can take the girl out of the aristocracy, but you can't take the aristocracy out of the girl." He held up a hand as I began to open my mouth. "And third, Miss Phillips, I couldn't think of a single person I'd rather dine with for four days in a row."

I corrected him. My family was of the monied class, but you had to be of a certain pedigree to be considered part of the aristocracy in England. I was not part of it. I told him about my father, and he immediately made a note. "What are you doing?"

"Noting that I've met Edward Phillips's daughter."

It seemed that my father was known even in the wilds of Canada. Then I told him about my years in Paris. I wanted to share with him my literary passion while not revealing my literary identity. So, I told him about the salons and how I'd gained access through a friend—which was entirely accurate. If it hadn't been for Christophe, I would never have been accepted.

"Literary salons, you say? Did you ever meet a guy named Hemingway?"

"The novelist Ernest Hemingway? Yes, but only very briefly. I met him once but have since come to know his work quite well. Why? Do you know him?"

"He had a brief but memorable stint at our office at the *Star* some years ago. He was a talented journalist, but I guess he's even better at the novel writing."

"I didn't know he'd ever lived in Canada." I sipped what remained of my drink. "Have you ever been drawn to writing fiction?"

"Me? No. I've never seen the attraction to writing what amounts to deceptions. I mean, fiction is really just made-up material, isn't it?"

It was clear that this would not be the moment to tell him how I made my money—if ever.

"Anyway," he continued, "maybe I'll write a book someday, but it will be about something real."

By the time we passed the Statue of Liberty as we sailed majestically into New York harbour on the first day of June, I felt I knew almost everything about Sam. I suspected he thought he knew everything about me. Of course, he didn't.

The Schiaparelli

Wife

TWENTY

*"Infatuation is when you find somebody who is absolutely perfect.
Love is when you realize that they aren't, and it doesn't matter."*
~ Anonymous

I WOULD BE IN NEW YORK FOR TWO WEEKS, during which I had a series of meetings that Christophe had set up for me. I still didn't know what the American publisher George H. Doran had in mind. I also didn't know what I was supposed to accomplish by meeting with a literary agent, but I was willing to participate fully. Sam, on the other hand, would be in New York for only a few days.

My publisher sent a driver to pick me up at the pier and deposit me at The Plaza Hotel. When I arrived in my room (small but stylish), I found a beautiful floral arrangement with a card from Christophe that read, "Knock their socks off, *chérie. Ils sont américains!*" Yes, they were, indeed, Americans. Sitting beside the flowers on the desk was a portfolio prepared for me by my publisher. There was a map of the city, including a map of the subway (I would have called it the Underground, and I had no intention of availing myself of American public transportation at this point in my life), a welcome letter, some restaurant suggestions and my itinerary. The following day, I had a meeting at nine a.m. with the literary agent Christophe had insisted I needed to consider working with. In the meantime, I planned to take a walk in Central Park across the street then meet Sam for dinner at that lovely Palm Court off the lobby. It looked magnificent, and I had an idea the food would be just as good.

In the end, Sam, who was staying at a somewhat more modest hotel three blocks away, suggested that the Palm Court was far too stuffy and that we needed to see a bit of the real New York. He had been here several times before on newspaper business. We ended up at a pizzeria in a part of Manhattan called Greenwich Village, and I felt like I had come home.

The Village was teeming with artists—each more Bohemian than the last—restaurants, galleries and excitement. I was in my element, and Sam seemed to pick up on my exhilaration.

We were just finishing up our last slice of pizza and polishing off a bottle of Chianti when Sam wiped his mouth with the red and white checkered paper napkin and sat back. "Okay, Frannie Phillips," (he had started referring to me as Frannie, something I liked the sound of), "it's time."

"Time for what?" I said. I was enjoying this cheap Chianti far too much.

"Time for you to spill." I said nothing. "I've interviewed too many people in my line of work not to pick up on when someone is holding back. I've told you everything there is to know about me. I'm an open book. But you have secrets." He held up his hand to stop me as I started to speak. "There's much about you I don't know. Maybe we could start with all those secretive meetings you have to attend in New York."

I wanted to tell him everything. I had never wanted to tell anyone my entire story—ever. But there was something about this man. Was I falling in love? Good lord, that wouldn't be good at all. There were so many obstacles, not the least of which was that I wasn't sure I could tell him everything. After all, I did have a contract that forbade just such behaviour, and then there was James. And a journalist? Dear god, what could be worse? But did I trust him?

I took the coward's way out. "You're right, Sam. I haven't told you everything. And I will. Just not now." If he bought that, then I'd at least have bought myself some time.

Sam didn't look happy, but he didn't press me. Now I just had to figure out when and perhaps even more crucial, how much I would tell. If we were to have any future at all, it would have to be everything. I knew that.

~

The following day at twenty minutes to nine, the impeccably uniformed bellman at the front door of the Plaza Hotel lifted his white-gloved hand and hailed me a cab. I loved how everyone in New York seemed to know just how to do that. I wondered if they had to learn the technique or if they were born with it. I climbed into the back seat of the cab, told the driver the address and settled back to watch the throngs of people making their way to work. I could feel the city throbbing, and its buzz was contagious. By the time I stepped onto the pavement in front of the building on West 29th Street and 6th Avenue, I was smiling and a bit in love with New York City.

I stood in front of the five-story red-brick building for a moment and watched men and women, all in light-coloured suits, hurry up the three steps that led to the front door. Then I followed them, stepping quickly to avoid being stampeded by the swiftly moving river of people.

The notes Christophe had sent to me the week before I left home had told me I'd find the agency on the third floor. I jammed myself in the elevator with the rest of the workers heading for their offices and squeezed myself out on the third floor. As I looked to the left, I could see a frosted glass door with the agency's name emblazoned on it. I walked toward it and opened the door.

Evidently, literary agents start work early because I could hear typewriters already madly clicking away from somewhere behind the reception desk. I told the receptionist I had an appointment with M.E. Benjamin, and she ushered me into a waiting area outside a private office just to the side of where women and a few men madly typed at wooden desks, each one with a look of concentration furrowing their brows. The receptionist brought me coffee and said someone would be with me shortly.

A few sips of coffee later, a tall brunette wearing a well-cut black and white houndstooth suit that looked warm for this beautiful June day approached and beckoned me into the inner sanctum. I turned to thank her when, to my absolute surprise, she took her seat behind the desk and gestured for me to sit. I had thought she was the agent's secretary—shame on me. But if I thought I was surprised, the look on the woman's face was one of utter confusion.

She looked down at the file on her desk. Then she looked up, folded her hands on the desk in front of her and smiled. "Well, blow me over. Why didn't I know? Of course, F.E. de Plessis is a woman. Welcome! I am delighted to meet you, Miss de Plessis. I'm Margaret Benjamin."

"I think we may both have been equally surprised," I said as I shook her hand. "I believe I expected a man as well. I should have known better. My friend Simone would not be proud of me." She looked puzzled. "Never mind. Just a friend whose work I'm sure we'll both appreciate as time goes on."

"Well, Miss de Plessis, you have astonished me again. I thought you were French. You're from England." It was more of a question than a statement.

"I am. And my name is Frances Elizabeth Phillips. Please call me Fran."

Margaret was the Benjamin of the Priestley & Benjamin Literary Agency note Christophe had sent me. As we talked, I realized that this woman I judged to be perhaps a few years older than me—maybe even forty—was entirely in her element. She was offering to represent me in America, but she was suggesting something more.

Margaret was a literary agent with a specialty. She did the usual things that literary agents do to sell her clients' books to publishers, but she also did something that I found thrilling. She explained that she was responsible for film rights sales of all the agency's clients' books to Hollywood. Just the year before, two of their authors had seen their books on film. My eyes opened wide at that thought.

"Surely my books are too risqué for film?"

"Not so. With a treatment by a script consultant, they could be just what Hollywood is looking for. And to think a woman has written them. It's almost too good to be true."

"You can't tell them that," I said. "I have a clause in my French publishing agreement."

"That won't be a problem if you write new material under your name here in America."

Under my own name? Was that possible?

"Do you see this book here on my desk?" She picked up a book that had been sitting on top of a pile of books on the side of her desk. "It's a new release, and I've had a chance to read most of it."

I took the hard-cover book with its straw-coloured dust jacket from here. The title was *Gone With the Wind* by someone called Margaret Mitchell. I had never heard of it, but it had just been released here in America.

"I predict that this will be made into a film, and that film will be something of a sensation," she said. "You could write something similar but with a bit more…" She paused as if looking for the right word. "Sex. Let's just say it. That's what you're good at."

She wasn't wrong. But I realized something at that moment. Although I had railed against not being able to use my own name when I first started publishing, now I realized what a gift that was. I could maintain my anonymity and keep writing. But it was clear I'd have to find a new American pseudonym.

As the meeting progressed, I felt more comfortable with this lovely, capable, impressive woman. I could feel her excitement about my work, and it reignited something in me. I was convinced that we could work well together and that she could add value to my career. We were just about to wrap up our discussion when her assistant poked his head around her door. (It turned out that her assistant was a young man—I loved that.)

"Peg," he said, "there's an overseas call for you. Want me to take a message?"

She nodded. "Sorry, Fran. Where were we?"

I was momentarily distracted by the interruption. Her assistant had called her "Peg," not Margaret. But, of course, Peg, or Peggy, was often an American nickname for Margaret. Margaret Benjamin. Peggy Benjamin. Where had I heard that name? Suddenly, before thinking through the ramifications of my thoughts, I blurted, "You don't happen to be Clifford Benjamin's wife?" What in the world were the odds of that?

Margaret's eyes lifted quickly from the folder on her desk, then straight at me. "Why do you ask?"

"Are you?" Oh, dear, we could very well have hit a snag in the negotiations.

Margaret sat back in her desk chair, crossed her legs and folded her hands in her lap. "Don't tell me. Let me guess. You met Cliff in Paris."

"As a matter of fact, I did, Margaret. So, you *are* his wife?"

"Yes, I suppose I am." She moved her chair closer to the desk and put her folded hands on it. Then she leaned toward me slightly. "Well, I must admit, you *are* his type."

I could feel my neck begin to redden as the flush then made its way to my cheeks. The annoying thing about blushing is that you can't control it. I had been found out, as they say.

She sighed. "And I suppose he told you we had an arrangement." She lifted her hands as if to put quotation marks around the word arrangement.

I nodded. "In my defence, if I may, I did ask him if you were aware of the arrangement."

Laughter erupted from somewhere deep within Margaret or Peg or Peggy. "I wouldn't have expected anything less of you, Fran. We do, in fact, have an arrangement, just not the kind that you might have thought." She calmed herself down and continued. "The arrangement is that I pay him a very generous monthly stipend, and he stays the hell away from me." I must have looked puzzled. "I know this sounds odd coming from a businesswoman, but I'll be forty years old this summer and having a husband somewhere in the background just makes life easier. And, because of my family situation, divorce is out of the question. I just hope you came out of any kind of relationship you might have had with my dear husband unscathed."

I told her I had. What I was wondering about, though, was how she could afford to give Cliff a generous monthly stipend (which, of course, explained his financial security even in the face of so many problems in the financial sector). Perhaps American literary agents did much better financially than I had thought. Since our meeting time was up, we decided to meet for lunch in a couple of hours at the Palm Court (I was determined to have a meal there!) to continue our conversation—but only if I agreed to call her Peggy.

Over lunch, I learned a couple of important things. First, Peggy's "family situation" to which she had referred was that she was a Vanderbilt—Ever heard of them?" she said. Hasn't everyone?—hence the bottomless pit of money and why she couldn't divorce Cliff. He could seek money that her family wasn't prepared to relinquish. Second, Peggy Benjamin and I both had secrets, and once I told her about James, which I did, and she told me she preferred women to men anyway, I knew we would become friends as well as colleagues.

Peggy Benjamin was now the only person in the world who knew my secrets. Abigail knew only about James. Kiki knew only about the writing. Two secrets. As I entered the elevator on my way to my room at the Plaza after lunch, I could think of only one thing: how would Sam feel about me if he knew I wasn't perfect?

TWENTY-ONE

*"Your task is not to seek for love, but merely to seek and find
all the barriers within yourself that you
have built against it." ~ Rumi*

WHY DID I CARE SO MUCH ABOUT THIS MAN I had known less than a week? Why, at my age (I was thirty-six years old), did I find myself wondering what he was doing at the most inopportune moments? As I sat in the waiting room at the George H. Doran Company, arguably the largest publisher in the world, I should have been excited that they had translated my books for the American market (and that they were selling) and that they wanted to continue the relationship in some way. Instead, the only thing that occupied my mind was that Sam was leaving to return home to Toronto the next day, and I had still not found the courage to tell him my secrets. Then, the next moment, something told me that I didn't need to bother—that I'd never see him again.

"Mr. Goodwin will see you now."

Charles Goodwin's secretary's voice brought me back to reality. As she ushered me into Mr. Goodwin's inner sanctum, it suddenly occurred to me that, like Peggy, Mr. Goodwin, the Executive Editor at Doran Publishers, might be expecting a man. This situation might get my mind off Sam.

The minute I walked into his office, I could tell that I had been right. Christophe had neglected to tell anyone that his author was a woman. The look on Charles Goodwin's face said it all. I immediately walked over to his desk and held my hand across it. "Good morning, Mr. Goodwin. I'm F.E. de Plessis, but you can call me Fran Phillips."

He started to splutter. Charles Goodwin was a big man. When he stood up, I saw that he was almost six feet tall, but his girth was even more impressive. Even his head was large. It suddenly struck me funny that I seemed to have been able to put this imposing man, a giant of the American publishing world (in more ways than one, it seemed), off-balance.

"Miss…Miss Phillips, you say." He finally found his tongue.

I laughed slightly as I sat down in the oversized chair across the desk from him and peeled off my gloves. Why, oh why did women continue to think it necessary to wear gloves even on a warm June day? "I gather that our Monsieur Lemieux neglected a small bit of description when he arranged for us to meet."

Mr. Goodwin sat down heavily in his chair and shook his head. "I've got to hand it to him. That little Frog got the best of me this time." He peered at me. "All these years," he said, shaking his head. "All these years, I thought that stuff he kept sending over was written by a man. And I've got to tell you that I had a moment or two of jealousy when I thought some man in Paris had such a way with women. I figured he could only be able to write this stuff if he'd done research—if you know what I mean. And you're not even French by the sounds of you."

Did he wink at me? Dear god, this was going to be awkward.

We chatted for a few minutes. He asked me what I was working on, and then I told him that Peggy had suggested I consider a slightly different direction in my work.

"So, you've got Margaret Benjamin working for you now, have you? That woman's a shark. She drives a hard bargain, but we generally get what we want from her authors in the end—lots of sales." He laughed.

Since my lunch with Peggy, I'd been giving some thought to my new American persona. She told me to think about a new pseudonym. I thought I'd come up with the perfect one.

I told Mr. Goodwin, who asked me to call him Charles, that I had decided I'd prefer to keep my readers in the dark about my true identity. He thought that was wise. Then I offered him my new *nom de plume*—Peyton Winter. I figured that no one could tell if that was a man or woman, and given the nature of my writing, most would naturally conclude that it was a man. He liked it.

"I think our American readers will take to that very well," he said.

So, over the next two weeks, with Peggy's help, Peyton Winter signed a three-book contract with Doran Publishing and a year later, his/her first book was released: *The Exhibitionist's Diary*. It made its way to the top of the *New York Times* bestseller list less than three weeks after publication.

But I'm getting ahead of myself. I need to tell you about Sam.

~

The telephone in my hotel room rang as I was getting ready to meet Sam in the lobby for dinner that evening. We were going to dine then dance the night away at The Rainbow Room. I was excited. The Rainbow Room had been open less than two years and was already the place to be in New York. I could almost hear the orchestra. Sam would be leaving the next day, and this was my last chance to have him near me. He could very well become nothing more than a memory by this time tomorrow evening. I was humming as I picked up the phone.

"You ready?" It was Sam, calling from a house phone in the lobby.

I looked at my watch. He was half an hour early. "Almost."

"Hurry up. I'd like to make a detour before dinner."

I scrambled to finish dressing and was in the lobby ten minutes later. I found Sam standing by the main doors, beckoning me toward him. I took his hand, and he led me out the front door and down the steps where a horse-drawn carriage was waiting. I had seen so many of these over the past two weeks, waiting for tourists across the street from the Plaza, then taking them through Central Park. Now, I was to have my own ride. I felt so "New York."

The driver helped me climb up, and Sam followed. It was a warm evening, still light, so the crowds were as thick as mid-day. The horse began clopping across the street and into the park, where we wended our way to the centre toward the lake. For the first ten minutes, Sam said nothing. I was enjoying the experience but soon began to get nervous about the silence. Was he saying goodbye? Had he decided against the Rainbow Room? That would disappoint me.

When we arrived at the edge of the lake, I could see couples strolling hand-in-hand, families sitting on blankets in the warmth of the waning day, and people rowing boats for hire. The carriage stopped, and Sam climbed down then reached up to help me. He asked the carriage driver to wait, and we walked toward a bench under an old weeping willow tree whose branches dipped low into the lake, touching the water.

"We need to sit here for a minute," he said as he looked around. "It won't be long."

"What in the world are you talking about? What won't be long?"

Just then, Sam jumped up as an elderly man approached. He was carrying a small package. As he reached us, he passed the package to Sam and began apologizing profusely. "So short notice, Mr. McLeod, but I did it." He then looked at me and touched his head as if in salute. Then he turned around and walked back down the path from whence he came.

"Okay," Sam said, making for the carriage, "We can go now."

I was so puzzled. "What? Are you buying illegal substances?"

Sam looked back at me. "What? No? Anyway, you'll see."

When we were back in the carriage, and the horse began clopping toward the main path once again, Sam turned to me. "I had hoped that I'd have this earlier, but better late than never." He looked down at the package on his lap. "Frannie, we've only known one another for a week, but I feel as if I've known you all my life. I felt that from that first night when I sat down beside you at the bar on the ship. Look, I know you haven't told me everything about your life—I know you have secrets—but I don't care. Tonight can't be the last time I'll see you. I won't let it, and if I have to do something drastic to make sure of that, so be it." He lifted the package and began to remove the brown paper wrapping.

I placed my hand on top of his. "Don't," I said. "Not yet."

And I started talking.

~

By the time we had completed two more rounds of the park, I had told him everything. He knew about James (and Elliott). He knew about Christophe and Cliff. He knew about my parents and Paris. And he knew about F.E. de Plessis. He said nothing.

He took my hand as we stood waiting for a cab when the carriage ride was over. He was still silent as we made our way to The Rainbow Room and followed the *maître d'* to our table. His first words were to order himself a whiskey and me a martini when the waiter came by.

Finally, I couldn't take it any longer. "Are you going to say anything, Sam? Please say something."

Just then, the Ray Noble Orchestra started playing "The Very Thought of You." Sam grabbed my hand and swept me onto the dance floor. "Yes, indeed," he said. "The very thought of you—F.E. de Plessis." And he started to laugh. "You are, without a doubt, the most interesting and inscrutable woman I've ever met in my entire thirty-five years on the planet, Frannie Phillips."

By the time the evening was drawing to a close, I hadn't a single doubt how I felt about Sam—or how he felt about me. And I had done the single most impetuous thing I had ever done in my life. I said yes when Sam MacLeod asked me to marry him after knowing one another for one week. And I left The Rainbow Room wearing the contents of the little package on the ring finger of my left hand.

~

Sam left New York the next day as planned, heading home to his job in Toronto and planning to visit me in London as soon as he could get away. I had another week in New York, during which I had several more meetings at my publisher and with Peggy. Today's meeting with Peggy was for lunch in the board room at her office.

The moment I walked into the room, she looked at my face and said, "What's going on? Something's happened."

I smiled and wondered—not for the first time—how it was that the two of us seemed to be on the same wavelength after knowing one another for such a brief time.

I put my handbag on the massive mahogany boardroom table that gleamed under the fluorescent lights.

"What's that?" Peggy said, pointing at my left hand. "You didn't have that the last time we met."

And so, I told her the story. When I had finished, she sat back in the oversized chair across the expanse of table from me and whistled. "That's kind of an unbelievable story, Fran, but then, much of your life has been exceptional. What part of it do you think will make it into your next book?" Then she laughed. "Just kidding. Anyway, when will you be moving to this side of the pond?" I must have looked puzzled. "You *will* be moving to Toronto, I presume? And it's so close to us here in New York. That could work very well, you know. We could meet regularly."

For the first time since I'd told Sam I would marry him, the reality of what lay ahead seemed to strike me. I suppose that somewhere, deep in my subconscious, I must have realized that I could not continue to live in London unless Sam moved there. If I were to move to Toronto, I had no idea what I'd do about Father—or James. And Canada? Who moved to Canada?

TWENTY-TWO

I BOARDED THE QUEEN MARY ONCE AGAIN for the return trip home. I felt vastly different than I had less than three weeks earlier when I started my journey in Southampton with the expectation of solitude. This time, I fully intended to spend the time alone, thinking about my life as it might unfold over the next few months and wondering how I would ever get Father to understand what I'd done. Did I have second thoughts about Sam? Not a single one. I only hoped he felt the same.

The journey was as I had hoped—solitary and smooth. I dined alone each evening and spent much of my time on deck in a teak deck chair, a rug over my legs, making notes for my new book. When I ran out of thoughts, I put my journal away and lay back, listening to the waves as they splashed against the sides of the majestic ship. The weather was pleasant, if not warm. After all, it may have been late June, but it was the middle of the Atlantic. We had sun for the first couple of days, but as we neared Southampton, the fog began to settle in around us, wrapping the ship in a layer of fluffy cotton wool. If it hadn't been for the dampness that also wrapped itself around me, I would have spent every waking hour on deck.

When the ship docked, and I retrieved my luggage, I retraced my trip back to London, first via the train, then a cab from the station. When I climbed out of the cab in front of the house, I stood there, a heavy suitcase in each hand, staring at the beautiful front in the drizzle and longed to see Sam's face again. I sighed and made my way along the walkway toward the house.

After I deposited my luggage inside the front door and peeled off my damp coat, I found my father sitting with a glass of brandy in front of a roaring fire in his study. Despite the calendar indicating that it was June, it was cool, almost cold. When my father looked up and saw me standing in the doorway, I could feel the chill increase.

"Well, Frances," he said, sipping his brandy, "I see you have returned to see what havoc you have wrought."

"Father, what's wrong?"

He put his glass down on the table beside his chair and sat up straight. "What's wrong? How dare you ask that. You know perfectly well what you have done. What on earth came over you? Why did you say anything to the boy?"

James. He was talking about James.

"And all without warning. You tell the child that he's been living a lie for his entire life, then leave? What kind of selfish person have you turned out to be?"

My father had never spoken to me that way before. He had always taken my side, but it was clear to me that he was right. I had been selfish not to have told him what I had done.

I crumpled into a chair. "I'm so sorry, Father. I didn't plan for it to come out then. What happened?"

"What happened was that James ran away." I must have looked startled. "Not for long. That child could not survive long without the comforts of his life. He was gone less than a day, and when he returned, I have never seen such anger spout from anyone in my life. I was almost frightened of him. When he calmed down, he agreed to go back to school at the end of his suspension, but not before telling me some nonsense about his putative forbears."

Putative forebears? Was he talking about the photograph of Elliott and his family? I simply was not prepared to get into this conversation with my father. James was a teenaged bigot, and there was little I could do about it at this stage. He would be seventeen years old in August—no longer a malleable child. In any case, my father didn't need to know the particulars. Perhaps the fact that James now knew the truth about his parentage was a good thing. I had other things on my mind, anyway. I just hoped I could get my father to let it go.

It didn't seem like the right time to tell my father about the impending changes in my life. It would pose yet another problem for him, and it was one I wasn't sure how we would resolve. I didn't quite know how to begin solving it, but I'd get there. It's a funny thing about life, though. We are often facing quite different choices than we think. This realization came as a shock to me.

I received a letter from Sam every week throughout July and August. He closed off each one the same way. "I'm waiting for you. Just give me the word." The word he was looking for was when he should board a ship and make his way to London for a wedding. I had now come to terms with the fact that I would be moving to Canada if this wedding was to go forward. I still hadn't told Father.

I was sitting at my desk upstairs in my room, tapping away on my typewriter—an activity I practiced only when Father was in his office at the bank—when Nora, who likely wondered what I was doing, knocked on my door.

There was a telephone call for me from Abigail. She and Ollie were inviting me to dinner the following evening. So, I started to formulate a plan. I would tell them the entire story since Abigail liked nothing better than a romance. Then I would engage them as my support system when I broke the news of my impending nuptials and departure to my father. It seemed like an excellent plan.

The next evening, as expected, both Abigail and perhaps even more so, Ollie, were shocked by my news. I think they had both begun to consider me to have spent my wild days in Paris and that they were behind me, leaving me as an ageing spinster with no hope of ever finding love in the long term. In any case, they agreed to provide moral support, and Abigail insisted on planning the wedding. They were both excited at the prospect of meeting Sam, my Canadian fiancé, but perhaps both had different reasons. With that arranged, I took my leave, intending to broach the subject with Father the minute I arrived home that evening. I had just enough liquid courage (I'd enjoyed a martini and several glasses of marvellous wine) to believe I could tell Father of my plans. I only hoped that he'd be in a good mood.

I heard muffled voices as I approached the drawing-room's double doors. It seemed Father must have company. I felt my plan slightly thwarted, but perhaps the visitor could be convinced to leave as soon as possible. I placed a hand on each doorknob and threw open the doors.

"Good evening, Fa…" I stopped short. I had no idea what I was seeing.

Two pairs of eyes bobbed up from the sofa. I could just see what appeared to be two bodies tangled up in a fur throw that usually draped over a footstool by the fireplace. What in the world was going on?

"Frances." My father's voice seemed oddly distant. Perhaps it was because my ears were buzzing as I began to put the tableau in front of me together in some sort of way that it made sense—because what I was seeing made no sense at all.

When I regained my faculties, I realized that I was looking at Father, half-dressed, writhing under a blanket with an equally undressed woman. And that woman was Nora.

I don't know how long I stood there in the doorway, my mouth hanging open while we stared at one another. Nora's eyes looked frantic as she began to gather her clothing close to her. Then I started to laugh. I couldn't help myself. The absurdity of the situation was beyond comic.

"Frances Phillips, please!" My father's voice now sounded pleading, but I still could not stop laughing.

When I finally calmed down, I backed out of the room and closed the door. I stood there staring at the door, trying to unsee what I had just witnessed. I took one step back and continued to contemplate the closed door and what lay beyond. Finally, a few minutes passed, and Father opened the door. Nora was now sitting primly on the sofa, fully dressed, sipping a glass of port.

"I think we need to talk," Father said as he ushered me into the drawing-room. Indeed, we did need to talk. At that moment, I realized that my news would likely pale beside anything Father might now have to say. And he had a lot to say.

It seemed that he and Nora had been taking solace in one another's company ever since "the incident" had left Mother in a precarious state. This revelation did go a long way to explain Nora's unwavering loyalty to our family in the face of strange expectations that only got stranger when James arrived as a baby. He had been almost exclusively in her care for years. After Mother died and I moved back from Paris, Nora had thought she would be sidelined, but their relationship continued to flourish, right under my nose. It seemed I and been far too self-involved even to notice. It occurred to me that I would not have minded in the least. I realized that I understood.

"Why did you never tell me, Father?"

"I didn't know what you would think of me."

"I would think that you were a man with a younger woman in his life, and I would have applauded you." I leaned over from where I was now sitting on the sofa with Nora and took her two hands into mine. "Now, why didn't you ever make an honest man out of him?"

Tears glistened in her eyes. "He asked me to marry him, Miss Frances, but I said no. I could never replace Mrs. Phillips, and I didn't want to offend you."

"First, you must stop calling me Miss Frances. I am Fran from this moment forward. Second, you must immediately tell Father that you will, indeed, marry him." I stopped and looked at Father. "And we shall make it a double wedding."

Of course, I then had little choice. It was time to tell them about Sam.

~

Sam arrived via the RMS Aquitania in late September. Father welcomed him warmly into our home and our London life. There was a week before the wedding date, and Father had decided he would take this colonial boy and show him the motherland—or at least the London of our life.

Father and Nora had decided that they wouldn't be married yet. Nora continued to protest that she didn't want to take Mother's place, but I suspected she was nervous about being Mrs. Phillips in Father's social circles. Their relationship seemed to work for them—and me.

Father and Nora would continue to play parenting roles for James, but he was now in his last year at school without much suggestion of what would happen the following year. Father told me to stop worrying. He said he had it in hand. I didn't have time to wonder what that was but suspected Father would tell me when the time was right. At this moment, there were wedding plans to make.

Abigail had insisted that she accompany me to find the perfect dress for this wedding. She dragged me to bridal salons, where none of the dresses seemed right for me at this point in my life.

We looked at many bias-cut satin dresses whose ivory folds shimmered under the chandeliers in the salons. We looked at white lace dresses with trains that measured six feet or more. None of them were suitable for me. More than once, I wondered what our new King's American girlfriend would wear to her wedding. The news was full of abdication talk—that our King Edward the VII, who had been our monarch a mere eight months at that point, would choose his American mistress over his duty to the crown. I had seen pictures in the newspapers of this Wallis Simpson and thought I was probably more like her than I was like young brides.

I had seen a picture of Mrs. Simpson on the front page just the month before. She and Edward were attending a function in Paris. Much was made of the fact that she was wearing a dress by the Italian designer Elsa Schiaparelli. The reporter who wrote the story had interviewed Schiaparelli herself and had quoted her as saying, "The clothes in themselves do not make a statement. The woman makes the statement, and the dress helps." I needed a dress that would help me make the statement that I was not a virginal bride. Instead, I was a woman who had proudly lived an independent, full life to this point and was now marrying for real love. I needed a Schiaparelli dress.

Abigail knew exactly what I needed. She made an appointment at *Salon Dupuis*, where the proprietor a Madame Dupuis (who, after I met her, I suspected was no more French than I was) had created a mystique surrounding her shop that it was an oasis of French style and gentility dropped into a tiny lane off Regent Street. I didn't care where we went for it: I just knew I needed to find a Schiaparelli dress.

As Abigail and I sat on a velvet-covered sofa drinking champagne from crystal coupes and munching tiny rainbow-coloured macarons, Madame Dupuis and her assistant brought the dresses in.   Although I had been specific that I wanted a Schiaparelli, she insisted that I also see a Lanvin, a Dior and a Balmain.

"Schiaparelli may be too unconventional for a wedding," she said in what sounded suspiciously like a fake French accent. "Perhaps too daring in style."

It was true that Schiaparelli was known for her daring details that, as far as I was concerned, lifted her tailored silhouettes into something entirely different and fabulous. I completely discounted all the dresses until she finally raised one in front of her. From the moment I laid eyes on that dress, I knew that it could have been designed only by Elsa Schiaparelli and that it was the perfect dress for my wedding.

'That's it," I said. "That's the one I will wear at my wedding."

Both Madame Dupuis and Abigail were aghast. They both started talking at once: it was too dark, it wasn't church-like, I hadn't even tried it on. I didn't care. It was the one.

The dress was black with a wide boat neckline trimmed in pink. On the front of the dress was a floral embroidery with pink petals tumbling down the front of the dress here and there, landing at the waist, the hip. It had short sleeves and draped beautifully to the floor in soft silk folds.

I tried it on, and the moment I saw myself in the full-length, three-sided mirror, I knew it was the one.

~

The wedding was small but beautiful. We held it in the back garden at the house where Nora insisted on arranging everything with Abigail's constant help. James came down from school and spent the entire weekend sulking, but he did attend the ceremony and stood around at the reception eating *hors d'oeuvres* and guzzling champagne. Sam, who knew the truth about James, tried to draw him out. Sam told me later that he found James quite impenetrable and doubted if James would ever like him—or anyone else for that matter. It didn't seem to matter to Sam, though. After all, James wasn't accompanying us to Toronto, so they wouldn't have much to do with one another.

I had invited both Jean-Christophe and Peggy to the wedding, not expecting either of them to make the trip, especially Peggy. It was a very time-consuming trip to get on a ship in New York to come to London for a weekend then return. However, much to my delight, she arranged for several meetings in London, one of which was with Christophe. He and Sabine came from Paris to share this day with me. I didn't' know if he was motivated by friendship or curiosity, and it didn't matter in the least.

At one point during the reception, as I stood at the edges in my black Schiaparelli gown, sipping champagne, I looked across the sea of faces, and I was struck with a thought. I was looking at all aspects of my life coming together at one point. I wondered if they might finally be colliding. That remained to be seen.

TWENTY-THREE

"I really believe my greatest service is in the many unwise steps I prevent."
~ William Lyon MacKenzie King,
Prime Minister of Canada, 1935-48

FROM THE MOMENT I SET FOOT IN CANADA, and specifically in Toronto, I didn't quite know what to make of it. Father had been adamant in his conclusion that Canada was a colonial outpost and that I would be begging Sam to move back to London with me within the year. Father even offered to arrange for Sam to take a position at the *Times* through an old friend who happened to be the managing editor. Sam was aghast at the suggestion since he was utterly opposed to the *Times* and its arrogant support of appeasing Hitler's demands, a position so contrary to Sam's perspective that it was almost funny. Besides, Sam had told Father, he was on an upward track at the *Star*.

As for me, it didn't matter where I lived for me to continue my work. So, I continued writing, publishing a book every eighteen months or so. One day, about six months after we moved into our apartment in Toronto, Sam came home to find me leafing through some papers scattered over the coffee table.

"Frannie, those look like houses for sale."

I nodded absently and continued to peruse the pages in front of me. "Here," I said, lifting one to show him. "This looks like a wonderful house."

Sam took the page from me and looked at it. "This house is in South Rosedale. I think I've walked by it. Wow! Look at that price." He gave it back to me. "Why are you looking at these? Doing some research for a book?"

I was sitting on the floor beside the coffee table. I looked up at him. "I thought it would be clear to you. I'm looking for a house for us. We can't live here forever."

Sam looked around. "Well, I don't see much wrong with this apartment. It's big. It has two bedrooms, a nice fireplace. Anyway, if we want to buy a house, we'll have to look in a cheaper neighbourhood."

I sighed. It was time for the talk. Although Sam knew I wrote books and knew the kind of books I wrote, he had no idea how much money I made. It was considerable, and I had saved much of it.

When I had finished making our substantial funds clear, he was speechless for a moment. Finally, he said, "Wow! I had no idea. But we can't live in South Rosedale. We'll never fit in."

What he wasn't saying was that he would feel uncomfortable. I knew that his colleagues didn't have the kind of money to permit them to live there. Thus he couldn't see himself there. I knew I had my work cut out for me to convince him that we could fit in wherever we chose to live—or live there and not fit in—the hell with anyone who didn't like it.

It took me a few months, but I finally convinced him of the wisdom of the idea once I had found the house I loved. We finally moved into our grand, red-brick mansion in South Rosedale in the summer of 1937. I set up my office in the back of the house overlooking the gardens where I liked to work. It was there that I spent my days while Sam was promoted to assistant editor, and we enjoyed our quiet life.

Father and I kept in close contact—or as close as you can when you must rely mainly on mail—so that I could keep abreast of James's activities. When James finished at Tonbridge, he went up to Oxford for two semesters. He hated it, and it appeared as if the rest of the student body wasn't enamoured of him, either. According to Father, James continually got himself in trouble for his opinions, which he obstinately refused to keep to himself. James left Oxford and returned to London, where Father arranged a job for him at his bank. Since James was good with numbers (more than good, it seems), it seemed a good fit, and he seemed to, if not enjoy, at least tolerate this new experience. He was working as an apprentice. Father's only concern at that stage was that James seemed to be always in need of money. Father had no idea how he could be spending so much money.

This concern of Father's went on for some time. I could do little to figure out what was going on since I was so far away, so I let it slide. I was thinking about this and the fact that Peggy had just telephoned me from New York to tell me that *Gone with the Wind*, the novel she had shown me when we first met, was, indeed, being made into a movie, which made her wonder if I had come up with a saleable idea yet. I thought I had, but I wasn't ready to share it. In truth, I had already largely completed the manuscript. She would see it in due course. These were the things on my mind when Sam and I met in the dining room for dinner that evening.

"I have news," he said. "And I believe this news deserves a champagne accompaniment." His excitement was contagious.

"Tell me. A scoop. Isn't that what you call them?"

He laughed. "It sounds so funny in your upper-crust British accent. And no, it's not a scoop. Something much more substantial." He popped the cork and poured two coupes, then handed one of them to me. "I have been offered a new job. Editor and publisher. Top post."

I was impressed. "At the *Star*?"

"No. Well, at least not the one you're talking about," Sam said, taking a rather large sip, perhaps even a gulp, of champagne. "It's at the *Halifax Daily Star*."

I put my glass down on the table and thought for a moment. "I don't think I know that one. Should I have seen it?"

Sam put his glass down on the table and clapped his hands together on the table in front of him. "No, I don't suppose you should have, but it's a well-respected Canadian newspaper. It just isn't in Toronto."

As it turned out, the *Halifax Daily Star* was, as you might expect, located in Halifax, a city I knew only because of having read the Titanic disaster stories back home in London when we returned after "the incident." Many of the disaster victims had been taken to the port of

Halifax, and some were buried there. That was the extent of my knowledge of the east coast of Canada. It also turned out that Sam had already accepted the position.

I was puzzled by this on several levels. First, I was surprised—perhaps even shocked—that Sam had gone ahead and made such a decision without mentioning it to me. He could defend this decision by suggesting that I had yet to integrate into my new community (he was right—I had met almost no one), and I could do my work anywhere. He was right on both counts, but I still bristled at the fact that he hadn't consulted me, and we had been in our new house for a mere two months. Second, Sam had lived in Toronto for his whole life, and given that it was the largest and most progressive city in this country, moving to a small town like Halifax seemed odd, to say the least. It had never occurred to me that he might be happy as a small-town newspaper editor when he could have moved up here at a major newspaper. It seemed he had a reason for this. Sir Samuel Cunard was his great-grandfather.

"Samuel Cunard?" I said, trying to piece this all together. "You mean the Samuel Cunard who started the Cunard Shipping company? The one who joined with the White Star Line of Titanic infamy?"

"That's the one." Sam got up from his chair opposite me and came over, pulling up the nearest chair so that he could reach my hands. When he had my hands in his, he said, "I'm sorry to have kept any of this from you. It's been on my mind for a while. I'm going to write a book."

"A book about what?" Then it clicked. He was planning to write a book about his great-grandfather.

"Samuel Cunard's life in Halifax. You know he was born there, don't you?"

I had not been aware of that fact. I had always thought Cunard was from London. I suppose it was because no one ever talked about the "colonies" or that someone who had accomplished what he had could possibly be from Canada. It was yet another revelation for me.

"Anyway," Sam continued, "I love Halifax, and I think you will too. I've been there three or four times, and every time I go, I can feel the pull of the ocean. I think this will be a good move for us." He stopped and looked around. "I know you love this house, but there are wonderful houses in Halifax. We could even have one on the ocean where we could see the rolling waves every day."

I shuddered a bit. I wasn't sure that seeing those North Atlantic waves every day was something I wanted to do, given my experience with them.

Exactly six months after we moved into our wonderful Toronto house, we packed up, sold it and boarded a train to take us to the ends of the earth, or so it seemed to me.

~

The Canadian National Railway train pulled into the station in Halifax on the second day of February 1938. My first impression of the city was that it was cold, damp and dreary, but I suppose I should have expected that at this time of year. Sam and I settled into the suite he had arranged for us at the hotel adjoining the train station. We would stay there until we found a suitable house to buy while Sam began his new position, and I finished the work on the book Peggy was awaiting anxiously.

Although it was colder than London by quite a lot, I found the weather in Halifax much like my home—damp and foggy. We stayed for two months in that hotel suite until, one day late in March when the sun was actually shining, Sam and I walked up to the gated walkway of a vacant house on Young Avenue in the heart of the city, far from the rolling waves of the Atlantic Ocean.

The house was thirty years old and bore all the hallmarks of that Victoria era. Built of red brick, the house had a welcoming porch wrapped around it on three sides, incorporating a round pergola at one corner. As I gazed at the house from the street, on the left, I could see a turret that looked, from where I was standing, as if it might hold an octagonal room that would make the perfect office.

I stood there with Sam in the sunshine and looked up and down the street. The houses surrounding it were just as impressive, especially the one next door. It was an enormous, formidable-looking grey stone edifice with a massive turret and a driveway that curved toward a colossal stone porch.

"Goodness," I said, "that one's impressive."

"Hope you don't mind living next door to the king of beer," he said. I must have looked puzzled. "Sidney Oland lives there. He owns a highly successful brewery and is also something of a well-connected philanthropist. I interviewed him a few years ago for a piece for the *Toronto Star*. You know, when prohibition was still in force, he went to Hollywood for a few years. He actually did some acting and directed a few films. He told me he was friends with Mary Pickford and Lillian Gish while he was there—even showed me a couple of photographs."

"Sounds as if he might be an interesting person to have to dinner," I said. We both laughed.

We opened the gate and walked toward the porch, where an estate agent was waiting for us. The moment I walked in through the double doors and stood there in the foyer, I knew I was home. This was my forever home.

We moved in a few weeks later when our belongings arrived from Toronto. I got straight to work decorating and arranging the house between editing the book whose contract with Doran Publishing Peggy had recently negotiated and writing a new one. As the soggy spring gave way to a lovely, sunny summer, I found myself falling ever more in love with this little city.

I loved walking down by the waterfront, strolling through the charming Public Gardens and meeting new people although the latter took much effort. I had settled nicely into a writing routine while Sam flourished in his new position. The only fly in the ointment was the rumblings of possible war coming out of Europe.

I corresponded with Abigail in London and Christophe in Paris, and both were becoming increasingly concerned about Hitler's actions on the continent, especially Christophe. I felt insulated, or perhaps even isolated, from the possibilities in my little cocoon.

Father's letters had a similar tone to those of both Christophe and Abigail. There was much talk of impending war. But even more troubling was the issue of what could happen to young men—young men like James—if Britain went to war. Eventually, the thing we all feared the most happened.

TWENTY-FOUR

"Only the dead have seen the end of war." ~ Plato

I RECEIVED FATHER'S TELEGRAM IN EARLY APRIL. "Conscription coming. Must do something about James. Cannot join the military."

I had a manuscript deadline facing me, and my initial thought was that my first obligation was to the contract I had signed. I, of course, felt a certain obligation to Father, yet I felt it would be a few months before I could get away. I put my trip off until later in the summer.

Father, of course, was right. On the twenty-seventh of April, the British parliament passed conscription laws, compelling young men from twenty to twenty-two to report for military duty if called up. Time was of the essence since James would turn twenty in August. I would have until then to do something about Father's problem. Despite Sam's concerns about my safety, I began to make my arrangements to go to London.

I told Sam I would book a passage from Halifax to Southampton to help Father and bring James to Canada. There was no other choice. Sam disagreed.

"Frannie, you can't go over there. Our stringers file stories almost every day, and they're full of the possibility of war. Real war, Frannie."

He was begging me to reconsider, but I knew I had to go. I also knew I would be taking a chance. I did wonder if he was opposed not only to me going but perhaps also to the real possibility that James might have to live with us. I had brushed away my own thoughts about that very matter, but I knew that I had an obligation to Father, after all.

~

From the moment I set foot in London in the third week in August, I knew that the atmosphere was utterly changed. I could feel it ooze from the features of every grim-faced Londoner I passed. I could see it clearly from the undertone of barely hidden bleakness evident in every deliberate movement they made. It reminded me of the ominous clouds of war that hung over London all those years ago, just before a war we thought would end them all. I had been a mere child then and could not truly feel it, but this time was different. I felt myself becoming increasingly disheartened as the few weeks I was in England played out.

As I expected, James was obstinately refusing to consider moving to Canada with me. As an adult, he did have rights, as he so carefully explained to me as loudly as he could manage. He seemed to truly like his job at the bank, a position that required him to sit alone in an office for eight hours a day accompanied only by ledgers and an adding machine.

The three of us, with Nora hovering close by, sat for the third evening in a row in the drawing-room, trying to work out what might happen next. James didn't seem to understand the gravity of the situation.

"I just won't go," he said when confronted with the idea of conscription into the military. "We aren't even at war. I shall simply refuse if I am called up." He held his fists tightly closed even as he sat on the sofa with a glass of beer, his new favourite beverage.

I could see the rage rise in a wave of angry redness creeping up the back of his neck. I had seen this before and knew that he would soon reach a boiling point. I had to find a way to defuse it.

"James, we are not at war yet, but it is only a matter of time." I knew this was unlikely to sway him.

"Perhaps," he said, holding his anger in some level of check, "but moving to an outback like whatever city you live in is out of the question. I have to stay here."

I knew I had once again lost the battle, but I was determined to win the war.

Father and I were having breakfast alone the next day when he suddenly slapped his napkin down on the table and began talking. "I am too old for this, Fran. Next year, I will retire from the bank, and I do not want that young man in my house any longer. He spends his days at the office, where he seems to be doing a reasonably good job, but what he does with his time off is a mystery to me. He goes out of here on Friday evening, and we don't see him again until he staggers in, drunk, on Sunday evening. He takes a bath, goes to bed then gets up on Monday morning as if nothing had happened. And the money! I have no idea what that young man does with the stipend I give him in addition to his salary. And he asks for even more. I am at my wit's end."

I told Father I would do whatever I could to help. There was no doubt in my mind that James would, indeed, be making the journey back to Canada with me.

~

I had one week to figure out how I would approach this dilemma with James. I felt strongly that the first step was to figure out what James did with all the money that Father gave him. I decided to take Ollie into my confidence and ask him for help. At his firm of barristers and solicitors, I knew there was often a need to make discreet inquiries of one sort or another, so I made an appointment and visited Ollie at his offices. He was surprised to see me there, and when I asked him about this service, he wanted a few answers first.

"I'd be only too happy to assist you, Frannie. You're my oldest and dearest friend if you must know. But, why in the world would you need some kind of investigator?"

"It's James. We don't know what he spends his time or money on, and I need to know this before I help my father by dragging him back to Canada with me."

Ollie's eyebrows moved up slightly. "You're taking him with you? How does your husband feel about this?"

I sighed. "I haven't told him yet, although Sam is quite aware of the potential situation here regarding conscription. James has just turned twenty, you know."

Ollie nodded. "I see. So, James won't go to fight for his country. Interesting." He tapped his finger on the papers in front of him on his impressive oak desk.

"You don't understand, Ollie. It's not that he won't—although I suspect you are quite right—it's that he should not be in the army. Or rather," I hesitated at this embarrassing revelation, "the army and the other young men in the army should not have to be subjected to him." Ollie looked startled. "The truth is that James has turned out to be a bigoted, entitled brat who is singularly unable to accomplish anything on his own. I do take partial blame for this situation. Anyway, it's a damn good thing he is so good with numbers."

Ollie hadn't known any of this. I wanted to blame my mother for how James had turned out, but I knew that there was no point in accusing anyone—except possibly myself. It was now simply a situation I had to fix in whatever way I could.

Ollie agreed to help me. He would arrange to have James followed for the entire upcoming weekend, and then he would have a report for me on Monday. I was relieved that at least I had one other person in my confidence.

~

By noon on Monday, my life had begun to implode. I knew with sickening clarity that my life would never be the same.

It had begun with my visit to Ollie's office, where he handed me a written report from his investigator who had followed James for the entire weekend. The summary indicated that James had a pack of equally entitled young men with whom he partied on the weekends—at the track.

According to the report, James had lost over £1000 on this one weekend, as far as the investigator could tell. One thousand pounds! It was inconceivable. I couldn't even have imagined that he had that kind of money. After he lost, he flew into a rage and had to be thrown out of the bar where he had been drinking with his friends. So, this was his dirty little secret. I knew I'd have to put a stop to it.

My resolve strengthened. James had to be brought under control, and short of shipping him off to the army against his will (from which he would likely flee), I knew that I'd have to do two things: cut off his allowance and ensure that he was on that ship next week when I sailed for Halifax. I would just have to hope that Sam would understand. But the implosion of my life had merely begun.

I was still shaking as I sipped a cup of tea at four o'clock that afternoon. I had asked Nora to join me, and we were sitting amiably in the breakfast room enjoying the sun's rays as they poured in from the window overlooking the back garden. The sun seemed such a rare commodity these days that I wanted to enjoy every moment of it. It was the third of September, and I knew it would be cold soon enough.

I was chatting with Nora, trying to avoid thinking about the inevitable confrontation with James that lay ahead, when Father burst into the room, his hat still firmly planted on his head, and slammed a newspaper on the table between us.

"It is done," he said. "And it shall go down in infamy."

I put my china teacup back down on its saucer so quickly that I almost dropped it. I picked up the paper and looked at the headline. I was so horrified at what I was reading that I could feel the sickening taste of bile at the back of my throat. I suppose I had known it was almost inevitable, yet the reality tasted even more bitter than I had imagined it would.

"Great Britain Declares War on Germany." The headline was so large that it filled up the entire front page above the fold.

"You must go, Frannie. You and James must leave. Go back to Canada. This minute."

Father was so overwrought that I feared he might fall ill. Nora immediately got up and was able to calm him down. She brought him a snifter of brandy then sat down with him at the table.

"Father, I have passage booked for next week, and I promise you that James will be with me."

He nodded weakly. "They will bomb us, you know."

An idea suddenly struck me. "Father, you and Nora must come with us."

Nora looked startled, but Father just seemed to calm down immediately. He looked at me. "Frances Elizabeth Phillips, that may be the most unselfish thing you have ever offered. But it is also one of the most preposterous. We cannot leave, but I insist that you do so."

That was the moment when the front doorbell rang. Nora immediately got up to answer it. She was gone only a few minutes, but when she returned, her face was white. "There's a telegram. For you, Fran." Nora, like many people, always thought the worst whenever a telegram arrived.

I opened it and read it quickly. The words made no sense. I looked at the sender's name, and I didn't recognize it for a minute—then I remembered that he was one of Sam's colleagues who had invited us to dinner when we first arrived in Halifax. Eugene. The telegram read:

"Heartfelt condolences. Accident at work. Sam dead. Will look after arrangements until you return. Eugene McMaster."

The Chanel

Woman

TWENTY-FIVE

"It's never too late to be whoever you want to be."
~ F. Scott Fitzgerald

IT WAS AS IF I WERE IN SOME KIND OF A DREAM, or rather a nightmare. I was so stunned by the news of Sam's death—and the fact that I hadn't been there—that I seemed to have suddenly hardened into a moving, emotionless statue.

By the time I cornered James in the drawing-room later that evening, I was ready. I was prepared to read him the riot act. In no uncertain terms, I told him that his days of gambling with Father's money were over and that Father was arranging for him to be made redundant at work. He would have no choice but to accompany me back to Canada, even as I was horrified at the thought of being alone with him now that Sam was gone.

It appeared that my ultimatum, the swift and merciless reversal of his fortunes and my stone-faced stance had some effect on James. If not cooperative, at least he didn't argue too much. He was initially incensed that I had him followed, but he couldn't deny his activities. And what I knew to be true about James was that he liked living in the lap of luxury, and that option was no longer available to him in Father's house. Then, when I slapped the newspaper down on the table in front of him, he visibly recoiled.

"I can't go into a war, you know. I just can't."

And so, it was decided. James was coming home with me. I knew, however, that given the war promised to be lengthy and massive, it wasn't outside the realm of possibility that he would be called up in Canada in due course. I chose not to mention that possibility to him.

As soon as Ollie and Abigail heard about Sam, they immediately arrived at the house and wanted to know what they could do.

"Please look in on Father and Nora from time to time," I said to Ollie.

"Won't you consider moving home, Frannie? Everyone who loves you is here," Abigail said.

I smiled at Abigail. "I can't make any decisions just yet. But Abigail, could you arrange for some suitable dresses to be sent along to the house so that I can select one for the funeral. There is simply nowhere in Halifax to find suitable attire for this kind of occasion."

The next day, Abigail arrived at the house with a rail of six black ensembles from which I would choose one.

Most of them were too matronly, in my view. I was still some months away from my fortieth birthday and wasn't ready to accept the inevitability of age. When I pulled up the Chanel she had brought along, I stood in front of my full-length mirror, holding it up against me.

"That one seems to suit you," Abigail said.

"Yes," I said thoughtfully as I looked at it.

The dress was black silk—almost a shirtwaist style—with a pleated skirt, three-quarter-length sleeves and buttons to the waist with a tie belt. The collar and substantial cuffs were of white silk satin, and it was finished with a white satin bow at the neckline. It was appropriate, yet not too funereal. When I tried it on, I stood again in the mirror and saw for the first time, not a daughter, a mother, a wife or a writer, or a friend. I saw a woman. I was ready.

~

James was sullen but cooperative for the duration of the voyage from Southampton to Halifax. I was lucky to have gotten him his own cabin since I was quite sure he would not have wanted to spend the several days in transit with me in my suite. I was also very sure I didn't want that arrangement. As I sat on deck in the biting cold wind, holding a wrap closely around me, I thought of Sam. The short time he had been in my life seemed like a dream that represented what was probably the happiest interlude in my life. I also found myself thinking about what to do next. Perhaps I ought to consider Abigail's suggestion to move home. Surely, I could not stay in Halifax. After all, the only reason I was there was because of Sam's job—and now that was no longer holding me there. The city had seemed like a little gem when I thought about the life Sam and I could build there into our old age. Now it just seemed to loom in my imagination like a lump of coal, and a small lump at that. It certainly didn't appear to be a lump of coal that I could use to keep me warm at night.

It occurred to me that I would have to decide if I would arrange for the funeral in Halifax or take Sam's body back to Toronto, where he was born, to bury him. Both his parents had long since died, and he didn't have any family that I knew about. As I sat there, staring out at the white caps rising and falling in the grey waves that reflected both the sky and my current mood, I realized with a start that I didn't really know anything about Sam's family. I remembered asking him about his family when we were planning the wedding, but we had done the planning over a long distance. When he had finally arrived in London, there hadn't been a moment to consider further guests from Canada. I supposed that I would have to seek family members now that he was dead. If there were any, they had a right to know about this. I would have to figure this out quickly. I wondered if Eugene might be persuaded to help me.

When James and I finally arrived in Halifax, James sat staring out the window at the passing buildings as the cab made its way from the pier to his new home, a mere five-minute drive away. When we arrived, he stood in front and just looked up at it. He still said nothing. I wasn't sure if I was annoyed or relieved at his silence. When I unlocked the door and entered the cold house, James followed me in and stood in the foyer, again looking around.

"Where's the staff?" he said finally.

Oh lord, I thought, *this is going to be a challenge*. "We—rather I—don't have staff save a housekeeper who comes in twice a week."

"You can't be serious," he said, placing his coat on the table in the foyer. "Good god, I've been dragged to the colonies, and it's worse than I thought." He looked around. "Who cooks?"

"I do most of the time," I said.

James snorted a bit. "You? People like you don't cook."

I didn't know what he meant by people like me, and I was sure I didn't want to know at that moment. I just wanted to get the house warmed up and take a bath in my own bath and sleep in my own bed.

Just then, I noticed a man's overcoat hanging on the coat rack. The coat was unfamiliar to me. I went over to it, and without thinking, I lifted the collar toward my nose and sniffed. Why do people do this? In any case, it did not smell like Sam. I walked toward the closed doors leading to the drawing-room and opened them to find a roaring fire in the fireplace and a man I had never seen before, sitting in Sam's chair. He was holding a snifter of brandy.

"What the hell are you doing in my house?" I said.

The man swirled the brandy, then put it on the table beside him and stood up. "Fran, I presume?" I said nothing. "I'm sorry we haven't met before this."

I looked carefully at this intruder as he stood there in the fire's glow. He was as tall as Sam, perhaps even taller, and there was something familiar about him. Perhaps we had met before, but that still didn't explain what he was doing in my house. I just stood there staring. By now, James had come over and was standing beside me, watching.

"I must apologize for letting myself in. I had thought your ship might arrive earlier, and I was cold waiting on the porch. And since I had a key—"

"Who the hell *are* you?" I said.

He took a step toward me, hand outstretched. "I'm so sorry. I'm Benjamin McLeod. I'm Sam's brother."

~

I wasn't sure what shocked me more—the fact that Sam had an older brother who lived in Halifax or that he had never mentioned it to me. I felt as if I might faint. Benjamin poured me a brandy, called my housekeeper to come over to make some dinner for all of us, and sat me down to tell me a story.

Sam and Benjamin had both been born in Toronto to parents who spent their time drinking and fighting, something Sam had never shared with me. The short version of the sad story was that Benjamin, seven years senior to his little brother, Sam, had left home at sixteen after a particularly nasty fight with his father. He had wanted to put as much distance between him and his father, so he had travelled to Halifax, where he worked as a stevedore on the waterfront. After a few months of manual labour, his boss noticed he was brighter than the rest of the colleagues and took him into the office to work. Eventually, he was persuaded to apply to university and attended Dalhousie University in Halifax on a full scholarship. After obtaining his master's degree and a doctorate in English literature, he took a faculty position and was now a full Professor. Sam had never forgiven him for leaving him behind.

When their parents both died in an unfortunate fire at a pub in Toronto one night when Sam was fourteen, Benjamin had reached out to Sam, asking him to come to Halifax. Sam had adamantly refused. He hadn't forgiven Benjamin for leaving him alone with his parents. They saw each other only once in the interim during one of Sam's several visits to the city that he'd mentioned to me when we were planning our move. According to Benjamin, it didn't go well. They never saw each other again—that is until two weeks ago when Sam appeared in Benjamin's office at the university while I was away in London.

"I was so startled that I didn't know what to say to Sam as he stood there in my office staring at me," Benjamin said. "Then he sat down and told me how angry he had been for so long and that he had taken this new editorial position in Halifax in the hope that we might mend fences eventually. It seems that your arrival in his life made him think about family and forgiveness. When he told me about you, I could see that you were the love of his life. I envied him. I was married many years ago, but it didn't work out."

I could feel my breath coming faster. "What else did Sam tell you about me?"

"Only that you had a son, James. I presume that was him?" He nodded toward the foyer and the staircase.

"Anything else?"

"Only that you work with a literary agency in New York. He wasn't specific. I just presumed you were an editor of some sort."

I nodded absently. At least my secret was still intact, and Sam hadn't even had to lie about it.

"We had made arrangements that I would meet you when you returned."

"How did you know he was dead?"

"Halifax is a small town, Fran. Word gets around. When I heard, I was devastated. I had just found my brother again, only for this to happen. I went to see Eugene McMaster at the paper—we went to university together. He gave me the house key Sam had left with him in the event of an emergency." He pulled the key from his pocket and laid it on the table next to the brandy glass. "It seems we're family now."

When Benjamin had finished talking, and I had finished my brandy, Mrs. Peveril, my housekeeper, arrived to begin dinner preparations. When I asked Benjamin to stay, he hesitated, suggesting that I might like to be alone this evening and that he would return the next day to help with the arrangements. I was so grateful—on all counts—that I nearly hugged him. There was much to do.

~

Of course, now that I knew Sam's background, there was no reason to consider holding the funeral anywhere but Halifax. True to his word, Benjamin was a great help. It seemed as if he knew everyone in town and made the arrangements swiftly and efficiently. Swift and efficient—this was exactly what I preferred with funerals. And since I didn't really know people in the city yet, I didn't have masses of people sending their condolences and flowers. Father and Nora sent flowers, of course, as did Eugene on behalf of the newspaper staff. That was all. Once all of that was out of the way, I had two decisions to make—one of them hinged on the other. Would I stay in the city that I knew hardly at all, and what was to become of James?

These things were on my mind as I read the daily news. How well I remembered this increasing feeling of unease about war from my teenage years. There were many questions about how the war in Europe would affect Canadian citizens at home in Canada. This disquiet was because six days after Britain had declared war on Germany, the very day James and I fled the country, Canada, too, declared war and became an ally to Great Britain. Conscription might very well sniff at James's heels, even here. As I read the newspaper every morning, though, it seemed that Canadian men were joining the army in droves, substantially reducing the possibility of any individual man being conscripted. Nevertheless, James would have to work—and soon.

As he had done since the day I returned from London, Benjamin came to my rescue. With little experience in the role—I didn't play the damsel-in-distress very well—the whole idea that I couldn't handle everything by myself grated on me. However, two days after Benjamin and I had discussed James and his limitations, as well as his one talent—numbers—Benjamin arrived for dinner bearing news. He had found a job for James.

One of his former students was now the chief accountant for Oland's Brewery, the business owned by my next-door neighbour. He had agreed to give James a try since his assistant had recently joined the army. So, my decision was made. I would stay in Halifax for the foreseeable future. I would reinvent myself as a Halifax doyenne—while keeping my real identity safely private. I could now be whomever I desired to be. I found the idea of reinvention oddly inspiring.

TWENTY-SIX

*"Isn't it nice to think that tomorrow is a new day
with no mistakes in it yet?"* ~ L.M. Montgomery

ON JUNE 14, 1940, I PICKED UP THE NEWSPAPER from where Mrs. Peveril had placed it on my breakfast table beside my place setting. Now that I was a widow (how I hated that description) and James was living with me (temporarily, I hoped), I had engaged Mrs. Peveril as a full-time housekeeper. I turned it over and scanned the headlines as I raised my coffee cup to my lips. My hand started shaking so badly that I could barely replace it on the saucer without spilling it. I sank into my chair and picked up the newspaper.

Paris had fallen to the Nazis. I was immediately engulfed with a fear that I could feel crawling up my back into my neck, encasing my head in a layer of anguish. I thought about my life in Paris, the beauty of the city and my friends. What about my flat? What would become of my friends? Where was Kiki? But the person I was most afraid for was Christophe, whose mother had been Jewish.

My best chance of finding out about Christophe was to contact Peggy in New York since they worked closely on various literary projects. Since America had kept itself out of the war—at least up until now—I even considered travelling to New York. In the end, by the next day, I didn't have to because Peggy called me, and we spoke briefly. She had news.

"Fran, darling, I'm so happy to catch you. I have such thrilling news." I was all ears. "In fact, I believe you should come to New York. You can fly from that place where you're living now, can't you?"

I honestly didn't know the answer to her question, but I did know that whatever thrilling news she had could not wait. I had to know. "I

266

think I could fly to Boston from here and connect to New York, but I'm not waiting. What's the news?"

"I've sold it! Warner's and MGM both wanted it, so I was able to have my partner in Hollywood negotiate an auction. We've sold the rights to Warner's Studio."

"Which book, Peggy?"

"Oh, Sorry, Fran. *When First We Kissed*. There are even rumours floating around that Katherine Hepburn may play the lead!"

"And who started those rumours, may I ask?" I knew that Peggy was well-known for her whisper campaigns to shore up support for both book and film projects. She was the best person in the industry to have on your team, and I was happy she was on mine.

She laughed. "Oh, I may have put the right thought in one or two ears," she said. "But it isn't outside the realm of possibility. You know Kate herself bought the film rights to that Broadway play she was in—*The Philadelphia Story*—she was wonderful in it, by the way. Anyway, she's just sold it to MGM. She's just the kind of talent you'd love to have on your project!"

At the risk of putting a damper on Peggy's enthusiasm and victory, I needed to broach the subject of Christophe.

"Oh, of course," she said more soberly. "I should have realized that you'd be worried given the news out of France. Anyway, as we speak, he's on—gosh, I can't remember the ship's name. I can ask Leonard to get me the name." Leonard was Peggy's assistant who had surprised me by being a young man when I'd first met her in New York. They were still a team. "Anyway, he called me a few months ago when he realized things were getting worse over there, and I helped him."

I heaved a sigh of relief. "And Sabine? What about her?"

"His wife? Oh, she left him for some Italian playboy. I'm surprised Christophe hasn't told you. It's been at least a year."

He hadn't mentioned it. I wondered why. In any case, I was oddly excited by this turn of events. Christophe would be only a few thousand miles south of me, on the same side of the ocean. And Sabine was gone. I hoped that her leaving hadn't made him too sad.

"By the way, Fran," Peggy said before hanging up, "there's a lot of money involved. I mean, there's a lot more money in the Hollywood thing than there ever will be in publishing. Just so you know—you'll be getting a cheque in the mail. It's the first of many."

I tapped my pen on the new manuscript in front of me on my desk and thought, *I wonder if Benjamin knows anyone who can help me invest my money*. I'd have to ask. I couldn't invest it all in France with Cliff's company.

~

In September, the first letter from Christophe arrived. He had settled into life in New York and seemed to be thriving as an editor at a new publishing house, but I could read between the lines. Nothing in the United States was as remarkable as Paris. And what could be? I often felt the same.

He wrote of the food he called mediocre and uninspired, the people he described as boorish and flashy, and the ambience loud. For Christophe's tastes, everything in America just seemed to be too over-the-top. I couldn't disagree. I only hoped that it would work out for him so he could return to our beloved Paris when this war business was over.

By the time his third letter arrived just before Christmas, it was clear that he was still in love with me. How did I know? He said so in as many ways as he could. How did I feel about him? I thought about this question a lot. I suppose there was no easy answer since I had convinced myself that Sam was the only man I had ever loved or ever would love in that way. It didn't matter, though. Christophe and I would always be friends and perhaps even lovers once again if the circumstances presented themselves. This war was undoubtedly getting in the way.

I was becoming increasingly frantic with the news stories out of London of the bombing campaign perpetrated on the citizens of my hometown by the Nazi air force. They were calling it the *Blitzkrieg*, and every story only amplified my worry about Father and Nora. When I tried to telephone him, I wasn't able to get through. I sent a telegram and finally got one in return. *"All well here. House still standing."*

I must admit that the terse words didn't give me much solace, but it would have to be enough. There was no way I could bring Father and Nora to Canada now, and there was no way he'd leave anyway. So I concentrated instead on my writing and my newly re-emerging interest in sewing. My writing was my passion: sewing became my necessity. I needed some clothes, and there was less and less to choose from on the shop rails. So, I bought lengths of fabric, a new sewing machine and a copy of the latest issue of the *Vogue Pattern Book*. I chose the patterns for two suits and went to work.

I set up a sewing room on the top floor of the house just above my second-floor bedroom. The room had a slanted ceiling and stretched the length of the house with a rounded widow on each end, one looking out over the street, the other looking out over the garden. It was here that I found the greatest solace in the midst of all that was going on in the world. I could lose myself in the lengths of fabric as I smoothed them out on my cutting table and in the seams as I motored my machine along. I found that I loved hand-stitching the linings into the jackets and sewing on the buttons. It was here that James found me one day late in November.

I heard his footsteps as they trudged up the stairs. He never came up here. *Whatever has brought him up here must be important,* I thought. I put my sewing down and waited for him to appear at the top of the stairs in the doorway.

"I've made a decision," he said, standing there with his fists clenched, as was his usual stance. "I'm changing my name."

This announcement sounded bizarre to me. "Whatever are you talking about? You can't just change your name."

"I thought you might say that. But it turns out that I can. I asked Benjamin, and he told me that I could do it. I've already begun the process, by the way." Then he turned to go as if our conversation were over.

"James, you can't just say that and turn to leave. What is going on?"

"It is quite simple and, I might add, should be clear to you. I no longer want to be a Phillips. Father has all but disowned me, and it seems you actually think you *do* own me."

I could never fathom what might be going on in that head of his. All he seemed to think about were numbers and money, which of course, almost seems to stand to reason. "So," I said, finally realizing that there was nothing I could do to change his mind, nor was it clear I even should, "what will your name be now?"

"I am James Wilson."

I suppose it was clever in a way. The name my mother had registered when she had adopted him was James Wilson Phillips. Wilson had been her maiden name. I shrugged.

"New beginnings, James."

TWENTY-SEVEN

"A bird sitting in a tree is never afraid of the branch breaking
because her trust is not in the branch but in her wings."
~ Anonymous

OVER THE NEXT SIX MONTHS, I was in weekly contact with Peggy as the plans for developing my book into a film progressed. The studio had engaged their in-house screenwriters to massage my prose into a script worthy of a big-name star. The whole process was so foreign to me that I found it thrilling. My only disappointment was that I couldn't share this excitement with Benjamin.

Ben, as he had told me to call him, had become a sort of fixture in my life. He came to dinner once a week, and we occasionally took a walk together when the weather cooperated. He often asked me to accompany him to one event or another—a concert or a public lecture at the university. I usually declined but had, on one or two occasions, attended a Theatre Arts Guild performance. They were a semi-professional theatre group in the city co-founded by my neighbour, Mr. Oland, the brewery owner. He had spent time in Hollywood during Prohibition, as I recalled Sam telling me.

It was this increasing number of invitations from Ben, my brother-in-law, that began to worry me. Although I had acquired several new friends in the city—a book club, if you must know—but there was no one with whom I could discuss Ben. We were not that kind of friends. And none of them knew that I was a writer. One month, I had some great fun when I suggested we all read *When First We Kissed* because I heard it was being made into a movie.

They were scandalized at first—the thought of reading such a racy book—but, in the end, they thought it might be thrilling. You cannot imagine how difficult it was for me to choke down my laughter when my book club colleagues began to speculate as to the sexual capabilities of the author—Peyton Winter. I wanted to shout, "I am Peyton Winter!" Imagine the shock that would have caused. I felt strongly that my social life in this small, rather parochial city would be over instantly.

So, I had to deal with the Ben issue alone. Well, perhaps not entirely alone. I told Peggy about it. She didn't seem to be bothered by the length of our long-distance telephone conversations. I suppose it was because she wasn't paying!

"So, you're telling me you think your brother-in-law is making a move on you?"

"Well, I might not put it that way precisely." I was thinking that I didn't really see Ben as my brother-in-law because I'd never seen him with my husband, but I thought better of saying this because she might get the wrong impression.

"Of course, you wouldn't. You're British!" Peggy's opinion of the British was that we were all just a bit stuck-up. She had often wondered out loud about how I developed my particular appetite for such a dubious writing genre as mine, given the obvious impediments offered by my upbringing. "Anyway, Fran," she continued, "if you're interested in the man, then let it happen."

"I'm not saying that he really is trying to do anything more than be my friend. I'm just saying—"

"You're just saying you don't know what to do. You're saying that you think it would be improper to engage in any kind of relationship with your brother-in-law. That's what you're saying."

"Oh, Peggy, you do have a way of clarifying things."

"You're welcome," she said. "By the way, Christophe has made some noises about taking the train northward to visit you."

"You're making that up," I said.

"Am I?" Peggy laughed and signed off.

~

One evening, late in November, Ben and I were sitting by the fire after dinner when he raised the subject of James.

"What's going on with James?" he said suddenly.

"Going on?" I said. "I suppose what usually goes on with James. He goes to work, keeps his head down as I've required him to do and comes home."

"His boss and I have dinner together a couple of times a month, and he's been wondering if James has a social life. He doesn't mingle with anyone at the company. In fact, he doesn't even talk to them. He eats lunch by himself, works and goes home. Is he all right?"

I explained to Ben that James had always been like that. I told him that James had some difficulty at school but omitted specific details, such as the one about him being a rabid bigot and occasionally violent. I hadn't seen any of that kind of behaviour since we'd moved to Canada, and for that, I was grateful.

"You know, Fran, he sounds a bit like someone I know. My colleague Henry Cormier's daughter Betty has a similar approach to life. He moans about it regularly. It seems that Betty took a secretarial diploma after high school and works as a secretary in a small legal office. She works all the time and shuts herself in her room at home when she's not working. Henry often jokes that her biggest strength is her ability to memorize lists. It's a bit like James's infatuation with numbers. He just wishes she'd find a husband."

"Sounds fascinating," I said absently. I was thinking about how long James could go on living here with me. It was about time he had an adult life of his own.

"Well, what do you think?"

"What do I think of what?" I had clearly not been listening.

"Of having a dinner party to get those two together. It sounds like they might make a good couple. At least they'd both have the semblance of a social life for a while."

I had little hope of James ever establishing an adult social life, but I felt there was little to lose. So, Ben and I set it up.

~

I planned the dinner for the seventh of December, a Sunday. Ben and I would host (was that an odd thing, I wonder?), and Henry Cormier, Ben's university colleague, and his wife Monique would come along with Betty. I convinced James to join us—after all, I told him, you have to eat. Mrs. Peveril was cooking and helping me serve.

I had planned a quiet, family-type dinner with lots of wine and conversation and Mrs. Peveril's roast chicken and gravy followed by her blueberry buckle, a kind of east-coast dessert cake. Then all hell broke loose.

Mrs. Peveril called me at nine o'clock that morning telling me how sorry she was, but she had to attend to her sister, a widow with two small children, who had fallen ill overnight. "Can we postpone until tomorrow?" she asked. I had no choice but to call everyone and ask if Monday evening would work. They all understood and agreed.

I spent the morning rearranging the food so that it would be fresh for the next day. I had just sat down for a cup of hot coffee when the telephone in the hall rang insistently. I put my coffee down and went to answer it.

"Fran?" came the so-familiar voice on the other end of the line.

"Christophe!" I was delighted to hear that voice. "Are you well? Is there literary news?"

"I am well, *chérie*, and I am here."

"Where is here?"

"I am uncertain. Permit me to look around for a moment."

This was puzzling.

"I believe it is a train station."

"A train station? Where are you going?"

"Going? *Non, non*, I am not going. I am coming. In fact, I am here."

Then the penny dropped. By here, Christophe meant here—as in Halifax. He had come to see me as Peggy had warned me. "Oh, you're *here*."

"*Oui*. Are you not happy to hear my voice? In any case, Peggy and I have talked—such a dear woman—and I have come to rescue you."

"I didn't know I needed rescuing. If you're here at the train station, why are you not here in my foyer?"

"May I be permitted to come?"

I rolled my eyes and told him yes, he was permitted to come. Ten minutes later, he was standing in my foyer looking even more handsome than ever with his salt-and-pepper hair and his grey cashmere scarf knotted around his neck. He was the picture of the self-assured, handsome, middle-aged Frenchman—and I adored him. And I would now tell him every detail about James.

If I'd had cause to wonder if Ben had designs on me, as my mother would have said, I was left with no doubt the next evening when Ben arrived to find Christophe ensconced in my sitting room, aperitif in hand, looking every inch at home. Not even our discussion about James had flustered him. He simply shrugged in that way of his and said, "*C'est la vie.*"

"Have you heard the news?" Ben said as he bounded in through the front door, peeling off his coat and thrusting a newspaper at me.

Christophe and I had spent much of the day catching up and working side-by-side in the kitchen as we had done so many times in Paris while Mrs. Peveril shooed us out. I had not read the news. Perhaps this was one day when I should have.

I looked at the headline and gasped. "1500 dead in Honolulu area. U.S. declares war on Japan!" So, it was truly another world war now.

When Ben carried on into the sitting room, Christophe stood up and extended his hand. "You must be Frannie's brother-in-law. I am delighted to meet you. I am Jean-Christophe Lemieux."

I could see Ben's brow furrow as he shook Christophe's hand. I could almost see the wheels moving. I may have mentioned Christophe's name to him once or twice—I may even have mentioned that we lived together for a time in Paris.

Is it possible to read jealousy on someone's face? I would not have thought so until I watched Ben look from Christophe to his half-finished glass of Kir now on a side table, to me, then to my glass which I was still holding. I swear I could see steam emanating from his ears.

There was no time to pursue further conversation because Henry, accompanied by his wife, Monique, and daughter, Betty, had arrived. I had instructed James to come downstairs when the Cormier's arrived, and this time, much to my surprise, he did as I asked.

I watched him walk slowly down the stairs to the foyer, sliding his hand along the railing. I could see his brow furrow deeply as he watched them remove their coats and prepare to enter the sitting room. When his gaze fell on Betty, I was sure I could see a slight change in his expression. Was it possible that he might be finding her attractive? Perhaps I was simply reading too much into it—seeing things I wanted to see. I beckoned him down, and we both followed them through the double doors, and the evening began.

Dinner was a horror show. There was little talk of anything but the war. The only good thing about it was that neither James nor young Betty, a mousy brunette who could have been pretty if she would just smile, seemed to have any interest in the conversation. They sat side-by-side for the entire first course without saying a word. Finally, I noticed James say something to Betty during dessert, causing her to turn her head toward him, then back to stare at me. I wondered what he had told her.

~

Although I was curious about what had gone on between James and Betty at dinner that evening, I said nothing. Christophe stayed for another week and then returned to New York, begging me to visit as soon as possible. I promised him I would try, then said goodbye.

A month later, I heard via Ben, who heard via Henry, that James and Betty had begun seeing one another. This news was something James chose not to share with me (no surprise there), so I tried to let it go.

One day in April, I was getting ready to leave the house to attend a book club session when I lifted one of James's coats that he had draped on top of mine on the coat rack, despite my continuing requests that he stop doing that. As I held it in one hand while pulling my coat out from under it, a small piece of paper fluttered to the floor.

I put his coat back on the rack and bent down to pick it up. I was about to stuff it into one of his pockets where I presumed it had been when my eye caught a glimpse of the note written on it.

There was no doubt about it. The note was for the odds on a harness race and a bet, and the date was from two days ago. The sum of money also shocked me. The bet had been for $150. My head was spinning—James was gambling again. I knew I would have to take control of this situation before it got out of hand.

When James arrived home from work that evening, he immediately went to his room, where it was his habit to stay until dinner. By the time he was halfway up the stairs, I called out to him. "James, please come to the sitting room. I'd like to talk to you."

He sullenly turned and made his way down the steps, his hands firmly in his pockets and presented himself in the doorway.

"Please, James," I said, "come and sit down."

"I'd rather stand," he said.

I stood up and placed myself directly in front of him. "You've been gambling again."

James glared at me. "You've been spying on me again."

"James, this has to stop. You are living under my roof, and I will not have it. You will ruin yourself."

"If you'd give me more money, it wouldn't be a problem, would it—Mother."

James had never before uttered that word. I had never been "Mother" to him. Hearing it threw me off balance.

"In any case," he continued, "you need not worry about me any longer. I shall be moving out from under your roof. Betty and I are getting married."

So, they had been seeing one another. Although under other circumstances, I would have rejoiced at the news, at that moment, all I could think of was that he'd ruin not only his own life but hers as well.

"Where will you live?"

"Betty's boss has an apartment above the office on Quinpool Road. We'll be living there."

"When is the wedding?"

"July 18. You can come if you want to—Mother." He turned abruptly and walked quickly out of the room and up the stairs.

TWENTY-EIGHT

"Things do not change; we change."
~ Henry David Thoreau

ON SATURDAY, JULY 18, 1942, IT RAINED—not just a gentle drizzle but a heavy downpour that lasted all day. As I arrived at the church with Ben, I thought about something my mother used to say at rainy weddings (and there had been many in London in her life). She always said, "Happy the bride the sun shines on." I had always thought this was a somewhat pessimistic view, but Mother had never been known for her optimistic, sunny view of life. I thought of this as I stood in my pew—acknowledged mother of the groom, no less, wearing my black Chanel dress (I will not be judged for wearing black to a wedding since it was the only appropriate dress I had—there was, after all, a war going on)—watching as the bride began her march down the aisle on her father's arm.

I thought of all the years I had spent in Paris in the couturier's salons, all the times I'd worn designer dresses fashioned from the finest fabrics, all the glittering parties I'd attended in my twenties and felt depressed. Betty looked sullen in her Woolworth's wedding gown with its short, puffed sleeves and its net skirt that seemed to crackle as it moved rather than sweeping lazily as fine fabric ought to do. I wasn't really worried about her sullen expression. As I mentioned, she usually looked like that. She looked more frightened today than anything else. Her father, on the other hand, looked pleased with himself. This wedding was what he had wanted for her—and for him.

The bride's parents hosted a cocktail reception at the Lord Nelson Hotel, where the family gathered in the main salon for the required photograph under the portrait of Lord Nelson himself. There we were, lined up in a row, posing as if this was a happy collection of like-minded individuals, as if no war raged, as if the future loomed bright for the newlyweds. Could I have been any more cynical?

When the bride's father called the assembled one-hundred or so guests to attention, he appeared considerably more enthusiastic about the union we had just witnessed.

"As we look at my lovely daughter today, marrying her sweetheart, I'm reminded of a wish I received from my own father-in-law when I married Monique so many years ago. May all sweethearts become married couples, and may all married couples remain sweethearts. To the sweethearts."

Dear god, I thought. *He really is happy to have her out from under his roof. I suppose I'll be struck dead if I tell him that.*

When the wedding was over, James and Betty borrowed Henry's car and drove to the Annapolis Valley for their honeymoon. They were an odd couple, for sure. I found myself hoping that the two of them never had children. What could that possibly be like?

~

The war dragged on for three more excruciating years. It was hard to read of the battles and the bloodshed while we sat in our comfortable homes. I travelled to New York on three occasions to meet with Peggy about my new work as Peyton Winter went from one best-selling novel to another. I remember remarking to Peggy when Betty Smith's new book *A Tree Grows in Brooklyn* was published a year later that I was surprised that the reading public was interested in such a wide variety of styles. This book was downright wholesome compared to anything Peyton Winter (I) might write. She laughed and continued to tell me about the opening of the film *When First We Kissed*.

Peggy told me now was the time—the time to peel the veil back from Peyton Winter. It was time for me to take the credit she said I deserved. She said it would be a remarkable publicity stunt if I were introduced as the real Peyton Winter at the opening in New York. Then she dangled the carrot. I would be seated with Miss Hepburn.

Yes, that Miss Hepburn. Peggy herself had circulated the rumours resulting in Katharine Hepburn reading the finished script and signing on as the star. It was almost too good to pass up. But I did anyway. I had long ago come to terms with the fact that no one knowing about the true identity of this writer was too freeing to give up. No, I told her, that would not happen. And as much as I wanted to be there for the opening, I told her I would wait. I flew to Boston, then on to New York two weeks after the opening and watched the film anonymously in a dark cinema one afternoon with Peggy and Christophe, who had come over just for this event.

As the closing credits rolled, the three of us just sat there as the rest of the audience climbed out of their seats and headed to the exits. Peggy had already seen it at the premiere, after which I had wondered why Peggy's reaction had been muted when I called her the next day. I concluded she was going to wait to let me experience it myself before gushing over it. I now knew better.

"Mon dieu. Qu'est-ce que c'était? Qu'est-ce qu'on vient de voir?" Christophe always reverted to French when overly excited. He did seem to be excited but not in a good way.

"Quite so," I said. "What the hell was that, indeed?"

"I couldn't tell you, Fran. I'm sorry, but you had to see it for yourself." Peggy was shaking her head as if to clear out the cobwebs of confusion. Neither of us had read the shooting script.

"Was that supposed to be based on my novel?" Peggy nodded unhappily. We were still sitting in our seats, alone in the auditorium, as the ushers began to clean up the aisles in preparation for the next showing. "Is this what a Hollywood treatment looks like?"

"I'm afraid it often is," Peggy said. "I had hoped they would be true to the story, but I suppose it was a bit too racy for Warner's. If it's any consolation, the reviews have been good, and you'll make a lot of money on the back end as a result of my negotiation. And mark my words, you'll have final approval of the script in the future."

It was small comfort.

~

James and Betty came to dinner on Sunday once a month. Every time we sat down to dinner, I marvelled at how she deferred to him in everything. I often tried to draw her out to see if she had opinions of her own, but she always seemed to glance toward James as if for his approval.

It was one such Sunday in May of 1945 when I asked Ben to join us since we were celebrating, and I hadn't seen much of Ben lately. The war was finally over. James and Betty dutifully sat in their usual seats in our dining room, and for once, the conversation was animated. At least Ben and I were having an animated conversation. We were just discussing when we might be able to once again travel to Europe—I could hardly wait to return to Paris for a visit—when James interrupted me mid-sentence.

"Betty and I have news," he said.

Ben and I both put our wine glasses down beside our plates and stared.

"Betty and I are having a baby."

I knew the war was over, but I felt as if a bomb had just dropped on my house. James and Betty, parents? It was unthinkable.

"Well, then," Ben said, raising his wine glass, "let's drink to the new parents." He looked at me. "And to the new grandmother."

I was thunderstruck.

"Where will you live?" I said. It was weak, but it was practical.

"Where we are now."

"We'll see about that."

There was no way on god's green earth my grandchild, unlucky enough to have James and Betty as parents, was going to be raised in an apartment above a law office. He or she would have the benefit of my wealth, and I hoped my influence. So, I did what any other desperate mother would do. I bought them a house—or to be more specific, I bought a house and let them live in it rent-free on the condition that James never again set foot in a gambling establishment. They agreed. I bought a new house a ten-minute drive from where I lived and helped them to set up by buying them a house full of new furniture. Betty was tickled at the house, the contents and the garden, which she promised to tend lovingly.

~

Katherine Elizabeth Wilson, eight pounds and two ounces, was born on January 8, 1946, and my life began again.

The Muir

Mentor

TWENTY-NINE

"One is not born, but rather becomes, a woman."
~ Simone de Beauvoir, *The Second Sex*

JAMES CALLED ME LATE IN THE AFTERNOON to tell me that he had just become a father, which, of course, made me a grandmother. Given that Betty had been pregnant for nine months, the news was not unexpected. However, until that moment, I had never really considered what this new role might entail. I had always thought about it as something that simply happened to most women, but it was really more of something one had to *become*. I became a writer, a wife, a woman, and now I had to become a grandmother. I wasn't sure I knew how to do that.

After James hung up, I poured myself a glass of Sancerre and sat at my writing desk looking out the window. I would visit little Katherine tomorrow, but I was alone with my thoughts about this new phase of my life this evening.

I had not been a good mother—of that, there was no doubt. No one looking at my track record could disagree. I suppose I had always thought that to be a good grandmother, you had to have been a good mother. Now I wasn't so sure. As I sat there sipping my wine and watching the sun as it set behind the trees, I began to take stock.

I had made what many would call (and have called) a mistake by putting myself in a position to have a baby at such a young age and without a husband. Despite the challenges, I hadn't seen that as a mistake so much as a learning experience. I never regretted my short time with Elliott—I learned so much about life and myself. I grew up quickly. I had made the best arrangements for James as I thought possible at the time, only to be thwarted by my own mother, a situation that began my life of living a lie. I was no longer anyone's mother—she was mine and my son's. Then I fled. I didn't stay to face that life, a life I believed was no longer mine anyway. I escaped to Paris.

I believe my life experience was my life's education. I suspect that old friends in London shrugged off my behaviour a running away to find myself. My mother blamed it on "the incident." They were all wrong.

I had run away—that I will admit. But I had neither been affected by "the incident" (except for my abiding disgust at the behaviour of certain members of my own class) nor was I trying to find myself. There was no need to seek myself. But I harboured a deep desire to *become* myself—to *create* myself. *Yes,* I thought as I sat there in the gathering darkness, *this is what I will teach little Katherine.*

Although few people in the world knew my true identity, I did create myself, and that was fine with me. I knew Katherine must also learn this: *you become yourself on your own terms.* I began to think about something I had read years ago. Something Aristotle once wrote. *There is only one way to avoid criticism: do nothing, say nothing, and be nothing.* Yes, I would teach my little granddaughter to stand up for what she wanted to do and say and be in life or risk accomplishing nothing. That was not an option. First, though, I had to meet this new little soul.

~

I arrived at the maternity hospital promptly at one p.m., just as visiting hours were beginning. I had sent flowers in advance from my regular florist, who had promised they would arrive before noon. I was otherwise empty-handed. Betty had gained weight even before the pregnancy, so it seemed cruel to bring chocolates—as much as she liked them. And Katherine was as yet unknown to me. Before the day was over, I would fix that and figure out what gift would be my first (of many) to give to this new child.

The Grace Maternity Hospital was a squat, three-story, red brick building on Summer Street at University Avenue, a grand name for a

288

small boulevard that claimed its name from the fact that it ended at the steps of an old stone building that housed the upper echelons of rarefied academics at Dalhousie University. The university's claim to fame was that it was the first such entity established in this country. Oh, and it was also Ben's employer.

The hospital was a mere ten-minute walk from my front door. When I arrived, I checked in at the reception desk to ask for my daughter-in-law's room number and where my granddaughter might be. The receptionist directed me to the second floor for Betty and the third-floor nursery for Katherine. I took the elevator directly to the third floor.

Despite my long life—I was now forty-six years old—I had never been in a nursery. I stepped off the elevator and turned left toward the large plate-glass window where I could see another older couple standing close to the glass, whispering and pointing. I made my way slowly and quietly toward the window, stopping just as the rows of tiny bundles came into view. I gasped.

What a sight! I felt as if I were viewing a department store window and all the tiny bundles, tightly swaddled in three neat rows of padded bassinets, were somehow for sale. As I looked down the corridor toward the couple still whispering, I could see, inside the window, a nurse, in angelic white from cap to shoes (I presumed this—I couldn't see her feet), holding up one of the tiny bundles for the couple, presumably the grandparents, to get a better look. All I could see of the baby was a tiny, wizened face that looked seriously unhappy to have been disturbed, poking out from the cocoon. I was thinking that the baby looked like a giant moth cocoon with a face. Then I had to search for Katherine—my Katherine.

"May I help you, Ma'am?"

I was startled by the voice so close to my ear as I stood there mesmerized by the display of such potential. That's what I was thinking—there was so much potential there. Which of these babies would be a ballerina? Which one a physician? A surgeon? A barrister? A pianist? At that moment, they all sat on a level laying field—only I knew that wasn't true. The moment they left this place, each of them would be subject to the vagaries of that lottery that is one's parents. No, the playing field was not level at all.

"Would you be looking for anyone in particular?"

I turned to look at the young woman—this one was, indeed, in pristine white from head to toe. "Yes, I am. Would you be able to point out my granddaughter?"

"Her name?"

"Katherine," I said.

"I mean her surname." She smiled indulgently as if she might be gazing at a dullard of some sort.

"Of course," I said. "It's Phillips." Then I stopped myself. "So sorry. It's Wilson."

The young woman stopped smiling. "Are you sure?"

"Yes, I am." I looked at the young woman's name tag. "Miss Talbot, is it?"

"Wait here," the nurse said as she turned toward the door leading into the nursery behind the glass window.

I gazed from one bundle to the next, thinking how they all looked alike. How in the world did the nurses tell one from another? Then I saw Miss Talbot pick up a bundle from the middle of the back row and begin walking toward me. Unaccountably, my heart began to race. I could hear the blood rushing in my ears. I was about to meet Katherine.

Miss Talbot brought her over to the window and held her up for me to see. Through the tears beginning to form, I stared at this tiny girl with the mop of dark hair among all the rest of the bald babies. She looked at me with a pair of penetrating blue eyes. The nurse began to unwrap her so that I could see the tiny fingers that were now gripping Miss Talbot's pinkie finger.

"Katherine, my darling girl," I said quietly so as not to be overheard. I looked at her as hard as I could. "Yes, I think that you are not Katherine so much as you are Kat. Yes. Kat, my darling child, I will always be here for you."

After a few minutes more, Miss Talbot nodded to me and took Kat back to her bassinet. I was in a fog of happiness as I stood waiting for the elevator. Before I knew what had happened, I was walking home, my daughter-in-law, who had just produced this darling girl for me, all but forgotten.

~

By the time Kat was six months old, I had begun to realize that I had undergone a kind of evolution—and an unexpected one at that. No longer did my life seem so much about me.

The first time I was permitted to hold her, I was sitting in James and Betty's living room in a large chair that provided support to both my arms. They insisted on it. I pretended that I was deferring to their wishes, but in due course, I would need to make it clear to them that I felt they were unequipped to be parents—on so many levels. They hovered around her with furrowed brows as if they expected her to break at any moment. I ignored them and simply began to get to know my granddaughter.

I felt an astonishing connection to this tiny human. There was so much that I would need to teach her about life that neither Betty nor—god forbid, James—could fathom. After Kat's birth, I had begun to make plans for a trust fund for her and had stopped writing. This decision to take a writing hiatus was the catalyst that caused Christophe to begin calling from overseas weekly to embark on a campaign to reverse it. He had, after all, returned to Paris to become the publisher at a new publishing house—his own. *Éditions Lemieux*.

"So, you are a *grand-mère*, Frannie. So, too, are many women," he said dismissively. I could almost see his hand in front of his face, brushing away the very idea. "It is simply a stage of life. *Mon dieu*, you cannot simply give up on your career, your life."

"And your career, Christophe? I do understand, you know. My writing does indeed benefit you as well."

"I do not believe you do. *C'est pour toi que je m'inquiète*. It is for you, I worry. You are a writer, Frannie. It is who you are. You can be a grandmother, but you still must be a writer."

I told him I'd consider a new project, but he had to give me more time. He continued his verbal assault and added to his insistence that I produce a new manuscript, then demanded that I come to Paris to see him. Not so much on business, he said. He wanted me to come to spend time with him. Now that the war was over, there was no impediment. I told him I would work it out. That wasn't the only thing I had to work out.

I had tried to distance myself from Ben ever since I realized his interest in me was less than brotherly. The very idea of any intimate involvement with him simply felt wrong. I realized this was not only because of Sam but also because of Christophe. The moment Peggy had told me about Sabine leaving Christophe, I had begun to see us once again becoming more than editor and author. So, I began to see less and less of Ben. He wasn't happy, but he had little recourse. Sadly, I felt even our friendship ebbing away.

By the time Kat celebrated her first birthday, I had begun a new book project. I also received a sad telegram from Nora. My father had died. Once again, I had to embark on a transatlantic voyage to take care of the business of his estate. He had left his estate in equal parts to Nora and me. While in London, I made arrangements to sell the family home while Nora found a cottage she loved in Oxford. Before I had a chance to make final arrangements with the estate agent, Ollie arrived at the house one afternoon to express his condolences and more.

"Frannie," he said, "I am so sorry about your father. He was a wonderful man."

As I looked at my old friend, a wave of nostalgia floated over me as I saw the white in his hair and remembered who we had been as children.

"I have a proposition for you," he said. "As it turns out, Oliver junior has always loved this house, as have I. He and I have discussed him buying it. You know I, too, am to become a grandparent."

I had not known, and I couldn't think of anyone I'd rather have in this house that was so full of memories—both good and bad—from my childhood. I certainly had no interest in keeping it as part of my real estate portfolio that already consisted of my Paris flat, an apartment in Manhattan purchased on my behalf as part of my real estate holdings and in which I had never even stayed (it was rented out) and the house in Halifax.

Once the house sale was finalized and Nora had settled in her newly acquired cottage in Oxford, I bid my home country goodbye for the last time, and I took the train once again to Southampton to board my ship.

When I arrived home, I sent Christophe a telegram. "New book coming along. Arriving in Paris September 7." His response, *"Enfin."* At last.

THIRTY

"I don't care what you think about me. I don't think about you at all."
~ Coco Chanel

Paris had changed. The war might have ended, but the evidence of it remained. Paris bore her wounds more deeply than London, whose blitz scars were horrifyingly visible reminders of what the Germans had taken from them. Things just seemed different to me. When I asked Christophe about it, his response demonstrated his usual Gallic "*c'est la vie*" demeanour. He shrugged.

"Well, Frannie, of course, the Nazis were inhuman in many ways, but never let it be said they failed to recognize perfection in art. It is said that one General Dietrich von Choltitz, the last of the Germans who had the privilege to be our military governor, refused to comply with the Fuhrer's wishes to have the city razed to the ground when defeat was imminent. It seems he was a connoisseur of art and could not bear the thought of such masterpieces being destroyed simply for spite. I have no idea if that is true, but as you have observed, our scars are not so visible."

We were sitting in the drawing-room of my flat on the left bank. I had not been here in many years. As I looked around, it occurred to me that I was a different person than the one who sat in the window discovering my identity as a writer. Much had transpired since then—much water under the bridge as I had learned in Canada.

I poured each of us another glass of wine. "But, Christophe, everything just feels different."

"Ah, *oui*," he said, savouring a long sip of the excellent Bordeaux. "It is deep in the souls of everyone I know who endured the Occupation. I almost feel embarrassed that I fled."

"But you had no choice. For sure you would have ended up in a concentration camp."

He nodded and shrugged again. "Yes, but I did not have to endure the daily humiliations faced by my friends who stayed. I have listened to them, and their lives were so precarious, never knowing if they would live to sunset of each day. And there continue to be shortages of this and that, as well as strikes. *Mon dieu*, the strikes! It seems the workers will never be happy." He took another sip of wine then turned to me. "Enough about the war. We must toast to your new project and that I will once again have you in my bed before the night is over."

Even at my advanced age, I think I blushed.

~

"I must see Simone while I'm here," I said to Christophe as we ate breakfast on the Monday morning of my second week in Paris. He furrowed his brow as if not recognizing the name. "Simone de Beauvoir? My friend?" I said. He nodded, and I continued. "I also have to find a copy of her new book. It's not available in North America yet. Even Peggy couldn't get me a copy."

"Yes, of course," he said. I could tell he wasn't listening. He was reading the morning newspaper. "Not much news, really," he said. "By the way. Have you purchased a new frock for Thursday evening?"

"Frock? Thursday evening? What's going on then? This is the first you've mentioned anything to me."

Christophe put the paper down on the table and looked pensive for a moment. "Perhaps I have forgotten to mention the party to you."

"I would have remembered a party," I said. "I could do with a party."

"Am I becoming forgetful, *chérie*?"

I stopped putting jam on my croissant and put my knife down. "Whatever are you talking about? You're not usually forgetful, Christophe."

"Ah, yes, not *usually*. Am I getting old?"

This conversation was one I did not want to have with Christophe, my dearest friend (and lover). I knew how important it was for him to remain youthful, and I would not be pulled into a conversation about our looming dotage. He was only a few years older than I was.

"We are all getting older, my love, but not necessarily old. Anyway, a party sounds like just the thing. What and where?"

We had been invited to a grand party in honour of the fashion industry and the new graduates of the *Chambre Syndicale de la Couture Parisienne* school at the *Grand Palais*. The party would consist of a fashion show featuring designs created by the newest members of the fashion design community, followed by dinner and dancing to the strains of an American orchestra whose name Christophe could not remember. There was no doubt that I'd need a new frock, as Christophe had so quaintly put it. And I was in the perfect city to procure one.

Since money was no object, I marched myself to the Pierre Balmain salon to select a dress. Known for the kinds of slinky, strapless gowns that a woman of a certain age (over forty in my view) ought not to wear, Balmain also did other work. As I sat in his salon looking at the mannequins parading through, I was startled by the poise and grace of these tall Amazons who were showing the designs to perfection. In particular, I was mesmerized by a tall, red-headed beauty wearing an ivory satin gown with a high neck, long slender sleeves and a billowing skirt. The dress was embellished with thousands of tiny sequins in a pattern that swirled around the bodice and spilled down onto the drapes of the skirt. It was stunning, but it occurred to me that I wasn't quite ready for that amount of coverage despite my advancing age. I realized that I was more taken with the model than the dress when the next dress arrived, and I gasped. This time, I didn't even notice the model. That was how I knew it was the dress.

It was also ivory, but this time, the dress was of silk crepe. The skirt was pleated and swished marvellously as the model made her way toward me. But it was the neckline that riveted me. It was a portrait neckline with a rolled back collar that fell off the shoulder, revealing the most provocative part of an older woman's body—her collar bone and neck. I had to have it.

After a hurried fitting during which the salon manager continued to tell me that there wasn't enough time to get it fitted, I left the establishment with her promise to have it ready for me to pick up the next day. It was safely ensconced in a cloth carrier, hanging on the back of one of the chairs beside me as I sat in a café the next day for lunch waiting for Simone to join me—and she was late.

~

"Qu'est-ce que tu as dans ce sac?" Simone said as she hurried to kiss me and take her seat. Of course, she wanted to know what was in the bag, even before saying hello.

I laughed. Despite our continued correspondence, we hadn't seen one another in so long, yet her first question was to wonder what I had bought. So, I told her.

"My dear Fran, you never cease to amaze me with your varied interests. You are something of a Renaissance woman, *non?*"

We ordered coffee and two *croque monsieurs*, then settled in to catch up. Simone had spent some years teaching at what would be called a high school in North America—she called it a *lycée*. After several successful books, though, she now made her living as a writer.

"You have been an inspiration, Fran. And I have a gift for you—to thank you." She leaned down to her bag that she had placed on the pavement under our table. When she sat up, she handed me a book. It was called *L'Invitée*, a novel by Simone de Beauvoir. "I know it is not yet available in America or—Canada? Anyway, it has a bit of a *menage-a-trois*, so you will understand why I thought of you. I believe it may be retitled when it is published abroad."

I took the book from her and would have opened it to begin reading right there and then if I didn't want to chat further—which I did. Simone was writing fiction, but I knew her well enough to know that there was more there than met the eye. She was a philosopher at heart and the most intelligent woman I knew, perhaps the most intelligent person. She told me she was working on what she expected to be her manifesto on sex and gender—no fiction this time, she clarified. I wanted to hear all about it, but she wasn't ready to tell me much. I only knew that I would have to read her book, and I knew it might very well change the world. She was that kind of person.

"All I can tell you is that, in my view, a man is defined as a human being and a woman as a female, and whenever she behaves as a human being, she is said to imitate the male. I will send you a signed copy when it is published." She drained her coffee cup and put it firmly on the table. "Shall we now have wine?"

So, we did.

~

It was a glittering party, to say the least. The evening was impressive enough just by being held in this magnificent building designed in the *Beaux-Arts* architectural tradition that was so much in fashion at the end of the last century when it was built. The *Palais* was never really a palace in the way someone like me who hailed from London might think of one. Whenever a Londoner thinks of palaces, Buckingham Palace and Kensington Palace spring immediately to mind, along with visions of royalty strolling the hallowed halls. This *Palais* wasn't built for royalty as much as it was built for the people—a grand edifice to serve as home to exhibitions that would showcase France and its many attractions to the world. I had walked past this building many times when I lived in Paris, but I never had any occasion to be inside. It certainly looked and felt like a palace to me.

"Finally, it is ours again," Christophe said as he took my arm. We were passing between the magnificent stone columns and up the steps to the entrance.

"What do you mean?" I said, trying to take in the magnificence of the glass-domed ceiling covering the enormous space just inside.

"What I mean is that when I returned to Paris, the *Palais* was just beginning to emerge from its humiliating service to the Nazis who violated it by turning it first into a truck depot—just imagine it! Then, worse, they displayed their vile propaganda exhibitions here. So, it is ours once again."

As I took in the magnificence of the surroundings, I couldn't even imagine how anyone could have desecrated such a glorious work of art. I didn't have much time to think anymore about this as the crowd gathered for the fashion parade that would begin within the half-hour.

An usher led us to our seats, where we could watch the models parade by wearing designs created by the graduating students. I was mesmerized by the glittering crowd. I prided myself in still being able to pick out specific designers' creations, but there were so many new ones since I had left Paris that I gave up. I did, however, see a few familiar faces in the crowd, Coco Chanel being among them. She was sitting in the front row, fanning herself with a program. I so wanted to see what she was wearing, but she was too far away, and the show was about to begin.

I was fascinated. The students were innovative—of course, they were. None of them would have been here this evening if all they did was copy other designers. Each of the new graduates showed two designs. Following along in my program, I watched them one by one, making a note by each name as a kind of personal prediction of their success. Some I believed were destined to be assistants for their entire careers, but one stood out.

I watched as the next model appeared and was stunned to see the redhead who had worked the Balmain salon earlier in the week. This time, however, I noticed more than her presence. I was also impressed by the design. Unlike most other students who had chosen to show cocktail and evening gowns, this designer showed suits—marvellous, tailored, beautifully cut suits. I looked down at my program. The student's name was Alfred Chang.

"Christophe," I whispered in his ear, "I must meet that young man." I pointed to a young Asian man who had just taken the stage and was standing beside the red-headed model who was at least two inches taller than he was.

"But, of course, *ma chèrie*," he said. "Whatever you wish."

The show was finally over, and we were invited to make our way to yet another wonderful room set up for dinner. Christophe told me he would return momentarily while I took the seat where the place card proclaimed my name in calligraphy. I introduced myself to my table mates while he was gone and promptly forgot all their names.

After dinner, Christophe took me by the arm and led me to a table where a clutch of people stood around the young man I wished to meet. Just outside the circle of people stood the red-headed model. I immediately went to her to introduce myself and tell her how wonderfully well she had done.

"Ah, Madame," she said. "I remember seeing you earlier this week." She stood back and looked at me. "You do justice to Monsieur Balmain's design. Oh, I am so rude. I must introduce myself. I am Caroline Chang."

I asked her about the young man.

"Alfred? He is brilliant, is he not?" She held up her hand and waved it in front of me. "And we have been married only one week!"

"Congratulations, Caroline! And I predict much success for both of you in the Paris fashion scene."

Caroline shook her head. "Oh no. Not in Paris. I have been offered a contract by a very new agency in New York. I am excited since it is owned by a woman named Eileen Ford. She will be the most successful of the modelling agents. You will see. I think women will be better in the business, do you not agree?"

We chatted for a few more minutes while waiting patiently for Alfred to be free. Caroline told me that the move to America was precipitated by her parents' disapproval of her marriage to Alfred and his acceptance at the prestigious Parsons Design school in New York. He planned to stake out his design territory in America, although, as it turned out, Alfred was, in fact, Canadian.

Finally, I met this up-and-coming fashion star. Alfred was wonderfully warm and self-effacing. I should have expected this since he was from Canada, but it still came as a surprise. Something about this young couple seemed to foreshadow great success, and I wanted to know them better. I was delighted when they accepted our dinner invitation. Dinner later in the week was fabulously entertaining, and after that encounter, we promised to see one another again in New York in due course. I wondered when our paths would cross again.

THIRTY-ONE

"The mind is not a vessel that needs filling,
but wood that needs igniting."
~ Plutarch

As much as I was determined to teach little Kat as much as I could about love, life and being who you are meant to be, it turned out that she taught me so much more. Over the next few years, I truly began to learn what it was to be a mother. I had not learned that lesson with James. I blamed my own mother, but I knew that was an excuse. The problem, however, was that my lessons in being a mother weren't viewed quite as positively by James. In fact, he took a dim view of most things I did when it came to Kat.

After years of minor skirmishes, the first major altercation happened when he arrived home from work one afternoon when Kat was seven to find the two of us sitting side-by-side on the sofa in their living room. Betty was in the kitchen baking. She always seemed more at ease in the kitchen than she ever did when she was with Kat.

"What's going on?" James said as he came into the room.

"Nan and I are looking at old photographs, Daddy."

I could see his face blanche ever so slightly. "What kind of old photographs?"

"I thought it was time Kat began to learn about her family. I was showing her some old family photographs."

I could see James clench his fists so tightly I thought he might injure his hands like he used to do when he was a child. "You and I need to talk, Mother." He looked at Kat. "Go help your mother, Katherine."

"But Daddy—"

"Go. This minute."

I kissed Kat on the top of her head as she left, sat back and folded my hands.

"First, Mother, her name is Katherine. Second, there is no need for her to know anything about her family—not now and not ever. She has quite enough of the old family with you around."

"I'll thank you not to speak to me that way, James. And there is nothing wrong with her learning about her grandparents in England. It seems only appropriate. After all, it is your birthplace as well, in case you've forgotten."

"I have not, but I'd like to."

Recently I'd noticed that James was losing his British accent. It occurred to me that he seemed to be making an effort to separate himself from his past. I couldn't argue with how sensible that might have been for him, but only if he moved in a suitable direction.

"Well, you can relax," I said as I got up to get ready to say goodbye to Kat. "I haven't shown her *that* photograph. She's much too young to understand."

I knew that there was only one photograph he wanted to keep from her—almost as much as he wanted to keep it from himself. It was the picture of Elliott and his family. James would never change, or so it seemed.

~

Kat never spent much time with me in my home. James objected to extended periods of the two of us keeping company. Yet, somehow, I was able to teach her to sew.

When Kat was ten years old, she asked me about a coat I was wearing one day. When I told her that I had made it myself, her eyes grew as large as saucers. "Nan! I must learn to sew! I simply must!"

For her next birthday, I presented her with a beautiful new Singer sewing machine, three lengths of fabric and three patterns for dresses I knew she'd like. Then we began our weekly sessions. She was a natural and wanted to learn more and more. As Christmas drew close, she wanted to make herself a red velvet dress for the season, but even more impressive was that she wanted to design it herself. The best we could do at that point was to help her make some changes to one of her patterns to make the collar and sleeves more like she imagined they should be. What was clear was that I'd have to find a sketchbook for her for Christmas.

On Christmas morning, as I sat with James, Betty and Kat under their Christmas tree, I watched Kat carefully as she tore the paper off my present while both her parents told her to be more careful so that they could fold it up and use it next year. I just rolled my eyes.

When she finally uncovered the sketchbook, Kat proclaimed that it was the best Christmas gift she'd ever received in her life. James was furious.

My darling granddaughter made good use of that sketchbook and the many more I lavished on her over the following years as she grew into a talented young woman. She made most of her own clothes, although she never made any of her own designs. When I asked her about this, she always said that she would someday.

When Kat was in high school, less than a year before graduation, I was having a pre-dinner cocktail on a Sunday afternoon. Of course, as usual, I'd had to make it myself since James refused to learn to make such posh drinks. He always said that with the edge of someone with a chip on his shoulder. I ignored him, and as long as he continued to have the ingredients in his bar, I would continue to make my own whenever invited to Sunday dinner. Kat and I were alone in the living room when she sidled over to me and started whispering.

"Nan, you have to help me."

"Darling girl, of course, you know I will always help you. But why are we whispering?"

Kat looked toward the dining room where her mother was setting the table. James was out in the yard smoking, a habit I despised. "I told Mom and Dad I wanted to apply to go to art college."

I put my glass down on the coffee table and hugged her close. "Kat, darling, that is wonderful news. You're so talented. There's no doubt about your acceptance."

"I'm not really worried about that. But I am worried about Mom and Dad. When I told them, Dad just said that I'd get over it. He said that art's not a real job. I told him I wanted to go to art college then to fashion design school."

"Of course, you do, darling. You have a god-given gift, and you should use it."

"Will you talk to them?" Kat looked at me pleadingly.

"I will, darling, but I can't promise anything. Let's see how it goes. You go ahead and apply, and we'll see what happens then."

Kat hugged me tightly. I hoped that I'd be able to help her, but the truth was that I knew I had only so much influence with James. And in the end, I wasn't her parent. He was.

~

Kat's acceptance letter from the Nova Scotia College of Art and Design arrived in April of the year she was to graduate from high school. I knew this because the minute she opened the letter, she called me. She was jubilant. Of course, at her father's insistence, she had also applied to Dalhousie University here in the city and the University of Toronto. She had already received her letters of acceptance to both those institutions, but she didn't want to study to become a teacher as her father told her she must. I had tried to talk some sense into James (Betty was no problem—she was frightened of me), but I feared that it might not have worked.

"Kat, that's wonderful news, but hardly unexpected," I said as she gushed about the possibilities.

"Surely Dad can't complain about this. I'll still be able to live at home. That'll save money," she said.

I didn't think money would be an object since I'd already told James that I had established a fund for Kat's education the week after she was born. I didn't mention that to Kat. I did, however, think I caught a slight inflection in Kat's tone that prompted me to ask her a question.

"You have told your father that you went ahead and applied to the art school, haven't you?"

Kat didn't answer right away.

"Katherine Elizabeth Wilson. This won't come as a complete surprise to him, will it?"

"I suppose it might, Nan," she said with far less enthusiasm than she had been demonstrating to this point in the conversation.

"Kat, you know how your father hates to be blind-sided."

"No, he shouldn't be blind-sided. I've been talking about my dream for years, but all he says is that I need to be a proper young lady and find a husband. I don't want to be a proper young lady—whatever that is!"

I briefly wondered where I'd heard that before! Like grandmother, like granddaughter, I suppose.

"Then why didn't you tell him you were also applying to art school when you sent off those applications to the other two universities?"

"Because I wanted to avoid a scene until I knew I was in."

I sympathized with her. There was nothing more I could do except wait for her to let me know how the conversation with her father went.

Two days later, she called me in tears.

"Nan, he just took the letter, crushed it into a ball and threw it against the wall. It was so awful." She sobbed. "He refuses to let me go. He says no daughter of his will be going to art school. He said I have to go to university to be a teacher and find a husband. I don't want a husband!"

I immediately wanted to tell Kat that I'd look after everything. I wanted to tell her that she could go to art school here in the city and live with me. But I didn't. I decided that I needed to bide my time.

First, it occurred to me that Kat had been brought up in a very sheltered environment. She lived in this small city where bigotry and insularity still flourished. She needed to see more of the world. Staying here wouldn't help her. Toronto would be a good place to start. Second, the local art college program wasn't really what she wanted (or should do) anyway. She wanted to study fashion design, and as far as I was concerned, that was what she ought to do. So, I made a deal with her.

"If you go to the University of Toronto for a few years then still want to be a fashion designer, I'll do everything in my power to help you. But don't stay here to go to school. Kat, are you listening to me?"

"I am, Nan." Kat sounded very subdued. "I guess I could do that. At least I'd be a thousand miles away from Dad."

In September, my beloved granddaughter left for Toronto, and I found myself floundering. I had just turned sixty-five—and we all know what that's supposed to mean. I decided it was time to visit New York for a bit of rejuvenation. That may not have been a good choice!

THIRTY-TWO

SOMETIMES, WHEN YOU DON'T SEE YOUR FRIENDS for long periods, it seems that the time has been nothing. You pick right up where you left off, still understanding each other and the subtle sub-texts of your relationship. It seems, though, that once you hit a certain age, those gaps become larger. It felt a bit that way when I met Peggy for lunch at our favourite spot, The Palm Court when I landed in New York.

I arrived first and sat at the table, glancing every so often at the entrance when I spotted an older New Yorker stop under the arch and look around. The woman was in head-to-toe black, which is why I knew she had to be from New York. Her hair was silver, and she was wearing four strands of something silver around her neck. There was also something else. She had a kind of hard edge that comes from a life of always having to be one step up on the competition, always better than everyone else. Of course, that woman was Peggy. The only thing I recognized was that edge.

Peggy saw me and waved. She began walking toward the table when someone at an adjacent table flagged her down. She spent a moment chatting before continuing toward me.

When she arrived at the table, she practically slammed her bamboo-handle Gucci bag on the table. I gawked. The design was brand new, and this was the first time I'd seen one up close. "Can you imagine the nerve," she said as she plucked her black gloves off one finger at a time. "Oh, sorry, Fran. How lovely to see you." She leaned over and pecked me on the cheek.

"Who was that?" I said just as the waiter arrived to ask if we wanted anything to drink.

"Martini, extra dirty," Peggy said. She looked at me. I held up a finger. "Two," she said, and the waiter scurried away. "Who was that? That was Jeremy fucking Bainbridge." I flinched a bit at her choice of adjectives. I still had no idea who he was. "If you haven't heard, he's the latest and greatest literary agent in the city—or more like the country if you ask him. According to the New York literati, he's the only agent worth working with. He represents all the bestselling authors. And, " she continued as the waiter set Peggy's martini down in front of her—she raised it to her lips and inhaled, "to add insult to injury, he refuses to represent women. He says they can't get inside men's heads, so no one wants to read their work. He's one of those men with a housewife to do his bidding every day, and he never wants anything to upset that applecart. What I wouldn't give to show him your accounts from the past few years."

I patted her hand. "Of course, you don't plan to do that, do you, Peggy?"

She suddenly deflated. "Of course not. You know I wouldn't do that to you. You still don't want to be outed, do you? Just imagine the publicity, though, for all those smug men to find out that they've been reading a female writer for all those years. Dear god, they'd pee themselves." She laughed.

I laughed along with her. "So, what's really bothering you, my friend?" I said. "You've never been disturbed by these kinds of perceptions before."

"Oh, Fran, just look at us. I'm going to be sixty-four years old this year, and what are you? Sixty?"

"I turned sixty-five earlier this year, Peggy."

Peggy stared at me. "Really? Well, it's all right for a writer, you know. You can write until you drop dead at ninety if you want. But I'll have to retire next year."

I felt the cold fingers of fear run up my spine. I couldn't keep on writing if I didn't have Peggy here in my corner. "Why? You run your own business. No one is going to force you to stop."

"Didn't I tell you? I have a new partner. At least he will be a partner soon. Remember Leonard?" She sipped her drink and waved at the waiter to bring two more. I wasn't sure I could manage another, but I didn't stop her. "Leonard, who I never thought would be anything more than my assistant."

I suddenly remembered how surprised I'd been the first time I'd met Peggy when I saw that her assistant was a young man.

"Well, he went off to work as an editor for *Simon and Schuster* for a couple of years, then started doing freelance agenting. It seems his business has grown immensely, and now he wants to buy the *Priestley & Benjamin Literary Agency*."

"Well, Peggy, he did have a great teacher in the business. You should be proud."

"Proud? I should be proud to know that I'm obsolete? A fossil?"

I just shook my head. "Peggy, I expect to continue to have you as my agent well into my dotage. Promise me you'll stay."

"You may be my only client," she said. Then she smiled. "Maybe that wouldn't be so bad!"

When she had finally recovered from her trip down the road to senility, we turned to other subjects. I asked her if she'd seen anything of Alfred and Caroline Chang lately. Peggy and I had become quite good friends with them when Alfred was at the Parsons School and later when he worked as an assistant designer for Claire McCardell, the sportswear queen.

"My god, Fran, haven't you heard? Alfred has his own atelier—in Toronto, of all places! He's done quite well, you know."

Then I remembered that Alfred was a Canadian. He'd returned home. I'd seen his designs in *Vogue* magazine in recent years, but I'd just assumed he was still in New York. "What about Caroline? Is she still modelling?"

Peggy waved me off. "They're old, too, you know. Not as old as we are, but they've grown up. They have a couple of kids. I think one of them is almost old enough for college."

Old. Were we really that old? Then I remembered reading my friend Simone's take on ageing. She said, "Old age is better for women than for men…they have less far to fall since their lives are more mediocre than those of most men." I truly wanted to be a woman who had far to fall.

"Are you in touch with them, Peggy?"

"In touch with whom?"

"Alfred and Caroline Chang."

"Oh, yes. Caroline and I talk from time to time. She's considering writing a book about her life as a model in Paris. I think it might be popular. What do you think?"

I told her I thought that could be interesting to readers and asked Peggy for Caroline's telephone number. I thought that I'd love to chat with her after all this time. Peggy wrote the number down on a napkin, and I tucked it into my handbag.

My lunch with Peggy had certainly not invigorated me as I had hoped. Her dour feelings about being an ageing woman were somewhat deflating, but they did give me much to think about. After we parted ways after lunch, I wandered down Fifth Avenue, gazing in shop windows and people-watching. As a writer, I often found myself watching and even eavesdropping on people. I guess I was a student of humanity, and much of that material often ended up in my books. That day, I was considering the current decade.

The windows were full of new mod styles, none of which seemed remotely appropriate for a woman of a certain age. I walked into Saks and was immediately assailed by a tableau of ten mannequins, all wearing the latest British designer, Mary Quant. As I stood there staring, I realized that Peggy was right—to a degree. There was so much about the world that was no longer part of our lives.

The dresses on the mannequins were bright, androgynous and very, very short. I remembered Kat showing me some recent sketches, and it occurred to me that her designs resembled this aesthetic quite closely. Yes, the dresses would look fabulous on my nineteen-year-old granddaughter. They assuredly would not look good on me. I had to accept that, despite not being quite ready to do so.

I meandered to the third floor of Saks and aimlessly wandered among the racks of brightly coloured clothing. As I turned to go back downstairs, my eye caught a section in the far corner of the store where the dresses on the mannequins were different somehow. I drifted over to take a closer look.

As I stood in front of three mannequins on a raised platform, I noticed the small, tasteful placard noting that these were also designs from Britain, but these were by Jean Muir. The placard also had a quote, presumably from the designer herself. It said, "The clothes in themselves do not make a statement. The woman makes the statement, and the dress helps." *Yes*, I thought, *it is, indeed, the woman who must make the statement, regardless of her age or station in life*. I realized that at that moment, I wasn't ready to accept that I was moving into the final act of my life. I still had Kat to oversee.

I reached out to touch the fabric of the green dress on the right. It melted through my hand like liquid. The lavender gown in the middle of the display was the same. My hand paused just as I was about to touch the fabric of the black dress on the left. I was struck by its square neckline and long, narrow sleeves with cuffs that hung languidly over the mannequin's hands. The fitted bodice gave way to a wide skirt that draped beautifully, ending just at the top of the calf. I had to have it. I had no idea where to wear such a dress, but I wasn't leaving that store without that dress.

Two days later, as I waited at La Guardia for my flight back to Toronto and then on to Halifax, I walked into a bookstore to find a book to read on the airplane. (I had discovered that I loved to fly, although living on the east coast of Canada meant that every time I wanted to go anywhere, I had to connect through either Toronto or Montreal.) I wandered up and down the aisles, my eyes finally falling on a translation of Simone's book, *The Second Sex*. I picked it up and looked at the back. Odd, I thought, the original was in two volumes. As I read the cover copy, I realized that much about her work wasn't deemed appropriate for the North American audience. What a pity that women and men everywhere couldn't access her remarkable work in its complete state. I felt honoured to have my original signed by the author, no less. I put it back on the shelf and ran my finger down the spines of the books surrounding it.

Betty Friedan was the author of the one I pulled next. I opened a page a began to read. "Aging [sic] is not lost youth but a new stage of opportunity and strength." I held the book tightly as I made my way to the cash register to pay for it—this was just what I needed. Indeed, a new stage was beginning.

~

Kat began writing to me from university almost the second she arrived. She told me stories about her dormitory house and her roommate Darla. When I received her letter telling me Darla had asked her to make one of her designs for her for a formal dance, I was ecstatic. Kat might have been studying to be a high school English and history teacher, but she had not lost her enthusiasm for her art. I would bide my time.

I kept busy throughout the fall, making notes for new books and looked forward to hearing all about Toronto when Kat came home for Christmas. I hadn't spent much time in that city, but it had made an impression on me all those years ago with Sam.

Finally, it was Christmas Eve. As I sat at my dressing table mindlessly spraying my *Shalimar* behind my ears and at the base of my throat, I was thinking about Kat and her dreams. I was wondering how the big city and university life might be changing her. I finished putting on my lipstick. I had always loved lipstick and had been wearing Chanel on my lips since she first launched it in Paris in 1924 when I had to have everything new. But it still had pride of place on my makeup table.

I heard the cab pull up in front of the house. I reached for my handbag (another New York acquisition—Chanel) and raced down the stairs to grab my coat from the closet while picking up my large pink and ivory floral carpetbag that held Christmas presents. I smiled when I thought about Kat's gift.

The cab dropped me in front of James and Betty's house ten minutes later. I stood for a moment and looked up the walkway toward the front door. James might not have been the son I hoped for—if I ever hoped for a son, which, to be honest, I never had—but he and his wife had kept the house in good condition. It even looked cheerful with its Christmas lights festooning the porch, and cheerful had never been a word I would have used to describe either James or Betty.

Betty answered the door, and I was just checking my lipstick in the mirror and thinking that I was delighted to share my love of lipstick with my granddaughter even if her father disapproved when I could hear familiar footsteps flying down the stairs. I was immediately enveloped in a bear hug.

"Nan! It is so wonderful to see you!" Kat pushed her face deep into my neck. "And you still smell as wonderful as ever. Maybe someday you'll tell me what that magic elixir is!"

Kat led me into the living room, where I placed my gifts under the tree. I knew that they would already have opened most of their presents this morning, after which James had dragged them all off to church. I had no idea where his sudden interest in religion had come from, but I found it off-putting. He seemed to have chosen some kind of fundamentalist Christian religion that was against almost everything except drinking (thank god for that). Mostly, they seemed to oppose any type of activity that made women equal to men. We had already had one too many arguments about it, and I wasn't about to ruin Christmas with yet another.

Once Kat had helped me place the presents under the tree to be opened after James passed out the drinks, I reached for a small box that I'd wrapped myself. It was for Kat—a little something I'd picked up when I'd been in New York. I didn't tell her that. *Let her think I'm a regular grandmother, staying at home, drinking tea and playing bridge*, I thought. *At least for now.*

"Kat, darling," I said, passing the brightly wrapped box to her. "This is for you to open right away. You are now ready for it." My nose started twitching, and even without looking, I knew James had walked into the room. "Really, James," I said, holding my hand over my nose, "For god's sake, stop smoking in the house. The smell is repulsive." Despite my attempts to appear worldly when I was in

Paris, I had never been much of a smoker myself and never did really get used to the smell.

He shrugged, took another long drag, then stubbed it out in the hideous turquoise ceramic ashtray on the coffee table. I leaned down to move it as far away from me as possible. I looked over at Kat, who was trying to take the paper off the package without ripping it, no doubt because of recent admonishments from her parents, who insisted on saving every scrap. She finally had it open and was looking at the little bottle sitting in its gold satin nest.

"Do you know what it is?" I said.

"Well, it's perfume, for sure." Kat gently picked up the flask filled with amber liquid.

"Of course, but to you *know* it?" She continued to look at the bottle. "I've been wearing it since I was twenty-five years old in Paris. You know, I had the pleasure of meeting Jacques Guerlain back then, just when he created it."

Kat's eyes widened. "You met Jacques Guerlain, the famous designer, in Paris? Oh, Nan, *Shalimar*! So that's what you've been wearing all these years!"

James sat down. "I don't think it's the kind of scent a young woman ought to be wearing, Mother."

I sat back and looked at him, daring him to persist. "Oh, and why is that, James?"

"It has a reputation."

"A perfume has a reputation? For what?"

"Luring men."

All I could do was laugh. Imagine a perfume to lure men. *Well*, I thought, *perhaps it does at that*! Every time Kat returned home after that, I could smell the exotic, woody scent on her.

As I readied myself to return home later that evening, I hugged Kat tight and whispered in her ear, "Darling, I know becoming a teacher isn't your dream, but you must remember that your life can take so many different paths. I know this from experience."

Kat pulled back for a moment. "Nan, promise me that you'll tell me about your experiences some time."

I hugged her again. "Think about your dreams, Kat, and never let anyone take them away from you."

I had never let anyone snatch mine. And no one would squash Kat's, not even her father. I would see to it.

THIRTY-THREE

"Women may be the one group that grows more radical with age."
~ Gloria Steinem

APART FROM THE COPIOUS NOTES I'D BEEN MAKING in my journals, I hadn't written much of anything for almost a year. I was deathly afraid that my ideas had dried up as I aged out of the kind of literature I'd been so passionate about for so much of my adult life. I had ideas, but none of them seemed to take shape. *Perhaps older women shouldn't be writing such risqué novels*, I thought several times as I sat at my desk without a scintilla of an idea of what to write about. Instead, I was spending more of my time sewing and tending my garden, and even—dare I admit it? —playing bridge with a group of widows enjoying the spoils of their late husbands' careers. In the middle of May, Christophe called from Paris. Unlike Peggy, who despaired of being able to work beyond age sixty-five, Jean-Christophe Lemieux, now the proprietor of one of the major publishing powerhouses in France, was starting a new era in his career.

"Frannie, *ma chérie*, have you read it? Have you ever seen such utter rubbish? Oh, you must start writing again. You can do so much better than this."

It seemed that he was wound up about a new book that had just reached number one on the *New York Times* bestseller list. It was called *Valley of the Dolls*, and Christophe believed I could give this Susann woman a run for her money.

"And have you seen the reviews?"

I had not, so Christophe embarked on fixing that omission. He began reading them to me. It seemed that *Publisher's Weekly* had called it "big, brilliant and sensational...if poorly written." Even Gloria

Steinem, a rising feminist activist, had written a scathing review in the *New York Herald Tribune*—I listened to him read her words.

"And that *Time* magazine," he said, "they have dubbed it the 'Dirty Book of the Month.' Imagine! It should be your book. You are the better writer."

By the time he had finished, I was laughing. I told him I'd find a copy and read it, and then I'd get back to him about a new novel. It was the only way to get him to stop talking about it.

I eventually did read the book and had to agree with the reviewers. Yet, there was an appetite for this kind of writing. That much was clear to me six months later when *Valley of the Dolls* had stayed number one on the *New York Times* bestseller list for twenty-eight weeks. I sat down at my desk, and the characters began talking to me again. I was back.

~

I spent most of the rest of that year working on my new novel. It was to be a *tour de force*—at least that was what Christophe hoped for—and so did I. Sometimes, though, as I sat watching the television news in the evenings, I had misgivings about the direction my life had taken—about the seeming triviality of the work I did. These qualms lasted for only a short time as I watched the horrific images of the Vietnam war and the American race riots fill the tiny screen. I sometimes wondered how I could have allowed my life to remain so superficial when so much deeply disturbing human activity filled the world. Even my old friend Simone was doing her part to ensure that the lives of women like Kat and her daughters would be all that they could be. And here was I, creating pornographic literature for its entertainment value. Then I'd consider how many women read my books, and it occurred to me that I might be playing a part in liberating women from the bonds of tradition. Yes, I liked that idea.

I was still hard at work on the new book when Kat arrived home for the summer. I could see, in so many small ways, that she was growing up. Her view of the world seemed to be expanding. I could hear it in her voice when she told me about how much she loved exploring the big city on her own (a fact she didn't share with her parents), working on Saturdays at a fabric store, going to coffee houses to hear folk singers in the Yorkville area of Toronto. I was almost jealous of that last one. I felt a bit nostalgic for my youth, remembering how it felt to be free of one's parents at last. My darling granddaughter was becoming a woman of the world.

As I sat with her on several Sunday afternoons in the back garden of her parent's house, Kat opened up to me about her mounting frustrations.

"The only time I'm really happy, Nan," she said, "is when I'm designing or sewing. I dread the thought of spending my life as a high school teacher. But I guess I have no choice."

As I sat there, sipping my cocktail, something seemed to shatter inside me. How could I let my son be the obstacle to his own daughter's dreams? How could I just sit there and watch a sublime talent wither away? I could not, and I would not.

Kat returned to school, and I finished my manuscript, which Christophe proclaimed to be my best one yet. It was called *La vie du désir, The Life of Desire,* and along with Peggy, we had decided that it would have more cachet if it made its debut in French for the more open-minded European readers. It would launch in the spring of 1967 in Paris, then later in New York. Peggy began shopping the film rights the minute I typed "The End" onto the final draft, hoping that she could persuade an up-and-coming movie star named Jane Fonda to play the role of Monique, the temptress. The very thought made me giggle like a young girl. And that made me think of Kat.

My granddaughter was a talented designer, of that there was no doubt. I felt I had something of an eye for this kind of talent after the years I had spent in Paris—an experience that I knew I ought to share with Kat, but something made me want to keep it a secret for the time being. I had felt her deep frustration with the direction of her life and knew that I had the wherewithal at least to give her the chance she deserved.

The week after Kat had left to return to school, I opened the double doors to one of my walk-in closets. It was the one that held my handbags, shoes and hats. I stood there looking around at the array of items that seemed to catalogue periods of my life. I wasn't what I would call a hoarder, but there were certain items from my life that I had kept through the years partly because they had been expensive and represented the design work of so many now-famous designers. Mostly, though, I kept them because they represented the layers of my life. They were like onion skins that continued to grow, layer upon layer. I hoped that someday my granddaughter would have fun peeling away those layers. But I wasn't standing here to reminisce. I was looking for a specific handbag—the one I'd been carrying when I'd last seen Peggy for lunch in New York. I found it tucked away on a shelf alongside the Chanel 2.55 quilted bag I'd bought when I was there.

I lifted it down from the shelf and rooted around inside. Yes! It was still there. I pulled the wrinkled napkin out of the bag, placed the bag back on the shelf and walked out into my bedroom. I smoothed the napkin out on my vanity table. Yes, the number was still visible.

I took the napkin into my office and sat down at my desk. I picked up the phone and dialled the number on the napkin.

"Hello? Caroline? It's Fran. Fran Phillips."

Five minutes later, I had Alfred Chang's office telephone number. After Caroline and I hung up, I immediately dialled Alfred's office. After explaining my identity to several people and waiting a few minutes, finally, Alfred was on the line.

"Fran Phillips, this is a wonderful surprise. I always love to hear from connoisseurs of fashion from my Paris and New York days. What can I do for you?"

And I told him. Between the two of us, we made a plan. Alfred's daughter, Abbie, a freshman at the University of Toronto, would be tasked with finding Kat on campus and ensuring that Alfred saw her sketches. Alfred would look at them and decide if they were worthy of encouraging her to apply to his alma mater, the Parsons School, where he still held some sway.

"I still mentor a few students each year," he said, "but my friend Simon, an up-and-coming superstar, is on the admissions committee. If she's good enough, I can help with getting her an interview. But the bottom line is that she has to be able to compete. She does have to be that good, Fran."

"Oh, she is, Alfred. Trust me. In any case, that is appropriate. You can open a door—Kat must be able to walk through on her own."

So, we had a deal.

~

I finished my manuscript and sent it off to the capable hands of my French editor—the one who worked for Christophe. Then I got ready for Christmas.

When Kat arrived home, she immediately telephoned me to tell me some news she didn't plan on sharing with her parents. She had received a letter from a famous fashion designer whose daughter, as it turned out, was a first-year student at the University of Toronto and lived in Kat's dorm house. His daughter had taken a few of Kat's sketches to him, and he was impressed. He would pave the way for her to have a portfolio review at the Parsons School in New York. Now, Kat was frantic about that portfolio. I was ecstatic. Alfred had been true to his word.

Throughout the Christmas break, I was conscripted into distraction mode to keep James and Betty from wondering too much about what Kat was up to as she spent hours at a time holed up in her room. I was sworn to secrecy about her work. I saw no reason why her parents needed to know anything at this stage. Later might be a different story.

Before she left to return for the winter semester at the U. of T., she showed me her portfolio. It was impressive, as I expected it to be. Thus, I wasn't surprised when she called me in April to announce that the Parsons School had invited her to an interview. But she had to find a way to get to New York. I bit my tongue before offering to set her up with Peggy, a relationship Kat knew nothing about. If I were to take her into my confidence at this point, it would completely distract her from her own life and her own dreams. It wouldn't be right. So, I said only that she would find a way. And she did.

I was never prouder than the day she telephoned her grandmother to tell her that the Parsons School had accepted her into their fashion design program, and she would be able to follow her dream. If only it were that easy, though. She still had to pay for it. I could not let this go. I immediately wondered if Parsons would accept a generous gift and set about finding out. Of course, they were only too happy to do so. Two weeks later, Kat telephoned from Toronto to tell me she had won a full scholarship and was going to study in New York—even over her father's strenuous objections. That made me smile.

My darling granddaughter went off to pursue her dream, and it seemed that her father, my son, might finally be evolving into a more accepting human. I was wrong.

THIRTY-FOUR

"There is nothing more frightful than ignorance in action."
~ Johann Wolfgang von Goethe

IN THE FALL OF 1967, KAT SENT THE FIRST OF MANY LETTERS from New York. She told me about her new roommates, her classes, a certain designer named Simon Carmichael with whom she hoped to work, and she told me about her new boyfriend. When we talked a few weeks later, I could hear something different in her voice when she mentioned his name. Chuck, Charles Cohen. I had never heard that before in her voice, and I knew, in a moment, that my darling granddaughter was in love. The more she talked about him, the more I began to think that I may never have experienced true love. I had thought I found that with Sam, but now I wondered.

When she came home for Christmas, she didn't mention a thing about her boyfriend to her parents, at least in my presence. When I asked her about it, she simply said she didn't want to be subjected to the third degree from her father. So, we left it at that. However, I dropped my own bomb on her. I told her I planned to spend my sixty-eighth birthday at the beginning of February in New York. She seemed pleased.

I had an agenda for this trip. First, I had to see Peggy. Second, I let Christophe know that I'd be in New York, and he immediately made plans to be there at the same time. Finally, I had to meet this Charles Cohen.

I arrived in New York two days before my birthday and spent the first day meeting with Peggy and doing much-needed shopping. As I stood in the lobby of the Plaza Hotel, waiting for Kat to arrive for lunch, I was thinking about how much my life had changed. I used to be at the centre of life, or so it seemed. Now, I was a small-town grandmother. Oh yes, I was still a writer—a famous unknown one if that were even possible—but my life was becoming ever more circumscribed, and I wasn't even seventy years old. I might have to do something about that. Then I remembered that Christophe would be waiting for me in my suite by the end of the day, and I looked forward to our coming tryst. Perhaps my life did still have some excitement and glamour, after all!

I spotted Kat as she walked slowly in through the door as the bellman held it open for her. As I watched her looking around, it occurred to me that she probably had never been here before. Then she saw me, and a smile broke across her lovely face.

We checked our coats, and as she handed hers to the coat check attendant and smoothed her dress, I noticed how stunning it was.

"Kat, where did you get that wonderful dress?"

She did a little twirl for me. "Do you really like it? I made it!"

Of course, she had made it. Although I had tried back so many years ago, Kat had much better skills in that arena than I ever had. I now hoped that I wasn't living vicariously through my granddaughter, supporting her pursuit of a design career—perhaps the career that had eluded me. That would not be good for either of us.

We spent the next hour and a half in the Palm Court among the ladies who lunch in their pearls and gloves getting caught up. She told me all the news from school and how much she loved the city. Then she told me about her budding friendship with a classmate named Suzanne.

"Nan, I really think we could be such good friends. I like her a lot, but we come from such different worlds. She seems to find it more of a problem than I do. I always seem to be saying the wrong thing."

"We all have such different experiences of the world, Kat. What makes Suzanne's world so different from yours?"

I noticed Kat hesitate for a moment before answering as if she might be trying to figure out how to say something. "Actually, she's black, Nan," she said finally.

"Well, then, she does come from a different world." I thought back to my few days with Elliott all those years ago and how our two worlds had collided. I started to open my mouth to tell Kat about my experience, but to do that, I'd have to tell her who her grandfather really was. Doing so would shatter the deep trust we had, but the story was more than germane to the conversation at hand. Instead, I steered the conversation toward the fact that Kat indeed needed to learn something about the world outside her hometown, where the bigotry wasn't daily news. Instead, it simmered just beneath the surface, always there, hidden from view, always threatening. I then tried to offer her a piece of advice.

"I cannot take credit for it, but it's worth considering. Dr. Martin Luther King once said, 'Shallow understanding from people of goodwill is more frustrating than absolute understanding from people of ill will.' Suzanne will know if your apparent understanding is shallow. Try to deepen your understanding." I drained my coffee cup just as the pastry cart came by. I selected two pastel-coloured macarons—one pink, the other mint green— and Kat took a cream puff as the waiter poured more coffee. "Now then, Kat, tell me just a bit about that Charles of yours."

The moment I mentioned his name, I could tell that my granddaughter was in love for the first time in her life. Her eyes lit up so, and she began to radiate a kind of aura. You could almost touch it. It almost made me dizzy just to see it.

"Oh, Nan, I've never met anyone like him. He's wonderful."

We decided that she shouldn't tell me much about him so I could draw my own conclusions, but Kat assured me I'd love him. I hoped she was right.

Just before I asked the waiter for the bill, Kat put her elbows on the table, clasped her hands and leaned her chin on them. "Nan, tell me something. You've been here in the Palm Court before, haven't you?" I nodded but said nothing. "Nan, when are you going to tell me about your life and why you seem to know New York so well?"

"Kat, darling, you know all about it."

"No, Nan, I don't, and I know Dad doesn't, either. I've always had a feeling you've had a life—a big life—that came before me. Why do you never talk about it?"

I reached for her hand and held it across the table. "I promise you this, darling granddaughter. One day, my life will become an open book to you. Just not yet." Then I turned to the waiter who had returned and paid the bill.

And so, we made plans for Charles to join us for my birthday dinner the following evening. Then we went shopping.

~

Later that day, after I put Kat in a cab at the front door of the Plaza after helping her with the bags and boxes of clothes and shoes I'd bought for her, I rode the elevator up to my suite. Just as he had promised, Christophe had arrived from Paris and was about to uncork a bottle of champagne. I could see that it was *Veuve Clicquot*, my very favourite.

"We have much to celebrate, *chérie*," he said as he expertly removed the cork with no more than a whimper from it. He then poured two coupes and offered me one.

"And how will we do that, Christophe?"

He raised his eyebrows and nodded toward the bedroom. Even at this advanced age, we still hadn't lost our connection. I drained my coupe and took his hand.

~

On Friday evening, I met Kat and Charles—Chuck—at what Christophe considered the best French restaurant in New York on East 50th Street. *Lutèce* had been open for only seven or so years, but it had already garnered a reputation as the place for French cuisine in America.

I arrived at the restaurant early and sat near the ornate fireplace under a sparkling chandelier enjoying the fire when I began to worry that this might be too grand or too European for a Brooklyn native who was a photography student at the Parsons School. After all, he was an artist, but it seemed to me that artists didn't have to enjoy starving, did they? I shrugged (to myself) and asked the waiter for a glass of Sancerre while I waited. I was enjoying my first few sips when Kat and her young man arrived.

I beckoned them over and stood up so that I could properly greet both of them. After hugging Kat, I turned to Charles, who reached out to shake my hand.

"Chuck Cohen. I'm delighted to meet you, Mrs. Phillips."

It was often odd to hear myself referred to as Mrs. Phillips. I had never used Sam's last name, and I wasn't "Mrs." anything, but it worked for me. I shook Chuck's hand firmly then stood back to have a closer look. He was just as handsome as Kat had said. However, she had not mentioned how dark and dreamy his eyes were in that extraordinary face with its smooth, dark skin framed by a wild mop of curly black hair. It wasn't only Suzanne who came from a different world than Kat did. I looked carefully then enveloped him in my arms for a hug. "I'm so happy to meet you, Chuck. Call me Fran."

I loved him from the first moment after I said, "Tell me about your family." And he did. The next day, when I talked to Kat, I realized the depth of her love and her fear. She wanted to take him home to meet her parents, which seemed the most natural thing in the world to me. But she was terrified, and she had good reason to be scared as far as I was concerned. After all, her father—my son—was among those bigots in the small city Kat called home, who harboured that simmering distrust of anything and anyone different. His prejudice needed only the right ignition to erupt. Chuck just might prove to be the spark to detonate the explosion.

~

The following summer, Kat finally brought her Chuck home to visit. Kat and I arranged for Chuck to stay with me, and I was delighted because I found him to be an excellent companion full of new ideas and the kind of zest for life held only by those with their whole lives still ahead of them. I also wanted to be there with Kat when James and Betty met Chuck for the first time.

The encounter was an unmitigated disaster. Chuck was polite, respectful, charming. But all hell broke loose the moment James said, "Well, *boy*, tell me about your intentions."

Chuck seemed unperturbed, but I flew into a rage. All the pent-up feelings I'd had, keeping Elliott's family identity a secret from his narrow-minded son through the years, suddenly erupted. I told James, in no uncertain terms, to stop his boorish behaviour. Then he dared to ask Chuck what his parents thought of Kat since she wasn't what James called "their kind."

"And precisely what does that mean, James?" I said, my teeth firmly clenched. "Proceed with caution."

"Well, you're Jews, aren't you?" he said to Chuck.

I got up and told everyone the evening was over. I took Chuck by the arm, and we departed.

When we arrived back at my house (Kat had stayed behind to try to set her father straight), I began apologizing to Chuck.

"I should have warned you about my son," I said. "I wish I could tell you that his behaviour was out of character, but the truth is that you saw the real thing this evening."

"Fran," Chuck said, looking at me kindly from the depths of those incredible eyes, "I've heard worse. And if it's any comfort, Kat did warn me."

Kat never brought Chuck home to Halifax again.

The St. Laurent

Sage

THIRTY-FIVE

WHEN MY BOOK, *LIFE OF DESIRE*, WAS FINALLY MADE into a Hollywood film starring the lesser-known actress, Barbara Bates, it was a box-office smash. I had nixed the idea of Jane Fonda since she was far too young to play a forty-something seductress. Miss Bates, whose previous credits had been smaller parts in a variety of movies, was perfection. In her early forties, with her lithe ballet-trained body, she played the character I had written with guile and a sub-text of the erotic. When I saw the film for the first time, her performance made me shiver. What I did not know at the time was that her off-screen life was unravelling. When I heard the news of her suicide not long after, I dropped to the floor and wept.

I remembered when she had first appeared on the screen. I was sitting in the middle of the theatre between Peggy and Christophe, wearing my new St. Laurent caftan-style velvet gown, which draped elegantly around me as befits a woman of a certain age—at least in my mind. This was the first time I'd ventured to a movie premiere, and it was fascinating to overhear the glittering crowd as they discussed all manner of trivia about their lives—where they had vacationed, who was seeing whom, how their children were doing (marvellously, if you must know). Then Barbara appeared. The costume designer had outdone herself. Draped in a filmy, silk Grecian-style dress, she moved across the screen with feline grace, luring in unsuspecting men one after the other. I couldn't take my eyes off her.

"You're going to make a fortune on this one," Peggy whispered fifteen minutes into the film.

The truth was that I didn't need a fortune—I already had one.

Christophe leaned closer from the other side. "You have arrived, Frannie. Welcome to posterity."

I laughed. Frannie Phillips might have written the novel, but, as the credits proclaimed, the screenplay was adapted from a novel by Peyton Winter. Mr./Miss Winter (no one knew even now) would enter the hallowed halls of posterity. When I realized that it didn't matter, I knew I had arrived at where I was supposed to be in my life.

~

In the summer of 1969, just six months shy of my seventieth birthday, I believe I truly began to feel as if I might have been born in the wrong era. How wonderful it would have been to be just beginning young adulthood then! I watched the moon landing in July and could only wonder at the extraordinary things that were to come in this world. It was as if I could see into the future, and that future was filled with innovations. I had read a recent magazine article about microwave ovens that could cook an egg in mere seconds, and I looked forward to the time (which I felt was coming) when every household—including mine—would have one in the kitchen. Just imagine the possibilities!

I was a news aficionado, a habit I think stemmed from my too-brief time with Sam, who was passionate about newspapers and journalism, as you can imagine. I had been reading the *New York Times* for years, and since it wasn't available where I lived in Canada, I had a local newsstand order it in for me. The only downside was that I read all my news two days late since it took that long to get here.

On a Tuesday morning in late August—August nineteenth to be precise—I opened my two-day-old copy of the *Times*, which my housekeeper Marilyn had left alongside my breakfast place setting. The headline story with the photograph at the top of the page was, "Tired Rock Fans Begin Exodus." The picture below was of masses of bedraggled but apparently happy young people making their way out of a farmer's field somewhere in upstate New York after a weekend-long music festival. Then I remembered Kat telling me that she and Chuck and two friends from here in Halifax were planning to attend something called the Woodstock Art and Music Fair. I wondered if this had been the same event.

I poured myself a cup of coffee and settled back in my chair in the dappled summer sunshine as it found its way through the rustling leaves of the trees just outside the window. According to the article, they were, indeed, departing the Woodstock Music and Art Fair, during which "security officials reported at least two deaths and 4,000 people treated for injuries, illness and adverse drug reactions over the festival's three-day period." Injuries and illnesses? Drugs? That didn't sound one bit like Kat's scene to me. But when I read about the musicians who had played, I put the newspaper down and sat back, wondering what it would have been like to be there. Despite my life that had been spent almost entirely in the lap of luxury, as they say, there was something about all that freedom, even amid a muddy field, that spoke to a part of me long buried deep inside. Although, one does have to wonder if my choice of genre in my writing might not have been a bit about that side of me. Perhaps I hadn't missed out on things as much as I thought.

Eventually, Kat did confirm that she and Chuck had been there and that it had been something of a watershed moment for her generation and perhaps even for her—at least, that's how she saw it. But she was so busy with her second-year design projects that she didn't have much time for me that semester.

I ate Sunday dinner with James and Betty once or twice a month. James had just sat down to his roast beef on one such Sunday when he began talking about Kat.

"Mother, have you noticed that Kat has changed?"

I put my fork down and looked at him. "Well, of course, she has, James. After all, her world has expanded so much over the past few years."

"You say that as if it's a good thing," he said, gulping his wine, a habit I had always detested.

"I *do* think it's a good thing. Even you had the benefit of living in another country."

"That was very different, Mother, and you know it. I was young, and I was a boy. And, that other country was England, not that den of iniquity that calls itself America."

I rolled my eyes. "What does being a boy have to do with any of this?"

"If you must know, we still expect her to come home to marry and have children."

"You mean your grandchildren, don't you?" I was getting far angrier than one ought to be.

"Fran, you know how nice it would be to have her here," Betty said quietly. "She isn't even coming home for Christmas this year." Betty rarely contributed to these kinds of conversations. I didn't blame her. You could never be sure how James would react.

"Of course, Betty," I said, "but as nice as it would be for her to be near to all of us, it is far more important that she has a life of her own."

Although I passionately believed every word I was saying, at the same time, I worried that Kat was losing herself to Chuck and the world he envisioned for himself. I loved Chuck, but there was little doubt he had a kind of power over her that wasn't conscious on Chuck's part but had a very real impact on how Kat made her decisions. James and I left our discussion of Kat's life at that, so when Kat called me in November in a frenzy of worry to tell me that Chuck and a friend had enlisted and were on their way to Vietnam, a cold dread descended over me like the icy mantle of an avalanche you don't know if you—or your companions—will survive.

Regardless of what happened to Chuck in Vietnam, I firmly believed that his experiences would forever change him. I feared that Kat might not realize this. I remembered listening to Elliott as he told me about the horrors of war he had experienced and how he would never see the world the same again. I remember sitting beside him in bed and feeling him shiver at the remembrance. Even then, I knew he was telling me an edited version of his experience. There seemed to be an unspoken rule among soldiers to keep their truest stories of their experiences buried deep inside. I felt strongly that if all those buried experiences and emotions ever bubble to the top, the reality would be so terrifying it might end war forever. But I knew that was not to be.

It wasn't long after Kat had called me to tell me that Chuck was now "upcountry" in some unknown reaches of an unknown land that the unthinkable happened. A little more than a week after my seventieth birthday, my worst fears were realized.

Before Chuck left for Vietnam, he had asked Kat to plan their wedding. She had made a few plans and had even cut out the pattern for her wedding gown. I knew these things. There was, however, something I didn't know.

"He never knew," Kat sobbed into the phone. "I never told him. How could I let someone die without telling him everything? I just want to die."

I was concerned about two matters: what it was she hadn't told him and, perhaps even more worrying, the fact she had just said she wanted to die. With that, all my fears about Kat losing herself to Chuck came back to me, and the icy fingers of the avalanche landed on my head.

"What didn't you tell him, Kat, darling?"

She just kept repeating, "I didn't tell him. I didn't tell him." And she sobbed hysterically. I let her cry and just stayed there on the other end of the phone, hoping she might calm down so that we could talk. Finally, she did.

"I don't know what to do, Nan. I'm all alone."

"You are not all alone. I am here. Your parents are here."

"My parents. Really, Nan? How do you think they're going to feel when I tell them I'm having Chuck's baby?"

And, there it was. Kat's bombshell. The thing she never had a chance to tell Chuck. I also knew exactly how James would react. He'd be furious that his child was bringing such shame on him by having a baby "out-of-wedlock." I'd heard him decry enough other unfortunate young women to be sure of that. I couldn't help but feel a more profound kinship with my granddaughter at that moment.

I was not wrong about James, but she was, after all, his daughter. So, he and Betty welcomed Kat home. Much to my regret (and I wondered about the cause of my disappointment), Kat left school without her degree, came home and holed up like a hermit. One thing led to another at home with her parents, who insisted she arrange to put the baby up for adoption (I wasn't entirely unsympathetic to their preference) to the point that she moved in with me to wait out her pregnancy. However, I agreed to have Kat come to stay with me on one condition—that condition was that she return to school in the fall after the birth, no matter what. She could complete her teaching degree here and at least have some kind of future. She agreed and was accepted into Dalhousie University here in the city with no problem at all. My heart ached for the loss of her dream.

As the fates would have it, the day the baby was born, I was not home. James and Betty took Kat to the hospital, and by the time I arrived several hours later, I had missed the actual birth—not that I would have been any closer than the waiting room, in any case.

I arrived on the third floor outside the nursery to find James and Betty standing in the elevator lobby engaged in a heated discussion, possibly even what you might call an argument. In all the years I had known Betty, I had never before heard her stand up to her husband. I was proud of her, although I hadn't the slightest idea what they were arguing about.

"He's my grandson," she hissed. "*Our* grandson. None of this matters."

So, the baby was a boy. That much I now knew.

"Oh, but it does," James said, clenching his fists. "It matters a great deal."

"What the hell is going on here?" I said. They both turned to look at me. Neither one of them had noticed me.

They said nothing but simply pointed to the window through which the rows of baby bassinets were on display. The baby was wrapped tightly in a blue blanket, his dark fuzz of hair creating a halo around his skin's beautiful chocolate-latte colour. He was breathtakingly beautiful, as I should have expected he would be. Kat's situation had just become more complicated, if that were even possible.

"It's for her own good, Betty," James said quietly now. "I've made all the arrangements. It's done."

"Katherine will want this baby. I know her," Betty sobbed. "Or at least she would want to know he's out there."

"No," I said before I even thought through what I was saying. "James is right."

James snapped his head around to look at me. "What did you say, Mother?"

"I said you're right. We need to protect Kat and her future."

James nodded. Betty hung her head as tears streamed from her eyes.

"Leave Kat to me," I said.

~

When Kat awoke in her room later, I was there. I was sitting beside her, holding her hand.

"Where is he, Nan? I was so groggy, but I heard them say it was a boy. He should be here. Where is he?" She sat up and looked around the room frantically.

"I am so sorry, Kat darling. By the time I arrived, it was all over. They said he wasn't strong enough. They had taken him away."

I watched her face with mounting dread. What had I done? But I knew there was no going back. Surely, it was at least the wrong thing for the right reasons. I would have to live with my belief that, in this case, the end justified the means. I didn't know if I could ever make it right, but I would go to my grave trying.

THIRTY-SIX

*"It is not the strongest of the species that survive, not the most intelligent,
but the one most responsive to change."*
~ Charles Darwin

KAT WENT BACK TO SCHOOL, AND I WENT BACK TO WORK. But as time
wore on, I realized that I was spending too much time sitting at my
desk contemplating the unlived lives of the characters who populated
my mind. So, I'd take walks. I walked every inch of the five or six miles
surrounding my house, which took me to the edges of the city. Yet, I
was still restless.

I was sipping on a glass of wine one evening, clicking through the
channels. I had heard about fancy television sets with remote controls
that allowed you to sit on the sofa and press buttons to change those
channels, but I didn't watch enough television to pay those prices. It's
funny how people with unlimited money often think about small
purchases. Anyway, I had to go over the television set and click the
dial, go back to the sofa, take another sip of wine, see what was on that
station, then repeat the process until I happened upon something that
looked interesting. I was engaged in this process when the telephone
rang.

I left to answer it, and when I returned, I wasn't sure what I was
looking at on the screen. I turned up the volume and listened to the
soothing voice emanating from the tiny woman on the screen. She sat
on the floor, cross-legged, wearing something that looked like what I
remembered Kiki and her fellow ballerinas wearing for practice
sessions. It was fascinating. I poured myself more wine and sat on the
sofa, mesmerized.

The voice had a very slight European accent—German if I was correct—and it was so mellow, it triggered a kind of meditative state. I watched as she moved into various positions, stretching her limbs like no one I had ever seen.

The next day, I turned on the television to the same channel at the same time, and there she was again. Her soothing voice coaxed and charmed the viewers into sitting on the floor with her to stretch their legs or to stand up and bend over to this side, then to that side. Before I knew what was happening, I was doing it with her.

I had always prided myself in my appearance and my physical capabilities. This young woman, however, challenged me. After the first half-hour program, during which I actually followed her, mimicking her movements, I found myself with sore muscles everywhere. But I persisted. Two months later, Kareen Zebroff and I were friends—at least that's how it felt. I had been introduced to yoga.

Over the next few months, I sought her books and bought each one as it was released—*The ABC's of Yoga, Yoga and Beauty*. I loved every one of them. And I had never felt better in my life. It was just what I needed to keep me alive so that I could make things right with Kat.

The secret I carried weighed heavily on me—every day of my life.

~

"Want to make god laugh?" I had said to Kat on more than one occasion. "Tell her your plans." Over the next few years, I could almost hear god laughing—often at Kat's expense. She made plans; life happened. I did my best to support her in so many ways, and on the day she married the love of her life, David Hudson, I was there, sitting in the front row at some peculiar church to which James belonged, in my St. Laurent dress. It was 1976, and women were expected to sit in the audience even at weddings, never saying anything. Kat was different. I knew this from the first moment when she told me that she intended to have a "man of honour" rather than a "maid of honour." I thought this was very progressive, especially given her father's near-stroke when he heard about it. Even my old friend Simone would have been proud. The second nail in her father's coffin (of his own making, I might add) was when he found out Kat had asked me to speak. I was more than delighted.

The wedding took place on a beautiful, sunny Saturday afternoon in July. My choice of attire was ill-advised, given the weather, but I felt as if the St. Laurent dress was just the thing a crone ought to wear. I had turned seventy-six earlier in the year and was beginning to feel as if I had landed on another planet—the planet where everyone shuffles around, waiting for god, as it were. It made me shudder.

Kat, David, James and Betty, along with a hundred or so of their nearest and dearest, gathered once again, as we had done when James and Betty married, at the venerable Lord Nelson Hotel for a reception after the dour pastor had finally declared them to be "man and wife." I could almost feel Kat's neck bristle. She had told me that she had instructed the minister that it was to be "husband and wife." He seemed to have slipped up. Anyway, we were now gathered with drinks and canapés, and I was looking at my beautiful granddaughter in her exquisite wedding gown that she'd made herself. Then I looked at David Hudson, the man by her side. I liked David. He was a solid man, and Kat had lived quite a life before she found him at the age of thirty.

I liked to think I had a hand in the two of them finding one another. A few years ago, Kat had come into some money—not from me, and it's a rather long story. In any case, I was well acquainted with the vagaries of wealth management by that point (although neither Kat nor her parents knew exactly how acquainted I'd become). I'd had more than my share of financial counsellors, but I had happily settled upon one in my later years and had been more than happy with the results. So, when Kat asked, I set her up with my investment advisor. It happened that David Hudson was a new addition to my manager's firm. When Kat told me about him after her meeting, I could tell from something in her voice that this man was different from the others who had played roles in her life to that point. I also knew her secrets and recognized her fears about laying bare her soul to anyone. I, of all people, knew how that felt. But here they were, and it was clear that my granddaughter was making a good choice. My gaze moved on.

I looked at James, who seemed to be happy—or at least as happy as he ever managed to be. I knew, however, from what Kat had told me just after we all arrived at the reception, that her father was still not happy about her "man of honour." James was more set in his ways than anyone my age.

Then I looked around at the assembled guests and realized that I knew very few of them. I was mainly searching for one of Kat's oldest friends with whom she'd had a falling out, although she hadn't told me why. Liz was nowhere to be found. Having such a falling out between such good friends seemed sad to me. I hoped that Kat would find a way to move on from whatever caused the issue between them. God knows I had left a litter of people in my own past. At this age, I was simply happy to have Christophe and Peggy still, although there were many miles between us. I wondered if those miles truly mattered when it came to long-standing friendships.

I was alone here, though, or so it seemed. I had made my choices—I had created my life. I was struck once again by the realization that so many people continued to search for themselves. It was a theme of the 1960s and was still a theme as we moved toward the end of the 1970s. I wondered if people would still be looking for themselves by the end of the millennium. When would they ever learn? No one could really ever find herself—she had to be the creator of her own life. Until that moment, I hadn't known what I would speak about beyond how wonderful my granddaughter was. I was ready.

We were sipping wine and eating canapés when Kat nodded to me. It was time. I put my near-empty wine glass on a tray carried by a passing waiter, smoothed my dress and made my way to the small dais, where the trio of musicians from the symphony orchestra was just getting up to take a break. There was a podium and a microphone. I stood behind the microphone for a moment, thinking, *I'm a writer, not a speaker*. At that moment, I realized that I had never done much public speaking. I knew the truth, though. What I was doing today wasn't public speaking at all—I was speaking publicly to my granddaughter, and she was the only audience member who mattered.

Someone began tapping a piece of cutlery against a wine glass. I had a brief moment of terror that we were about to begin that wedding abomination that struck horror into my very being every time it started—the revolting call to see the bride and groom kiss. *Such a vulgar practice,* I thought. In any case, I was saved from the spectre of such boorishness by the call to attention that the glass tinkling was intended to accomplish.

I adjusted the microphone and looked around at the wedding guests, each one poised, glass in hand, to hear another in a long line of boring yet gushing tributes to the bride and groom. All such tributes are required to gush, aren't they? I believe there's a directive somewhere in the rulebook for wedding toasts, isn't there? Since I wasn't speaking to the guests—only to Kat—the rules didn't matter.

I realized that standing behind a lectern wasn't where I wanted to be, so I lifted the microphone from its stand and came out from behind. I stood squarely in front of the lectern and turned to Kat, where she was standing under the portrait of Lord Nelson, holding a glass of champagne in one hand. David was holding her other hand.

"Katherine, my darling granddaughter," I began. All eyes were on this spectacle of a woman—a grandmother no less—speaking at a wedding, a task usually given over to the best man and father of the bride. "Kat, I have loved you from the first moment that I laid eyes on you and your mop of dark curls in the nursery, mere hours after you were born. You stared at me with those insightful blue eyes—and we connected, creating a bond that continues to this day. There is a continuity of life in meeting one's grandchild, I think. This continuity reminds us that life goes on no matter what we do. It reminds us that life will go on even after we are no longer here.

"I realized at once that you were an old soul, that you connected me both backward and forward—backward to the life I had before I even knew myself and forward into a future not yet known but likely already written on some level. When I met you, I felt the pull of a kind of love that I had thought I would never feel. And really, today is about nothing so much as it is about love, isn't it? It's about the love you have found in your own life, and it's also about the love I know you will give as you and David move through life together. At weddings, I often wonder if the bride and groom are merely infatuated with one another and the idea of love or if they genuinely love one another. I believe that the difference is that infatuation is that intensely consuming emotion one has when one finds that perfect person—that person who is absolutely flawless, who completes them, as they often like to say. That isn't love. Love arrives only when you realize that your perfect person is not perfect, but rather is flawed, an imperfect being just like you—and it doesn't matter.

"Kat, you have always been passionate about your talents yet pragmatic about life. I look at you now and know in my heart that what we are celebrating today isn't infatuation but love—real, deep, enduring love.

"There are two ways to live your life, Katherine, at least if one listens to Albert Einstein. You can live it as if nothing is a miracle, or you can live it as if everything is a miracle. For you, I wish you only miracles, my darling granddaughter."

I placed the microphone on the lectern and stepped down.

~

"That was an incredible wedding speech, Mrs. Phillips."

I turned toward the voice to find myself looking at a beautiful woman, about Kat's age, dressed in a floaty, silk caftan that reminded me of an exotic eastern costume. But it somehow worked on this wisp of a woman who couldn't have been more than five-feet-two inches tall. Her sharp pixie-cut hair was jet black. But it was her dark eyes that seemed to be able to penetrate all the way to my soul. I shivered slightly.

"Thank you so much," I said. "It's not difficult to speak when one is speaking about a cherished granddaughter." I extended my hand. "I'm Fran, by the way. I don't think we've met."

"Not in person, at least," she said as she took my hand and squeezed it slightly before letting it go. "I'm Elspeth. Elspeth Savant."

"How might you know me if not in person, Elspeth?" I was as curious about this as I was about how she knew Kat or maybe even David.

"I don't know Fran Phillips as much as I know Peyton Winter and F.E. DePlessis," she said, a small smile playing around her eyes. "It would be difficult to imagine any of them not being able to write something quite beautiful."

My jaw dropped, and I could feel the blood drain from my face. "How...? Who...?"

Elspeth took me by the hand and led me to a sofa along the wall. She took two glasses of champagne from a passing waiter, gave me one and sat down beside me.

"First," she said, then sipped her champagne, "please know that your secret is safe with me. Second, I was at the University of Toronto in 1965 for a year when Kat began her studies there. We lived in the same dormitory and were in several classes together—history and ancient and medieval art, I think. After I left to go to McGill to finish my studies, we continued our long-distance friendship for the past decade. It's funny, isn't it?" Elspeth looked around the large salon. "Some people can know someone daily for a long time and yet not know them. But true friends never lose touch even when they are never in the same room for more than a few moments throughout life."

I was reminded of Christophe—and of Peggy. Then I snapped back to reality. "Elspeth, about what you have referred to as my secret—"

She took my hand. "No need to worry. It's just a part of the work I do."

"And what kind of work would that be?" As I listened to myself, I hoped I wasn't beginning to sound desperate—yet I was.

"I discover the truth behind secrets. Some people refer to me as a forensic historian. Mostly I'm just a historian with a serious love of certain types of literature."

I swallowed a sip of champagne and tried to quell my mounting panic. "Does Kat know about my—work?"

Elspeth shook her head. "Of course not. I perceived that you had maintained this secret for a reason. It is not my story to tell. I am wondering about something, though." I nodded for her to go ahead. "Will you ever tell her?"

I didn't have an answer.

THIRTY-SEVEN

"I take pleasure in my transformations. I look quiet and consistent,
but few know how many women there are in me."
~ Anais Nin

IN MY VIEW, KAT AND DAVID SEEMED TO BE MADE for each other. When they returned from their Caribbean honeymoon, they settled into a beautiful life. As the fates would have it, Kat didn't spend her entire career as a high school teacher. Instead, she found a way to pursue her almost-lost dream. I continued to spend time with Kat and to write. Since I was getting older—or so the world seemed to keep pointing out—I spent less and less time travelling. I saw Christophe only once a year when I was able to slip away to Paris. The saddest moment came when I received word from Leonard, now the owner of Peggy's literary agency, that she had died. I cursed myself for not getting to New York one last time. But time does seem to move faster as we age, and the next thing you know, it's too late. Occasionally, though, you get a reprieve.

Kat and David never expected to be parents. I suppose that's the conclusion you draw when you've been married for ten years, and it's still just the two of you. I had never wished to be a parent myself, but I sometimes thought Kat would be good at it.

Then, one day, right out of the blue, Kat called me to say she was coming right over. I was sitting in my office, staring into the screen of my new computer system, just hoping for a distraction. She was there within half an hour.

We settled into our coffee and muffins that my housekeeper, Marilyn, had just set on the table.

346

"Don't you think Marilyn looks like Marilyn Munroe would have looked if she'd lived this long?" Kat whispered as Marilyn left the breakfast room.

"I doubt that you came over here to discuss Marilyn's doppelganger," I said, biting into the cranberry muffin. But Kat was right: my Marilyn did look like the other Marilyn.

"No, as a matter of fact, I didn't," she said. "I have some shocking news."

"Darling girl, there is very little in this life that shocks me anymore," I said. "I'm not sure there ever was. But try me."

"You're going to be a great-grandmother!"

I told her that was wonderful news and hardly shocking, but it seemed that she and David had been the shocked ones. I also felt a weight lift slightly from my shoulders. Kat would have the experience of motherhood, after all.

"I'm worried, Nan," Kat said, suddenly becoming serious. "I'm forty years old, you know."

I nodded. I knew only too well how old she was—after all, I was eighty-five myself. She was worried about the baby, but she was also concerned about her career. She began to chatter about giving it up. I held her hands tightly and told her in no uncertain terms that it was too big a burden to put on any child to know that he or she had been the cause of a mother giving up her dream.

"If you choose to abandon yourself," I held up a hand to silence her as she tried to interrupt, "your child will not be any happier, and if you think about the consequences, you know that your child will be worse off, too."

Seven months later, I met my new great-granddaughter, Evelyn. She was a wonder of energy and single-mindedness. From the moment she was born, I could see a great future. As I looked at this feisty little one, I wondered how long I would have to see her grow. I set up a trust fund for her and hoped that she would use it well. I wouldn't be around to know.

Two years later, another surprise—Kat was expecting another baby. Her due date was shortly before my eighty-ninth birthday (eighty-nine! How does one get to be that old?), and I hoped that I could be around long enough to meet this new great-grandchild. It was by no means a foregone conclusion.

I had felt unwell for a few months. I was still practicing yoga—these days with a private instructor who came to the house weekly. Her name was Audrey. Audrey was a middle-aged woman, a dedicated yogini (she had taught me that word) who taught classes to underprivileged children, suburban housewives and prison inmates in addition to her private clients—like me. When I asked her how she felt about these disparate student groups, she often quoted revered yoga master B.K.S Iyengar.

"Fran," she would say as she gently encouraged my back to bend just a bit further, "remember what the master says: *Yoga does not change the way we see things; it transforms the person who sees.* I am transformed by being open to everyone and every experience. I think you might be the same."

One day, while she and I worked through a flow—a vinyasa, as she called it—she seemed to notice something about me. "Fran, are you in pain? If you are in pain, you must stop that movement immediately. Your body is not meant to be manhandled by its owner."

I smiled. I was not that far from my ninetieth birthday, and on some days, I felt every one of those years. Audrey was right. I was in pain, but it had little to do with the yoga poses. I had been ignoring it, but it was getting to the point where I could no longer pretend it wasn't there, especially when it seemed that I was no longer covering it up as well as I had thought.

After Audrey left that day, I called my family physician. When he saw me the next week, he sent me for some tests. In the end, my doctor was sorry to tell me that I had fairly advanced pancreatic cancer. I knew I'd not live to see my ninetieth birthday after all. But I did want to meet my new great-grandchild. I kept my diagnosis to myself and hoped for the best.

~

It seemed that the gods were smiling down on me, letting me have one last hurrah.

The day I met my new great-grandchild—another girl—the sun was shining in through the window of Kat's private room at the Grace Maternity Hospital, the same place I first saw Kat as a newborn baby. I stood up straight as I pushed open the door to Kat's room, expecting to see the new addition to the family with her mother. These days, the babies didn't spend much time in the nursery, although most of the new mothers (the smart ones, in my estimation) permitted them to return to the nursery overnight to get a better sleep. However, as I moved into the room to hug my darling granddaughter, I looked around and didn't see a bassinet. Kat caught me looking.

"Oh, Nan, she's not here. She was looking a bit jaundiced, so the nurses decided she ought to be assessed for a few hours. They'll bring her back later." I must have shown my disappointment on my face.

There was a gentle knock on the door at that precise moment, and a nurse in head-to-toe white pushed a bassinette into the room.

"Well, Nan," Kat said, "it seems you're in luck. Kat eased herself out of bed and picked up her little daughter. "Sit over there, Nan." Kat directed me to a large, comfortable chair with wide armrests.

I sat down, and Kat handed the little bundle to me.

"Would you mind spending a moment or two with your new great-granddaughter while I go for a short walk? I need to get moving."

Mind? Of course, I didn't mind. And I knew my granddaughter well enough to know that this was her way of letting me have a moment alone with her new daughter.

"Oh, by the way, Nan, I'd like to introduce you to Charlotte Elizabeth Hudson, but you can call her Charlie." Kat leaned over toward the beautiful little face I held in my arms. "Charlie, this is Fran, but you can call her Nan. I do." And she left me alone with little Charlie.

I unwrapped her tiny hands and held the little fingers in the palm of my hand. I gulped back the lump forming in the back of my throat and tried to stop the tears that welled up in my eyes. I hadn't felt this way in over forty years—not since I'd met my granddaughter, Katherine. "Hello, little Charlie," I whispered.

Charlie looked up at me with dark eyes that seemed to hold the promise of generations to come. I could feel a connection to the future, an irony that was not lost on me as I looked into the abyss of the final period of my life. I knew in that moment that I would not be here other than in spirit, to see the flowering of what I sensed would be an artistic soul, not unlike her mother's.

"Charlie," I whispered, "remember this. Life isn't about finding yourself. It's about creating yourself. Create one for the ages, child, create one for the ages."

When I walked back into my house after leaving Kat and Charlie, I felt alone for the first time in my life. I had always been alone, but I had never felt alone. I could feel the edges of my world beginning to ebb. I didn't know how much time I had left, so I began getting things in order. There was much to do when you had amassed as much as I had in my life and began arranging trust funds and real estate transactions as quickly as possible. In the end, I decided to keep both my flat in Paris (which was now worth a small fortune) and the one I'd bought in New York about twenty years earlier. When I thought about which of them I would bequeath to which of my great-granddaughters, there was no question about it. Evelyn was very New York, and Charlie, the artist of my soul, was Paris. I believed that each of them could better appreciate the gift if they waited until they were adults. So, I set out in my will that they would both receive the deeds to their properties the year Charlie turned thirty-five, along with the cash. I would leave my house to Kat and David, although they certainly didn't need it. I would suggest in my will that they sell the house and move on, pocketing the substantial profit that David, the astute businessman, could likely accomplish for them. So, it was arranged.

When I returned home from my solicitor's office after signing my will, I was tired. I sat on the bench in the middle of my walk-in closet and looked around at the items of clothing that marked the eras of my life. I lifted myself from the bench with some difficulty to search for a marking pen in my office. When I returned, I separated a rail of dresses, exposing the wall behind. I took the marking pen and wrote:

"À ma belle Evelyn et Charlie. J'ai l'air calme et cohérent, mais peu savent combien de femmes il y a en moi. Tu es toujours dans mon cœur. F."

I hoped that it might inspire the new owners when they saw it. "To my beautiful Evelyn and Charlie. I look quiet and consistent, but few know how many women there are in me. You are forever in my heart. F."

"There," I said out loud to myself when I had finished. "When David sells this house, the new owners will find that and wonder who Evelyn and Charlie might have been. And that might be a great story!"

~

It took the better part of a year for all of this to come together—thank god, I had the time. I had written a letter to each of my great-granddaughters on the day they were born. I reread my letter to Evelyn and was happy with it, then tucked it into one of my diaries. I reread my letter to Charlie. As I did, my eyes filled with years of unshed tears. I hoped she would have an easier time than her mother did of finding her artist's way. I hoped that someday when she finally read this letter, she would understand what she had to do. But there were a few things I'd have to tell her.

I picked up the linen-finished paper and read it one more time to make sure it was right— because I had to get it right.

"… I have just looked into the eyes of the future—your future. Oscar Wilde once said: "To live is the rarest thing in the world. Most people just exist." Existence is not enough, darling Charlie. If you do not know that already, you soon will. I wish for you to do as I have done—to live every day as if it is your last."

Charlie

THIRTY-EIGHT

"If you have yet to be called an incorrigible, defiant woman,
don't worry; there is still time."
~ Clarissa Pinkola Estés

IT WAS ONE OF THOSE DREAMS that you can't seem to awaken from. I could hear someone calling my name, but I couldn't quite figure out who it was. I could feel the story receding like a wave on a beach, but I couldn't be sure it would return. It had to come back to me. I was frantic. Where was it going? Where was she going?

Finally, I awoke to find Tom shaking my arm. "Charlie, wake up. You must be having a nightmare."

I raised my head and looked around. I was confused. "Tom, what?" I seemed to be lying on the sofa, surrounded by books and papers.

"You never came to bed last night. You must have found some fascinating reading," Tom said, picking up one of the books beside me on the couch.

I couldn't quite get my bearings. *Have I been dreaming everything?*

"Hey, this one looks racy. Did it belong to your great-grandmother?"

Tom was holding up the copy of *Life of Desire*. I looked at the cover closely now. The author's name was Peyton Winter.

"I don't know…I guess so," I said. My head was so foggy, and I wasn't sure what was real. I had obviously fallen asleep in the middle of reading my great-grandmother's notes and journals, but now I seemed to be walking a tightrope between the real past and my over-active imagination.

"You know," Tom said, thumbing through the book, "I think I saw a movie based on this one back when old movies were all the rage in university." He stopped at a page somewhere in the middle of the book. "Hey, look at this."

He passed me the book. There was a circle around two words and a hand-written note in the margin. It read, "Tell P. to get this fixed." The circle seemed to surround a typo. I shook my head, wondering why this looked familiar.

I reached for the large leather-bound diary that was half-covered by one of the giant-sized cushions. I opened it to a random page and placed it on the sofa beside the other book, still open to the hand-written note.

"See this?" I said to Tom, my excitement mounting.

He leaned over. "Yeah, it looks as if they were both written by the same person. The handwriting is identical. So, if that's your great-grandmother's diary, why is she pointing out a typo in an old book by some dude named Peyton Winter?" He looked at it again. "Did she know him? It does say to tell P. to get it fixed."

I was still processing all of this when Tom sat down on the arm of the sofa. "Hey, you don't think this Peyton Winter was her lover or something? Maybe he's your great-grandfather, Charlie."

I slowly picked up one of the other books beside me—one of the French ones. The title was *Secrets du pas-de-trois* by author F.E. de Plessis. The publication date was 1923. Yes, this one had been on the reading list in that women's studies course I took in the first year of my M.F.A. program, but we had read a paperback reprint. This one was a first-edition. I remembered heated discussions of the patriarchal arrogance of male writers writing female erotic characters. Dear god, we were so wrong!

"No, Tom, not my great-grandfather. My great-grandmother."

"What? Your great-grandmother? Who is?"

"Peyton Winter. Peyton Winter *is* my great-grandmother. My great-grandmother was Peyton Winter." I was beginning to feel frantic. I lifted the other books, several of which were written by F.E. de Plessis. "And these, Tom. They're hers, too." I knew he wasn't following, but things were beginning to fall into place for me. "Here, Tom," I said, holding up a copy of a book titled *The Secret Life of Adaline*, an English translation published in New York. "See the author's name? F.E.?" He still wasn't following. "F.E. Frances Elizabeth, my great grandmother's initials. She was F.E. de Plessis!"

It was all too much to take in. I was suddenly possessed of an idea. My mind was full of Frannie's journal entries, and they seemed to be playing havoc with my rational thoughts. I thought about Frannie's house where she had lived and died. There was no way this could be true, but I had to find out.

I raced out of the room, Tom trailing behind, no doubt wondering what I'd been drinking through the night. As I raced up the stairs, I was more clear-headed than I had ever been. At the top of the stairs, I turned to the left and ran down the hall toward our bedroom. The bedroom boasted two walk-in closets (as realtors like Tom liked to say). I opened the first one where Tom kept his clothes. I rifled around behind his suits and sport jackets and shirts of every hue imaginable. Nothing.

Then I raced over to mine and flung open the double doors. It was a long shot, I knew, but I couldn't let the thought go. I separated clothes hanging on the left and looked behind. Damn it! Wallpaper. Not to be deterred, I began picking at the edge with a fingernail just as Tom appeared at the door.

"Charlie, what the hell is going on? What are you doing?"

I pulled off a long swath of wallpaper, but there was nothing underneath. My disappointment was so palpable I almost cried. But there was another wall. I turned to the opposite side and repeated the procedure.

"Okay, Charlie. Don't you think you owe me an explanation of why the hell you're destroying the wallpaper?"

I wasn't listening. I was staring at the black inscription under the wallpaper. It was faded, but there was no doubt about it.

"À ma belle Evelyn et Charlie. J'ai l'air calme et cohérent, mais peu savent combien de femmes il y a en moi. Tu es toujours dans mon cœur. F."
"To my beautiful Evelyn and Charlie. I look quiet and consistent, but few know how many women there are in me. You are forever in my heart. F."

I sat back and sobbed.

THIRTY-NINE

"If you would not be forgotten as soon as you are dead,
either write something worth reading or do something worth writing."
~ Benjamin Franklin

"YOU'RE TELLING ME THAT I BOUGHT your great-grandmother's house? That you and I are living in your great-grandmother's house, and you didn't know it?" Tom and I were having breakfast on the back terrace to enjoy the June morning. "Charlie, how is it possible that you didn't know?"

"Tom, what can I tell you? My mother never mentioned it, and if she did, I must have been too young to be interested. Mom and Dad must have sold it right after Fran died. I was a baby. And you know how my family was."

At that point, Tom did. My mother had gone to her grave with secrets that Evelyn and I discovered only after she was gone from our lives. Now, this. It should hardly have been surprising.

I could scarcely keep my mind focused on my students that week as we moved toward the last day of school as if we were moving through jelly. It was so close, and yet it seemed a long way off. I just wanted to hole up in my office with Fran's books and journals and see if I could get my head around the details. And I still had to call Evelyn.

Finally, Friday arrived, and the school year was over. Before leaving for the summer holidays, I decided to take a bit of time to clean up my desk and computer. The desk and office space didn't take long. Despite being an artistic sort, I was scrupulously tidy. The same couldn't always be said about my computer—specifically my email. I had a habit of leaving emails that should have been trashed in my inbox for weeks—occasionally for months. So, I diligently went back through them, one at a time to be sure I hadn't missed anything. While I was doing this, I happened upon one I'd remembered from a month or so ago that I thought was probably spam, but I wanted to check it out when I had more time. That time never materialized.

Just before I trashed it for good, I took a closer look and remembered that I'd left it because it was in French and, despite years of French classes in school, my French was abysmal. Given my recent discovery of great-grandmother Fran's French connection, I was more interested in taking a closer look.

As I began to examine it more closely, I couldn't really understand it, but I saw a name I thought I recognized. The email was signed by someone named Etienne Lemieux. *Lemieux*, I thought. *I know that name.*

I looked at the clock. It was getting late, and I had promised Tom that I'd meet him for a drink at a wine bar downtown to celebrate the end of the school year. I forwarded the email to my personal account and powered off my computer. I gathered my belongings that had to come home with me over the summer and locked the door behind me.

~

When I arrived at *Oh-Blah-Dee* wine bar, I could see Tom through the window as I rounded the corner. I loved sitting in that window with its great view of the tiny interior and the street outside. He had ordered a bottle of champagne—*Veuve Clicquot*, if you must know—to celebrate the end of my first semester as a writer-in-residence and writing teacher. He didn't know it yet, but we were also celebrating the call I'd gotten from my editor in Toronto earlier in the day. She loved the manuscript and was fast-tracking it for publication. We might even have advance copies of my novel *Kat's Kosmic Blues* before the end of the year.

Once we settled into the comfortable seats with a glass of bubbly and I'd had a chance to savour it for a moment, I told Tom about the French email and the familiar name.

"Well, let's translate the sucker," he said. He pulled his laptop out from under the table. Since he had walked from his downtown office, he hadn't stopped to drop it in the car. He turned it toward me, and I logged into my email.

"There it is," I said, turning it back toward him. "Is your French any good?"

Tom smiled. "Even if it isn't, there's nothing quite like an online translator. We'll get the gist of it, anyway."

So, we began.

« *Chère madame. Pardonnez mon intrusion. Je cherche les descendants de Mlle Françoise Phillips.* »

"That's easy," Tom said. "Dear madame. Then he's apologizing for intruding on you. It seems that he's looking for Frances Phillips's descendants. That's your great-grandmother, isn't it?"

"Dear god," I said. "Why didn't I notice that when it came?"

"Probably because you weren't clicked into your great-grandmother like you are now. Shall we continue?"

I nodded. The two of us muddled through the rest of the email. As far as we could figure out, Etienne Lemieux, the email's writer, was the publisher at Éditions Lemieux in Paris. Tom looked it up and found out that it was one of the oldest and most revered publishers in Europe at this stage.

"It says here that they gained their initial success in the 1920s and 1930s publishing the famous erotic literature by F.E. dePlessis, a writer whose real identity was never revealed." Tom looked up from his phone and smirked at me. "Well, I guess you come from a long line of writers, Charlie!"

I ignored him. "What else does he say?"

"He says they're looking specifically for the offspring of Katherine Elizabeth Wilson Hudson," he pointed to a specific passage. "Let me see if I can figure out a more specific translation." He clicked a few keys. "It says he has an envelope that he has been instructed to give to your mother's descendants on the occasion of her death if her death occurs before 2024. He says he knows nothing more."

Things were getting murkier by the minute. Mr. Lemieux asked that if he had found the correct person, I was to call him.

"I guess you better call him, Charlie. Whatever this is about, it's a great mystery." Tom loved a mystery.

So, I called Etienne Lemieux in Paris on Monday morning.

~

"Please forgive me, Miss Hudson. I should not have subjected you to a correspondence in French. I have made the incorrect assumption, have I not? I had just assumed that since you were in Canada, that you would be fluent in French. Please forgive me."

"People often make that mistake," I said dryly. It was ironic, though. We live in a bilingual country, so it does seem natural to assume that everyone speaks two languages. That couldn't be further from the truth. "My high school French seems to desert me whenever I need it most. Don't apologize. I should apologize."

Then we got down to business. Etienne explained that his great-uncle Jean-Christophe Lemieux was the founder of Éditions Lemieux. When Jean-Christophe died in the 1990s, he had left these odd instructions about finding Mom's children. To be more specific, though, they were seeking F.E. de Plessis's—Frances Elizabeth Phillips's—successors. Etienne had done some research and had discovered me.

He had an envelope for Evelyn and me. I asked him to put it in the mail.

"That I cannot do, I am afraid," Etienne said. "I have strict instructions that I am to hand it directly to you."

"Are you suggesting that I come to Paris to receive it?"

"But of course, Miss Hudson. I cannot hand it to you unless you are here. When may I expect you?"

Paris? I had to go to Paris. I told him I'd get back to him.

When I told Tom about the conversation, he said that, of course, I had to go. Unfortunately, he wouldn't be able to get away. Summer was a big season in his industry. The more I thought about it, the more I felt like it was something I had to do on my own anyway.

When I called Evelyn, she was just as perplexed as I was. I thought I heard a bit of something in her voice when I told her that Etienne had been instructed to give the envelope to me although it was intended for both of us.

"Well, I can't go anyway," she said. "I'm not supposed to fly."

Evelyn was nearing her due date as she waited to welcome her first child into the world, so I told her I'd keep her updated on everything. The moment I hung up, I booked a flight to Paris for the following week. Then I went back to Fran's diary to see if I could figure out what this mystery might be all about.

~

I had never been to Paris. As the Air Canada flight banked and prepared for its landing at Charles De Gaulle International Airport just outside the city, I could feel my anticipation mounting. At one point, I looked out the window and saw the Eiffel Tower in the distance, and I knew I was really here. *What more do you have to tell me, Frannie Phillips?* I thought. *Whatever it is, I'm ready.*

On the taxi ride into the city from the airport, my face was practically plastered against the glass, taking in everything as we drove through varying neighbourhoods, finally emerging into the city. It was as if I had landed on a different planet. *Why in the world have I never been here before?* I wondered.

Evelyn, who had been to Paris several times, insisted that I stay at the Marriott Hotel on the Champs-Élysées, but I was aghast when I looked at the prices online. I phoned her back to ask her for a more reasonable recommendation, but she insisted that I use some of their points. When I suggested that I should probably stay somewhere a bit more authentically French than an American chain hotel, Evelyn snorted.

"For the love of god, Charlie," she said. "Trust me on this. You'll be in the middle of authentic Paris at this hotel. And trust me. When they make fun of your French in that condescending way some of them have at that hotel, you'll know you're in Paris. "

So, Evelyn, in a fit of unaccustomed generosity, had booked me into her favourite hotel for four nights. I had told her I didn't need to stay that long. After all, I was only there to pick up an envelope of some sort. She insisted that anyone who is going to Paris for the first time needed to stay a minimum of four nights. So, now, I found myself standing just inside the hotel lobby, gazing up at the magnificent glass-covered atrium that soared for how many stories I couldn't count. The hotel was in a glorious heritage building directly on the most famous street in the world. I thought I'd died and gone to heaven. I didn't care at all about Etienne and the letter. I was just happy to be here.

My overnight flight had arrived before eight a.m., and it was now only nine-thirty. I couldn't check in so early, so I left my luggage with the bell desk, had a bite of breakfast at the lobby bar, then set off to do a bit of exploring. I didn't have to be at Editions Lemieux until nine o'clock the following morning.

As I stepped outside the hotel, I was immediately assailed by the sense of controlled urgency all around me. It was so unlike other cities I had visited. There was a buzz (like I always felt in New York—at least on the two occasions I'd been there), but it had a kind of elegance to it. It was as if the city itself were an elegant woman who knows exactly who she is and doesn't need anyone to tell her. I liked that feeling.

As I stepped out of the hotel with my phone showing the map of Paris clutched in my hand, I turned right. I could already see the *Arc de Triomphe* a few blocks in that direction. It beckoned me.

As I walked along, I was astonished at the traffic. Cars were speeding in every direction—or at least that's how it felt to me. I noted the cobbled street that stood in contrast to the shops along this famed avenue. I was more than a bit surprised to walk past Sephora, Levis and H & M, all shops that seemed more at home in a suburban mall than in downtown Paris en route to a famous landmark. As I neared my first destination, I was gratified to see a few sidewalk cafés (one of them did, however, belong to a McDonald's).

When I arrived at the traffic round-about that surrounded the arch, I stood there staring at the traffic as it made its way around and around without any apparent lanes or anything else to guide the constant flow of vehicles. There seemed to be much dodging and ducking, all aided by honking horns and shrieking tires. I loved it.

The streets fanned out in spokes from the centre of the arch. I consulted my map and made a decision. I would take Avenue Victor Hugo because I'd had to read *Les Miserables* when I was in high school (I hated it) and walk down that street to what the map told me was a garden on the bank of the Seine. The park was directly across from the Eiffel Tower. I expected that I could get the quintessential selfie right about there. I was right. It was magnificent.

After staring at the tower directly across the bridge for a while, I turned left to meander along the river. I knew I could turn on just about any street, and it would lead me back to the Champs-Élysées and eventually my hotel. By the time I arrived back at my hotel, my room was ready, and I was famished. I had a combined lunch and dinner, then fell into bed to try to ward off jet lag. It seemed almost criminal, though, to sleep when I had such a limited time to get to know this beautiful lady whose charms had already started to suck me in. Tomorrow was another day, though.

~

Éditions Lemieux's offices were located *Rue des Rennes* on the left bank of the river Seine. The left bank, the Latin Quarter, is the home of Sorbonne, that seat of higher learning, and such shops as the storied *Shakespeare and Company*, an ages-old bookshop frequented by such luminaries as Hemingway, F. Scott Fitzgerald and other glittering members of what we now called the "lost generation." As a writer (albeit one of a much lesser echelon), I was itching to soak up the ambience of the left bank. I'd take some time to do that after my meeting with Monsieur Lemieux. I only hoped no one there expected me to speak French with any degree of proficiency.

Frightened of being late, I opted to take a taxi rather than the Metro. I would have loved to have that experience, but I couldn't be sure I'd get off at the right stop. When I alighted from the taxi in front of the building ten minutes before my nine a.m. meeting, I stood looking up and down the street. Coming from North America, I found the city to be amiably low. In other words, there isn't a skyscraper to be seen. The building I stood in front of was six stories of yellow-beige stucco. It looked as if it contained nothing but flats, with its row upon row of small windows, each with a black, wrought-iron Juliet balcony. It was charming. If I hadn't known the offices were here, I might have missed the little card beside the doorbell proclaiming their presence. I rang.

After a few minutes, a young woman dressed head-to-toe in black despite the July heat (at least her flowing tunic was sleeveless, a good thing since the black scarf wound around her neck looked warm, indeed) opened the door. She told me her name was Anouk and beckoned me inside. We took an elevator to the top floor. It was one of those I'd seen in 1930s movies with the metal cage that she pulled across to close the door. When we emerged on the top floor, we were in a different world.

The place was dazzlingly bright, a situation enhanced by the massive amounts of LED lighting and three immense skylights. The décor was also surprising to me, given the building's outward appearance of historic solemnity. It was all white leather, shiny white metal and a few touches of blonde wood, mainly the floor. As Anouk and I walked through the door, a handsome man, about mid-forties, with a shock of blonde hair falling into his eyes over the round frames of his very stylish glasses, emerged from an office and came over immediately. He grasped my shoulders firmly and planed the inevitable double-kiss on my surprised face.

"Miss Hudson, it is so wonderful to meet you. I almost feel as if I know you!"

I most assuredly did not feel as if I knew Etienne Lemieux. "It's nice to meet you, too, Monsieur Lemieux. And please call me Charlie."

He raised his eyebrows slightly. Either this was surprisingly informal for a French publisher, or my name was surprising. "It's short for Charlotte," I said.

A smile broke over his face, lighting up his eyes so that they were magnified even more than they were by his lenses. "But of course! And I am Etienne. Please come with me."

I followed him into his office, where the nameplate on his desk said, "Etienne Lemieux, Publisher." He was the boss. He bid me sit down on a white sofa, and he took the chair to the side. Anouk came in with a tray containing two espressos and a basket of fabulous-looking croissants. When Anouk left, and we had both settled into our coffee, he began to tell me about his publishing company.

The company was loosely established in the late 1920s by his great-uncle Jean-Christophe Lemieux who moonlighted for himself while working and learning the business in the employ of what would become his competitors. He had built the company—and its current media empire— over the course of a seventy-year career. Etienne himself had begun working for his great uncle in the early 1990s while still a student at the Sorbonne.

"Your great-uncle must have been in his nineties then. Was he still working?"

"Oh, very much," Etienne said as he sipped his espresso. "Indeed, he was very much in charge until the day he died. He, himself, appointed me to succeed him." He picked up the croissant he had placed on his plate and bit off the end. I could see chocolate oozing from it, making me rethink my choice of a plain one. "I was very young then, you know. I still had much to learn. I had to graduate and gain some experience. The editor-in-chief acted as publisher for those years. When he retired, I took over. And here I am."

Etienne then told me that F.E. de Plessis and his (her) work had put the publishing company on the map.

"You may already know this," he said, picking up a folder I hadn't noticed from the table in front of us. He opened it. "But the royalties from the many F.E. de Plessis books have grown over the years." He stopped to read for a moment. "I must tell you something," he said, taking off his glasses and polishing them on his pristine white shirt. "I was very shocked when I learned that de Plessis was a woman. In any event, your great-grandmother, Mademoiselle Phillips, had not touched the money in many years. They have grown substantially, and even now, many enthusiasts of erotic literature continue to buy them. The money continues to grow."

I told Etienne that I had been required to read one only a few years earlier in graduate school. He laughed and said that the market for these books as course reading was a substantial one.

"I believe the royalties are to be transferred to you and your sister, but I also believe that the details may be contained in the envelope I have been tasked with putting into your hands."

He first passed me the royalty statement and a bank statement. The name on both documents was "Estate of Mademoiselle Françoise Phillips." My eyes bulged out at the sum. He then reached behind to a small side table and picked up a large white envelope. I had expected something small and flat. This one was large and fat, clearly stuffed with documents. He passed it to me. I immediately began to open it.

"No, no, Charlie. You must not open it here. I have been given strict instructions that you are not to be accompanied by anyone on our staff when you open it. With that being said, I will be at your service until you depart France."

I put the envelope in the large purse I had put on the floor beside me. We finished our snack, discussed the weather in Paris, and I left with my bag firmly tucked under my arm.

FORTY

*"Begin at the beginning," the King said, very gravely, "and go
on till you come to the end: then stop."*
~ Lewis Carroll, *Alice in Wonderland*

I WALKED OUT OF ETIENNE'S OFFICES WONDERING what had just happened. Perhaps even more to the point, though, I wondered what was about to happen. What was in that envelope that made it so mysterious? That required everyone to follow some kind of protocol? All Etienne had been able to tell me was that the instructions came directly from Frannie, my great-grandmother, sometime in the 1980s. I walked down the street toward the Luxembourg Gardens, where I planned to find a place to sit in the sunshine and open the damn thing.

I stopped at a small shop along the way and bought myself a bottle of wine and two wine glasses. Why did I buy two? I don't really know. I was, in fact, alone. I also picked up a baguette (although I didn't need it after the croissant) and a block of white cheese.

When I reached the edge of the park, I decided to venture into the centre, where my map said there was a water feature—a pond as far as I could tell. And there it was. Surrounded by a pea gravel-filled space, the concrete pond glistened in the midday sun. Here and there around it were chairs, generously supplied by the city of Paris, or so I surmised. I spotted a lone empty chair, off by itself near the grass and a flower bed. I reached it quickly so as not to lose it to a harried office worker looking for a place to have a sunny lunch break.

Finally, I was settled. I poured myself a glass of wine (thank you, France, for being so much more progressive than Canada and letting me have a glass of wine in a park) and tore open the envelope.

As expected, it was stuffed with papers—and other things.

The page on top of everything was an instruction sheet of sorts. At the bottom was my great-grandmother's signature. I would have recognized that anywhere now that I'd read her journals. It referred to her will that had evidently provided my mother with a significant sum and her house in Halifax, the house my parents had obviously sold when I was less than a year old. My grandfather James, her son, received only the house where he lived (this puzzled me) and a much smaller sum of money. Then came the astonishing part.

In 1989, the year I was born, she had set up a trust fund for me and one for Evelyn. Several of the attached pages detailed the current value of those trusts. The sums of money were in the seven figures. I almost choked on the piece of cheese I was mindlessly chomping on. We were also to become the owner of her copyrights and her book royalties. The reason I knew nothing about them was that they were to be kept secret until I turned thirty-five. Evelyn was about to turn thirty-five, but I was two years younger. So, why did I come to know about them now? The reason was that there was another provision. If Katherine Elizabeth Wilson Hudson, my mother Kat, died before I turned thirty-five, we were to inherit immediately. Mom had died a year and a half earlier, but Etienne told me they had difficulty finding us. He, along with Fran's French lawyer, had worked for over a year to track us down.

I sat back and watched families strolling along, their children running ahead. I watched couples, arm-in-arm, taking in the July sunshine. I saw the office workers taking a much-needed break from work. I sipped my wine and thought about the fact that my world had just changed. I was now a wealthy woman. Why didn't I feel any different then? *It struck me that money doesn't change how we feel about ourselves.*

I reached down to pick up the envelope and put the papers back when I realized I hadn't removed everything. Still inside were two letter-sized envelopes that seemed to contain documents and more. I opened the first one.

It was a deed to a property in New York—and a key. There was a sticky note on the deed. It said, "Deed transfer completed." I looked at the name of the owner. It was Evelyn Hudson. My god, Evelyn was now the owner of an apartment in New York! I quickly looked up the address on my phone map and discovered that the deed was to an apartment in Manhattan's upper east side. I whistled. It must be worth a fortune. I wondered what it was like.

Then I opened the second one. Another deed and another key. This time, it was to an apartment in Paris. Another sticky said the same thing. With my heart pounding in my ears, I scanned the page. There it was. The owner of the flat was listed as "Charlotte Elizabeth Hudson." Me.

~

It was still early in the afternoon. Naturally, I couldn't slow my racing heart and knew that I'd have to see the apartment that very day. I checked the address: *rue de Vaurigard*. I could hardly believe it when I realized that I must have passed it on my way into the gardens. I gathered up the remains of my lunch and stuffed as much as I could in my bag. Then I set out to find this apartment.

Less than ten minutes later, I stood on the street looking up at my great-grandmother's Paris flat. No, I wasn't, was I? I was looking up at *my* Paris flat.

My hand was shaking uncontrollably as I tried to put the key into the lock. Finally, I opened the door to the flat and walked inside. A memory of the day I walked into my mother's atelier after she had died flooded my thoughts. I felt her presence everywhere. This feeling was the same in one way, yet different. My mother had been a very real presence in my life for three decades. Yet, as I stood here in an apartment I'd never been in before, on the left bank of Paris, I felt as if I were not alone.

I looked around at the dust covers on the furniture and began walking around, removing them as I went. I ran my hand over the sofas and the tables and the Chinoiserie screen with its inlaid enamels of red and peacock blue, so like the ones I'd seen in pictures of Coco Chanel's home in Paris. I walked into the tiny kitchen and tried to picture Fran pouring a glass of wine or mixing a cocktail. Then I walked into the bedroom and pulled off the dust cover to reveal an enormous four-poster bed hung with raspberry-coloured silks. I felt a slight breath on my neck.

I turned back toward the door and wandered into the next room, a turret room with a view toward the gardens where I'd just had lunch. When I pulled the next dust cover off to reveal an enormous desk and solid-looking metal typewriter, I gasped. It looked as if the desk's owner had just left to join friends at a bistro and planned to be back momentarily. It was Frannie's desk—the desk where she wrote those magnificent books. I walked around and dared to sit in her chair. I ran my hand over the leather blotter and opened each drawer. In the bottom drawer, there was a pile of pages. I reached down to pull them out.

I placed them in the centre of the desk and just looked. I began to shiver. It was a manuscript—a manuscript that looked as if the pages had just been pulled from the jaws of the typewriter that had pride of place on the desk. With a shaking hand, I picked up the first page and began reading.

An hour later, I sat back. "Where the hell is the rest of it?" I said out loud.

The book was like the old F.E. de Plessis books, and yet it wasn't. Even now in the twenty-first century, the story was what post-fifty shades we would classify as racy, risqué, hot, perhaps. But it wasn't pornography. And it was beautifully written prose. And it had a story. But it wasn't finished!

"What the hell, Grandma Fran?" I said. I got up and walked over to the chair where I'd laid my tote bag earlier. I took out the half-full bottle of wine and the two glasses. I went back around and sat down in her chair—my chair and poured myself a glass of wine. Before I lifted it to my lips, I had second thoughts.

I put it down and poured a second glass.

"This one's for you, Frannie."

And it came just as it had once before when I sat among my late mother's unfinished projects.

"Finish it."

It didn't sound the same, but I shivered as I sat there, listening; it was like a breath of air, a whisper in my ear, faint but unmistakable. I knew.

"Finish it."

ABOUT THE AUTHOR

PATRICIA J. PARSONS has written nineteen books, including health and business books, a memoir, two historical novels, and women's fiction. She has been a fashion design and sewing fanatic for most of her life, a passion she writes about online at *The GG Files* blog. She lives, writes, designs and sews in Toronto.

Connect with her on Instagram @patriciajparsons or @pjparsonswriter

Join her on Facebook @patriciaparsonswriter and at facebook.com/groups/12dresses

Visit her web site at www.patriciajparsons.com

* 9 7 8 1 7 7 7 2 4 3 1 8 0 *